Views of *The Name*

CW00567152

"Debut collections rarely exhibit such literary ⸻
less Dark is brutally poetic and poetically brutal. The shadows evoked by T.E.
Grau have teeth, and they shall endure."
— Richard Gavin, author of *At Fear's Altar*

"Some authors become contemporary favorites of mine on the merits of only a
story or two. Such was the case with T. E. Grau. With his first story I was exposed
to, 'Free Fireworks,' he seized my attention, and when I read 'The Screamer' I was
flat-out sold. He's never disappointed me since. Even as a relative newcomer, he's
writing stories that can stand tall alongside those of much more established writers of modern weird fiction. His stories are sometimes tragic, sometimes blackly
humorous, often cast a probing gaze at society, and may very well do all these
things within the borders of a single tale. His range is especially to be admired,
his settings diverse but always convincing and immersive. A story like 'The Mission' reads like a feverish blend of Cormac McCarthy and H. P. Lovecraft, but is
all Grau: wildly imaginative, fiercely gripping, brazenly unpredictable."
— Jeffrey Thomas, author of *Punktown*

"In *The Nameless Dark*, T. E. Grau finds the sweet spot between terror and accep-
tance, horror and beauty, the unusual and the familiar — both frightening and
touching at the same time. Not an easy task. These unsettling stories grab your
heart and squeeze — a sensation that is both terrifying and like coming home."
— Richard Thomas, author of *Disintegration*

"T.E. Grau's odd, edgy stories shine a new light into the dark corners of human
experience. These stories shine with smart prose, clever — often quirky — in-
sights, and enough weirdness to make any genre fan froth at the mouth with glee.
Start reading Grau before he hits big, then you can say you were one of the first."
— Gary McMahon, author of *Pretty Little Dead Things* and *The Concrete Grove*

"More than any other genre, perhaps, horror is defined by its places — from
the snowy streets of Lovecraft's Kingsport to the windswept beaches of James'
Seaburgh or the ancient hills around Machen's Caermaen. In such places the
alien exists alongside the familiar and the horrific mingles with the beautiful.
T.E. Grau's *The Nameless Dark* follows in this same tradition, evoking within its

pages a world of haunted landscapes: blasted cities and barren deserts, suffocating jungles and sun-bleached plains."
— Daniel Mills, author of *The Lord Came at Twilight*

"*The Nameless Dark* is a horribly good collection from the incredibly versatile T.E. Grau, featuring stories ranging from the nihilistically bleak to the darkly humorous. You'll find harrowing accounts of modern day life alongside stories of an old west that's wild with monstrous things, Lovecraftian horror holding hands with the Ligottian. Each story is written with a clear love for language, the prose evocative, heartfelt, and often heartbreaking, providing observations of human nature that are wickedly astute and well considered. The stars must have been right when he wrote this because Grau has created magic here, magic of a very dark kind. *The Nameless Dark* is an excellent collection — I loved it."
— Ray Cluley, author of *Probably Monsters* and *Within the Wind, Beneath the Snow*

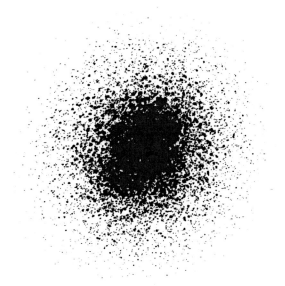

THE NAMELESS DARK

A COLLECTION

T.E. Grau

Foreword by Nathan Ballingrud

Published in 2015 by Lethe Press, Inc.
118 Heritage Avenue • Maple Shade, NJ 08052-3018
www.lethepressbooks.com • lethepress@aol.com
ISBN: 978-159021-463-3 / 1-59021-463-3
Cover image by Arnaud de Vallois.
Cover design: Inkspiral Design
Interior design: Silvia Moreno-Garcia

"The Screamer," first published in *Urban Cthulhu: Nightmare Cities* (ed. by
Henrik Harksen, H. Harksen Productions, 2012) / "Clean," first published in
The Fog Horn #2 (ed. by Quinn Emmett, 2014) / "Return of the Prodigy," first
accepted for publication in *Cthulhu Fhatagn!* (ed. by Ross E. Lockhart, Word
Horde, 2015) / "The Truffle Pig," first published in *Tales of Jack the Ripper* (ed.
by Ross E. Lockhart, Word Horde, 2013) / "Beer & Worms," first published in
The Best of the Horror Society 2013 (ed. by Scott M. Goriscak, 2013) / "White
Feather," first published in *World War Cthulhu* (ed. by Brian M. Sammons
& Glynn Owen Barrass, Dark Regions Press, 2014) / "Transmission," first
published in *Dead But Dreaming 2* (ed. by Kevin Ross, Miskatonic River Press,
2011) / "Mr. Lupus," purchased for publication in *Mark of the Beast* (ed. by Scott
David Aniolowski, Chaosium Inc.) / "Free Fireworks," first published in *Horror
for the Holidays* (ed. by Scott David Aniolowski, Miskatonic River Press, 2013
/ "Love Songs from the Hydrogen Jukebox," first published in *The Children of
Old Leech* (ed. by Ross E. Lockhart & Justin Steele, Word Horde, 2014) / "The
Mission," first published by Dynatox Ministries/Dunhams Manor Press, 2014.

Deep into that darkness peering, long I stood there, wondering, fearing, doubting, dreaming dreams no mortal ever dared to dream before.

Edgar Allan Poe
The Raven

◎

"I do not love men: I love what devours them."
André Gide
Prometheus Illbound

For my two girls

For Ivy, my bones, my home, my Dream Girl waiting for me on the last ring of Saturn. I am yours and you are mine. Tout est noir, mon amour. Tout est blanc. Je t'aime, mon amour. Comme j'aime la nuit.

And for Angelina, my magic child, my sunrise and eternal source of hope in this world of dancing brutes.

To the stars, my loves. To the sea. This book belongs to you two alone.

The Nameless Dark *is written in loving memory of Michael and Kathleen Powers, Charles "Chip" Grau, Nubar Papazyan, and Mikael Hovanessian.*

ACKNOWLEDGEMENTS

Many have aided me on this journey into prose, culminating with this first collection of fiction, and rightly have my deepest gratitude for their support and generosity, but I especially want to thank Steve Berman, Nathan Ballingrud, Laird Barron, Paul Tremblay, Jordan Krall, Ross E. Lockhart, Jeffrey Thomas, Michael Marshall Smith, Adam Nevill, Matt Cardin, Ray Cluley, Michael Kelly, Thomas Ligotti, Lawrence Block, Ellen Datlow, S. T. Joshi, Tom Lynch, Brian Sammons, Michael Abolafia, Paul Carrick, Scott David Aniolowski, the Grau/Curtis families, the Telalyans, the Papazyans, the Oganesyans, The High Plains/HT Crew, Grigor & Vardui, Angelfish, and, of course, Ives Hovanessian, who steered me onto the track, coached up my stride, and then ran far ahead, twirling and singing and forever showing me The Screamer. Her fingerprints are all over these tales.

CONTENTS

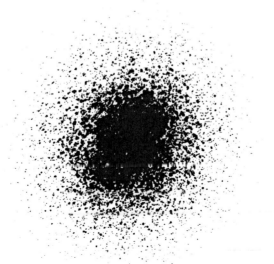

WHAT CALLS US TO
THE DARK

Imagine a church. Not built by any human hand, not enclosed by any structured walls nor a place of sanctuary in any inhabited city, this church is felt rather than seen. Imagine you have descended into the earth to find it. Volumes of stone separate you from the surface of the world, where you have left the light behind. To bring light to this place would be a sacrilege. You're a pilgrim, and this is a holy place.

But you're not alone; many have come. We've come because someone is down here telling stories, and stories that come from the nameless dark come with their own peculiar illumination, a kind which can't be found in the sunlight. We need them, as much as we need the fables which give us our illusions of order and safety. Maybe we need them even more.

In the hands of the best storytellers, there is no greater pleasure than losing yourself in horror.

Case in point: T.E. Grau.

The first story I ever read by Grau was "The Mission." It's a tale set in the Old West, about a group of unlikely soldiers tracking two Lakota warriors across the Nebraska plains, and who eventually stumble across something fantastically strange and terrifying. I didn't know what to expect. What I got was prose moving across the page with the lean, efficient elegance of a dancer.

"Ebke snorted. Didn't care for a damned thing in the whole wide world, including his own hide. The kind of man who was just born hollow, who just went where he was supposed to. Didn't matter, though. When the chips were down and the dander up, it's always light versus dark. To hell with this New World."

Crisp, tough language. It suggests the pared cynicism of the gathered men, their resignation to unhappy truths and a disdain for the florid and inessential. One does not imagine they would tolerate a gregarious soul in their company.

And, a short while later:

"Farm boys ain't exactly expert trackers. Good to have at your side in a saloon dust up, as those coffee can fists always found purchase, but rosy-cheeked plowboys weren't born bloodhounds like those with a more suspicious nature."

Read that paragraph aloud. Listen to the rhythm of it. It's full of rolling muscle. The cadence of it is picked up repeatedly by clusters of stressed syllables, pounding like an old steam train: "coffee can fists," "rosy-cheeked plowboys," "born bloodhounds." It's elegant, strong, and precise. Consider, too, the expert use of figurative language. I'm more jealous of "those coffee can fists always found purchase" than I can tell you. Prose like this is a pure joy to read.

It comes early in the story, and although I'd been enjoying it right from the start, it was when I came across that line that I knew for sure I was in expert hands. Grau knows what he's doing, and he does it damn well. After that, I surrendered completely to the story, like slipping into a river's hard current, and was carried to further unexpected rewards.

I won't tell you what the soldiers find at the end of the story — that's a pleasure I'll leave to your own discovery — but I will tell you that when they did find it, I think I might have actually exclaimed aloud with happiness. It's straight from the old school *Weird Tales*-style pulps, something which might have crawled out of a Clark Ashton Smith fever dream. This story would have delighted Farnsworth Wright, and might have nestled comfortably in a table of contents between CAS and Robert E. Howard.

Except, perhaps, for one crucial detail, which I'll come to in a moment.

The Nameless Dark is an unapologetic love letter to the ghoulish adventurism of the old pulp aesthetic. The ghost of H.P. Lovecraft haunts many of these tales, drifting brazenly through stories like "The Truffle Pig", one of the most audaciously inventive Jack the Ripper stories I've ever read; "White Feather", an examination of cowardice and outrageous courage in Revolutionary America; and "Free Fireworks", a war story shot through with love, beauty, and glory-laden horror. "Beer & Worms" is a simple tale of friendship and fishing, with a stinger ending you can envision being illustrated by Jack Davis in an issue of *Tales From the Crypt*. In "Transmission" and "The Screamer", isolation and the constant simmering insanity of contemporary life are the hinge-points for transcendent horrors. The bleak cosmology of Laird Barron is the backdrop for "Love Songs from the Hydrogen Jukebox", another period piece, this one set in '60s San Francisco, where so many lost or damaged souls became fodder to the appetites of more powerful, dangerous personalities. It's one of the best stories in the book.

But there is, as I said, a crucial difference that sets Grau's writing apart from the grandfathers of the weird tale. He is cognizant of the cultural assumptions and short cuts his characters indulge in. The racism and the misogyny that can make reading Lovecraft and Howard such a vexing experience are replaced here by a cultural self-awareness that forever eluded those writers. You'll find those traits in some of the characters, to be sure; Grau is too honest a writer to engage in the wish fulfillment of a truly democratic depiction of the world. But, as is especially clear in the contentious relationship of the soldiers in "The Mission" — and in the terrible insight which accompanies their final discovery — the author refuses to relegate anyone to a caricature. Everyone bears the weight of a life.

In this way, he is the writer I wish Lovecraft and Howard could have been.

T.E. Grau is a large-hearted writer. He's a generous writer. The themes that unite these seemingly disparate stories — loneliness, isolation, threats against the family, or the desire to belong to a family — are made potent by this. This is what gives the horror its teeth.

And we want our horror to have teeth. We need it to. It is designed to hurt us even as it thrills us, so that we may survive the hurt and become wiser because of it. This is what brings us here, to this unlit church, down in the black belly of the earth. We're here to weep over the doomed love which entangles us all, and to suffer for our hopes. We're here to feel the cool air of the crypt, and to tremble at the way it calls our lives to attention. We're here to honor all the beauties and the horrors of the world.

We're here to bend the knee to the nameless dark.

Nathan Ballingrud
Asheville, North Carolina - April 8, 2015

TUBBY'S BIG SWIM

T he fat horsefly flew in a wide circle, tethered by a length of thread taped to the desktop. The buzz of its wings was deep, sonorous, more majestic than flies are often given credit.

Alden's chin rested on his crossed arms and his small eyes followed the insect. "Bertrand," the boy said, giving proper name to the airborne thing. A small dish of sugar water was set up on the edge of the desk, as was a miniature perch fashioned out of picture wire. "Bertrand the Fly Boy," Alden announced. The naming was complete.

The boy continued to watch, noting the change in flight path, the figure eights, the frustrated zigs and zags, marveling at the variety. But after a time, the circles became concentric, growing tighter and tighter, until Bertrand spiraled downward, pitched to one side and landed in the dish, legs twitching, wings rippling the surface of the thick water.

Alden sighed, pulled back the tape and held up the dripping fly in front of his large, perfectly round face. The leash had become a noose. All of them died. Every single one. No matter how much care and effort and love he put into their survival. They all eventually died right in front of him.

He gave the fly one last look, before letting it drop out of the open window onto the noisy street below. "So long, Bertrand."

◎

Alden opened the front door to the three-story brownstone and trudged down the steps on thick ankles squeezed into last year's shoes, a large glass pepper jar under his arm. He was hunting bigger game this time, and needed a receptacle worthy of his prey.

He walked up the sidewalk, trying to fold in on himself to avoid the attention of the older kids gathered across the street, laughing and cursing just loudly enough to infect the block while keeping out of earshot of their parents almost certainly screaming at each other somewhere inside their building. School would be starting soon, and kids were overheated and under-stimulated after three months away from their studies, itching for an excuse to take down a straggler that didn't fit the herd.

Alden and his mother Regina had moved to this downtown neighborhood two weeks ago after the owner of Pinewood Park grew tired of wrestling with his mother in her room. The night before they left, the man gave her a black eye. An hour later, she gave him a gift in return—a dropped match on the shag carpet soaked in vodka. The cloud of black smoke that rose in the distance behind their station wagon as they sped out the gate was beautiful, like the breath of a dragon. Alden sure wished he could trap one of those, because dragons lived forever.

Now in this new city that looked so old to him, he missed the trailer and its rectangular simplicity. It was just him and his mother, for the most part, and there were lots of critters living in the chaparral on the other side of the chain link fence. Lizards, spiders, rolly pollies, earwigs—even scorpions, when he could find one. He caught each of them in turn, but they all eventually went the way of Bertrand, the way of the trailer and the smile in his mother's eyes. Things died so quickly, which made Alden wonder how many days any of us had left.

Across the way, the group of boisterous kids gave chase to a neighborhood cat, hurling soda bottles and insults at the terrified feline as it skittered toward the other side of the street, leaping over the curb and passing right in front of Alden, stopping both of them. The cat and the boy stared at each other.

"Hi, kitty," Alden said, bending down to offer his hand for a sniff, just as an untied high top kicked the animal out of view. The cat screeched bloody murder as it arced through air, landing awkwardly on its side with a weird thump, before limping into the alley and disappearing behind a pile of stuffed trash bags. Alden thought that cats always landed on their feet. This one sure as heck didn't. City cats must live by different rules.

Four sets of shoulders moved into Alden's view, topped by sweaty, excited faces. They all wore swimming trunks, the plastic fabric rustling between their sunburned legs as they jostled for position, slinging their towels over their necks or wrapping them around their arms. Three of the boys smiled. The fourth, bigger than the others, wasn't. "Where you goin'?" the tall one asked.

"Yeah, where you goin'?" the shortest one echoed.

Alden's heart was pounding. He didn't like confrontations, and he knew this was a major one. He was the new kid, always the new kid, and so he had to take his lumps. Maybe this time wouldn't be as bad as the last.

"Looking for pets," Alden said, holding up his pickle jar, as if in explanation.

The boys looked at each other, confusion quickly giving away to sneers and laughter.

"What are you, a fucking retard?" one of the other boys asked. Aside from the tall one and the short one, the two other boys looked very much alike. They might have been twin brothers, or just both really ugly.

"Yeah, you a fucking retard?" Echo Boy said.

Alden founds this question odd. Both times. "No," he said.

"Well, you look like a fucking retard," Tall Boy said, slapping the jar out of Alden's hand, not watching as it smashed on the sidewalk, spraying them with shards of glass. The shrapnel surprised the other kids, and even kept Echo Boy quiet as he dug a chip out of his shoe. Tall Boy leaned in close to Alden, breathing the sour smell of strawberry soda into his face, and poked Alden in the stomach. "Tubby."

Echo and the Two Others who had moved back to avoid the glass now closed in, hands balling into fists, lips stretching over missing teeth. One of them wound up his towel into a tight twist, holding it low, ready to unleash it like a whip.

"You get on outta here, now," a voice called from above. The boys looked up and found a wiry woman with ash gray hair leaning out of her window, gesticulating with one hand, her other holding a phone. "Breaking glass on a public sidewalk? What in the *world*? I'm calling the police!"

"Come on," one of the Other Ones said to Tall Boy, grabbing him by the shirt. "That bitch is crazy."

Tall Boy's peeved grin widened into smile of anticipation. "See you around," he said.

They ran up the street, laughing and high fiving and bumping into each other as they veered around the corner, heading toward the dilapidated strip of boardwalk built atop the beach.

Alden stared down at the collection of glass that had been his pepper jar. Crystals glinted around a perfect tin circle lid with holes poked through it, which would have allowed those things trapped inside to breathe. It would have been the perfect environment. The ideal home. Alden would have made sure. Now it was just trash.

A bus squealed to a stop in the street, offloading a cluster of exhausted people in various stained uniforms. A faded banner ad on the side of the bus, marred by unimaginative graffiti, announced the unveiling of the new primate exhibit at the city zoo. *Come experience the WILD!* the advert dared.

"Are you hurt, son?"

Alden peered up at the woman in the window staring down at him, the phone receiver held limply in her hand. There was no cord attached to it.

He wiped his nose with the back of his hand. "Which way to the zoo?"

The route she gave him was wrong, and after an hour of walking in a gradually widening square, he noticed that there weren't any more gulls circling overhead, nor could he smell the fishy brine of the ocean. He was far from his apartment, and probably nowhere near the zoo. Maybe that bitch *was* crazy. Crazy enough to get a kid lost without batting an eye.

Alden sat on the curb and took off his shoes to let his cramped feet breathe a little. Blood from a popped blister on his big toe stained his sock. He'd need to soak his foot in Epsom when he got home. *If he ever got home*, he thought to himself, weighing his excitement against his gnawing fear of being lost in a strange city, full of mean kids and old women who gave crummy directions. The sun was going down, and he thought about forgetting about the zoo and asking someone for a route back to his apartment, even entertaining the idea of calling his mother to come pick him up at one of the major cross streets. Maybe he could find a dime in one of the payphones guarding each block, most of them surrounded by shouting men and crying women in short skirts. But tonight was Friday, which meant that Uncle Duane was staying over for the weekend. Uncle Duane didn't like Alden, which suited Alden just fine, as he didn't like Uncle Duane either. There was something about him—the disjointed tattoos, the band of pale skin that circled the ring finger of his sunburned left hand, the way he looked at Alden when Regina was in the bathroom.

Alden gingerly put his shoes back on and stood up, raising a fleshy chin with determination. After approaching a hairy man who smelled like whiskey bottles, an old woman sitting on a park bench under an enormous blue hat, and a fruit vendor who Alden thought looked exactly like Bruce Lee, Alden got the proper directions to the zoo, and arrived minutes later just as it was closing.

It was a drab, tiny zoo, as zoos go. He had snuck into so many all over the country, wherever he and his mother had stayed, and would do the same here in this city. Security for caged animals was never very good, so Alden circled the perimeter of the property until he found a cut in the fencing. Other kids had been here before. Maybe even the ones who broke his jar. The Beach Bums. Alden hoped they hadn't, remembering the way the cat landed on the cement, the sound it made. Fleshy and embarrassed. They could do so much damage in a place like this.

Alden waited by the fence, guessing at the contents of the buildings he could see and planning his route once inside. You always had to have a plan. After a half hour, just as the sun went down, the main lights along the thoroughfare blinked off just as the pale blue overnight lamps came to life. A humming refrigeration unit behind the snack bar suddenly went quiet, creating that weird sensation of removing a sound that you never heard in the first place. This was the power down. The main staff would be gone in a few minutes, leaving just the cleaning crew and whatever security detail was tasked with watching over animals that had nowhere to go, and no interest in going there anyway. These were broken creatures, robbed of everything that made them wild. Puppets for the public, reenacting the Nature play in a grotesque spectacle of enslavement and exhibition. Several cars drove out the front gate to his left. Time to start his visit. Alden squeezed through the opening in the fence, tearing his jacket on the jagged edges of metal, and walked up the deserted pathway.

The zoo was even drabber on the inside. Cracked paint and rutted pavement. Faded signage from before Alden's mother was born. And the stink of tar, stale popcorn, and urine shrouding everything. That zoo smell. They didn't know how to take care of their pets here. Not one bit. He wanted to burn this place to the ground, but only with the customers in it. The animals needed to be boarded onto parade floats and moved to that farm upstate that takes all the unwanted dogs and cats and lets them run free in the country. Alden vowed to visit that farm someday. Maybe they'd even let him work there. It would be a fine life. Alden the Pet Farmer.

He tried the doors to several buildings, but they were all locked. No sounds came from inside. He found the primate house, adorned with a picture of a baby chimpanzee. He liked baby animals. Easier to carry. He grabbed the knob. It was sticky, but he turned it anyway. The door clicked loudly, echoing off the deserted corners of the zoo and sending a shiver down his spine, then creaked open. He looked behind him and entered.

It was humid, almost stifling, smelling of feces and rotten fruit. He walked to the sole exhibit window in the room, and put his hand on the thick pane of cloudy glass, scratched with initials and an assortment of R Rated words. The enclosure was dark, with two fake tree trunks scattered randomly across the stained floor. Alden peered inside, making out a figure huddling in an alcove, blacker than the darkness around it, faced away from the glass. It was large, with bulging shoulders, and a low-slung head pressed against its massive chest. Alden knocked lightly on the window, careful not to make too much sound. Animals could hear things we couldn't, and didn't like loud noises. The gorilla didn't move.

Alden wandered outside behind the primate building, glumly wondering what had happened to the baby chimp from the advertisement. Thoughts of a smoky card game organized by the loser overnight crew to determine the fate of the baby chimp spun in Alden's head. Bunch of sweaty roughnecks in cutoff shorts, bandanas, and sleeveless shirts. They probably force-fed it beer and made it dance to disco songs when the rest of the staff went home. They probably sold it off to some black market collector of sad baby chimps. They probably threw it down into a culvert during a rainstorm, and watched it tumble out to sea, screaming until it drowned, dreaming of the jungle and its mama waiting in the trees. People did such things all the time, and not just to baby chimps.

While Alden tried to erase these depressing thoughts, he detected the low purr of filtration equipment, the lapping sound of water. He brightened, regained what bearings he had in this strange place, and followed the sound, heading up a switchback ramp, arriving at an open-air pool at the back of the zoo.

He rushed to the edge of the raised tank and looked down into the water, which reflected the bluish security lamps above like snatches of broken lightning. Just below the surface, black shapes moved and roiled in that slow motion way of underwater life, active now that the sun had gone down and all of the groping hands and horrible pink faces had gone home.

Alden watched the creatures slither over each other like intertwined tongues. Nurse sharks and stingrays. A few skates, with their smiling alien faces. Prehistoric cousins, all of them, stuffed too densely into this shallow pool. Bisected eyes stared up at him with cold accusation, as if he had designed this small enclosure for so many live bodies. He reached out a hand, realizing too late that he was now just as bad as all the rest of them. The stupid idiots who groped and grasped at animals that just wanted to be left alone. But he couldn't help it. How could you not touch them? They were so beautiful, even angry as they were. So unlike their clumsy, two-legged descendents. How could one not touch human flesh to aquatic hide that still held the blueprint? Alden leaned forward, reaching his hand further, bringing his face close to the swirling water. A flippered wing of a ray broke the surface of the water and slapped against his forehead, sliding all the way down to his nose and mouth, before disappearing back into the black water. Alden stepped back, eyes wide. He touched the wetness on his forehead, brought it to his nose and sniffed, but it didn't smell like anything.

The sound of footsteps coming up the ramp sent him scrambling into the thorny bushes surrounding the pool. A gangly security guard with bad skin and his skanky girlfriend whose skin was worse stumbled to the edge of the pool, where they smoked a joint and giggled. Alden grimaced, imagining the greasy pair giving the baby chimp some drugs before they did away with him. The young man unbuckled his heavy belt that was too large for his slight frame, unbuttoned his pants, and clicked on his flashlight, pointing the beam at what was growing in his underwear. His girlfriend took the wad of pink gum out of her mouth and flicked it into the pool, then crouched down quickly, losing her balance and skinning her knees on the concrete. She cursed. The man laughed.

Alden turned away, hoping nothing in the water ate that gum.

Alden climbed through the hole in the fence and made his way back into the city. It looked different at night, with new sights, sounds, and smells, not helped in the least by the fact that he had to flip his mental map and make opposite turns to retrace his steps back the way he came. Even with his best efforts and his normally excellent sense of direction, he ended up getting lost. He wasn't so much scared as he was disappointed, as he had to come to grips with that fact that a point of pride had taken a blow.

As the city got louder and the air more interesting he turned down this alleyway and that, running from strange grunts in the darkness, cackled laughter, empty bottles rolling on wet cement. He looked for a pay phone, but there weren't any around here, just broken windows and boarded up doorways. Remnants of posters were everywhere, on every fence, wall, and street lamp, leading Alden to believe that in the not so distant past, a great era of poster-making and display ruled the land, most likely replaced by magazines, and then television. The boy wished the posters were still up, in all their old timey grandeur and fantastical colors. Maybe one of them would have been a poster of the zoo when it was brand new, accurately explaining what sort of animals they had on exhibit. Maybe one of them would have been a map of the city, which would have come in real handy at the moment.

Alden stopped and pondered. He would have liked to think that his mother was at their apartment at that very moment, worried sick about him, pleading with Uncle Duane to set out on a search and rescue mission for her poor lost son, but he knew deep down that that would never happen. Not until his mom and Uncle Duane's secret meeting in her bedroom, which sometimes took hours, and ended with something breaking behind the locked door. Alden didn't like those secret meetings. Alden didn't like Uncle Duane, and was pretty sure that he wasn't really his uncle. The ones back in Pinewood Park always were. They were *his* people, every single Uncle of them.

The scuttling of an insect next to his shoe brought Alden to the realization that he had been staring at his feet. His eyes refocused and he followed the three-inch cockroach as it trotted up the alleyway, proud as the King of Siam. Alden followed, making room enough for a royal roach in the pocket of his jacket, cursing that tall kid for smashing his pepper jar. He'd call this one Sam of Siam.

Alden rounded a corner, just as the roach melted down into a crack in the pavement. He jammed his fingers into the slimy opening, but the insect was gone, disappearing into the bowels of the city, where all cockroaches lived and where Sam of Siam lorded over his own secret empire. Alden sighed and sat back, catching a smudge of light out of the corner of his eye. He turned and faced the most beautiful sign he had seen in weeks, basking in the fizzing pink glow of its faded neon. Maybe this crappy city wasn't so bad after all.

OK Pets 'n More was a cramped, dingy affair, with very few pets, and too much of the "more," which in this case meant boxes of cheap electronics filling most of the front section of the room. But, to keep the promise of the name, a few cages were stacked in the back of the shop, flanked by a wall of filthy aquariums kept humming by a tangle of extension cords and three prong adaptors that bristled from the wall outlet just above the scuffed tile floor. Men with dark hair and fierce features walked in and out of the back room, grunting under the weight of more boxes of cheap electronics, which they carried to the front of the store. None of them paid any heed to the pets arranged in the corner, or to their lone customer.

Alden reverently approached the collection of cages. He'd only been inside two pet stores in his entire life prior to this day, so he marked the occasion as a chance encounter with divine providence. Alden walked slowly past each cramped pen that smelled of unwashed animals and bladdered ammonia. It was a wonderful odor, this musk of furry things, and he breathed in deeply, making sure to establish eye contact with each creature, looking past the mange, the cracked teeth, the gummy eyes. The cages were labeled with hand scrawled breed names, but Alden didn't need any help. Douglas the Dachshund. Pinky the Poodle of Crying Castle. Feline Fiona. Gerald the Gerbil Knight. He nodded at each in turn, paying his respects, ignoring the fact that they ignored him. Fiona may have been dead. Gerald certainly was.

A light tapping brought Alden's attention to the aquariums. He scurried over to the wall of segregated glass and moved his round face over each tank, peering inside, looking for any signs of life. In the middle aquarium, a small white fish emerged from the cloudy water and banged its nose into the glass, before shimmying back into the murk. It did this over and over, every twelve seconds. Alden knew this because he counted. Other than that lone fish—Twelve Second Charlie—and a few sluggish goldfish in the top row, the aquariums seemed empty, making liars of the stained tags advertising such exotic species as Kissing Gourami, Clown Loach, and Sailfin Molly. Alden didn't see a thing in any of the other tanks. Not even a garden variety Guppy. The bottom tank, wider than the rest by three, was empty, aside from dust bunnies and a wolf spider that had taken up residence in the back corner.

The sound of expensive shoes clicking on tile turned Alden around. One of the men, who looked indistinguishable from the others, walked toward him, carrying a rusty tin bucket that sloshed water onto the floor. Alden stepped out of his way as the man stopped at the aquariums and set the bucket down. He slid the lowermost tank forward on its metal rack, and unceremoniously dumped the contents of the bucket into it. The man clicked on the fluorescent light inside and flicked on the water pump, before slamming it back into position under the rest of the tanks and walking away, his shiny leather shoes squishing through the pools of water on the floor.

Alden took one look at what was now living in the aquarium and opened his eyes wide, air hissing through his lips like a deflating balloon.

"Sir," he called out when he collected himself, raising his hand like he was in school.

The man turned and glared at the boy with a mixture of irritation and surprise, as if noticing him for the first time. He said nothing.

"What is this?" Alden said, pointing to the tank. "It's not labeled."

The man shrugged before walking off, disappearing in a flap of plastic dividers that led to the back room

Alden bent to the bottom tank, his mouth opening slowly. On the other side of the glass, swaying with the movements of the settling water, was a bright orange bulk the size and shape of a decorative pumpkin. Almost the same color, too, but even more vibrantly orange. Eight arms unfurled beneath a stout body—the bloom of a fiery flower. A noble brow ridge topped two yellowish eyes, drawing down in the middle of the rounded cranium, giving the impression of a perpetual scowl of irritation or contemplation. It was an octopus. A big, round, beautiful octopus. It was real, and it was in the tank in front of him. And it was for sale. Alden touched his forehead, remembering the feel of the stingray's wing on his skin. He made a gurgling sound that must have resembled the contented cluck of an infant, if anyone in the room was listening to the chubby boy huddled in front of the aquariums. Which they weren't.

Alden put his finger into the water and brought it to his mouth, tasting it. He smacked his lips a few times, just to make sure. "Fresh water," he murmured. After a moment of processing this discovery, his eyes once again grew in their sockets. *Fresh water octopus?*

He heard the tap on the glass again, this time sounding more forceful, like the blow of a tiny hammer used to cobble tiny shoes. Alden stood, just in time to see Twelve Second Charlie drift to the bottom of the aquarium, its face smashed and tiny eye discs dangling from a thread on either side of its tiny ruined skull. Alden rolled up one sleeve and slipped his arm into the water, his hand creating a swirl that pushed the dead fish out of reach. He finally cornered it and pinched the slippery body between his fingers, pulling it from the water. He bent down and slipped Charlie into the octopus tank, watching its twirling descent, coming to rest in front of the octopus. Its two golden eyes registered nothing, and it made no move to eat the dead fish.

Several of the dark haired men were talking in low tones in a foreign language at the front of the store, gesturing at the boxes of electronics with lit cigarettes and writing down figures on a notepad. Alden waited for a break in the conversation, but after none came, he decided that he had to forego his manners. "Excuse me."

They all stopped talking at once and glared at him, as if Alden was an interloper who had stumbled into a dire family discussion. With their faces lined up together, the boy realized that they looked almost identical, thick eyebrows knitting together with the same irritated expression as the creature in the back of the store.

"How much for the octopus?"

After a brief pause, they returned to their discussion.

Alden took a deep breath, embarrassed that he needed to be so forceful. It wasn't his style, especially with adults. "I beg your pardon, gentlemen." He held up his green Velcro wallet, lined in black and stitched with the outline of a cartoon grasshopper.

"What is it?" the closest man asked in a heavy accent, drawn even heavier by exasperation.

"I want to buy the octopus," Alden said, gesturing behind him. "The one in back. The orange one." He waved his wallet, as if some sort of enticing promise. "I don't have any money on me right now, but I'll get it and bring it back tomorrow." Again, nothing from the men. "So how much?"

"Twenty dollar," one of them said, turning back around.

Alden couldn't believe his good fortune. "*Twenty* dollar?"

The man wasn't going to repeat himself.

Alden grinned. "Okay!"

He shook each of their hands in turn, and ran back to the aquariums to make sure the octopus was real and still there. It was. The white fish was gone. "It *is* alive," Alden whispered. He kissed his hand and pressed it on the tank, smudging the glass, took a deep breath and ran past the men and out of the store. They paused for a second, then picked up their discussion where it left off.

A few seconds later, Alden reemerged in the doorway. "Which way to the bus stop?"

After three transfers and a mad dash, chasing down the last Number 9 of the night, Alden arrived home well after 11:00 pm. He didn't have a curfew, but if he did, he was pretty sure he would have broken it by an impressive margin.

Alden unlocked the door to the apartment with a key that didn't yet feel familiar to his fingers. He never wanted it to become familiar. Back at Pinewood Park, they never locked their door. Never even closed the metal door behind the screen. People looked out for their neighbors there. They socialized, had parties, holed up in the back room together for hours on end, as smoke that smelled like burnt plastic filtered through the door while Alden played video games. They were doing science projects in there, Regina had told him. Those must have been some kind of important experiments, because they'd sometimes go on for days. Real go getters, those citizens of Pinewood Park.

Despite the television blaring an old Western, Alden crept into the living room. He wasn't worried about getting grounded for coming home so late, he just didn't want to be seen. Being invisible, he knew, was the best course of action on any Uncle Night. He noted the greasy jeans flung in one corner, next to worn cowboy boots and wadded up socks the color of dishwater. A long wallet attached to a chain stuck out of the back pocket of the jeans. It had a skull set against a confederate flag stitched into the leather. It was perfumed with motor oil and cigarette smoke. Alden remembered the smell.

A bluish light leaked from underneath his mother's shut bedroom door, together with the screamed lyrics of some stupid heavy metal song buzzing through cheap speakers. Alden pressed his ear against the door and held his breath, combing a furrow through the sounds of the television behind him and the music within. He wondered if they were doing a science experiment in there. Hoped, actually. The sound of yelps and moans that didn't match with the music told him otherwise, and he was ashamed for listening. But he didn't move.

The next morning, Alden was awakened by a hand around his foot and dragged out of bed. Almost before his head hit the floor, he was whipped across the legs and backside with that very same chain from the long leather wallet. Uncle Duane stood over him, wearing only his underwear, and hollered at him between lashings, asking where the ten dollars went. Alden's room was ransacked, what few belongings he had scattered and broken on the floor. The boy flinched with each strike, but didn't make a sound. He concentrated on the bulge in Uncle Duane' underwear, which looked like an upside down carrot flopping inside a pillowcase. Alden got whipped a few more times, before his mother ran shrieking from the bathroom and leapt onto Uncle Duane like a wolf spider, twisting her own arms into his so he couldn't deliver another blow.

They tussled a little, but Regina was much smaller than Uncle Duane, and as soon as he got a hand free he punched her right in the face. Closed fist and everything, just like he was hitting another man. She crumpled to the floor and started crying, while he staggered to the bathroom, breathing heavily, and threw up in the sink. He didn't even have the common courtesy of making it to the toilet. City Uncles just didn't have any class.

From the bathroom, Uncle Duane yelled something about leaving and never coming back, calling Regina all sorts of Rated R words. She got up and ran to the doorway, pulled off his concert t-shirt that she was wearing and threw it at him, coming up with a few Rated R words herself. Back and forth they went, until Uncle Duane grabbed his clothes and headed out the door, still in his underwear with that carrot leading him outside. He didn't close the door behind him, which would have been the proper thing to do. But no, it remained open, and his nasty, untruthful words echoed down the hall and up the staircase, ending with a description of her privates and the final repetition of the words "worthless cunt." He most likely wouldn't be back, Alden thought, as who would return to the home of a "worthless cunt" with obviously substandard private parts?

Regina hugged her son close, pressing his face into the side of her breast and wetting the top of his hair with her tears. She apologized and made promises, holding his perfectly round face in her hands and looking into his eyes, pushing his hair back from his wide forehead. But Alden knew even before she went off to the kitchen to find the first aid kit for his legs that there would be another Uncle in the house by the end of the week. Alden figured out long ago that his mom couldn't live very long without an Uncle around, no matter where they stayed. Alden began to feel that he couldn't live very long *with* another Uncle. He was all Uncled-out.

Later, when Alden was alone again in his room, he gingerly moved to the floor, wincing at the long red welts on his thighs and calves, and pulled up a bit of the thin carpet that always seemed wet, as if whatever had melted into it refused to dry up and go away. Underneath, between the sticky underpad and the scarred hardwood was a folded up ten dollar bill. Alden brought it to his nose, smelling the warm minty bite of the green paper, combined with the odor of motor oil and cigarette smoke. A last gift from Uncle Duane.

While his mother took one of her long morning naps, Alden decided to use some of the tenner as an investment in his long-term plan, and did just that at the corner store which was nowhere near any corner, but actually a dozen blocks away, jammed between a foul smelling Chinese restaurant and boarded-up wig store with bubble-rounded graffiti words covering what was left of the show windows. Inside, rows of wigless Styrofoam heads lined dusty shelves, all facing the back of the shop. Most of the heads were painted brown. A few of them were knocked over. A few more were missing.

Alden needed a mode of transportation for both the front and back end of his plan, so a wagon was definitely in order. Luckily, the Round Th' Way Store sold a Radio Flyer, which turned out to be a knockoff on closer examination that included wiping away a layer of dust. *RODEO FLYER* was painted across the side, with a little stick figure man perched atop a horse instead of a wagon. And it wasn't even red, more a pinkish orange. A crooked sticker on the undercarriage proclaimed *Made in China*. Alden sighed.

The cheapo plastic wheels detailed every crack and rut in the sidewalk as Alden pulled the wagon through the city, parking it outside alleyways and behind taverns and restaurants, where he climbed inside dumpsters and rummaged through battered garbage cans in search of his temporary cargo. In no time at all, he had filled up the wagon bed. Thick Coke bottles, crushed Budweiser cans, brown, green, and clear beer bottles, with the green ones always smelling like a skunk. The entire haul was carefully arranged in the Chinese Rodeo Flyer. After he could fit no more into the wagon without the conglomeration unraveling and tumbling to the pavement, Alden headed for the recycling center that the shopkeep at the Round Th' Way Store assured him was at the cross street of Howard and Hodgson, on the outskirts of the industrial district and spitting distance from skid row. Sure enough, it was. Finally, someone with a sense of direction. Alden made a mental note to thank the man later, and began to construct a thoughtful compliment to reward the clerk's superior geographic orientation. Birds of a feather needed to be supportive of one another.

The recycling center was a vacant lot in the shadow of a corroded warehouse, its machinery of commerce consisting of a tagged up semi trailer stuffed with bales of smashed cans and a small industrial scale, surrounded by a labyrinth of orange traffic cones, ostensibly to keep the customers away from each other. Alden maneuvered his Rodeo Flyer through a slalom of plastic bags and plastic bag people, finding that executing the transaction of prime recyclables was more trying than the actual hunt, as this was a busy, complicated place, teeming with activity and shouts and arguments, demanding a heightened level of alertness. After ignoring several muttering homeless men who gestured at him with hands made of beef jerky, it was Alden's turn at last, and he tried to haggle glass prices with the stone-faced recycling center employee, pointing out the attributes of clear glass over colored, which the man insisted should be weighed together. It was no use. The cretin wouldn't listen, and all grades were weighed the same. Such a waste. No wonder wagons were all made in China now.

As he trundled away with an empty rig, Alden looked down into his palm at the first reward for his morning's work: $2.78. With the tight, satisfied nod of a saddle bitten working man, he carefully folded the bills around the loose change, and slid the monetary package into his pocket, patting it with his hand. Only six more runs to go, he reckoned. Seven if he found more bottles than cans. Aluminum was where the money was at.

Alden worked every back alley he came across, whistling past rodents the size of Schnauzers (clearly not suited for domestication), and diving into hellish receptacles of rot and stink the outside world would never believe. But he stayed true to the plan, gritted through the dirty work, and made his trips back and forth as the sun rose as high as it could and then began to set with red-faced resignation.

On what proved to be his last haul to the recycler, he came across the owner, an honest to goodness African man who actual came from Africa, so black that he shined blue in the dying light, with tiny glasses and an unusually wide part in his close-cropped hair. It was like seeing a zebra, which coincidentally was also native to Africa.

"Too much hot," the African man cried as he pulled in the scale and stacked cones a full hour before the closing time promised on the hand painted sign taped to the trailer. "Dees hobos get the crazy and start to rob when it get *dis* hot!" He grinned, and a crescent moon of white cut through all the black. He was beautiful.

Alden made several commiserating clicks with the side of his mouth as he received his last essential payment, pocketing a paltry $1.62. But it was enough. More than enough, actually. He'd cleaned out this corner of the city, going after bottles and cans that the transients couldn't reach. And in the end, he had enough. His clothes were filthy. His back ached. There was a strange cut on his hand that leaked red in a perforated stitch. But he had executed his plan and achieved his goal.

"Too much hot," the African man said again for good measure as he slammed the trailer door shut.

When Alden arrived back at the apartment, the Rodeo Flyer gripped under his arm like a surfboard, the door was unlocked and it was silent inside. No mother, and most importantly, no Uncle. Alden didn't panic. His mom went away at night sometimes, working the night shift at the factory. Alden assumed there were many factories in this stupid city, as it was old and dirty and wheezy, like a mean grandpa dying in his bed. She'd be back in the morning, before he even woke up. He'd open his eyes, and she'd be lying behind him in bed, the two of them pressed together like two spoons in a drawer. Her makeup would be smeared, her breath would smell like bleach, and her heart would be beating twice as fast as his. Regina always told him that she was having bad dreams about the factory, which made her heart beat like that. Alden didn't care. He just liked the feeling of waking up with her arm wrapped around him, the Tweety Bird tattoo on her forearm smiling up at him as he opened his eyes. His mom had a pet of her own.

◎

The next morning, Alden woke up alone. No mom. No Tweety Bird. They both must have put in overtime at the factory. At least she wouldn't have any bad dreams about that place. No sleep, no dreams. There was a silver lining hidden inside every cloud.

Alden made himself a breakfast of mayo and Wonderbread, not hungry and hardly tasting it. He was too excited. Today was the day of the Big Purchase, and he needed fuel for the journey.

He took a quick bath and put on his Easter suit, a white tuxedo Regina had picked up at Boy Wonder Big & Tall two years ago for a visit to his grandparents' house that had gone horribly wrong. It felt a bit snug—okay, a lot snug—but it fit well enough for the occasion. Alden dabbed some shaving cream on his cheeks for cologne, filled his palm with a mound of white foam from his mother's canister of mousse and slicked back his hair like in those old black and white gangster films. *It's all about respect*, most of them said in most of those movies. Alden agreed. Respect was a dying virtue, and he'd do his best to keep it alive in these dishonorable times.

In his bedroom, Alden pulled up the carpet and removed the folded bills and the baggy containing $3.17 in coins. All told, he was now in possession of twenty-one dollars and seventeen cents. A king's ransom, even after factoring in roundtrip bus fare. Heck, he could probably treat himself to a celebratory Shasta on the way home, purchased from the geographically savvy shopkeep at the Round Th' Way Store. He'd toast his new title, reborn as Alden the Octopus Man. A parade would be waiting for the two of them outside his brownstone, he just knew it. All the critters in the neighborhood would line up to welcome the conquering hero and his orange companion, bowing low in homage. It would be a fine affair. Alden smiled as he crammed the bills into his tight trousers, opting to stow the baggy of coins in the interior pocket of his blazer. He didn't want to tempt the fates holding his pant seams together.

The octopus. The parade…. That's the great things about critters. You can always count on them.

Alden carried his wagon down the steps of his apartment building, resting its four wheels on the sidewalk. The air was clean and salty, full of promise. It was still early yet, not even past nine, but the Beach Bums were already sitting on their perch across the street, filling the block with their quarrels, crude noises, and uninspired insults. They must set their alarm clocks, to be the first ones outside before the rest of the neighborhood could get into position. Seagulls circled overhead, monitoring the situation. *My crown for a very long net*, Alden thought. *And a birdcage.*

Making himself as inconspicuous as he could in a white suit with a lime green bow tie, Alden pulled his empty wagon to the bus stop, quickly plotting the reverse route to OK Pets 'n More on the transit map, making note of bus numbers and times. The chatter from the Beach Bums suddenly stopped, and Alden knew without looking that they were staring at him. From the corner of his eye, he could see them getting up, rising high and ugly, and making a move toward the street. Alden forced himself to not look their way, even though every atom in his being was already pointed in their direction.

Their beat-up tennies made contact with the asphalt of the street. They weren't dressed for the beach today. They were geared up for neighborhood work, which included punting cats and beating up all the new kids. Alden was just about to run back into his apartment when Number 9 hummed into existence down the block, sliding toward the bus stop in that slinky, soundless way peculiar only to busses and vehicles in science fiction. Air brakes squealed, and with a whoosh, the door folded open. Alden leapt into the bus and landed on the second step with a heavy thump, his wagon clattering against the railing.

The bus driver frowned and whistled low, sizing up Alden's stout frame. "Goddamn, son, you gonna put a hole through the floor."

Alden crouched down and dug into his blazer pocket for the fare, trying to apologize, but nothing came out of his mouth as his jaws worked around the words. Four Beach Bum-size shadows passed in front of the bus, looking up inside. Searching.

"You okay?" the bus driver asked.

Alden tried to answer, as he wanted to tell this man about the marauding Beach Bums, his napping mother, the cruelty of Uncles and what lay in wait for him at OK Pets 'n More, but the fear that had grown in his stomach reached up and choked his throat, making speech difficult. "Close…door." Alden croaked.

The bus driver made a face, shrugged, then closed the door as Alden pulled the baggy from his pocket, poked his fingers inside, and dropped a quarter into the metal basket. It dinged. A coin for the ferryman.

"Keep that wagon out the aisle," the bus driver said, clicking on his blinker. "Ain't got time for no lawsuit."

Alden pulled his wagon through the open front door of OK Pets 'n More, breathing hard from his near run from the bus stop several blocks away. He blinked several times, seeing stars as his eyes adjusted to the low interior light.

The store looked different in the daytime. Thick rays of luminescence cut through the front windows like butter knives, revealing a dance of dust motes and pet hair that frolicked in the air, normally invisible without the revelation of the sun. The boxes of electronics remained stacked up at the front of the room, and the aquariums hummed in the back, flanking the cages. But today it was completely quiet. No serious-faced men moving merchandise and disappearing through doors and arguing with each other in a language he didn't understand. The place was devoid of human life.

"Hello?" Alden called out. "I'm here to buy the octopus." He waited for a sound from the back room, the approach of clicking leather shoes. Nothing.

He noticed tiny pools of water on the floor, dotting the tile all the way back to the aquariums. Alden pulled his wagon behind him, following the trail, which led him to the cages. All of the slatted doors were open and every cage was empty. Douglas the Dachshund. Pinky the Poodle of Crying Castle. Feline Fiona. Gerald the Gerbil Knight. The whole sad royal court was gone, leaving behind only puddles of urine and smears of feces.

The trail of water continued to the aquarium wall. No goldfish swam in the top row. In the lowest tank, the orange octopus brooded, composed in the exact same position as it had been the night before.

"Hiya, boy," Alden said, bending low with a dangerous creak of non-breathable fibers stretched tight over knees and backside. "I'm taking you home."

The octopus neither regarded nor ignored him. It just stared out with a directionless gaze from those strange golden eyes. Alden didn't take it personally.

Cephalopods are a notoriously stoic lot. You don't survive hundred of millions of years by giving it all away for cheap.

Alden got to his feet and looked around again. "Is there anyone here?" he called through cupped hands.

No answer. Maybe the men were all on break. At church, or something. Was there church on a Thursday morning? Alden certainly didn't know, especially when it came to whatever country these fierce looking fellows came from, or what sort of church they would attend. For all he knew, they went to church every morning, and maybe at night, too. And left the door wide open to their shop stuffed with chintzy electronics and empty pet cages. It could happen, Alden told himself, half believing it. People were different. His other, more skeptical half wasn't buying it, though, and made the decision for both sides to get out of this place as fast as they could. But not without finishing the deal for which he had worked so diligently.

"I'm going to take the octopus," Alden announced to the empty room. "Purchased fair and square. I'll leave the twenty bucks on the counter, okay?" No one agreed or disagreed. He took this as a binding contract of assent.

Alden set to work transferring the aquarium full of water and a very impassive orange octopus into his Rodeo Flyer. After several minutes of grunts and sweat and numerous sloshes of water onto his Easter suit and all over the floor, the deed was done. The tank and its cramped inhabitant were now in Alden's wagon, resting where the cans and bottles that purchased creature and tank had lain just days before.

It took some effort to get the wagon moving, now accommodating a good thirty extra pounds. Alden hoped the axles would hold, but who could be sure when it came to Chinese engineering. On television, they said China put poisons in their kid's toys, for goodness sake. Probably into their wagons, too.

As Alden pulled his possibly toxic vehicle outside the store, he wondered how long the unguarded electronics would last. Considering how valuable these items would be in this neighborhood, or any neighborhood with a workable wall outlet, Alden found it strange that none of the items were disturbed, let alone carted out of the store without the owners lording over their product. They must have been the world's worst electronics piled up at the front of the store, closely matching the world's worst collection of pets shoved into the back. Not including the octopus, of course. He was a show pony. The cream of the crop, and he was all his.

◎

Back at the apartment, Alden readied his room for its new occupant, which was waiting out in the hallway next to the bathroom. He swept and tidied, whistling while he worked, which was what all good animals lovers did. The whistling also helped fuzzy the memory of the deal he made with the neighbor man who lived a floor above them, who was sitting out in front of the building, and offered to help carry the heavy aquarium up the two flights of stairs. He wanted to come in and help set up, but Alden had a firm rule about allowing no strangers in the house. The man from upstairs seemed to want to say something or do something, then smiled and shrugged, reminding Alden about his promise. The boy told the man he didn't need to worry. Alden always kept his promises.

Alden's legs and feet were sore, as he had to pull his wagon all the way home, without aid of mass transit. He knew he'd never be able to haul the half full aquarium onto and then off the bus. He didn't know how he'd get the tank up the stairs until the helpful man from upstairs came to his aid. That guy was always hanging around, offering to help the children in the neighborhood. Some people are just hard wired that way.

After the last square inch was dusted, and the desk properly cleared off, Alden dragged the tank into his room, wrapped his bulky arms around it, and hugged it off the floor, using the bed as a halfway point to the top of the desk. Breathing hard, he pushed it back in front of the window, and sat down on his chair, watching as the octopus rocked back and forth with the water as both slowly stilled.

Alden wiped sweat from his brow, and ran his stubby finger down the front of the aquarium, taking in ever knotty detail and rounded curve of his new pet, which caught the light from the window and lit up like a captured flame.

"Tubby," Alden said. "Your name is Tubby." The boy smiled wide. This one would last. He just knew it.

"The fuck is that?"

Alden's face went pale. He didn't turn around, as he recognized the voice coming from his bedroom doorway. "What are you doing here?" he said.

Leaning against the doorframe was Uncle Duane, shirt off, exposing faded prison tats, greasy jeans unbuttoned, letting out a tuft of hair that hid underneath his underwear. He stretched his arms wide. "I'm home. That's what I'm doing here."

"This isn't your home," Alden muttered. "You don't belong here."

"You got your facts all sidefucked, kid," Uncle Duane said, casually biting his nails that were rimmed in black and receded deep below his fingertips. "Your mom asked me to stay here with y'all. Make a proper family. Raise you right. Apply a little discipline to an unruly child."

"You're not our family. You're just another Uncle."

"I ain't uncle to shit, 'specially not you. I live here now, and you're going to have to deal with it, *comprendo*?"

Alden could see Uncle Duane walk toward him in the reflection of Tubby's golden eyes. "Three's company, four's a crowd," he mumbled, stroking the outside of the tank with the tip of his finger.

Uncle Duane stood behind Alden, then bent down and loudly flicked the glass. He smelled like the dirty old beer bottles he pulled from the bottom of a dumpster, probably with twice the germs.

"Ugly fucker."

"He's beautiful."

"It ain't stayin' here."

Alden turned on him, standing between Uncle Duane and the aquarium. His eyes bulged, his heart pounded. "Yes he is. He's my pet."

"Bullshit. I ain't feedin' that."

"You don't have to. I will."

"With what money? Your ma says you don't work. Can't work. Too fat and three steps past lazy."

Alden's cheeks flushed. "My mom didn't say that."

"Sure as shit did. You should hear the garbage your mom says about you." He whistled. It didn't sound anything like the way Alden whistled, while he worked or otherwise.

"You're a liar."

"Yes sir. Yes sir, I am. But I ain't lying about this. Don't have to."

Alden felt tears well up in his eyes, squeezed out from several different directions at once. His skin went hot, started to sweat. "Tubby's staying here. You're not."

"Oh, is that right?" Duane removed his belt and folded it in half, gripping the buckle end in his hand, testing the leather with the other.

"Where's my mom?"

"Sleepin'. Get that thing out of here before I throw it out the window."

"You can't make me."

"I can whip your ass!" Duane lunged for the boy, stopping when he heard the groggy voice behind him.

"What's all the hollering in here?" Regina shuffled into the room, eyes half open. One of them had a ring of purple underneath it.

"He's making me get rid of my pet," Alden said, body blocking Tubby from the rest of the room.

She walked over to the aquarium. "What is this thing? Where did you get it?"

"He's Tubby and he's mine."

"I ain't raisin' no kid *and* his stupid fucking fish," Duane said. "You think I'm made of money?"

"He's a cephalopod, you jerkoff!" The cuss word nearly caught in Alden's mouth, but felt good on the way out.

Duane reached for the boy, but Regina stood in front of him. The man made choking sounds, almost a whimper of frustration. He held up his hands and stalked out of the room. "I'm out."

Regina reached for him. "Baby, wait!"

"Mom, mom," Alden said, pulling on Regina's satin robe. "Did you really say those things about me?"

"What?"

"Fuck that fish!" Duane shouted from the other room, loudly gathering his things, knocking over bottles.

Regina headed for the door. "Baby, don't go!"

"Mom, did you really—?"

Regina grabbed Alden by the shoulder and shook him violently. "Just get that thing out of here!" She released the boy and dashed into the other room, talking quickly, making promises.

"Where am I supposed to take him?" he called out to the other room.

"Take it back where you got it!"

The tears were released, and streamed down thick cheeks bunched wide by grief. Alden wiped his nose with the back of his hand and stared at Tubby. He would've liked to believe that Tubby was staring back at him, encouraging him as he fought for his honor, for his new turf, but he wasn't so sure. Stoicism cut both ways, and was a mysterious mistress.

Uncle Duane helped move the aquarium outside, dropping it on the cement sidewalk as he set it down, resulting in several cracks spidering along the bottom of the glass.

"Sorry, hoss," Uncle Duane said as he bound up the stairs without a glance behind him.

Alden watched these jagged fissures sweat water as he made the return trip to the zoo, which had the distinction of being the single most depressing zoo trip of his short life. He wasn't going there to see the animals. He wasn't even going there to touch the animals. He was going to the zoo to abandon his pet. He considered taking Tubby back to OK Pets 'n More, but he was worried that the store was abandoned. Besides, even if they were still in business, he was starting to realize that those guys didn't even like pets, and should have renamed their sign to Lousy Electronic that Nobody Wants 'n a Couple of Ignored Pets in the Back. That would have made Alden giggle on a normal day, but today was no normal day. It was the day he was giving away Tubby, his best friend, bought fair and square.

Alden waited outside the zoo, just like last time, and snuck through the cut in the fence at closing, just like last time. But this time, it took him longer, because he had to fit an aquarium through the opening with him. And, he had to admit, he just didn't have the same enthusiasm on this go around.

He skipped all the mammal and reptile houses and went straight for the open pool set aside for the skates, rays, and sharks. The skates and rays were not a threat, and none of the species of sharks in that pool could eat something as large or as handsome as Tubby, so Alden figured he'd fit in just fine, spending the rest of his days glaring at his new family, and ignoring all the stupid spectators while he waited for dead white fish to float down in front of him for dinner.

Alden stared at the enclosure for several minutes, trying to figure out how he was going to lift the aquarium high enough to pour Tubby into the water, as the top rim was about a foot above his head.

He reached inside the aquarium and picked up the octopus, holding him on either side of what could only be its head. The physiology of mollusks was a challenging area, Alden had to admit to himself, and he was no zoologist, after all. Not yet, anyway. The boy held the orange creature out in front of him, its tentacles writhed slowly beneath it. They stared at each other, this boy and his octopus. Alden's round face seemed to pulsate, as various muscles reacted with despair and set the flesh above them dancing. Tubby's eyes remained fixed and taciturn, regarding the boy in that emotionless way Alden found so endearing. The boy's arms began to shake, as much due to holding up this hefty creature as it was with the woe he was feeling throughout the entirety of his being. Tubby was his Everest, his perfect companion, quiet and shrewd and loyal to a fault inside his fortress of three hundred million years, and Alden knew he'd never find another pet of quite the same caliber.

Alden hugged him close, feeling the rubbery hide press against the flush of his face. If viewed from afar, it could have appeared as if eight tentacles wrapped around the boy in return, but that would have been impossible. Octopi didn't give hugs, especially bright orange ones about to be cast into a dungeon of sharks. Alden understood this, and knew that Tubby preferred to keep his emotions hidden, folded away inside that tiny pocket called a soul, just like him. Brothers shared these sorts of traits.

With his last bit of strength, the boy reached up his quivering arms and carefully released Tubby into the pool. Alden was hoping that a tentacle would hold on, grasping at his arm with one of his suckers in what would make a truly cinematic moment. But it just plopped into the water like a bag of sand. Alden scrambled to the glass sidewall, and watched the octopus slowly sink to the bottom, an orange star adrift in a black abyss. Its tentacles fanned out just before it touched the bottom. Within seconds, the swirl of shark and ray and skate erased it from sight.

"So long, Tubby."

Alden turned and pressed his back to the glass, sliding down the side of the pool. He needed to rest for a few minutes before he headed home. His arms hurt. So did his feet, his heart. The crying made him dizzy. He didn't cry much, just like he didn't vomit much. Both really took it out of him. Alden leaned his head against the rough concrete and closed his eyes. Just a few minutes to recharge was all he needed, before he'd set out for his mother's stupid apartment he'd never call home.

Alden woke up because the seat of his pants was wet. For a moment, he thought he was at home, but not that apartment across town or even in his bed in the trailer in Pinewood Park. He was in another bed, a much bigger, fluffier, fancier bed, and he had just peed in it, wetting the biggest, cleanest, softest bed in which he'd ever be allowed to sleep. He'd ruined it. Again.

But he didn't ruin it, because he wasn't at home, which he discovered after opening his eyes and clambering to his feet in the dull gray of pre-dawn. Nor was the front of his pants wet. Just the back, on which he had sat the entire night before in an upright position. He regained his bearings and remembered where he was. The zoo. He'd fallen asleep next to the shark and ray enclosure, which was surrounded by shallow pools of water dotting the pavement around it, including the spot where Alden had spent the night. Water on the ground. Just like in the pet store.

He crawled to the glass and pressed his face against it. The entire pool was empty. The water was still there, of course, but nothing living swam inside of it. Completely cleared of every single shark, skate, and ray. Just like in the pet store. But this time, Tubby was gone, too.

Panicky, Alden knocked over a nearby trashcan and rolled it to the edge of the pool. He climbed on top of it, and pulled himself with much difficulty (his arms were terribly sore from the day before, as were his legs and backside from sitting on the cold pavement all night) to the lip of the pool, shakily got to his feet, and walked the six inch tightrope of cement around the edge of the pool on his wide, thick feet, scanning the water. From this vantage point, he spotted Tubby, resting gently on the bottom at the very back of the pool. Alden jumped in.

Back at the wagon, Alden splashed water into the tank from inside the pool. It took several minutes. Realizing the ruckus he was making, Alden paused, expecting the zoo's gross security guard to come running, buttoning up his pants. But no one came. Certainly the overnight guards were just around the corner. But they weren't. Nothing seemed to be moving at all anywhere on the grounds. Not a chirp or a hoot or a howl. Just the gentle lapping of the empty pool. Empty except for Tubby.

After waiting for a bit longer in that weird silence, just to make sure, Alden continued splashing water into the aquarium, until it was adequately filled, then submerged under the water, feeling around for Tubby. He found him exactly where he was supposed to be, and he gripped the octopus with both hands. Alden broke the surface, sputtering out fishy tasting salt water, and held Tubby aloft like a chosen son.

"We're meant to be," Alden cried, his voice echoing back from the cement around him.

Balancing Tubby on the back of his neck, Alden awkwardly, painfully, climbed out of the pool, and slid down to the ground below, scraping the skin on his stomach where it bulged out from his waistband. Alden normally would have thought about the rash he was bound to get, and plan for the treatment of it, but today his mind was soaring above his battered body.

He could barely stop the quavering of his hands as he plopped the octopus back into the aquarium, and within minutes, he was out of the zoo, pulling Tubby to freedom in the back of the Rodeo Flyer, a good hour before the first of the day staff would arrive to find nothing living inside the zoo—aquatic, animal, human or otherwise. Just water on the floor. Everywhere, water on the floor. Just like in the pet store.

◎

Alden made it back to the apartment building two hours later just as the neighborhood was waking up and the gulls took to the air to circle the boxes and valleys of their daytime benefactors. He had walked the whole way, not even feeling the soreness in his limbs or the chafing between his legs as his clothing dried. He told stories to Tubby the whole way back. Tubby was a good listener. Taking it all in, wise as a sage.

But while he was talking, his mind was piecing together the reality of the situation in which he now found himself, based on the evidence of the last two days. Tubby was special, to be sure. He could do things nothing else could. *Had* done things nothing else could. He had a destiny. And it seemed, for the very first time, so did Alden. The two were connected now. They were family.

As the boy approached the front stoop, he stopped, his brain jammed loosely back into his body by the sight of the motorcycle parked at the curb. He ached, felt the blood pooling in his shoes. Felt the blisters filling up on his wagon hand. Most painful of all, though, was the reality of his living situation, which bolted his mind tight inside his skull.

He couldn't go back in there, with that Uncle setting up shop. They'd never let Tubby stay. Alden couldn't let Uncle Duane stay.

Then again, he could take Tubby inside. Hide him in the tub overnight. The next day, Uncle Duane would be gone, just like in the pet shop. Just like at the zoo. This most repugnant of all Uncles would be gone forever, but then so would his mother. Alden didn't want to think about that, even if it meant never seeing Uncle Duane again. He only had one mother, and she only had one son. Mutual orphans, fitting together like spoons laying on a bed late at night. If he kept Tubby inside the apartment overnight, *he* might be gone in the morning, too. Although that hadn't happened at the zoo. Was that just an oversight? Had he been missed? Was Tubby planning on doing what he had done to all the rest when Alden woke up?

Alden bent down to gaze at Tubby, who rocked gently with the cloudy zoo water in the cracked aquarium that was leaking into the wagon. "You wouldn't do that to me, would you, boy?" The octopus was predictably quiet on the subject. Classic Tubby.

Finding himself in quite the pickle, Alden decided to sit on the stoop and think. Through his numerous—and always brief—stints taking care of a zoological menagerie plucked from an immeasurable number of vacant lots, yards, and stretches of desert, the boy understood that pet ownership brought its own set of challenges and unique responsibilities not understood by those sadly unacquainted with pet ownership. Still, he wasn't prepared for such an arduous decision on what to do with the crawly creature resting in the back of his Rodeo Flyer. He couldn't just dump him off somewhere. He wouldn't. The octopus was in his care now, and he was therefore bonded to Tubby.

Alden's ruminations were interrupted by the familiar cackle of the Beach Bums, back once again in their uniforms of tank tops and nylon shorts, yanking down heavily on the towels wrapped around each neck. It was the last day of summer vacation, and they were keen to get in one more day of sand and salt water and shoreline harassment, befitting their name and reputation. The four of them—Tall Boy, Echo Boy, and the Other Two— were across the street, and hadn't seen Alden yet. Today, he was hoping that they did. Today, he was hoping that they'd come over to his side of the street. Maybe he could get them alone. Alone with him and Tubby. See how the night went. He'd promise things to make them stay. It worked for the man upstairs, so why not these four brutes? But they were engaged in tormenting two skinny kids unfortunate enough to live on the other side of the street, one wearing glasses underneath a tall, unruly brown afro, the other with tiny, beady eyes, buck teeth, and a squared-off head. They smacked the afro kid across the back of the head, and his glasses flew off and broke on the sidewalk. The Beach Bums howled in delight.

"Psst." The man from upstairs stood just inside the door to the building, motioning to Alden. He pointed up with his finger, to the floor above, and smiled.

Alden waved him off irritably. "Later." He returned his attention to the Beach Bums, who had their fill of local pestering and were now clearly fulfilling their namesake, heading toward the shoreline the next neighborhood over.

"Hey." Alden refused to turn around. He now knew the next step in his destiny. The man from upstairs' face darkened, twisting into something hideous and hateful as he moved back into the darkness and climbed the stairs, where he'd wait.

The boy didn't see any of this, nor would he have dwelled on it if he did. It was time to move again.

The Beach Bums ran across the street, blocking traffic in a complete disregard of the law. Tall Boy shoved Echo Boy's face, spit on the ground. "Last one to the beach is a rotten egg!"

Alden got to his feet and bent down over the aquarium. "You ready for a swim, boy?"

Tubby refused to answer, but it didn't matter. Alden knew what Tubby wanted to do. Knew their shared destiny. Pinewood disappeared in the rearview.

Picking up the wagon handle, Alden pulled Tubby down the sidewalk, the cheap wheels protesting, leaving a trail of water in his wake that collected in pools on the cement.

At the end of the block, Alden turned right, following the route of the Beach Bums, heading toward the beach, the ocean, while gulls circled overhead.

THE SCREAMER

It had been a week since Boyd first heard the scream, and after that, nothing had been the same.

At least it seemed like a week. It was hard to tell, shut up as he was inside an empty apartment that creaked and popped with awful intent, like a stiff hand ready to make a fist and squash what remained. Time outside had stopped, while things moved within the walls, on the roof, under the floors. Slithering veins and twitching tendons. Scuttling feet. He had brought the scream home with him, and it drove out everything alive. All that was left shifted and shook, waiting to fall to the dust or launch into the sky that always loomed yellowish gray and starless.

In Los Angeles, the stars were below. Everything above was just a poorly lit backdrop.

There were two of them here, before the scream—three, if you count the bunny. But even then the apartment was vacant, lost within a housing complex cowering in the rent-controlled backlot of dirty Downtown. The apartment had more room now, and the fist wanted to close before the last of them slipped away. Leave no one to whisper the tale.

Boyd had to get out, had to get back to Century City. He needed to hear the scream one more time, because he finally knew what it meant.

Just another hour. As soon as the sun would allow, he'd escape this tomb and make it in time to hear the last stanza before the stage went black.

◎

Boyd's aging Pontiac sputtered, hacking to life with an exhale of bluish smoke sure to piss off his granola neighbors nuzzling their exotic morning blend. He looked up at the balcony of his third floor apartment, wondering if she'd be there to see him off, like stalwart wives lining the docks back in the good old days. All he found were dried vines clinging to the rusted railing. She never waved to him anymore. Romantic notions died with the mystery.

Boyd gave the four banger some gas. The Detroit engine block oscillated dangerously on its shoddy frame. It was just a matter of time before this bullshit car broke down, and then he'd be sentenced to the bus. Urine soaked seats and squirming transients. The claustrophobic crush of musty bodies and sewer breath and windows that only cracked a few inches. Boyd put his head on the wheel, tasting last night's Jameson, and reached into his messenger bag. Forget quitting. Forget two. It was going to be a three cigarette ride, for sure. He lit up, sucked in and held it in his lungs. It was the burn he would miss the most.

The car chugged away from the curb and onto the rain slicked streets of Echo Park, greeted by a circle of vomit outside the local hipster haunt. The sort of bar that didn't have a sign, because proper promotion was so passé. It never rained enough to clean the city. People just stepped over the mess and continued on, texting like they were writing the next Great American novel 140 characters at a time.

Boyd rolled down his window, exchanging cigarette smoke for a dank carpet of exhaust. He moved through the traffic on autopilot, planning his caseload for the day while flipping back and forth from NPR and classic rock stations, looking for anything interesting. He found a mournful song on the forgotten end of the dial, occupied by pirate radio and Rowland S. Howard. *"I'm soaring through outer space... There's no better place to be."*

The lyrics faded to a murmur as Boyd gazed sightlessly out his windshield. Eclectic boutiques, tattoo shops, and taco stands, all fighting to define the neighborhood for whichever magazine was doing the write-up that month. Los Angeles always looked better through the lens of a camera, but it really didn't matter to Boyd. He didn't see any of it anymore. He'd gone blind from navigating the same route five days a week, and sometimes a sixth, when college football wasn't in season. He was a rat, racing toward a mirage of overpriced cheese, hoping to make it to the branch office on the swankier side of town, where you could actually smell the ocean. He needed those negative ions and coastal gloom. Blue skies year-round could drive a transplant insane. *"No better place to be—"*

Without warning, a flatbed truck over-laden with shopping carts shot out of an alley and cut in front of Boyd. He kicked his brakes, swerved, and punched the horn. It didn't work, and he was left bashing his steering column while the truck puttered away without reproach. No honk. No satisfaction. A ropey arm cartooned with cheap prison tats gave him the thumbs up from the driver's side. Boyd flipped off the disappearing taillights, cursing shitty ink and flatbeds everywhere. Definitely a four smoke trip.

Boyd turned off of Sunset on the east end of Hollywood, favoring less trafficked side streets as he continued west. The passel of cars was just going to accordion the closer he came to the sea. Along a neighborhood block of stucco housing and barred windows near Santa Monica Boulevard, two tall, wiry transvestite prostitutes—real go-getters, considering the hour—clattered over the gummy sidewalks, the night shift bleeding into the morning as they bled into their heels. Gaunt faces scanned every slowing car, looking for another trick. A last dip to carry them through the harsh sunlight into the dope sick dusk, just to do it all over again. One of them whistled at Boyd. They made eye contact. Never lock eyes with anyone who calls the streets home. The tranny grabbed his crotch and yelled something foul and unintelligible. Boyd sped up, almost running over a shapeless woman bound to a wheelchair crossing the intersection. She said nothing.

Boyd turned up the radio and lowered his rear view mirror.

Back into the teeth of the main drag and cresting Vermont Avenue, Boyd approached Mid Wilshire, which was once a glittering area favored by the Golden Age of Hollywood elite. Now, it was just scarred wallpaper covered over by the capitalistic creep of Korea Town. Swatches of grand old Tudor homes broke up long expanses of unreadable neon atop BBQ joints, pool halls, and insurance companies. At every corner, young K-Towners in Gucci shades reclined low in their German cars, blasting house music and yammering into cell phones, while grandparents strolled the sidewalks, bewildered by this weird new world from under wide-brimmed visors.

Lights changed, as did the scenery. Vermont turned to Pico, then Olympic. The landscape blossomed from grit to green, Indo-Asian to Hebrew and Arabic, until Boyd pierced the invisible radius of Century City, a carefully planned municipal workspace on the pampered backside of Beverly Hills.

Century City's four block by four block stamp of white collar purgatory was lined by rows of featureless, uninteresting skyscrapers filled with featureless, uninteresting people. The bland, 9 to 5 little brother of far funkier Downtown.

Similar buildings sprouted up in regular patterns, enveloping the celebrity-heavy shopping mall at the heart of it all. In the latest round of the never-ending phallus measuring contest between the five major movie studios, construction on a new edifice—one to dwarf all the rest—had commenced on Avenue of the Stars last year, but was abandoned when the economy went tits a few months back. Now, a half-formed shell reached 900 feet into the air, like the bones of a long-dead dinosaur bleaching in the sun. A massive crane with its precariously outstretched arm stood guard on the east side, just in case the call came to finish. Sometimes it's just cheaper to walk away.

The twin towers on Olympic marked the southwest border. *Conquest of the Planet of the Apes* was filmed here, as Century City—hailed "The City of the Future" —was so advanced for its time back in the optimistic 70's. Now it just looked bored, like a middle-aged woman who cut her hair into a Q-tip and slid into oatmeal frumpiness for the rest of her life.

Streets were kept clean. No riff raff. No flavor. No talking monkey handing out weapons to other talking monkeys. Lawyerville wouldn't have it any other way. The place overflowed during office hours, then became a ghost town after 6 pm. Even the lone tavern closed by 9. Century City wasn't about aesthetics or nightlife, it was about making money, and it did so in large, obscene stacks, thanks to drones like Boyd, working for less educated but savvier superiors who had the balls to stake their claim, back when the West was still wild.

Nearing Constellation Avenue, Boyd's building came into view. Twenty-eight tastefully lit floors of steel and glass encased in a white lattice of cement. There were rollers in the foundation for when the Big One hit. The Big One was long overdue, Channel 7 promised. The locals couldn't care less.

At the entrance driveway, a street repair crew stood around watching a man with wrap-around shades and a handlebar moustache, leaning his belly into a whumping jackhammer, silently critiquing his technique. Boyd nodded at one of them, sharing that put-upon look of two worker bees struggling inside the hive.

He flicked his card in front of the electric eye and burrowed down into the parking garage that smelled of pan-seared garlic from the first floor restaurant. The Pontiac pulled in behind Neil's car, a sunburst orange convertible Volkswagon Cabrio. The license plate read NEILIST, and was surrounded by Leftie stickers supporting a number of vague yet intensely earnest causes. Neil was the kind of guy who believed the moon landing wasn't just faked, it was a live stage show funded by the Illuminati. Neil believed a lot of crazy shit.

Boyd hopped out of his car, dashed to the elevator, and stepped in just as the doors were closing. He seemed to arrive just a bit later each day.

Inside, he punched the twelfth floor button, rested against the mirrored wall and faced front, like any right thinking person would. The other occupant, a short man, was gearing up for conversation. He was one of *those* guys. Feeling the last shred of his personal space invaded, Boyd looked over. The little man smiled.

"Fuck a Monday, am I right?" the man announced, as if uttering a profundity on par with Plato. He was ridiculous, with slicked-back hair and a shiny new suit. Large, green and white wing tips, polished to a wicked sheen. Like the Lollipop Guild sent out their best-dressed representative into the workforce. Who wore wing tips these days?

"Yep, they're for the birds," Boyd muttered, concentrating on the ticking floor count. The man laughed, far too loudly. Boyd regretted saying anything.

Just then, the lights dimmed and the car shuddered, halting their ascent. The silence was thick, in that peculiar way when two strangers stood too close.

"Earthquake?" the man asked, his voice gaining an octave.

"Brown out, maybe," Boyd offered. The elevator wasn't moving. The guts of the building went quiet. Boyd almost hoped the cramped box would plunge to the basement instead of locking him up with this clown.

The walls trembled, and the car began to climb again,

"Fucking politicians," breathed the diminutive fellow, adjusting his cape of Napoleonic machismo. The elevator dinged.

"Check you later, guy," the little man said, a wink and finger pistol in his voice. Boyd was gone before the doors slid back together.

At exactly 9:14, Boyd trudged the path least traveled by his boss, past file cabinets and chatty cubicles to his office that was still cold from the weekend. Two tall windows looked out at a carbon copy building next door. The limited view was his reward for dumping a decade of his waking life into the firm. He sat down at his desk, fired up his computer, and waited for the day to end.

It was about ten minutes 'til lunch when he heard the scream.

One of the florescent lights was buzzing and blinking. Something must have been trapped. A moth, most likely. The illumination it coveted so desperately would eventually kill it. Boyd leaned back to ponder the slow death on the ceiling, when a scream came from outside. He thought nothing of it. The valets often communicated with a series of woops and catcalls. Curious sounds weren't uncommon in this town.

But it came again.

A scream. A loud, strange scream.

Boyd spun around in his chair and scanned the perimeter. Nothing but industrial brown, with a sliver of opaque blue above and a ribbon of charcoal below.

Another scream penetrated the air. Boyd surveyed the buildings, but no one else was looking out. Windows didn't open in Century City. Suicide wasn't billable, and should be handled on your own time.

The screaming continued. It seemed masculine at first, but grew to transcend gender. Such an odd sound... Sometimes joyful, sometimes anxious. It had no terror in it. Just an expression of... *something*. Inscrutable, but surprisingly tantalizing. A scream wasn't supposed to sound like this.

Boyd sat at his desk and listened. The screams came every ten seconds for about two minutes, then ended abruptly. After several moments of silence, he stood in the doorway, looking up and down the hall at his passing co-workers. There wasn't a mention of screams in the snatches of conversation, usually devoted to obscure films playing at the Nuart or the latest article in *Slate*. Uppity bunch, or at least pretending to be. Though it made sense that the rest of the office didn't hear what Boyd did. Most didn't have windows with a spectacular view of nothing. Still, those on the same side of the suite would have heard it, too.

"Holding up the wall, Stansfield?" Boyd flinched. His boss, Mr. MacIntosh, squinted at a quivering sheaf of papers he always held in front of him like a corporate shield. MacIntosh never looked anyone square in the eye.

"No sir," Boyd fumbled. "Did you, uh... Did you hear?"

MacIntosh shoved a portion of the invoices at Boyd. "Make these calls. It's the end of the month, and seven... no, *eight* of your clients haven't paid."

Boyd took the bills, as MacIntosh shuffled down the hallway, his face buried in statements, like a vulture fussing over a carcass. "You gotta stay on people, Stansfield," he added over his stooped shoulders. "That's the only way to reach the top."

"Capitalism is for killers," issued a voice from the next office. Boyd ducked inside, where Neil nested amid a cluttered womb of files. The walls were plastered with bits of French philosophy, maps of forgotten French cities, and various ironic and rarely funny Internet memes. France and irony were very important to Neil.

With his earbuds firmly in place, Neil banged away at his keyboard while spooning brie onto those fancy crackers from Trader Joe's. He somehow kept everything straight in this junkyard of paperwork and vegetarian snacking. The slovenly order of chaos. "I wonder how many bodies MacIntosh has stashed in his bank account," Neil said, grinning through a mouthful of soft cheese.

Boyd smirked. "They died for our sins." He enjoyed their wry banter, but couldn't imagine having a beer with the guy. It just seemed like too much god-damn work.

"At least somebody did," Neil said. "Jesus had better things to do."

Boyd chuckled, then remembered why he came in. "Oh hey, did you hear that this morning?"

"Hear what?" Neil said, rummaging through a folder.

"The screaming."

Neil shrugged, pointing to his ear. "All I heard this morning was Claude François and lectures from MacIntosh." The Uppity Bunch had found their king.

Boyd walked to the window. Neil only had one. "It was coming from some-where outside." Boyd looked out at the intersecting geometry of building, roof, wall, and sky. "There aren't any hospitals around here, are there?"

"Hospitals?"

"Yeah. You know, like, mental hospitals." *Of course there weren't.* The insane were secreted away inland, amongst the dust and hills of the "other" California you never see on Entertainment Tonight. "And no one lives in Century City. Not even the homeless." They all lived in Boyd's neighborhood, he thought. By now, Neil wasn't listening. This was obviously more interesting to Boyd. "Seems weird to me," he said quietly.

"It's a weird city, man," Neil mumbled, his flight from the conversation punctuated by a belch. "You hear about the sink hole?"

"Hmm?" Boyd wasn't listening either, internally mapping out the suspect points on Century City's coordinate plane.

"Took out a whole block of warehouses in Commerce last night. The ground just imploded." Neil's chubby fingers danced over his keyboard like a concert pianist. "The Mayor took a break from banging news ladies to show up and de-clare it 'a cause for concern'," he air quoted, shaking his head. "I mean, can you believe—?" Neil looked up, realizing he was alone.

"Asshole."

◎

Boyd walked into the file room to grab a cup of coffee before heading off for his lunchtime smoke. He never ate lunch. Didn't have the stomach for it. Mar-garet, the doughy office lifer collecting chins instead of wedding anniversaries, stood humming by the copy machine. She unconsciously counted along with the sheets of blue G-28 forms spitting out of the Sharp X3400.

"Hiya, Boyd," she chirped, without even turning. 25 years of surviving company politics gave one extraordinary peripheral vision.

"Heya, Margaret. How goes it?" Boyd said. He found himself putting on a chipper attitude when he talked to her. He had a gift for adapting to the postures of those around him. "Professional blending," his girlfriend called it, trying to hide the irritated roll of her eyes. But it seemed to serve Boyd well, as his reputation for affability would attest. Boyd's girlfriend thought it left him indistinct, like a reflection in a bowl of milk, and about as deep.

"Oh, you know…" Margaret said. She always answered the same way, as if on the verge of launching into a string of uninteresting complaints that thankfully never came.

"Yeah," Boyd said, reaching for the door. He always answered the same way, too.

"Crazy screams, huh?" Margaret said absently.

Boyd stopped. "You heard it?"

"It sounded like a little girl."

No, it didn't, Boyd thought. *It sounded like anything <u>but</u> a little girl.*

"I called the police," Margaret said, lining up the edges of paper on top of the copier. "They said they'd search the area. They're always so nice."

"That's probably a good idea," Boyd said, still baffled by her description. He saw this woman more than his own mother. More than anyone in his life outside the office, but didn't know one thing about her other than her penchant for mauve nurses shoes and bedazzled QVC blouses. He opened the back door to the suite.

"Spooky, right?" Margaret said as Boyd walked out into the hallway. "Poor little thing," she added, returning to her hum. The door shut slowly behind him.

Outside, Boyd gathered with the other smokers, standing the legislated twenty feet from the entrance, as to not offend anyone's already smog-tainted innards. He took a drag of his cigarette and looked up at the buildings rising like colossal rectangular pillars. He checked the streets. Nothing out of the ordinary. No one who looked capable of emitting such a queer sound with such dedicated regularity. So, where were they coming from?

Boyd's contemplations were interrupted by the appearance of his boss inside the building's glass lobby. He was returning from a lunch meeting, seeming smaller and more fragile under the glare of the sun. MacIntosh shook hands with an equally aged gentleman sporting a shock of silver-rinsed hair, costumed in what looked like a natty yacht captain's jacket and ascot, sans hat. They guffawed about an inappropriate anecdote told over well-done sirloin. The monied old owned the world, flapping their stingy wattles at the doe-eyed plebs. Neil might have said that once.

Boyd turned, hiding his cigarette. He had been working at the firm for over ten years, but still felt like a shamed child if the boss saw him smoking, even on his lunch break. He didn't know if it was a moral worry, or that Mr. MacIntosh would think he was chain-smoking on company time. Either way, it was something to be hidden.

Boyd returned to his apartment just as his girlfriend was getting ready to go out for the evening, wearing the kind of outfit he forgot she owned. "Girl's night," she squealed. Sometimes she didn't come home from "girl's night" until early the next morning, citing "breakfast at IHOP" as an unimpeachable explanation. She was probably seeing someone else, or a series of Someone Elses, but Boyd didn't really care. This was the natural progression of things. When one of these Someone Elses impressed her enough, she'd leave him, and that would be it for this sophomoric experiment in playing house. Some people didn't belong together. Some people didn't belong with anyone.

Boyd poured himself a drink and let out the bunny, which dashed under the table to ignore him for the night.

The television blared some insipid network reality show. Boyd clicked it off, and sat in front of the window. It wasn't as big as the ones in his office, but at least it opened. He battled the weathered side jambs and pushed it halfway up, letting in the sounds and smells of Echo Park, which was just starting to fill with trustafarians and commuting wannabes. Boyd quaffed his drink and lit a cigarette, not bothering to blow the smoke out the window like he normally did. As the chilled poison chewed through his stomach lining, he watched the outside world behind a haze of swirling white, hoping that someone would scream.

All week, Boyd heard it. The more he listened, the more he understood, detecting layers. Nuances. It seemed to have a music to it, a melody folded inside dissonance, like a structured Baroque refrain woven inside jazz.

His work suffered. Mr. MacIntosh noticed, shoving even more papers at him accompanied by loud rebuke. MacIntosh was a master of making an example of layabouts. Boyd's co-workers noticed too, occasionally peaking into his office with concern. But he didn't see them.

He faced the window, waiting for the next scream.

Wednesday came, but the Screamer didn't, and Boyd was forced to focus on his work. Two people didn't show up that day, complaining of a migraine and intestinal troubles, respectively. MacIntosh grumbled an oath about "brown bottle flu," leveling a knowing glare at Boyd. Normally, he would have blushed, having fallen victim to the similarly virulent "green bottle flu" more often than was prudent. But today, Boyd barely registered the judgmental sniff. He was distracted. Something was missing.

It was ten minutes to lunchtime, and Boyd stopped pacing long enough to grab his smokes and exit the office, which was starting to feel like a quotidian morgue. Stiff bodies stuffed into small boxes. He walked right past MacIntosh, who was delegating case files while chastising Sandi, the childlike receptionist just out of junior college. She hunched sadly at her desk, crowded with stuffed animals, felt flowers, and pictures of unfortunate-looking children. "Hi Boyd," she squeaked. He grinned and avoided eye contact as he slipped into the file room.

Margaret stood post at the copier, a flurry of pink I-907 forms gathered at her feet. Boyd paused. "Margaret?"

She stared at the wall, a blank look in her eyes. She seemed far away, her lips slightly pursed, rounded into a soft 'o'. Reams of paper piled up in the copier collating bin; bending, crumpling, slumping to the floor.

"Heya, Margaret," Boyd said gently. She didn't look up. He repeated her name.

She turned her head slowly, gazing at Boyd without recognition. Then, her eyelids fluttered, and the practiced smile slowly etched across her face, bringing her back to life like a re-wound toy. "Hiya, Boyd," she said dreamily.

Boyd pressed the 'clear' button on the copier, picked up the collection of forms, arranged them as best he could, and handed them to Margaret. "I think that's enough," he said.

"Yeah," she replied, "I suppose it is." She walked away, pink paper falling from her pink, flabby arms.

Boyd lit a cigarette and fidgeted. He couldn't sit still, even outside. The screams came from out here, but they hadn't today. His neck felt tense, his muscles restless. The air was loud, and the sky garishly bright. Every conversation a vulgar shout, mixing together in a cacophony of flattened noise. He stood unlawfully close to the door, and blew out a fast hiss of smoke, enduring glares from the PC Nazis for his effort.

A woman walking by stopped at Boyd's right. He saw her out of the corner of his ever-sharpening eye, and figured she was glowering at him like the others. He turned to his would-be accuser, expecting jackboots guised in a scowl.

But she wasn't looking at him. She was looking up, entranced by something Boyd couldn't see. Then, with a sublime calm, she sucked in her breath and closed her eyes, her feet lifting at the heels. Then, she rose, passing over the sun like a human eclipse. It blinded him. He blinked, then found her again. She was walking away.

"Sneaking off for a cigarette, Stansfield?" MacIntosh had noted his burning grit.

Boyd hid it between his fingers, the smoke wafting up in the static air. He waited for the panic of discovery, but it didn't come. "Yep," Boyd said casually, taking another drag and squinting off into the distance like the Marlboro Man.

"You know," MacIntosh said, his voice oddly conversational, "I used to smoke, too." The old man was smiling, a devilish sort of expression on his normally dour face. "Picked it up in Korea, along with as many village girls as I could get my hands on," he chuckled. "I gave up both when I came back to the States." He looked at Boyd conspiratorially. "Our little secret."

The elevator opened and Boyd walked back up the hall, passing Mr. Resnik, the family law attorney from the opposite side of the floor. He was a kindly man, pigeon-shaped and endearingly dorky. Wore a fanny pack and a baseball hat with his rumpled suit. Always carried a thermos filled with some sort of benign soup. "The Dodgers really flubbed the 9th, didn't they?" Mr. Resnik said.

The Dodgers were their connective small talk, even though Boyd hadn't watched an MLB inning since collecting Topps baseball cards as a kid. Ron Cey and Davey Lopes and their substantial moustaches were the last Dodger references Boyd knew anything about. "Couldn't believe it," he exclaimed with faux outrage, imagining his dopey mug staring back at him in a bowl of milk.

Mr. Resnik patted Boyd on the arm. "We'll get 'em again before the play-offs."

"Sure will," Boyd said. "Next time, we bring out the big bats." Resnik smiled and moved on, in that labored waddle of the chubby kid walking alone on the playground.

On the way home, Boyd deviated from his ingrained course, driving down filthy alleys and seedy backstreets, hoping to get lost. But he knew the city too well. At one point, on a burned-out avenue in Lynwood, he stopped the car and wept like he did the day they pulled him from seventh grade track practice and told him about the accident. No one noticed.

Boyd tried multiple keys to unlock his front door, but none seemed to work. His first instinct was that he was drunk, but he wasn't. Not yet. His second was that the locks were changed while he was gone. It felt like a long time since the morning, when he stumbled down the staircase, heading for his dusty car. Finally, the right key shimmied in, and the door swung open.

His girlfriend was on the phone in their bedroom, talking in low, giggling tones. *Her* bedroom, actually. Boyd slept on the couch, in front of the computer or on the floor, depending on where he blanketed his brain. He felt like a stranger in his own home, creeping to fetch his outdated office togs after his shower. He didn't want to wake her. It only got nasty when he did. *Stranger in a strange land, land of ice and snow.* The radio never played Iron Maiden. Boyd hadn't turned his on in days. Cracking the door, he snuck his head in to let her know that he was home. She ignored him, laughing at what was obviously the most hilarious joke ever told on the other end of a phone line. Boyd closed the door.

Out in the living room, Boyd eyed the bunny sprawled out in its cage. It appeared to look back, but Boyd knew better. This bunny hated him, looking for a vulnerability... an exposed soft spot. It would lunge at his vitals if he ever laid too close. It never made a sound. Never screamed. It just squatted in its own filth and watched him, weighing its chances.

Boyd got up and walked to the cage.

... An endless labyrinth of interconnected skyscrapers replicated tortured fractals... They rose to fantastic heights and melded into a murky darkness that cast shadows blacker than the hue ever dreamed. Massive shapes undulated in the mist overhead.

His shoes squished against the pliant obsidian stone, cutting through the frantic barks and cackles echoing within the twisting maze. Cyclopean buildings broke free from one another, sagging to the ground like branches of miles-high weeping willows. They wanted to snatch him up and take him away. They wanted to rend him limb from limb.

Boyd tried to run, but dimensional space was melting away, replaced by a furious chaos, a void without direction or meaning. This infinite *nothingness* was more hideous than anything that came before it. Boyd was starting to lose himself in the fear and entropy.

Just then, an unnerving scream punctured the maelstrom, injecting fullness into the inky vacuum. Gravity returned. Boyd writhed, inching forward like a mealworm. He opened his mouth and extended his tongue, trying to touch it, taste it; bring it down deep where it belonged. The scream. Boyd screamed. Their voices fused as the churning abyss roared all around them…

Boyd sat up with a jerk, his throat dry and sore, as if he'd been screaming all night. He didn't know where he was, until he saw the empty rabbit cage. He closed his eyes, trying to recapture the exact state of sleep from seconds ago. He heard a scream, but it was that of a woman. It had no music in it. Only horror.

Thursday arrived, and so did The Screamer. Perhaps Boyd brought it back through his dream. He excitedly closed his door, taking in every note, every nuance. He was studying.

Boyd wasn't sure how long he was enthralled, when he noticed that someone had opened his door. Poking his head out into the hall in search of a culprit, he didn't see the man fall past his window behind him. A snap shadow of violent descent.

The scream came again, and Boyd set his jaw.

Find The Screamer.

Sidestepping new temps had become a full-time job. Hired to replace the six veteran employees who had recently quit, they flitted to and fro, eyes sparkling with the enthusiasm of new walls and unformed impressions. MacIntosh was in his office with his door closed. He never closed his door, unless he was arguing with his wife. His wife died three years ago.

Boyd sped toward Sandi's desk, where the phone rang incessantly, all the lines lit up, all unanswered. She paid it no mind, glued to her computer screen with sunken eyes, tapping her mouse so quickly it sounded like chattering teeth. The phone continued to ring, irritating Boyd enough to pause in his quest. "Um, is anyone hearing these phones?" She said nothing, scratching a bleeding groove into her arm as she clicked through hundreds of images of death, dismemberment and mutilation on several websites at once. Sandi's desk had since been cleared of its usual cheery accoutrements. Her eyes darted over the gruesome pictures as she clicked and scratched. "Sandi?" Boyd said.

"*No...*" She drew the word into a carnal groan, consumed by her obsessive mental upload of atrocity. Boyd missed tacky felt flowers and pictures of children he didn't know.

Just then, screams filtered in from the lower levels. They weren't the screams Boyd cared about, because everyone in the suite heard them, too.

He pushed through the stunned horde assembling outside. A semi-circle had formed around a spectacle. Cell phones sprang up to capture the moment for posterity, dispersing the tragedy into the networked ether.

A pulpy mound of gore and blown out fabric lay in front of him. This was the body of a man, splattered onto the scrubbed marble fronting the building. The impact of the fall had pulverized his body and exploded it through his suit. Large hunks of bone and flesh and brain diffused in a wild but vaguely human shape, like smashed tubes of crimson oil paints arranged into a crude chalk outline. Rivulets of blood ran unimpeded across the smooth stone, leaking toward feet that scurried back from the creep of warm fluids. A bright red stream collected around an ejected shoe. It was a white and green wing tip, its immaculate shine reflecting a glint of sun.

Boyd looked at the lump of tissue and skin. His eyes opened wide, remembering the last thing the exuberant little man said to him. He smiled.

"Check you later, guy," Boyd said aloud, his voice ringing out amongst the hushed din. A collective gasp, then frowns of disgust. Everyone backed away as he started laughing. The cell phones turned on him. A beefy man in gym wear shook his head ominously. He laughed harder, rattling his organs, before approaching sirens drowned him out. Boyd's explosive laughter seized up his pharynx and he started to choke. He fell to all fours, spitting phlegm onto the tile, frosting the sanguine ponds that were beginning to coagulate like day old pudding.

Boyd rolled over. The broken window 18 floors up gaped like a missing tooth in a titan's skull. A few floors below, Boyd could barely make out Mr. MacIntosh looking at the scene from his corner office. Security emerged, moving everyone back into the building, entreating the crowd to go home. But Boyd didn't want to leave, even though Century City was now a deafening mess of gossip and bullhorns.

A beefy shadow towered over him, and a foot came down hard on his face. This guy wasn't wearing wing tips.

In the car, Boyd held an ice pack to his fractured cheekbone. Only an hour before, he had regained consciousness as the trauma crew scraped the body off the ground, scooping remains into plastic bags. The area was free of civilians, save for a few haunted co-workers being questioned by police. Boyd got to stay 'til the end. The EMT suggested a ride to the hospital, but he refused, insisting he was fine and had to get home to let out his incontinent Labrador. Boyd didn't have a Labrador, and he certainly wasn't fine. Worse, he had missed The Screamer, and now had to wait one more day.

A speeding police car whizzed by, nearly clipping Boyd's side mirror, its lights flashing and sirens yelping. Feeling woozy, he opened his window to get some air. The raw howl of ambulance and firetruck came from a dozen different directions, but only a few headed toward Century City. There were other acts of disorder occurring nearby. Maybe a wildfire in the hills. Maybe a riot…

Something was heating up in the city.

A honk startled him. To his left, Mr. Resnik waved from behind the wheel of a sensible tan Volvo, smiling like he was on a pleasant Sunday drive through Amish country. Boyd waved back. They were too far apart to talk about the Dodgers. He looked ahead, still sensing Resnick's ghastly grin aimed at the side of his face. He tapped the steering wheel impatiently, desperate to move forward, to flee this awkward stand-off. The light changed, but Resnick's smile didn't, as he pealed out, raced up the street and disappeared around a curve.

Boyd clicked on the radio, trying to fog over his hyper-alert brain with the clang of instruments, but all the music stations were overtaken by emergency broadcasts, reporting scattered acts of violence and gathering mobs. A bombing at the Mondrian Hotel. Mass stabbing on 3rd Street Promenade. Heavily armed man holding hostages at a Brentwood school. Burning buildings in the Beverly Hills shopping district just off Doheny.

He slammed on his brakes, narrowly avoiding rear-ending a line of stopped cars at the green light ahead. He squeezed the steering wheel, steadying himself, as traffic lurched forward. Boyd followed suit, joining the slow moving parade of rubberneckers as they passed an accident. A tan Volvo had plowed into a café on Pico. Broken bodies were laid out on the sidewalk. The injured lined the curb, heads in bloody hands. As Boyd crept by, he saw a man lying under an insulated blanket, receiving oxygen and medical treatment. It was Resnick. His body convulsed as if hooked up to an electro-shock machine. He was still smiling.

The apartment was cleared of most of his furniture, including his girlfriend. She likely fled to a different, now familiar home with all of her belongings and the body of a dead rabbit sealed in a freezer bag. Boyd took in the vacancy around him. Three rapid gunshots came from outside.

He sat in the middle of the floor, unable to feel the grooved hardwood beneath. He was expanding, hovering in-between worlds. His skin tightened, ready to burst through a throbbing eye socket, spraying fizzy goo onto the peeling wall. Something in the foundation moved, like ancient larva coming to the surface, eating sinkholes into decaying urban blocks. The four corners moaned, as the building vibrated ever so slightly. It was trying get up while it still could. The giant movie screen, refracting all the light and noise down to the near-sighted city that created it.

Something detonated a few miles away. Boyd wanted to run to his car, drive back to his two cold windows, but he had no key.

So, he'd wait, as he had been waiting all his life. If he could only get through this night in one solid piece, he'd find out everything tomorrow. The ticking seconds of hermetic time were suffocating.

With his good eye, he stared down the horizon until it sweat and broke, grudgingly giving up the first rays of dawn with a defeated shrug.

Boyd was on his way before the sun could wax hesitantly from behind the bluffs ringing Hollywood. He'd survived the night, and now the day was his. He'd find The Screamer, and demand an explanation.

The streets were devoid of the usual bustle at this hour. A dark silhouette loped from an alley. Flailing arms seized something heavy from the sidewalk and pulled it back into the shadows. At the next light, Boyd spied someone at a bus stop waltzing with what looked like a floppy, life-size rag doll, twirling it 'round and 'round like an enraptured dervish.

Morning slid from gray to pink, framing plumes of smoke lazing up into the sky like slowly unspooling phantasms. The radio played a song that Boyd once knew but no longer recognized. *I'm standing next to a mountain, chop it down with the edge of my hat.* These chords, the end of the world. The lyrics, a eulogy. *Pick up all the pieces, make an island, might even raise a little sand.* Skinny palm trees, on fire, swayed like dancing birthday candles.

Boyd's autopilot had disappeared, replaced by an innate magnetic pull to a destination lying due west, flagged by the framework of a hulking crane. He felt his eyes closing, but still saw everything that lay ahead of him in stark relief.

As he neared Century City, abandoned cars littered the streets, strewn about like Hot Wheels around shuttered shop fronts. The Scream had escaped, taking in the surrounding neighborhoods, turning all life into specters. The second story of a nondescript synagogue spewed ash, as flames licked out from blackened holes. No one attempted to douse them. Ghosts didn't like water. They liked synagogues even less.

From Pico onto Century Park East, Boyd dodged debris: discarded clothing, a gutted snack cart. A long, broad streak of scarlet stained the pavement, as if someone hit a deer and dragged it under their drive train until it ground down to nothing.

Up ahead was a wall of demolished trucks, stacked thirty feet high two blocks in front of his building. Boyd killed his engine and got out of the car. He looked at this bulwark of crushed steel not in shock, but as a challenge. The sound of a muffled jackhammer zigzagged off the skyscraper canyons. He began to climb.

His arms and legs torn, Boyd jumped from the barricade and jogged toward the front entrance. A disheveled woman roamed aimlessly, naked from the waist down. Her tank top covered in blood, a clump of white hair in each hand. She passed a man slamming his head against a dumpster, trying to scream. Nothing but a dry wheeze came out.

Boyd dashed across the driveway, approaching the street crew somehow still hard at work. They were splattered with what looked like tar, jackhammering something spongy into the asphalt. Something giving and wet. Viscous chunks of matter splashed up onto their tattered coveralls. Boyd didn't meet their eyes, didn't care to be amongst them anymore. His business was elsewhere.

◎

The lobby was devoid of security and the elevators were out. Boyd kicked open the emergency exit doors and took on the stairs, bounding up three at a time. He had to get higher, to his two cold windows. He had to be in position when it came.

◎

He entered the suite through the back, past quiet cubicles and barren offices. Nothing seemed out of place. Everyone was just gone, even Margaret. Her absence, and the silence of her favorite copier, made the depopulated workplace all the more desolate.

At the end of the hall, Mr. MacIntosh's door was closed. Boyd went for the handle.

Amongst the bad art and impressive diplomas adorning the walls, MacIntosh hung in the center of the room, his head nearly severed at the shoulders by a garrote of wires reaching down from a tear in the ceiling. His fingers, gripped like talons, had come to an unholy rest clawing the air for paper.

Boyd felt dizzy and staggered to the couch. He hadn't slept in days. The world was closing in on him. The buildings were bending again.

He wasn't sure if he heard it at first. The mind sometimes doesn't want to give up the intoxicating apprehension and accept the moment.

The eerie wail reverberated through the panes of glass, immense in its inexplicability. It cocooned him, soothing his spirit while igniting his thoughts. From the converging wall of windows ending in a sharp isosceles point, Boyd could see where it was coming from. This was the catbird seat, taking in the full measure of the Scream. He could feel it, drawing him in, daring him to fly. He knew that he could.

The thud of MacIntosh's body hitting the desk snapped Boyd out of it. He moved back from the windows, away from the hungry triangle, and stumbled over the decapitated corpse of his boss draped over a high-backed chair. The head had rolled to a stop in a corner, regarding Boyd with mushy eyes and a swollen, jutting tongue. MacIntosh must have known all along, and kept it inside. Goddamn him.

The Scream came again.

From somewhere in the office, a hint of elegant typing gave him pause.

Neil sat completely naked at his computer, his ears free of their pretentious music. He was surrounded by a bunker of inked-up parchment stacked like sandbags, protection from the outside world. Blood caked his truck-tire belly, smeared down to his knobby genitals and matted pubic hair. The thick ankle of a middle-aged woman stuck out from behind a cabinet, away from its usual post at the copy machine. Neil looked up, his eyes fevered with insanity. "I heard it, Boyd! I heard it!" Boyd yanked a fax machine from the wall. "They died for our sins," Neil said. Boyd raised the machine high over his head. *"They died for our sins!!"* Neil's sweaty face caved into the back of his cranium, as fragments of plastic and brain decorated French philosophy.

Ignoring pockets of slaughter and destruction, Boyd sprinted to the cusp of Century City, where his magnetic pole awaited. Nothing barred his way. Everything within earshot was wrapped up in their own private hell.

Boyd barely touched the grated stairs as he climbed upward, ever upward, in his ascent to salvation. Though, he wasn't safe inside this beast. It had no skin and couldn't hide him, which made it the perfect place for The Screamer to be. No one ever looks at the bones when there's so much else in full rot.

At last, Boyd stood at the top of the unborn building. He could see the ocean, the mountains. He could see where he'd never live again.

The whole world was ablaze, and it was beautiful.

Just then, something moved. A figure, huddled on the end of the crane's gargantuan arm. The Screamer.

Boyd scrambled toward it. He needed to get close, needed it to scream again. The shape stirred. It was a child. A little girl, pale in complexion and eye, as if all her color had been drained. She looked at Boyd, then through him, her lips beginning to part. He couldn't believe it. This was the scream.

Without making a sound, the girl rocked back onto her heels and dropped from the crane. Another small thing, falling like hail from the blue skies, born to paint the world below.

Boyd ran to the edge and watched her flutter gently downward, as if she weighed nothing. A husk of skin, sketched as a human but empty inside. She caught an updraft and began to twirl like a helicoptering maple seed, drifting off into the smoldering horizon. Boyd never knew if she touched the ground.

He fell to his knees in anguish. He never got to hear the last scream, never got to know what it wanted.

Just then, another scream split the air.

He leapt to his feet and searched frantically. It was close... It had to be right here. Where was it?

The scream erupted again just yards away, knocking him flat with a blast of concussive modulation. His ears ringing, he peered around the platform, discovering a minute dent in the thick concrete spine that held up the ribs of the building.

On closer inspection, he found that the divot was really a small hole bored into the super structure, corkscrewing down into the stone and steel. Something tiny scurried out of the aperture and stopped at the lip of the opening. Boyd squinted and leaned in, making out the details of a delicate arthropod creature a centimeter long. At first glance, it resembled a hatchling praying mantis influenced by the lingering genes of the cuttlefish. Its body was firm, yet malleable and totally translucent. Indescribable colors whirled and pulsed inside, and the sense of a boundless intelligence radiated outward. It was exquisite, yet horribly alien in its erratic gestures. More unsettling was the play of the rising light, which seemed to arc around the organism, displacing the air, as if our reality recoiled from it in revulsion. It didn't belong here. It was antithetical to everything in our existence.

Boyd had never been so terrified in his life. Not of death, but of a destination more inconceivable, from which this exiguous being had sprung. The sheer idea of what was before him threatened to heave Boyd into unconquerable lunacy. His skin crawled with the sensation of a million needling legs. Bile clogged his throat and his heart hammered his chest, yet he still sensed himself moving closer to the miniscule thing, compelled by a primal yearning that he couldn't understand. Boyd reached out a hand...

When his quavering finger nearly touched the creature, it froze, hunkered down and released a sonic discharge, which in this place was understood in terms of longitudinal waves, translated into a booming, sonorous scream.

This was The Screamer. *This* was what screamed.

Boyd's mortal shell disintegrated. His consciousness catapulted through space, moving inside an immeasurable helix of compressed notes; a cosmic symphony where light had not yet reached. A resonance that bred madness when poured into a single shriek, created beyond the rim of comprehension.

He wanted to shut it off, but it was too late. The information came in painful tides... Born in the elemental swirl of the unquiet void... Sent across the gulf of Space and Time... Do the bidding and spread the chaos...

It screamed, as Boyd groveled in supplication to something no larger than a silverfish, which possessed the knowledge of a billion spent galaxies and paths to dimensions unimaginable.

His ears burst and red tears dripped onto the platform, as it screamed again and again. He'd never hear anything else. Boyd felt something crack inside him, below him, as his brain filled to the saturated brink, intertwining with the sentience of the tiny entity.

The Screamer was a pawn, utterly alone in a place so incongruous and insanely aligned. So it screamed, as would a confused and frightened child banished from home. Its very presence here didn't fit, and that which sent it knew this. It would tear through the carefully stitched order of this insignificant rock.

This tiny thing, unaware of its own power, was pulling our world apart.

Boyd wanted to die, praying for a heaven or even a hell instead of the roiling continuum that waited just beyond this sphere. Nothing was sacred. Science became myth. Only death would preserve ignorance before the canopy was ripped down. He wanted to die to turn it all off.

As the city below was being eaten alive, Boyd thought of insipid reality shows, hoping he'd still be heavy enough to hit the ground.

The Screamer took flight, spiraling into the air with impossible speed, following the lean of the rising sun. It would land elsewhere soon and scream again, as it screamed here. That which brought it over was gone. Some locks never shut twice.

Boyd could no longer move his limbs. His body wasn't his anymore, just a jumble of meaningless nostalgia. His changing eyes were aimed into the starless sky that should have been blue, but was now a dome of ash, gathering below the nighted eternal. The firmament over Los Angeles had never looked this way, and would never look this way again.

But Boyd didn't see it, his vision focused on places further away. He only saw two windows. Behind neither were Heaven or Hell.

The earth cracked and opened beneath the crane and the towering skeleton. The brittle bones split like matchsticks, caving in on themselves, taking everything with them. The fissure spread like a gaping maw. The City of the Future pitched and collapsed, shattering into the stardust that built it up and tore it down countless times before, rejoining all the forgotten things in the profound silence below, as everything above it screamed.

CLEAN

Billy typed the name of the town into the search browser, careful of the spelling, and pressed Enter. Red pinpoints popped up on the electronic map, clotting together like a wound.

He scribbled down a long list of addresses into his notebook with the stumpy yellow pencil provided by the library. A group of bored middle school kids clomped by behind him, eyes glued to their phones or blurting loudly under the scowl of their teacher, who had given up trying to draw attention to the burnished walnut ceilings and Victorian stained glass arcing above them.

After filling up several pages, front and back, Billy clicked off the computer, returned the pencil to the coffee can painted to look like tree bark, and carefully folded the sheet of paper.

"Hey kid."

Billy turned. A library worker with black porcelain plugs weighing down each earlobe was staring at him from behind a cart of books. "You're going to miss your bus."

Billy grinned, slinging on his backpack. "I doubt it."

It was a beautiful autumn day, with the last of the falling leaves collecting under shrubbery and in grated gutters, piled in yards awaiting the bag. He had three neighborhoods in mind, and focused on a few specific locations in each one. The warmth would mean everyone would be outside, which made Billy's job easier.

He got lost twice, but arrived at Maywood Elementary School just in time, as children flooded from the double guarded exit and ran to open arms and open car doors. He curled his fingers through the chain link fence hemming the playground and watched a group of children chase each other on the spongy blacktop. They were all talking, shouting, playing made up games with just enough rules that everyone knew. Laughter and words blended together, until Billy couldn't understand any of them. He turned around and faced the street, crossing one foot over the other and digging his hands deep into the pockets of his snug khaki shorts. He pushed his sock down a little lower on one ankle.

A stumpy kid with the shape and consistency of a potato hurried up the sidewalk. He wore an orange mesh vest, nearly matching the color of his hair, and handed another one to Billy.

"You on with me?" The potato boy huffed under his freckles.

Irritated, Billy looked down at the vest, then up at the boy's face. "No, not today."

The boy sighed, crumbled the vest into his hand, and lumbered up the block toward the intersection, mumbling to himself about the inequities of crossing guard duty. Billy leaned back into the fence, noticing the first hint of sunburn on his freshly shaved legs.

Around three o'clock, most of the children had disappeared and all the non-native cars had driven off from the surrounding streets. One silver sedan remained, a silhouette perched behind the wheel, watching Billy. The boy pretended not to notice, until the engine started and the car drove slowly up to the sidewalk, crunching on dead twigs next to the curb.

A window lowered. "Hello there," the man said with a smile. He was well dressed. The smell of air freshener radiated out from inside the car, reaching Billy. The expensive kind that you can't buy at gas stations. The man had the AC on, even though the afternoon had turned brisk.

"Hi," Billy said.

"Whatcha' doing?"

"Just waiting, I guess."

"Waiting for your parents?"

"No. My parents aren't coming. I thought a bus would take me to my aunt's house, but I think I missed it. My aunt watches me these days…" Billy looked up the block, searching for a beat-up minivan that wasn't on its way.

The man followed his gaze. "You new here? At school, I mean?"

The boy nodded his head. The man rubbed his jaw, lips tightening over his white teeth.

"Hey mister, can I burrow your phone? I need to call my aunt, but.... She drinks a lot and all, and those meds she takes..."

The man looked at Billy for several moments, then raised his window. He drove off a bit faster than was normal for the neighborhood, bottoming out his Hyundai on a speed bump with a scraping sound. Billy watched him go, annoyed by the cloying air freshener smell stuck in his nose.

The Ezee Mart had bars built into the glass, and posters of heavily made up girls wearing tube tops posing next to giant bottles of beer.

Billy walked out the front entrance holding a small plastic bag. He opened up his list from the library and scanned the notes, unwrapping and shoving a neon green Blo-Pop into his mouth before heading into the neighborhood behind the store.

Billy sat on the curb, the white lollipop stick jutting from between his lips, cheek bulging out on one side. He could feel the weight of the house just two lots down. The vertical blinds sagged in one corner, and then tightened back into straight, black lines. The light in the window went off. The blinds didn't move again for many minutes, which stretched into much longer than that, as dusk turned to nightfall, marked by the blinking of the streetlights that came alive in disjointed unison up and down the block. Billy got up and walked away, leaving the Blo-Pop on the sidewalk, the exposed pink ball of gum glowing yellow on the cracked cement.

He hit a few reliable spots after that. A shopping mall, a local park with rusted swings. A dank video arcade with crappy old games and missing windows. An adult book store with no windows at all. Finally, he gave up for the night, found the main drag, and headed for the motel, both hands gripping his backpack straps, bony elbows poking out behind him.

It grew late, but being a Tuesday, traffic was light. He made his way toward the familiar Ezee Mart sign to pick up a few things for dinner, and maybe a little something for dessert. Money was running low, but he had faith.

Billy walked to the frozen foods bin at the rear of the store. A man with thick glasses and thinning hair stood in front of the beverage cooler, squinting at the rows of brightly lit bottles. Billy came to a halt and stared at him. The man felt the attention, and glanced over. Billy smiled at him, before turning slowly and walking to the register.

Outside, the man got into his car and clenched the wheel, his eyes glued to Billy standing next to the pay phone by the side of the building. He couldn't believe his luck. The man looked at the bag on the passenger seat, got out of the car, and walked back into the store.

◎

A key rattled on the other side of the motel room door before Billy pushed it open and walked inside, placing a plastic sack on the dinette table. The man poked his head in from the parking lot outside.

"Come on in," Billy said, carefully removing each item from the sack. Two packets of beef jerky, two bags of Cheetos, two cans of grape soda, and two ice cream sandwiches, Neopolitan style - all neatly arranged and grouped by twos. Billy set down a box of cinch tie trash bags last.

The man entered the room, carrying a bag of his own, and quickly shut the door behind him. He touched the lock and paused, unsure about what message he might send. "Can you lock it, please?" Billy asked without looking. "You never know anymore."

The man locked the door and sat on the bed, clearly more relaxed. "Nice place."

"Thanks," Billy said, lining up plastic forks and knives next to the food.

The man pulled a pint bottle of whiskey from the bag and dangled it with his fingers. "You want a little of this?"

Billy walked over, took the bottle and unscrewed the top. "Make a man out of ya," the man said with a grin.

The boy sniffed the open bottle, made a face and shook his head. "No thanks."

"Aww, you're no fun." The man grinned and took a swig, swishing it around in his mouth and playfully wiggling his eyebrows before swallowing. He smacked his lips. "Okay, how about this?" He produced a wine cooler from the bag and popped the cap with a lighter. "It's sweet."

Billy's eyes opened wider. "I like sweet stuff." He took the bottle and downed a gulp. He grimaced, then smiled.

The man smiled back. "So do I."

More things were taken from the man's bag, including a comic book, a pack of baseball cards, and three more wine coolers. Other things stayed inside at the bottom, at least for now.

Billy sighed as he lay back on the bed and paged through the comic. It was the Green Lantern, which he never liked much, but he didn't want to appear rude. The man sat in a stiff chair in the corner, placed his hands on his knees and looked around the room, out the window. He took another drink from the bottle. The Green Lantern's ring blazed and threatened cosmic magic on the page.

He glanced up at the man, who had taken his coat off and was checking his hair in the mirror, bobbing his head while humming power chords.

"Do you like boys or girls?" Billy asked.

"Well," the man began, combing through the question, looking for snags. "I guess you might say I like boys *and* girls."

Billy nodded, thinking about this.

"What do you like?" the man asked.

"Girls, I guess."

"You guess?"

"I mean, I don't really like anyone, but if I had to like someone, it would probably be a girl."

"Boys can be just like girls, and girls just like boys."

"Really?" Billy looked at him, intrigued.

"Really. I—" A thumping sound from behind the closed bathroom door across the room startled the man, who shot to his feet. "Who's that?" The man clutched the bottle to his chest like those frightened damsels in old black and white movies.

"That's my sister," Billy said.

"You never said anything about a sister."

Billy looked the man square in the eye. "You never asked." He returned to the comic.

The man went to the bathroom door. As he reached it, the sound of water in the shower started from within.

"I wouldn't go in there if I was you," Billy said.

The man looked at him suspiciously. "Why not?"

"Because she's taking a shower."

The worry on the man's face eased, and his grin reappeared. He took a deep breath and clapped his hands together. "We'll just let her finish up then, huh?"

Billy shrugged. "She likes to be clean."

The man laughed, somehow finding this funny. "Yeah, I'll bet." He picked up the bottle, roughly tousled Billy's hair, and strolled around the room with a cocky gait, like a general familiarizing himself with new spoils.

Billy smoothed out his hair. "You like them clean, right?"

The man held up a large surfer's wetsuit that was resting on the dresser next to a motorcycle helmet with a tinted faceplate. "To be honest with you, I don't." He sniffed the suit. "I like the...the essence." A pair of balled up women's underwear was underneath the suit. He glanced at Billy, and stuffed it in his pocket. "I like to know what I'm dealing with."

"Yeah, I suppose you do," Billy said absently. "That's only fair."

"Whose is this?" asked the man, holding out the wetsuit. "Your dad's?"

Billy laughed. "Yeah, right. My dad wouldn't wear that for a million bucks. That's my sister's."

The man held the suit up to his body, the slack of the lower leggings curling up on the brown shag carpeting. He cut his eyes to the bathroom door, a slight frown on his face. "She's tall," he murmured.

"And still growing."

"How old is she?"

"Eleven, or thereabouts."

The man moved across the room, checking drawers as he took larger and larger gulps from his bottle, before returning to the chair in the corner. His knees bounced. "When did you say your parents were coming back?"

"A week or so. They have some errands to run."

"And they trust you two here alone?"

"Oh yeah. We can take care of ourselves. They know that. We're not babies."

The man grinned again and began untying his work boots. "Mind if I take these off?"

Billy shrugged, took a swig from the wine cooler, and positioned his comic book in front of him, staring at the same page he had for minutes.

The man pulled off his boots and removed his socks, putting both near the door. He flexed his toes, digging yellowed nails into the shag. "Cozy in here, huh?"

"I guess," Billy said. The water in the shower stopped, making the room quieter than a moment before. More still.

"I like getting cozy. You want to get cozy with me?" the man asked, walking toward Billy's bed. His eyes were hazing with tiny veins, the bottle almost gone.

"My sister goes first."

The man stopped. "Is that right? You done this before?"

Billy nodded.

The man couldn't help but laugh. "Couple of pros, ain't ya'?"

"Like I said, we can take care of ourselves. She's waiting for you in the shower. She likes to be clean."

"Her first, then you?"

Billy nodded again, holding up three fingers in salute. "Scout's honor."

The empty bottle landed sideways on the dresser, and the man opened the bathroom door. Steam boiled out and collected along the ceiling, temporarily hiding the water stains in the drooping tiles. "Hello there," the man said into the mist as he stepped gingerly inside the bathroom.

"Can you close the door, please?" Billy called out. The man craned his head around the corner, his glasses fogged, sweat or condensation or both collecting on his face. "My sister likes her privacy."

The door closed slowly and the shower curtain swished open. There was a sound of impact against the wall, a long, choked scream, and then silence.

Over the next several minutes, soft grinding and clicking sounds came from inside the bathroom, rising just above the humming of the air conditioner, before the shower started again. Billy got up, removed a trash bag from the box, and tossed in the comic book, then the man's shoes, socks, and empty bottle. He set the trash bag next to the bathroom door, sat down on the bed and ate the food, two at time, starting with the ice cream sandwiches, which were beginning to melt.

Billy emerged from the hotel room, carrying a full trash bag with a Gideon's Bible under one arm, holding his sister's hand with the other. She towered a good three feet above him, and was wearing the wetsuit and the motorcycle helmet. Her body was lumpy, thin in parts that should be thick, and thick in parts that should be thin. She moved with an odd, jerky gate, like a puppet learning to walk.

He led her to the man's truck, tossing the tied trash bag in back, before helping her into the cab. Going to the driver's side, he opened the door, placed the bible onto the seat, and sat on top of it, using it as a booster to see more fully over the dash, making him look less like a child behind the wheel of a half ton pickup with several thousand dollars worth of tools in the back. Billy knew where to take those, as he'd been all over town. That and the wallet would keep them going, and keeping going was what it was all about.

After a night of haggling with hard-eyed men in a vacant lot next to a trailer park, Billy drove the truck to the train station and parked in the farthest stall, right under a stunted acacia tree that offered shade and a blanket of bird droppings in the coming days. He used the wet naps he requested with breakfast to wipe down the steering wheel and interior as his sister uncurled from the now empty bed of the truck.

When he was finished, Billy took her by the gloved hand and led her across the parking lot and toward the non-pedestrian side of the tracks. They wouldn't be buying a ticket. Inside Billy's backpack was a library chart of every industrial train route across the country, so now it was just a matter of finding a rail car that had room to spare, either outside or in. It didn't matter. Billy was used to the elements, and his sister had the wetsuit to protect her. And she was strong.

RETURN OF THE PRODIGY

I t was over the "Complimentary Anniversary Cake For Two!" that Gary
sprang the news.

Just minutes before, the Vahlkamps were wrapping up another predictably
silent ceremonial dinner at The Drover, where they had memorialized each anniversary for the last thirty-four years. The occasion was once again ushered in
with identical iceberg salads, butter grilled Omaha steaks, and long looks around
the room over smeared cocktail rims, searching for familiar faces and forgotten
gossip.

But this night was different. This was the thirty-fifth, and after enduring exactly 12,775 days of intermittent harping on the fact that he had never taken his
wife Gladys on a honeymoon following their traditional Lutheran wedding, Gary
decided to man up and do the right thing, if only to find a little goddamn peace.

You see, Gary was a frugal man, but not inappropriately so, considering the
circumstances of his upbringing. Born with the sluggish blood of German stock
on the cusp of the Platte River Valley, he wore his innate thriftiness as a badge
of honor. It was the right thing to do. It was the *Nebraska* thing to do. Gladys,
a former Kansas City socialite and theatre actress of little renown, was quite the
opposite, and although she loved her husband as a historian loves a bygone civilization, she always chafed at his chintzy ways. But the heart doesn't deal out fairly,
so she suffered his shallow pockets mostly in wifely silence. Mostly. That would
be her story, anyway.

But on this night, Gary bit the bullet. He didn't like the taste, mixed as it was with the floury chocolate he was trying to work out of his bridgework, but he understood that men sometimes do things they don't want to do. The burden of the masculine, and all that jazz.

Gary finished his Beam and water, placed his hands on the tablecloth, and made the pronouncement. Gladys was ecstatic, spilling a bit of her Mai Tai as she leapt with surprising speed across the table and planted a series of awkwardly received kisses on her husband.

"Hawaii, right?" It was more a declaration than a question.

Gary, long since accustomed to her odd fascination with Don Ho, tiki parties, and all things Polynesian, just smiled. "You'll see," he said with one of his patented, ex-jock winks that first wooed Gladys all those years ago.

Gladys blushed and hugged him tight. Gary inhaled her Avon perfume that always smelled like Raid on her skin. "I love you," she whispered. Gary grunted and patted her arm. Gladys released, clapped her hands like a schoolgirl, drawing much needed attention from the room, and trundled off to the bathroom, squealing happily through tears.

Gary sat back, exhaled, and ordered another drink.

When they arrived home, Gladys hustled to her laptop to purchase a whole new wardrobe of "nouveau chic cabana wear" from QVC online, while Gary logged onto his desktop, searching out "affordable vacation options in Micronesia." Hawaii wasn't even an option. Fiji and Tahiti were out, obviously. Money-sucking tourist traps lousy with shirtless newlyweds and Eurotrash stuffing their uncut manhood into Speedos. Murderous. Guam would be fitting in a way, as a former Navy man, but he knew Gladys would see right through this, and nag him into suicidal thoughts he'd long since put behind him.

Clicking through various slick tourist sites, Gary came upon a promo page for Walakea, a flyspeck peeking up from the water nearly equidistant between the Philippines and Easter Island, which sported "A cozy resort nestled upon a dreamy, secluded island of exotic, black sand beaches." *"Cozy,"* Gary grumbled at the thought of such forced intimacy. Worse, a backwater like this probably wouldn't even serve proper liquor. But before he could move on, his gaze was caught by *"The most affordable vacation value in the Pacific!"* highlighted inside a flashing gold star. Nice. These islanders were speaking Gary's language, and doing it with class. Cross checking a few reputable news sites, he discovered that Walakea had experienced a spate of underreported "ecological incidents" that had nearly ruined the local fishing economy late last year. Gary nodded with satisfaction. If he had to hand over his hard earned greenbacks to foreigners, might as well do a little charity work amongst the godless zipperheads while he was at it. Two birds with one stone, moonlighting as a Christian imperative.

Gary now had to sell Walakea to his wife. He whipped up a batch of Malibu Rum Runners and presented them to Gladys as she stood in front of the mirror, going way easy on the condition of her pear-shaped body while babbling about various crash diets "that all the actors do." Gary kept the cocktails flowing, and after a less than an hour, his wife was on board.

A belated honeymoon on Walakea. Let the angels sing.

The creaky SouthPac Airlines 737 circled the tiny, mountainous island a few times, shedding altitude like a bad habit as it began a tight, controlled corkscrew. Gary, who hated flying with a white-hot passion normally reserved for illegal immigrants and tax hikes, steadied himself as his stomach rose into his throat. He glanced nervously past Gladys, down on the lush greenery below, which seemed to chew its way up to the lip of the pitch-black beach, as if wanting to retake the land from the sea. From above, Walakea looked like a sooty History Channel graphic of the islands of the Pacific theater in WWII. Guadalcanal. Palau. Okinawa. Back when America won its wars.

The plane shuddered, jerked nose down and careened toward the tragically short landing strip. Gary gritted his teeth, tasting the bourbon and club crackers that served as his breakfast after waking up mid-flight, hoping that it was already over.

After a screaming descent that felt more like a free fall, the plane skipped, skidded, then thudded onto the asphalt, and wobbled toward the lone gate of the one horse airport. The AC was cut, and Gary mopped his brow, feeling the creep of the unencumbered sun that beat down on the winged metal cylinder. This was heat without season.

"Wow, wasn't that something?" Gladys chirped, clutching Gary's leg. "What an *adventure!*" Gary was just hoping their baggage made it into the guts of this rattletrap during their layover in LA, and that the rooms had central air and plenty of ice. He had vacation drinking to do.

The passengers disembarked across the boiling tarmac, and were met by a garishly painted golf cart that took them to the Sea Pearl Resort, where they had booked three nights of "fun with the sun," as the confirmation agent assured him in choppy English.

The room was modest and smelled musty, which he thought was odd for the dry, kiln-like conditions of a Pacific islet squatting on the equator. Gladys flopped on the bed with a laugh, and paged through the faded brochures left on the nightstand. Gary set about inspecting the room, checking for faulty wiring and load bearing beams behind the walls. This was earthquake country, and he'd be good god damned if he'd breathe his last under a pile of cheap roofing smack dab in the lap of slanty-eyed heathenism.

Satisfied that the walls would hold for the next three days, Gary rang down to the front desk while Gladys peeled off her Spanx and launched into a clumsy fashion show, ripping off tags and dangerously stretching new, non-breathable fabric. As she kept calling for Gary to look, he scanned the television, finding nothing but bizarre Japanese game shows and incomprehensible regional news, which seemed to be covering yet another natural disaster somewhere along the dark Indochinese Peninsula. Retribution for the godless Socialists, Pat Robertson always said, before he lost his mind and started talking about legalizing dope. Gary clicked through the channels a few more times, hoping for a different outcome, but found nothing remotely resembling ESPN or Fox New. Hell, he'd even settle for the Trinity Network, just to get a little home cooking. *"Jesus Christ,"* he hissed, hoping to high heaven that they sold Tom Clancy at the gift shop.

There was a knock on the door. Gary leapt up to open it, moving past Gladys, who was in the middle of asking his preference between a TrimShaper skirtini and something called a "sarong." Gary opened the door and found a pineapple standing at shoulder height in front of him, decorated with a wispy moustache and mirrored sunglasses. It was the room service attendant, a huge grin etched across his wide, pockmarked face, making it seem wider and more pockmarked than Gary thought possible. Must be some strange genetic quirk, he thought. *Inbreeding*, he deduced with a nod of finality, as the walking botany experiment held out a red and white plastic bottle and two Dixie cups.

Gary glared at the label. "The hell is this?"

"Language, Gary," Gladys trilled from the bathroom.

"Whiskey," the attendant answered with a smile before putting the bottle to his mouth as if instructing this confused round eye what to do with it.

"I asked for Jim Beam," Gary growled, taking the plastic container of Black Velvet and holding it out in front of him with disdain. The total lack of understanding of decent distilled spirits was worse than he feared.

"Whiskey," the Walakean repeated, handing Gary the Dixie cups, and held out his hand, palm side up.

Gary looked at him with disappointment and shook his head. "It's already starting," he sighed as he dug into his pocket and pulled out some loose change, which he dropped into the man's gnarled, net-scarred hand. The attendant bobbed his head, and loped away, walking in a manner more accustomed to being on the deck of a pitching skiff than solid land. Gary frowned at the shabby bottle, most likely airlifted in during the Reagan administration. Better than nothing, he surmised, and a definite necessity to survive the next half of the "beachwear for the mature woman" burlesque going on inside their room. When in Rome, drink low.

"He kind of looked like Don Ho, didn't he?" Gladys called out from the bathroom.

Gary sighed and closed the door.

The sun dropped behind the island's volcanic peaks, and under the burden of jetlag and cheap bourbon, Gary was soon ready for a nap that would hopefully extend into an early bedtime. Gladys had other plans, and finished her fashion show with the grand finale, waddling out of the bathroom in an ill-fitting, matronly nightie cut from way too much shiny material. She slunk over to the bed and shook Gary awake, purring something about "consummating the honeymoon." Gary knew the drill, and got down to business, turning the light off while he fought through his boxers.

"No," Gladys cooed. "Tonight I want us to see each other, like the natives on the Island of Blue Dolphins."

Gary looked for his Dixie cup as her eveningwear hit the floor.

In their intertwined, post coital positions, the couple listened to massive waves crashing down on the beach below. "I think I felt the earth move while we were... *you know*," Gladys whispered.

Gary, feeling buzzed, smiled. "Yeah, I have that effect on women."

She giggled. "Can you believe these waves?"

Gary scratched at his jaw. "Must be high tide," he muttered, dozing off.

Gladys listened as Gary began to softly snore. "We could get washed away at any moment," she said quietly, delighting in some imagined danger on this forgotten reef thousands of miles from civilization. Now that he was asleep, she snuggled up close to Gary's thick torso and exhaled happily, running her fingers through his chest hair that always reminded her of Tom Selleck.

That night, Gary dreamt that the whole world was heaving and pitching around him, then disintegrated like a sand painting into an endless, howling abyss below. But as everything melted away, Gary stood tall in the middle of nothingness, balanced on a six-fold circular pattern shimmering bright yellow below his booted feet. He looked down into the void, and found a comfort in the emptiness. He paused for a second, trying to remember his waking life, then leapt off the edge.

Gary fell, but didn't experience a plunging sensation. Instead, he felt himself twirling, tumbling upward amid a cloud of oily bubbles. His body softened, becoming pliable, and clove into a double helix. Even through all of this, Gary didn't try to wake up. He just watched, inside his dream, as his body separated into minutia, wondering how it would all end.

The next morning, Gary awoke with a start, threw off the smothering covers, and tried to press himself back together. He couldn't remember his nightmare, which was strange. Gary was inclined to bad dreams and cursed to remember them all, filing them away in a dark vault deep inside. He'd seen a lot. In the haunted jungles of Vietnam. In his private, shameful thoughts since then. But this was different. Stark flashes came to him, yet he couldn't make heads or tails of what he actually dreamt last night. Just fractured glimpses. Suffocation. Choking. Drowning in the sky.

Gary blinked his eyes and crawled out of bed, careful not to wake Gladys, who slept with a contented smile on her face. God bless her little mind. She never dreamed.

He pulled on some baggy swimming trunks and padded to the dresser, where he poured himself the last of the Black Velvet into his limp Dixie cup. Gary took a sip, trying to burn away the strange feeling nagging at him, and looked in the mirror, squeezing a portion of his hardened gut. *Not bad, sailor.* His self-examination was broken up by an unholy racket coming from outside, down by the beach. The frantic squawking of birds.

He walked out onto the patio and looked down at the waterfront, where a jabbering cloud of sea fowl were dive-bombing the sand. Gary reached for his flip-flops.

Gary made his way down to the beach, approaching a gathered group of locals watching the feeding frenzy in silent mourning. A few shooed away birds in hopes of salvaging the fresher carcasses, but most were ruined, chewed up before they hit shore. It was the same scene up and down the beach—black sand hosting a twisting colonnade of the ocean's gleaming dead. Gary examined the heaps as the first squirm of rot began to set in. Amid the mass of dismembered commercial fish and knotted balls of kelp, he spied some very unusual creatures. He'd watched plenty of Jacques Cousteau with his oldest in the 70's, and knew that what he was looking at wasn't your usual collection of supermarket filets. Here and there were the pulpy, many-legged remains of bizarre creatures from the darkest depths, possibly never before seen by human eyes. Whatever violence drove these things to dry land must have dredged them up from somewhere impossibly deep.

Wanting a souvenir, Gary bent down to pick up a bony specimen sprouting what looked like a dozen eyestalks and feet-like flippers, when a hand stopped him. He looked up, and found a squatty, strong shouldered Walakean gripping him tightly by the arm. The man shook his head and pulled him back. Irritated by this close contact but not wanting to make a scene, Gary scowled, stood up and gave ground, while the man shook his head again and crossed his arms, continuing his silent gaze at the unhallowed funeral in front of him.

Suddenly very thirsty, Gary turned and headed back to the room and his deteriorating Dixie cup, passing a rusted front loader belching smoke into the screeching sky as it headed toward the shore.

After a continental breakfast of slimy eggs and bacon ostensibly hewn from shoe leather, Gary took initiative and proposed that they go for a swim, which had the added bonus of allowing Gladys to show off her new "Day One" bathing costume.

Hoping to gain wide berth from the aquatic holocaust that choked their side of the island, Gary and Gladys caught a scooter-drawn rickshaw to the opposite, undeveloped side of Walakea, which, according to the desk clerk—an oddly proportioned man with puffy hair and sideburns who looked like a villain in those knock off Bruce Lee films—boasted a secluded beach not even used by the locals. That suited Gary just fine. It had been forty years since he swam in the ocean, and he'd be damned if some grinning native or snickering tourist saw him trip over a rip tide or lose his shorts in the undertow.

In a dusty trinket shack just outside of town, Gary picked up some antiquated, Navy-issue snorkeling gear that must have come from a returning American brother, freshly emerged from the slimy hell of Vietnam, his sanity left behind in a bloody jungle pill box.

The scooter puttered up a bumpy dirt road that meandered into the hills, affording a view of the oblong island and the never-ending water that tried to swallow it every high tide. Even with the underpinnings of black sand, the surrounding sea just beyond the breakers seemed darker than most volcanic islands in the South Pacific, hinting at an unusual depth, positioning the island of Walakea as just the tip of a capacious ebony spear thrust fast and hard from the sea floor.

Gladys slipped her arm under Gary's, interrupting his musing. "Isn't this romantic?" she sighed.

"Yeah, it's something else," he said.

She rested her head on his shoulder. "I want to be buried here."

Gary knew she was just caught up in the moment, but his thoughts turned to the grim faced locals gathered on the beach, watching as his wife's swollen, naked body sank slowly to an unreachable ocean bottom. Patting her absently on the head, he surmised that Gladys wouldn't find a watery grave, chewed to the bone by unclassified fish, as romantic a notion. Moving his gaze to the hills to his right, he scanned the ridgeline of the leveled off peaks. He did the same just outside of Da Nang. The zips cut them to fucking pieces that day, raining down hot death for eighteen straight hours. Ghosts of the past never rest, especially in heat like this.

Just then, something not altogether natural in the shadow of the mountains caught Gary's attention. Shading his eyes from the blazing sun, he spotted a ring of tilted, worn statuary on a sloping hillside. Aside from their greenish gray color, they looked similar to those silent monoliths found on Easter Island. But that couldn't be the case, as Easter Island was 4,000 miles away.

"What are those things?" Gary asked their driver. Gladys looked around and fumbled with her camera, hoping to shoot something interesting enough to impress the gals at Sunday brunch. The driver turned around to Gary and motioned to his ears. "What are those things? Up there!" Gary yelled, jutting his finger at the hillside.

The driver shrugged and smiled.

Gladys began snapping pictures at random, not sure what Gary was talking about. "What is it, honey?" she called. The driver glanced up at the hills and made tiny movements with his hands. Gary noticed this, and looked up at the worn, discolored monoliths, sneering at such superstitious nonsense. But just as they rounded a curve and were out of sight, Gary could have sworn that one of the statues looked vaguely amphibian, which would clearly make them *not* like the exaggeratedly human effigies carved on Easter Island. "What did you see?" Gladys asked again, checking her shots.

"Nothing," Gary said, trying to convince himself by clearing his throat and swallowing.

Every place has its ghosts.

Gladys set up a picnic on one of her mother's quilts atop the rocky beach, dotted with large basalt rock formations, polished smooth by endless years of determined wave and weather. It wasn't the most comfortable stretch of sand, but at least the natural bowl of the cove protected if from the fickle tide and the onslaught of dead fish that plagued the Sea Pearl-side of the island. After a snack of venison summer sausage and Colby cheese brought from home, lubricated by a clay jug of room temp Jap sake purchased locally, Gary stood and beat his chest, grunting like a silverback, which elicited a giggle from Gladys. He grinned and marched to the water, determined to make contact with this unruly, foreign ocean. Gladys watched him go, trying to remember the exact year when the fullness of his backside suddenly evaporated.

Gary stopped at the lapping water's edge and dipped in a toe. Not bad. Easing in, the water became surprisingly frigid just yards from the beach, much colder than he expected. Shivering, he waded out to his chest, then pushed off and began to tread water, working forgotten muscles. Gary leaned back and kicked his legs, staring up at the infinite blueness of the sky above. For just a moment, floating weightless, he felt like an infant inside an immense, frigid womb of dark fluid. His dream whispered back to him. Gary smiled for a second before something long and thick slithered between his paddling feet. He froze, allowing his toes to touch sand, bringing the waterline to just below his upturned mouth. Gary tried to recall the list of sharks native to the area. He came up with nothing other than scenes from *Jaws 3D*, his favorite installment of the series. Gary held his breath, feeling the tightness of water around his submerged body. Nothing moved, save the gentle rise and fall of the waves. Maybe he imagined it. This island set the mind to strange things.

He was just about to continue his swim, when something large and powerful bumped into his lower back, and stayed there, pressing against him, nuzzling. Gary thrashed his arms behind him, striking something hard and ice cold that shot away quickly, the force of its propulsion dragging him under. He surfaced and swam/ran with a panicked stiffness to the shore.

Breathing hard, he rushed from the water and jogged toward Gladys, who looked like a bell shaped porcelain doll lying on a stretch of black nothingness. With leaden legs, he made it to the blanket, and collapsed next to his wife, who was "sunbathing" under a thick slathering of 50 SPF. "Jesus Christ," Gary let escape between labored breaths.

"You almost drown again?" Gladys asked without concern behind her absurd sunglasses two generations too large.

"No!"

She shaded her eyes and peered at him.

"No," he repeated, lowering his voice. "I just…felt something out there."

"The ocean is full of all sorts of things, honey," Gladys said. "Remember Jonah and the whale?"

Gary rose to his knees and toweled off, keeping an eye on their scooter driver, who smoked and watched them underneath squinted eyes on a cliff above. Gary laid face down on the quilt, not noticing what was higher up, on the sloping hillside in the shadows of the mountains, where a collection of motionless, naked human figures stood and watched the two stark white visitors lay on their black beach below. From this elevated vantage point, the basalt along the shore showed clear evidence of careful cutting and shaping of massive stonework, which lay half buried in the sand. The ruined columns outlined a foundation of an immense structure, as if scattered in a fit of rage by a colossal child in a time when the world was still young and wild.

Back at their room, following a silent scooter ride from the far beach, Gary and Gladys showered together for the first time since before their grown children were born, and remarked with laughter at how shower stalls must have been more spacious in simpler times. Their intermingled feet danced over the rivulets of dark grit that collected on the tile, before slithering down the drain, joining their billion year old brethren under the sea.

Gary found himself inside the same dream, only this time he was an amphibious creature rising from the abyss that had taken him. Higher and higher he climbed, only to be birthed onto a burnt, sandless shore recently cooled from the fires that raged and smoked on mountaintops looming in the distance a thousand miles high. The domed sky above was copper colored and veined with crimson gold. Triple moons, soft with youth and fat in their close orbit, jockeyed for prominence in the starless expanse of space just above. The Gary creature moved with pain, his soft bones protesting against dry gravity. He struggled for breath, feeling his neck tighten and his chest about to explode. He coughed, drew air into tiny lungs, and exhaled a roar of victory, declaring himself a prodigy.

Gary awoke from his dream, coughing onto his pillow and scratching at the sides of his neck. He sat up, staring sightlessly at the wall opposite of him. But he wasn't afraid. He felt like a conqueror. Looking down and noticing the bulge in his boxers, he nudged Gladys awake.

In an unusually jovial mood that evening as they dressed for dinner, Gary announced that they were to dine away from the resort, finding the finest place on the island that served only the most authentic Walakean cuisine. Gladys was as shocked as she was overjoyed. "You really mean it, Gare-bear?" she asked.

"Sure do," he said. "Let's soak up a little local color, huh?"

Gladys squealed and hugged him close. She rushed over to the closet. "Let's *really* have a safari tonight."

Gary slumped into a rattan chair, immediately regretting his generous idea as Gladys unveiled a gaudy Hawaiian shirt for him, and a matching dress of the same flowery material for her. He knew it was no use arguing, nor fighting it, for it had arrived. They were THAT couple. They'd be power walking in the local mall every morning in matching sweat suits the day after they landed back in Omaha. Gary's mood darkened. His thoughts turned to whiskey.

"You think we can find a place with a luau?" she asked. "We can pretend we're Mr. and Mrs. Ho!"

Ho indeed. Cuckolded by a dead Hawaiian. Again. Gary excused himself and headed for the front desk, praying to the Christian God for the discovery of another plastic bottle of Black Velvet. Even this far out, no matter how hard he tried, some things would never change.

They set out from the Sea Pearl an hour later. Gary walked several steps ahead of Gladys, who was taking pictures of every neon-lit tourist shop and gaudy storefront she came across. He scratched at the tag irritating his neck inside the back of his stiff shirt, which still had that hollow, stale smell of a Taiwanese warehouse. He felt ridiculous. Walking about, in this loud, garish get-up that strategically matched his woman's. If he had a tail, it would have been tucked deeply between his chaffed legs. Gary glanced behind him at his wife's enormous purse, wondering if anyone else could hear the clanging of his testicles against her bottle of Avon perfume better suited for pest eradication. Walking alone, wrapped inside the old, comfortable blanket of boozy gloom, Gary searched for the first place that looked presentable, just wanting to get off this strange, black-rimmed island that seemed so at odds with the rest of the civilized world. Honeymoons are for suckers. He was right the first time.

Rounding a corner, Gary came across a glowing sign for the Seven Seas Grill, nestled between two large warehouses. He peered inside, and saw that the joint was sparsely populated and seemed more or less clean. Good enough. Gary prepped his case and turned to find Gladys, but she was nowhere to be found. He darted his eyes up and down the cramped street, feeling an unexpected rush of fear.

Gary headed back around the corner, and found Gladys bent over a legless transient propped up on the curb. She handed the wrinkled old man a few dollars, rewarded with a toothless grin. Gary's face soured. He called out to her, and she trundled over. "That sweet old man just gave me the most wonderful thing." Gladys held up a spiny shell hanging from a hemp string, featuring a six-fold circular pattern shimmering bright yellow.

"Put that away," Gary said.

Gladys was taken aback. "Why? It's so pretty, and that old man told me that it would protect us on the island. Isn't that *neat*? He didn't even have any legs."

Gary scowled. "It's pagan jewelry. 'Neat' has nothing to do with it. You think Pastor Thune would want you wearing that around town? Come on! Toss it out."

Pouting, Gladys walked to the nearest overflowing trashcan and laid it atop the pile. Gary was distracted, his mind delving into his memory, trying to uncover his certainty about this cheap trinket. Gladys glumly rejoined Gary. "Party pooper," she mumbled.

Gary pulled at his itchy shirt. "Let's go eat."

Gary and Gladys were seated in a corner booth next to a murky aquarium. Cuttlefish swirled along the bottom, hiding from the sputtering light, while tiny eels slithered to and fro, taunting their older antecedents. A sea snail clung to the inside of the glass, unable to keep up with the filth, or had merely quit trying.

Gladys read the menu aloud to no one in particular. Gary stared into the tank, once again remembering the death scene on the beach, remembering a tiny sliver of his dream…

"So, what will it be?" The question caught Gary off guard, and he jerked his head to find a tall, darkly handsome Central Asian man that definitely didn't look local standing in front of them. Still Asian, though. Asian enough. Gary glanced at his wife, flexed the faded green anchor tattoo on his beefy forearms and opened the menu.

"What's the best thing in the house?" Gladys asked, avoiding her husband's glare.

The waiter smiled broadly. "Devil Fish, ma'am. Best in all the islands."

Gladys' permed hair seemed to shiver with excitement. "*Oooo*, that sounds yummy, doesn't it Gare?"

Gary shook his head, squinting at the prices on the right side of the menu. "I don't like the sound of that."

"Oh, *poo*," Gladys chided. "Live a little."

Gary glowered and handed the menu to the waiter without looking at him. "I'll have the special."

The waiter nodded and turned to Gladys, who continued scanning the menu like it was the goddamn Rosetta Stone. "You're supposed to let a lady order first," she said, as if an afterthought, but which clearly wasn't.

Gary cracked his neck. "You have any whiskey here?"

"No sir," he answered coolly. "Only rum."

"Oh goody," Gladys clapped. "I'll have a Mai Tai, *and* the Devil Fish." Gladys handed off the menu and smiled sweetly at her husband. A barb dipped in honey.

According to Gary's Timex, the food arrived exactly twenty-eight minutes after the waiter disappeared into the silent kitchen. Gladys was already on her third Mai Tai, served in a ceramic cup fashioned into the mouth of an exotic fish. Gary was absently rubbing his stomach that burned with sugary indigestion from nine shots of cheap rum. This is what you get for traveling, he ruminated dourly with a burp.

The waiter set a plate in front of Gary that featured a thick, inscrutable slab of grilled marine life surrounded by seashells and a giant clutch of parsley. "What's this?" Gary demanded.

"Special," the waiter assured him with a pleasant smile.

"I mean, what *is* it?"

The waiter shrugged as he set a sizzling plate of braised Devil Fish in front of Gladys. "Catch of the day."

Gary was about to protest, when his wife cut him off. "Don't complain, Gary. You get what you pay for."

The waiter nodded and bowed slightly. "*Bon appetit,*" he said in a perfect— perfectly annoying—French accent as he retreated.

Gary frowned at Gladys as he snapped open his napkin. "Can't you be on my side, just once?"

Gladys slurped up the last of her Mai Tai. "Oh, don't be silly." She held up her glass to the waiter hovering by the bar, as Gary pick up his knife and fork and tucked into his meal. The skin was a bit rubbery and tough, resisting Gary's efforts.

"Shark," Gary said. "I like shark."

"Of course you do, dear." Gladys said absently, receiving her fresh Mai Tai from the waiter with a suggestive smile.

"Gonna need a bigger boat," Gary mumbled to himself with a chuckle as he sawed with his knife. Gladys just hummed tunelessly to herself. Finally, the plated skin parted under the blade and revealed a pinkish flesh underneath. Gary frowned, cut off a slice and put it in his mouth. He chewed hesitantly at first, but found the flavor surprisingly agreeable. "Not bad," he said. "I guess I do get what I pay for." Gary cut off a larger hunk, smiling as he chewed. "How's Satan's ding dong over there?" he asked, poking his knife at her plate.

"Absolutely *sinful,*" Gladys enunciated in that theatrical way that emerged when she drank in mixed company. She took another exaggerated bite while keeping wobbly eye contact with their swarthy waiter.

By the end of the night, Gary felt like he was warming up to the island. The dinner was spectacular, and reasonably priced. Even the bar bill was a pittance, as their waiter seemed to have comped half the drinks poured with a heavy hand. Island hospitality, Gary reckoned. Maybe he was wrong about this place. They left the restaurant and headed back to the resort. Gladys seemed heated up, so Gary let her go on to the room, determined to comb the shops for whiskey.

He only made it a few blocks before his extremities turned to jelly and he pitched to the sandy pavement, skinning his hands and tearing the knees of his linen trousers. The heartburn had dissipated in his notoriously iron gut, but his head felt like it was packed in cotton. Worse, his heart was pounding like he had shotgunned a pot of Folgers. Sweat coated his brow, soaking through the flowers of his stiff shirt, making it feel like an exoskeleton he needed to shed. He crawled to his feet and clutched a corroded street lamp for support.

He spit something thick and unnatural and looked around, trying to get his bearings. The streets were deserted, but he felt eyes on him, hundreds of them, and not all of them in pairs, peering out through grotesque pineapples from deep in the dark places away from the isolated circles of light and the neon glow of the storefronts. One window display featured naked female mannequins, arms arranged into obscene poses, topped by hideous tribal masks. He hadn't seen this on the way home, but it was all he could see now. Distended necks and tiny breasts with nipples like fingers. Unnatural, primal postures as suggestive as they were threatening. The vacant eyes that seemed to have depth and purpose shot their darkness deep into him, and he reeled, falling backwards without moving. He saw clouds of exploding napalm flatten smears of green, rising triumphant into a mushrooming horror show of angry soot and burned trees and skin and innards and dreams that were no different than his own. White phosphorus melted into the ground, eating up the bones of ancestors and their buried secrets. Gary clawed at his face and blinked his eyes dry, only to see lolling tongues quiver from underneath plastic teeth and lick toward the window, tasting the glass and streaking it with blackish gore.

He turned to flee the other way when he stumbled over something lying in the gutter. At his feet was the body of the legless transient, his skin gray, as if mummified, his mouth wrenched open sideways, gums crawling with insects. A final scream, or a last desperate bite.

Gary careened back up the sidewalk, hoping he was heading in the right direction. Behind him, the poorly lit street narrowed, waiting.

After what seemed like hours, Gary threw open the door to their room. Gladys was snoring in a rattan easy chair, dressed in a crooked grass skirt and bunched up pink nylons, a string of Puka shells balled in her hand, succumbing to the Mai Tais mid primp. Gary collapsed to the ground, clothing soaked, heaving for breath.

"I'm sick." he wheezed, trying to wake her. "I'm—" His voice failed.

Gary slumped into the bathroom and pawed at the switch, jarring the six walls into painful, sudden white light. He propped himself up in front of the mirror and saw bloodshot, yellowing eyes staring back at him like a demented stranger.

He bent down over the toilet bowl and held on tight. He hated vomiting, but he had to get this liquor out of him. Just like when he was twelve, when he took on an entire fifth of gin for his debut. He had almost died then. That was before he went pro. Maybe he had lost a step. He just had to get through this and start fresh tomorrow. Man up and do the deed, goddamn it.

Gary stuck his finger deep into this throat, which gurgled and contracted, as his stomach prepared to empty against its will. He pushed deeper, eyes gushing tears, until his guts seized and pushed upwards. Gary leaned into the bowl, his body clenching as if shot through with a cattle prod. Paralyzed with the effort, he choked a scream into a high-pitched rasp, yet nothing but foamy saliva came out. He tried again, and only quivering drool dripped through his strangled shriek into the toilet water. He sat back, gulping air, fighting back the tremor as his body attempted to resume normal functioning. The ceiling spun, the water stains in the tiles taking on demonic shapes. Goat-faced faerie folk fucking on clouds. A whale swallowing a city. Someone must have spiked his cocktails with enough LSD to melt a buffalo. The waiter. That fucking waiter. Gladys.

Anger burning through his revulsion, Gary bellied up to the commode and jammed his finger down his esophagus, nearly fitting his fist inside his mouth, stretching and cracking the skin around it. Jaw wrenched sideways... Crawling insects...

His stomach convulsed and expelled whatever was left inside, which felt like nothing. Gary feared a night of dry heaves, with that span of trapped time that never seemed to end, freezing him in panic forever. Veins bulged in his neck and forehead. Blood vessels burst in his eyes. Gary's face turned purple and the light dimmed. Finally... a dribble of black ichor dripped past his lips and dotted the water like ink. In it writhed what resembled a dying tapeworm, but it had tiny legs, like a millipede. Parasite brought up from a tangle of guts.

More bubbled out of him and everything went dark.

Gary woke up on the bed as Gladys was getting dressed in a high wasted denim jumper. It was still dark outside, and the ocean sounded closer than before. Right outside the patio door, underneath the ground. The sheets chaffed his skin, the terrestrial cotton strands clawing at him. "Oh, there you are," she said cheerily. "Did you feel that shaking?"

"What—?" Gary said, a deep-body shiver stealing his words that felt rounded and unfamiliar on top of his rubbery tongue. The rest of him felt numb. He tried to move but only quavered like a Mad Dog drunk drying out in an alley after a forty-year bender.

"Between the walls moving and those noises you were making… Scared the *dickens* out of me. I ran into the bathroom and found you on the floor, all frozen and stiff with a bloody mouth. I was afraid you were having an aneurysm!" She laughed, but it came out shrill, like a bird.

"I…" He put the ball of his hand to his throbbing head. He felt worse than before. "Fuck."

"Language, Gary. You should have seen what was in that toilet. All sorts of weird things." She sat next to him on the bed and placed a moist hotel towel on his forehead. "I think all those toxins are leeching out of your system. Must be this fresh air and organic seafood. I told you that we should start juicing. It worked for Jack LaLanne."

"He's dead."

"*Well…*"

"I feel like…" He didn't know how to describe it. Didn't have the strength.

"I know you do. Rest now. You'll feel better in the morning." She bent down, removed the towel and felt his forehead for a fever. It was clammy, cold. She paused for a second, then grabbed her purse and headed for the door.

"Where're…you going?"

"Just out for a walk."

That fucking waiter.

"Be back in a jiff!" The door closed behind her and he heard her mules clatter away faster than he thought possible. Gary closed his eyes and felt a thousand others opening up inside of him. He prayed for no dreams and knew that his mumbled pleas would fall on deaf ears, or maybe no ears at all.

Gladys hurried up the deserted sidewalk, an address written on resort stationary clutched in her hand. She peered anxiously at the street signs. Something large and low to the ground shifted back into the shadows without making a sound. She never noticed as she moved on, the lines in her face carved deeper under the sodium lights swaying on poles above. Farther up, amid the jagged shadows that marked where the mountains bit into the sky, tiny fires burned and bobbed like dancing sparks escaping a smoldering log.

She came to a set of barred windows decorated with a wired plastic sign. The painted cross had faded from red to a pale, unpleasant pink. The bulb was turned off. Gladys banged on the bars. "Hello?" Someone moved inside the clinic. She banged again. "Is anyone in there? My husband's sick. He doesn't..." She didn't continue. Didn't know how. She heard another sound, and peered through the window. A pair of wide, staring eyes looked back at her from the gloom. They were rounded and buggy, not like anything she'd seen on the island. They moved toward her without blinking, or giving away what was attached to them, even as they reached the bars. Gladys stumbled backwards, falling out of one of her shoes. She left it on the sidewalk behind her and hobbled on one heel further down the street.

Gary forced himself to sit up. He wanted to be awake when she came home, smelling of garlic sweat and Oriental fuckery. He knew that stink all too well, from Burma to the Philippines. He'd be damned if his wife did too. He'd kill the bitch first.

All of his old impulses born in piles of maggot choked jungle corpses flowed back into him, firing his limbs and putting salt back into his spine. He stood up and strode to the dresser, taking off his clothes. He flexed in front of the mirror, muscles bulging with a youthful strength and vitality left on the college gridiron. He felt massive, transcendent. He felt like a goddamn monster.

It was then that he saw the tiny black needle poke through the skin just above his unruly nest of pubic hair surrounding his erection. He stared at it, detached, as other spiky tendrils emerged from his rounded belly that swelled by the second.

The room shuddered, or maybe it was his cells shouting out in protest and the walls never moved. A low tone rumbled deep below him like the last bass note on a million key piano, reverberating from somewhere far beneath the ground. As if breaking a spell, Gary's body sagged, and he puked up blood, holding it in his mouth under glassy, terrified eyes, and then swallowed, taking down skittering chunks that laughed at him...

The island swallowed with him, stealing the air and leaving everything deathly still. The incessant sound of the crashing waves was gone, sucked back home, away from the shoreline that hated it.

Jarred inside a cocoon of profound silence, Gary felt his chin dip and gore leak from his mouth as he looked down at the spreading forest of black writhing spines sprouting from his body. In a moment of instant clarity, Gary realized that he was about to see exactly what his insides were made of. And he wasn't afraid. He was curious.

◎

Gladys was lost, but that was the least of her apprehension. The entire city suddenly seemed deserted. Even the ocean seemed to have fled, as she couldn't hear the surf, just an occasionally creaking, like her grandmother's old porch swing. It was a thick, pregnant silence, amplifying her sobs.

She moved one way, then the other, wiping at her eyes, looking at the mascara that clumped on her fingertips. It was black and runny, like what she found in the toilet next to her comatose husband.

She turned to run, then gasped, hope flickering in her face. Gladys kicked off her remaining shoe and ran toward the familiar restaurant. Up on the hills, far above town, thousands of people, not all of them local Walakeans, stared down at the lone woman running through the street. Their naked flesh was decorated from toe to forehead with Polynesian tattoos of swirls and spirals, meshed with patterns far older and more ominous, of teeth and eyes, twisted geometry and forgotten glyphs. None of them moved as they watched, not even the waiter, who stood taller than the rest, his face painted yellow and green and dotted with black, his protruding eyes following Gladys below.

All the signage was turned off in the window of the Seven Seas Grill, but the front door was open. Gladys ran inside and found it just as empty as the rest of the town, but there was no sign of a hasty exit. Tables were arranged neatly, chairs left on the floor, awaiting business the next day.

"Hello," she called out, startled by the sound of her own voice that seemed to echo back at her from a soft barrier. She rushed through the swinging double doors and into the overly bright, spotless kitchen that seemed to be missing most of its appliances and utensils. She looked around, not sure what to do. Out of reflex, she grabbed a butcher's knife resting on a white plastic cutting board.

Gladys noticed an insulated door slightly ajar at the far corner of the room. Moving as fast as her trembling legs would take her, she followed the knifepoint into the walk-in refrigerator, and found that it was more of a corridor, lined with prepackaged and canned food. More than one would expect to find on an island surrounded by an ocean teeming with fish.

She emerged into a spacious cooler the size of a small plane hanger, her feet splashing in a pool of oily water on the floor. The smell of gasoline mixed with a noxious, heavy odor that stank more like a filthy reptile house at the zoo than the docks at high tide. A generator puttered and smoked just outside a window that provided the only light, blocked by a prodigious bulk that took up most of the room, rising to the high, reinforced ceiling.

At first it looked to be a mound of dirt, or maybe a bus covered in a sprawling tarpaulin, held fast to the floor by small hillocks of melting ice. But as she moved forward, Gladys noticed a glistening quality to the shape in the low light. An almost phosphorescent glow, lined with creases and furrows. The smell was overpowering, and the water deepened the closer she crept, but she was drawn to the enormous mass. Just feet from it, she discerned deep cuts into one side of the deeply wrinkled hulk and large slabs of missing tissue, conjuring images of old whaling footage and the gashes left in the sides of great beasts by blades the size of a man. Gladys reached her hand forward, compelled to make contact with what could only be called wounds, when a shiver seemed to run across the surface of the shape. She froze, just as the colossal thing clenched and thrashed, booming against the corrugated roof.

Gladys shot backwards and landed in the stinking slush. Outside, an emergency warning siren gathered itself into a scream from somewhere high and far away.

"Oh my God…"

Gary moved to the bed, his legs somehow still working but disjointed and jerky the way a marionette flails under the control of an inartful puppeteer. He lay back slowly onto the comforter, his skin bubbling like a latex balloon stuffed with beetles. The siren was blaring outside, then wound down to a long, extended murmur. Gary wasn't breathing, just waiting with something resembling a smile pinched under his bloated face. He felt the sudden urge to roar, and did, just as his body imploded, falling in on itself as a mass of writhing creatures emerged from what was once him to feast on what was left, on each other.

Gladys ran like she hadn't since childhood, her arms flailing and breath caught in her chest. She moved on instinct, barreling onto a side street that angled downward, taking her to the seashore. Looking up the beach, she spotting the resort with a scream of joy, when her attention was caught by the sinking expanse of pitch black sand stretching out to her left, dropping out of sight where the water once was. The ocean was gone, exposing the lip of the island and nothingness beyond. She was suddenly standing on a box butte in Central Nebraska, like the ones she and Gary marveled at outside of Salt Creek on their way to

Denver as the pink sun faded to dusk, and the prairie yawned like a brown abyss below.

Gladys flung open the door to their room at the Sea Pearl, and found the wall facing the sea eaten away. A trail of blood and debris lead down to the ocean. She ran to the patio and saw a twisting mass slink toward the waterless beach, expanding as it went, moving from what looked like a pool of slime to actual shapes, growing erect, evolving with every quivering second, worming toward the shadow that was forming high in front of it.

Gladys gaped up at the towering bulwark of water bearing down on the island. It was a mile out, and what looked like a mile high, and it made no sound. It didn't have to.

She turned and walked back into the room, lying in the blood and black soaked bed, resting her head next to the desiccated eggshell skull that once belonged to her husband, who broke the mold and decided to take her on the honeymoon she always wanted.

Gladys smoothed out the denim of her outfit and folded her hands over her stomach. She tried to pray, but forgot the words.

EXPAT

I woke up staring at the sagging tile of a ceiling I didn't recognize, emerging from a roaring fog that quieted in direct proportion to the reality of things firming up around me. This wasn't an unfamiliar sensation, as I often woke up in strange places in strange positions without remembering how I'd gotten there. Where that bruise came from, or how I'd lost a tooth. The furred creature taking up residence in my lungs. But this time was special, if one can call it that, because of the dead body lying face down in the middle of the floor.

Calling it a "dead body" was an assumption, to be sure, but what other conclusion can one draw when the back of man's head has been caved in like a cheap tin can? To soften up the shell like that must have taken some effort, or some pretty damn inspired intent. Inside the broken bowl, hair and skin and brain and bone were all mashed together, like when you knead raw egg into hamburger before balling it into patties. Tiny chips of reddish white were everywhere as if someone shattered a candy cane with a hammer – attached to odd things in odd places, like on the edge of a matchbook, dripping down the side of empty beer bottles, dotting the dull brass of the trombone propped up in the corner. The imitation Oriental rug was now decorated with a deep burgundy stain the shape of a perverse thought bubble issuing from the man's mouth crushed against the floor. He was naked aside from a white t-shirt, like Yogi Bear, or any of the Saturday morning cartoon characters that lived by a twisted morality where torsos must always be covered and damn the rest below.

It was odd that I was thinking these things. About cartoons and candy canes. It was odd that I was so calm, considering that I was sitting upright on the vinyl couch—one of those rigid European jobs from the catalogues everybody gets in the mail but no one really reads—and the corpse was inches from my bare feet. I had never been so close to something so big that was so profoundly dead. If you didn't count the scrawny, four-point buck with velvet horns I'd shot when I was fourteen, aiming through the tears while my father danced behind me like a moonshined hillbilly. He never danced. And he certainly wasn't a hillbilly. He was a regional sales rep for a second tier pesticide company. The deer twitched and bleated as it bled out on the ground until a bullet to the brain finished it off. I never knew deer could make noises like that. Cartoons and candy canes and screaming deer.

I stared at the floor, my feet coming into focus. I wriggled my toes. What happened to my shoes? My socks? What happened last night? The memories were fuzzy, interspersed with jarring flashes of noise and commotion, vomiting, shouts in foreign tongues and tongues stuck straight out shrieking. Green in glasses, flames and sugar and silver spoons hovering just above conversations I couldn't understand, even when it drifted back to English. Heat down my throat, glasses scattered, stumbling, hitting the ground, stairs, stars, laughter, the smell of smoke and sweat and cologne and leather and a pungent otherness that can only be found in places far, far from home. The last full scene I remembered was of a terrifying taxi ride in a very old part of the city, watched as if it were on television. They were all laughing. I wasn't making a sound.

I tried to rewind the movie in my mind, to find the beginning, and arrived at something close, elbowing out the black and lighting jade candles in the corners.

I was sitting at a table full of North American exiles at the Bluebird, a precious little pub on the bad side of the river, carefully arranged to look a goddamn mess when everything was incredibly expensive and spotlessly clean. The Czechs were many things, but sloppy wasn't one of them. The expats were predictably smug but loose enough around the hips to let in a newly uprooted outsider. Philosophy was discussed, cut through with pointedly vague book and music references that sounded like they came from philosophy books about music. Or maybe philosophical music about books...

It was hard to recall correctly, this muddle of practiced snobbery, spun inside a cloud of green. I remembered, I didn't remember, my head felt like it was stuffed full of ether-soaked cotton balls...

I remembered asking them what they did for employment. And I remembered asking them about the absinthe, as the Bluebird was notorious on the trail for selling it to those familiar and trusted by the staff. I was neither of those things, so I figured getting cozy with some who were could get me to where I wanted to go, as a guy like me didn't come all the way to Prague and *not* try the absinthe. It would be akin to skipping Charles Bridge and holing up at the Kentucky Fried Chicken that just went up on the corner of the museum district.

I had been drinking at a pretty steady clip all day, starting just after breakfast, as I had done all across the Continent. I would have liked to say if anyone asked (no one did) that I was a semi-pro drinker before landing on the runway at Schiphol, and by the time I had snaked my way across a dozen countries, winding down my trip on the eastern edge of Hitler's European theme park, I had become a full fledged professional. No job and a blank daily itinerary lent itself to just such a matriculation. I was thirty-two years old, but always drank like I was a decade younger, when I was supposed to have first taken Le Grand Tour du Backpack, but was held stateside by the quicksand of small town routine and the expense of breaking through it. Ten years on, my body felt the age and weight of every day of it, and couldn't shrug off the onslaught of toxins like my mind was convinced I could. And so, the blackouts, the discovery wakeups in strange locations, the curious bruises in unexpected places. But I've already covered that. That's the thing with drunks, they get stuck on autopilot when they fall backwards into the dark, and start repeating themselves. Annoying habit, but it is what it is, especially when they have the time. And I did. And I do.

But none of that explained the body on the floor. And none of it helped me figure out a way to escape this apartment, this *flat*, find my way back to the tidy hostel in east Prague, grab my pack, and get the fuck out of town before the trail of bloody breadcrumbs found my door.

It was time to get up. I had to get up, stand on my feet and run. No, not run. *Walk*, goddamnit, looking like a good, untroubled Ugly American, clutching a fanny pack and taking measured Teva sandal steps over those small rectangular bricks in careful effort to not draw attention from the Policie or Interpol or whomever the fuck kept law and order in these frontier European countries. Walk away from a nightmare that I couldn't remember, like so many that left glimpses on the edge of the brain and hid the true horror only revealed to the subconscious mind as flashcards, while the forebrain was looking the other way, grinning like a fool. Insidious, these nighttime monster makers. Toying with sanity, allowing just enough rope to squeeze the neck but not enough to break it.

But this nightmare followed me home, or to wherever I was now. Someone else's home. Maybe the guy slowly decomposing on the floor in front of me. Hard to recognize a face macerated into an imitation Oriental rug.

Had to get up, *stand*, but my body felt like cement, trying to convince me that I was one of those sculpted figures reposing on park benches in art-conscious cities, creeping out tourists who never knew if the statue would move. Some things test reality, and we can't take our eyes off of them. *Had to get up*. My mother didn't raise no statue. My daddy didn't raise me at all. But he did dance, out in a dead December cornfield eighteen years ago this December.

Statues. Museums. Hamburgers. Rewind again to a new part of the tape, where the expats are sneering about the opening of a McDonalds down the block, and the rumors of a Planet Hollywood going up next year. As if they were local now. As if McDonalds and Planet Hollywood and Blockbuster weren't local to them in the places where they grew up, used up, and cast aside like a spent juice pouch. Faces frowned, beards were tugged, and talk began about how Prague went bust in just three years, and then about the next holy destination for the eternal outliers. Krakow, one offered. Istanbul, countered another. Bratislava, Estonia, Albania, Kiev... The locations got progressively more isolated, the plans increasingly absurd, yet the solemn tone remained, as the nostalgia for uncut European primitivism by these professional hobos on perpetual cultural safari thickened in the air with the smoke from their blue pack Gauloises. I soon realized that these self imposed exiles weren't just Americans living each day in avoidance of their Americanism, they were living each day as a competition with each other, trying to "out vague" each other. Life as a daily statement of the safely exotic. Odd, but not weird. Edgy, but not dangerous. A half ass cultural rebellion by half ass bourgeois warriors.

My opinion of this whole scene started to sour, and I was concocting an exit strategy—out of the Bluebird, and possibly out of Prague—when the absinthe arrived.

It was brought to our table (how quaint that I considered it "our" table then) without much ceremony. I wasn't surprised by this, or concerned. Quite the contrary. I was hoping I could indulge in a bit o' the wormwood in a city notorious for it. My quest for Big Experience demanded it. Drinking a banned substance in the open air at a legitimate establishment was just what the doctor ordered, and why I paid so much for airfare to get me far away from the Puritan's New World. Smoking weed at Amsterdam "coffee shops" and getting down with a hash fondue on the deck of a backpacker canal boat in front of the Ann Frank

House seemed quaint in comparison to imbibing a fairy tale poison that fueled the writing of Rimbaud, Wilde, Poe, and Baudelaire, and the paintbrushes of Manet and Degas, Van Gogh and Toulouse-Lautrec, as well as anyone worth a damn who spent any time in Paris in late nineteenth century. All of my icons. All of everyone's icons. How could I not add my DNA to such a proud bloodline, veined green with the promise of some fertile enlightenment?

But it was just after the brief, unceremonious absinthe ritual that everything went sideways, and pulled me into a spiraled trajectory with dead-eyed strangers. Jaded, these animals. Jade. Deep, burnished green, cutting a hole into my brain and excising eighteen hours of my life, which could now steal the rest of it. I wasn't an icon, and the green dark knew this, punishing me in due course. Flight of Icarus without even attempting to apply the wax in a brief, unceremonious ritual. I was as bad as they were. No different and just as guilty. Worse because they were gone, and I was the punk left with the body, to suck up the blame like a sponge while they went on scoffing, trying to stay one step ahead of deadly boredom that had already murdered them years ago. They were the Ennui Professionals, while I was just a bullshit dilettante, sacrificed on the altar.

And here was a new murder. The latest, maybe. I didn't know. I didn't know shit. I couldn't even feel my body, as the green had gotten under my fingernails and down deep into my core. My head didn't even hurt. I just felt numb. A new chapter written in a textbook of hangovers.

I got to my feet and stepped gingerly over the body, careful not to leave a footprint in the pool of blood. I couldn't—*wouldn't*—touch anything with my hands. The less I left of myself in this place, the better. I was getting out of this freak show, by whatever means.

The apartment was small and plain in that former Soviet Bloc sort of way. Functional. A tiny kitchen with meager supplies, a back bedroom, which was empty. I found the bathroom. The light was still on, alleviating the need to paw the wall to turn on the light switch, which were always slightly confounding in old European apartments like this. I stood in front of the sink with my hands at my side and looked into the mirror, seeing a bruised, pale face staring back at me. I touched the blood pooling under my left eye and couldn't yet feel the pain that would surely come. My hands were covered in nicks, but so were the man's hands on the floor. Must have been a battle. I must have won. I must have killed him.

Good Christ. Good *fucking* Christ. I killed a man.... That's why everyone was gone. These jaded expats must have bugged the fuck out when it all went down and the body hit the floor. The ultimate party foul. What started it? Good natured ribbing gone horribly awry? Possibly. Stranger things... An insult to my manhood? Bullshit. I'm not the macho type. An insult to his? Maybe. A woman? I couldn't for the beating life of me remember a woman anywhere in the mix last night. There certainly weren't any at the table at the Bluebird. That gathering was an ironclad boys' club. It must have been something, through. Something intense, biting. Something to turn Intrepid American way past Ugly American to Horrifying American right before their widening eyes. Goddamn Hulk, paling their green to a sickly shade of Campbell's pea as I caved in the skull of a smug former citizen of some New World cultural bastion that wasn't sorry to see him go. The bored elite feel the way they do about life because they've never had to struggle, to chase survival. When shocking violence erupts around them, or comes for their teeth, they fold like cheap suits and run screaming toward the light like bitch moths. Or they die on the floor, left as a trophy at the feet of a murderer.

Murderer. I, murder. Murder, I.

This had to be a dream. Hangovers can sometimes feel that way. Nightmares, actually, but the gist is the same. Illusionary creations of the subconscious brain. But that body back in the living room was no illusion, and no goddamn joke. Nor was the reality that I had to face. Face mashed into the bloody floor. Murderer, I.

I nearly collapsed onto the sink but caught myself before I touched a thing. I needed to start thinking clearly, push away that fog and a weird hum in my ears. The whispers. Needed to get my bearings. Figure out where I was and how to extract myself. I went to the tiny, half open bathroom window above the toilet and peered outside. The day was overcast, making it hard to tell what time it was. The light traffic on the narrow streets didn't help, either. The flat seemed to be about three stories up, in a low rent part of town, suffering from graffiti on walls and refuse on the sidewalks that you never saw in the touristy parts of town. I had only been in Prague for a little over a week, so I was certainly no expert, no *expat*, but I didn't recognize any of the *Let's Go* landmarks from my tiny rectangular vantage point. This was just another dingy city spared by the Nazis but not by the Soviets. Brown buildings and blackened streets without end. Signs written in a language that made no sense, no matter which way I looked at it. I was lost, just as I had gotten lost one night in Paris when too much liquor gave me the confidence of a homing pigeon, and I ended up sitting on a park bench in a decidedly non-French part of town, warding off stares and gestured propositions, waiting for the sun to rise and the city to awaken to the point that I could butcher the native tongue just enough to get back to my hostel.

I crept out of the bathroom and headed for the back bedroom, careful to not make a sound on the scarred wood floors and alert whomever lived below. If they'd caught any of the noises generated just prior to and definitely during the murder that happened mere yards above them, they might not ignore the footsteps coming from above, especially if –

Mid-thought, I rushed back up the hall to the living room and stopped near the body. The pool of blood that had leaked out of this poor sap's head was still wet, and well soaked into the rug. Once that was saturated, the blood would have filtered down through the wood floors, collecting on the top end of the ceiling of the resident who lived below this room. It would stain the cheap stucco ceiling common in buildings of this sort, and then it would drip. God in heaven, would it drip like a motherfucker. Drops of dark red coming from the flat above, together with the weird, slow, creaky footsteps.

From out in the hall, I heard a door slam in the stairwell one level below, and the sound of unsure feet climbing the steps in a slow, careful manner. I darted back into the bathroom, making surprisingly very little noise as I went. Not that it mattered now anyway, as the most perfectly imagined noisy neighbor who ever lived below a person in an Eastern European block of flats now stood in the partially opened doorway. She was a short, stocky old woman swaddled in a formless dress and slippers, with the face of dried apricot, close-set beady eyes peering into the apartment, moving slowly inside as she did. She held a snow globe in her hand, possibly as some sort of neighborly offering for an unexpected visit, but more likely brought as a crude weapon to bludgeon an even more crude killer who was stupid enough to allow his victim to bleed out on the cheap wood floors while strolling around the flat, creaking with every step like they were announcing their presence to all the world. Or at least to the beady-eyed apricot lady who lived below.

She made her way into the living room and stopped. A wrinkled puncture of a mouth set into a flattened slit, somehow showing determination rather than shock. After a moment, she doddered forward, stepping between the dead man's bluish white feet, and set down the snow globe on his lower back. She stood up with difficultly, folded her hands and prayed in hushed Czech, making what appeared to be the sign of the cross over and over again, as she backed slowly toward the door. I was no Catholic, and was a bit out of my head at that moment, but I could have sworn that she was doing the sign of the cross, only upside down.

Everything inside me clenched as I tried to calculate the equation that had sprung up around me like a fat fingered white kid pawing an abacus. I looked from the snow globe resting on the dead man to the front door to the old woman, gauging her speed in relation to the distance for her escape, divided by the possibility of reaching the heavy piece of glassware, jogging ten feet to my right and bashing in her brittle skull before she could reach the hallway and scream bloody murder. Then carry the one. I was always shit at math, even on a good day. And I was no murderer, contrary to the evidence. So I just let her go, listening to the rasp of threadbare slippers as they descended the stairs. The front door of the building opened, and then slammed shut. The silence after the last echo reached me in the bathroom was as heavy and foreboding as that of a tomb. Or perhaps a solitary confinement cell in a Czech prison built miles underground by the most diabolical mind ever birthed by Khrushchev's KGB. Being shit at math left lots of time to study history.

I returned to the bedroom, not worrying about my footfalls on the floor. There was a bare mattress shoved into a corner, but nothing else in the way of furnishings. No nightstand, no lamp, no dressers. Not even a clock radio. There was, though, an unusually large spider perched in the far corner of the room, ensconced between the wall and the ceiling. It was a big fucker. No web held it in place. Instead, it gripped the wall with five-inch legs, supporting a thorax striped in brilliant shades of pale jade set against a shiny black. I stared at this insect— no, dummy, an *arachnid*—for longer than I should have and could have sworn that I heard it giggling. But that would have been impossible. More impossible still was that these tiny, high pitched laughs knitted themselves into more structured sounds that were interpreted as simple words in a language that made no sense to my ears. But they were words nonetheless. Words. This spider was *talking* to me. No, not talking. *Mocking* me.

Suppressing the urge to mash this insolent little fucker against the faded beige wall paint, I went to the open closet and looked for my clothes. The closet was devoid of clothing, had not even a wire hanger or rod. Had the expats stolen my clothes when they left me alone with the victim of my wormwood rage? Had they even taken my Tevas? My fucking *sandals*? I realized about the time I hit the tarmac several months back that Tevas were a rubbery smudge of American upper middle class fuckery on the Grand Old Continent, casting me in league with a merry band of juiced up frat boy assholes and package tour embarrassments that I was trying to leave in my rearview. That's why I came here. That's why I was debating if I should stay. But new footwear wasn't in my fixed Traveler's Cheque budget, not when there were so many fermented grains and berries to purchase under the guise of "exploring Europe." A drunk is a drunk is a filthy goddamn drunk. That a drunk wore Tevas was just the shitty icing. American splendor.

The chug of a large automobile engine approaching down below drew my attention away from the spider. I blinked away the splayed pattern on the bug and returned to the matter at hand. *Escape*. The fuck out of here.

I rushed through the living room and out the open front door, again careful not to touch any part of it. The cold of the hallway slowed me, and the board-ed-up door across the landing brought me to a full stop. Three slabs of discolored plywood had been nailed haphazardly over the frame some time ago, judging by the fade of the graffiti and the sunset hints of what appeared to be human feces smeared across the eyehole and down the length of the door's facade. No sounds came from any of the hallways or apartments above or below. I looked up the stairwell that wound skyward in a squared spiral to a pane of stained glass keeping watch from the roof, and saw that each door facing the dusty stairs was also boarded up, tagged by profanities spelled out in a dozen languages and twice that many depictions of genitals. Condemned, the whole damn place. This was a dead building. Nothing lived here, except for me and the apricot woman, who was now God knows where, saying God knows what to God knows who.

Time to bail, pants or no pants. This was Europe. I'd probably be hailed as some daredevil cocksman or half assed exhibitionist on the street by mildly amused Praguites or Prahaians or whatever the denizens of this city were called. Or they'd all point and giggle at Yogi Bear.

I dove down the first flight of stairs that would carry me to freedom from this cold, foreign place. Reaching the second floor landing, I heard the sound of two heavy car doors slamming in near unison outside. I froze. It could just be a resident, parking out front and heading inside their apartment building for a lovely day with the family. They would have no reason to remember my face should they glance at it as I walked quickly and purposely by. Why would they? They weren't apricot women. Or were they? Was this whole blasted building filled with stoic old ladies who kept small arsenals of snow globes to place on recently murdered bodies? But that was madness. No one lived here. It was dead. I could *feel* the deadness, not even needing the confirmation of the boarded up doors. I knew it as soon as I woke up on the couch. I could feel it in my bones more than I could feel my bones lurking inside that greenish fog.

The front door below opened. I leapt back up the stairs, taking three at a time on bare feet as light as air and ran back into the apartment, skittering into the bedroom and hiding behind the door. I waited, listening for my breath, my heart. I couldn't hear anything. The buzz inside my brain drowned out all sounds coming from my poisoned body.

Two sets of firm footsteps on the stairs, then on the landing, then walking into the apartment. Something heavy landed on the floor in the living room. It sounded like a body.

I closed my eyes to become invisible—an old trick from my childhood that somehow came back to me. Maybe it would work this time. It never did then. They always found me, eyes opened or closed. In the black of my mind, I heard voices talking in low tones in the living room, too quietly to make out the language. I also heard something else, much closer to me. Next to my shoulder.

Someone giggling.

I opened my eyes and turned my head. A man was standing right next to me, smiling. He was naked and pale, bruised. Like I was. His cock hung straight down from a ring of sparse black pubic hair. A bloodless wound hugged his neck, exposing the meat inside. I could see his esophagus pulsating, holding in that weird giggle. His eyes were large and perfectly circular, showing too much white above and below his flat black pupils. I opened my mouth to shout or scream or just generally vent the disquiet that bubbled up inside of me, when he placed his finger to his lips. The international symbol for shut the fuck up. His scabbed lips curled up into a smile behind his finger, looking out of place dangling just under those round, expressionless eyes.

A bluish flash came from the beyond the door. The naked man moved past me and peered out into the living room. I was about to pull him back when he motioned for me to follow suit. I shook my head. He scrunched up his face, exasperated, then stabbed his finger toward the next room, his eyes somehow growing larger. I moved hesitantly past him, and glanced into the living room, where a man was bent over the body, snapping pictures with a camera. Flash and click. Flash and click. The light hurt my eyes. I blinked rapidly, momentarily blinded. My vision returned just as the other man in the living room walked right toward me.

I cried out, but no sound came from my mouth. The man continued walking, passing within inches of me without noticing. He examined the empty bedroom with a critical eye, checking the closet, lifting the mattress. He was about to leave when he noticed the spider in the corner. At this he grinned, turned, and left the bedroom, this time passing right through me, as I stood shaking on my bare feet. I felt like I should have pissed myself, but I had no sensation in my bladder. I had no sensation at all. The naked man was gone.

I walked out into the living room, suddenly unafraid, feeling nothing other than a vague sense of ownership of something. They had turned the body over and were taking pictures with expensive looking cameras, like those used by the paparazzi to batter celebrities. Big lens and bigger flashes. The hair was slicked back with a pomade of blood that covered the dead man's face like a mud mask. The outline of the profile seemed familiar. More than familiar.

It was my face. The body on the floor was mine.

Me, murdered. Murdered, me.

I thought the evil green hangover fucked with my vision. The features I knew so well, which had pushed back at me from mirrors and photographs enough times to construct my own self image hologram inside my brain, for good and bad. That was me on the floor, even as I stood across the room looking at me.

I gasped soundlessly and felt as though I was falling, but hadn't moved. I heard the giggle again. The naked man squatted on the top of the couch like an obscene ape. He put his hand over his mouth and pointed to me, then to the body, and back to me again. Then he stood and danced on the top edge of the couch. Just as my father had danced. A weird, jerky, hillbilly jig, his heavy penis still pointing straight down, like the business end of a divining rod. He never lost his balance, and his feet made no sound on the narrow piece of furniture, nor any dent into the thin padding.

My head swiveled like a wind-up robot back to the two men working soundlessly over the body. *My* body. They positioned it at the far edge of the rug, then rolled it up like a lumpy crepe, exposing a thick layer of plastic on the underside. The wood flooring underneath was spotless. Not a drop of blood stained it. No drip. No trace.

The naked man wasn't watching them work. He was watching me, his flat eyes feverish, waiting for a reaction. Waiting for anything. One of the men unrolled the new rug in its place, which was identical to the one that now held me inside it, while the other wiped down the room with a spray bottle and rag, removing all the candy cane fragments of my skull and brain. Cleaning away every last trace of my living self, balling it up in a dirty cloth. When he was finished, he picked up another plastic spray bottle and coated the room from floor to ceiling with an invisible mist. His partner pulled a small portable work light from a duffel back, plugged it in and turned it on, shining the purplish bulb carefully around the room. Nothing showed up in the luminescence. I was all gone.

They packed up their bags and checked the kitchen. The refrigerator wasn't plugged into the wall, lightless and devoid of any food. The cupboards were stacked with empty cans of soup and tinned meat, boxes of pasta and cereal, all resealed after their contents were drained. They were props, hollow on the inside. Dead between the packaging. Meant to make a person feel at ease for those few minutes that it would take to get everyone inside and take up positions.

This wasn't a home. It was a kill room.

The naked man was now perched on the kitchen counter, watching me watch the men, as they shouldered their bags and lifted the rolled rug with me inside. They were speaking English, but I couldn't understand a word of what they were saying. Without a look behind them, the men headed out into the hallway, closing the door behind.

I ran after them, and dove between the closing door, arriving too late. I should have been lodged between the door and frame, but it closed and I passed through and found myself walking step for step with the two expats as they carried my remains down the stairs, to dump in some brackish swamp or dark stand or trees or vacant lot strewn with broken glass and feral dogs.

I recognized them now. My memory of the night before was all pouring back into my head like a pitcher of cool water into a washbasin. These were the two that invited me over and kicked out a chair, that ordered the absinthe and suggested a change in scenery. The two ringleaders of the expats. That look in their eyes, it wasn't boredom, it was malevolence.

I moved between them on the stairs. Above, alongside, in front. They were ugly, these Americans. Truly, truly ugly. Their arrogance choked the air, and the underpinnings of their smugness wafted off of them like the stink of rotten meat. I wanted to get inside them, hurt them from the inside out. Tunnel into their brain and start cutting wires. Get into their organs and open up walls, flooding the whole system with blood and bile and shit and pain that would go on for days. I wanted partial brain death. I wanted sepsis. I wanted to fuck them up on a cellular level, but I didn't know how. I was dead, but I was moving, seeing, thinking, goddamn *feeling*, and yet I didn't know how it all worked.

I followed them down the flight of stairs, and started to follow them out into the street, those quaint looking streets made up of the little bricks that never showed what filth had soaked down through them over the centuries. But I found that I had stopped at the front door. I couldn't leave. Didn't want to, more likely. But I couldn't even if I'd wanted to. I'm not sure if I tried. I don't remember now.

I walked back – *drifted* – up the stairs, and noticed a face several flights up looking down at me over the railing. Then another face, further up, and another. There were dozens of these faces, little and big, male, female, and of varying ages. They all looked down at me with those same flat, black eyes, and I looked up at them. I'm sure my eyes would become as black and flat as theirs, if they hadn't already.

They could see me, these face. Of course they could. I was one of them. An expat. The real fucking deal.

I walked back into the apartment, moving past the snow globe placed just outside the door. The naked man was standing in the kitchen, looking out the window at the ground below, where the two men loaded the lumpy roll into their white van. "Someday we'll get them," he said, his lips not moving. But his voice was in my head. Thin and tuneless. "Haul *them* away, to the places *I* know about."

I opened my mouth to reply, worked my jaw, but nothing came out, as if the words were plucked from my tongue. I didn't know this language yet. Wasn't allowed to know until I had paid my dues, I reckoned, just like at the table at the Bluebird. I was just newly arrived, coming from the New World to the Old. Heading back. Still wearing those sandals. But I would learn. Become a proper native instead of a tourist. I'd have the time.

THE TRUFFLE PIG

I am a ghost, a curl of smoke, a whisper told to children to shut stubborn eyes until sleep comes to take them from their sheets. A shadow of a thing that casts none.

I am the wave that washes away the sand castle when the father turns his head. I am a saboteur, a tracker. I am a killer of women, and of men. But so many women.

I am reviled by all who don't know me and hated by the very few that do. And I am the only thing that stands between how our world remains, and how it could be. No one wants to know how it could be, because it will mean the end of everything.

I have been given many names from many quarters, yet none that really matter. Bloodhound. Monster. I know myself as the 42nd of my kind, and the success of my art is the last barrier that keeps us from falling into the soundless crush of the eternal abyss.

Presently, I am on the deck of a ship tossed by the North Atlantic, following those whom I and my forbearers have always followed, keeping six measured steps behind, which is close enough to see but not be seen. They never know who I am, or when I am going to strike, although I see them clearly. That is my edge, and the only reason why we are all still alive.

I would kill every last one of them if I could, but I am one, and those behind me very few. We must keep our numbers low, as secrets abhor a crowd. Yet there are so many of them, with their numbers multiplying around us, while ours dwindle in private, as all rare things do. Total eradication was attempted in the 7th century, and our order was nearly wiped out when we emerged from the shadows, drunk on hubris and the lotus of righteousness. We were cut down like chaff and chopped to pieces. Souvenirs made of our bones. So now I follow them like a bloodline curse, do not engage, and destroy their work in whatever way I can.

They make their rounds, and so do I, tailing them on their circuit of ancient outposts, established before time had meaning. After a stint in the red hill country of Southern France, they recently arrived in London, blending in with the bustle of the shrouded city, close enough to their communication base at Solsbury Hill and those things that still live deep in the Pictish Highlands above the Antonine Wall. The calculating Romans never built a wall without reason, let alone two. They knew what was lurking in those caves, what howled from the bottom of deep crags. But those bulwarks had crumbled with forgetfulness, while what they were built to repel waited for the stars to sing to them in melodies none of us could hear.

My work in London attracted more attention than we anticipated, as none of us could foresee the butchery of a few random spares igniting a national scandal that soon spread across the globe. Information moved so quickly these days, and we were guilty of underestimating the modern lust for depravity. During times past, such events would be muttered across a tilled row, accompanied by a sign of the cross or prayer to an ancestor. Murder was still hot in primal limbs back then, and untimely death was an unfortunate neighbor to every house. It was endured, a wintered dip in daily lives. But in these days of lace and buttermilk, death was marched into sitting rooms and made to dance, as a brush with oblivion became exclusive to the point of aristocratic fetish.

Accordingly, in a matter of hours, London exploded with interest in the first girl I took apart. This made my remaining task more difficult, demanding a hastily prepared misinformation campaign to distract the insatiable thirst of pen and populace from my bloody casework on the cobblestone of Whitechapel. Make it appear isolated, spiced with a bit of royal intrigue, so no broad-minded Scotland Yardies would put the pieces together. Princes, Freemasons, palace doctors. Occulted journalists and Polish Jews. A smear of horseshit over the lens, ensuring that the puzzle would remain scattered upon the floor while the full picture bled invisible into the planks underneath.

They who continually force my practiced hand year after year are followers of the Dark Man, who was last documented by public record—since destroyed—

striding out of a screaming Egypt after blanketing the land with pestilence three and a half millennia ago, before fading into the sand at a Delphic place still marked by the wandering Kharga of the great Western Desert. He had punished his former hosts for turning their backs on him in the name of river superstition buoyed by slave theology, while his legacy of plague was co-opted by various holy books in the years that followed. The Dark Man cared not for the truth or the lies, waiting for his next re-emergence on a timetable only he knew, dictated by the stars and those things that lay in wait far beyond them. In his absence, a growing coterie of acolytes disappeared underground with him, anticipating his next mission of celestial cataclysm, and often taking initiative, sowing anarchy to pave a path of advent. Multitudes went with him. Houses were cleared. Villages. Families within families that kept alive the Elder Ways, and those willing to sacrifice everything they knew to learn. The allure of the glinting black is irresistible to anonymous eyes choking on the monotony of the neverending gray.

That is when we were born, like seeds fertilized by rotting flesh, rising delicate into the morning air, yet still tasting death in our veins. We grew in secretive greenhouses, shaped by the blade, and then were released one at a time to follow across the planet the spoor of the Dark Man and those followers who glorified in his peculiar taste for destruction. But chaos begs for order, and order can only live to stabilize chaos, as water looks for the glass. And so I and others before me were tapped and trained, called by forces that no one fully understood yet dared not question, as the reality presumed by the rational mind is just an onion skin surrounding the deeper mysteries spiraling at the core. We were trained in the secret fighting arts and built a mental foundation grounded in the philosophies of dead moons, before graduating to anatomy and vivisection, memorizing the human form inside and out, as this was the battlefield on which our modern wars would be waged. The flesh. It always came back to the flesh. To hone our skills, we leaned on esoteric surgical techniques far more advanced than those of contemporary physicians employed in the enterprise of saving lives, as our craft was always practiced in the pursuit of death. Removal of corruption on such a minute level could end in no other result, for the sake of the infected and the greater world. Much like the Romans and their concealed knowledge of what lay north of their Britannia walls, we had to keep in place a shade over our work and real reasons why we willingly play this game of fox and goose, hoop and stick. Marbles. Bloody fucking marbles.

And so we studied as we fought and learned as we died, finding that the servants of the Dark Man are dedicated, and not merely human. Things that slither, scuttle across the dust, and swim in lightless waters heed the call of this ancient numen, who happened across our reality incalculable eons past, before human and mammal, before the birds and thunder lizards and bright things of the sea. He has been with us since before the beginning, and much like us, named a thousand labels. One for each tribe. Trickster, Loki, Lucifer. He isn't any of these things, yet is all of these things. He is older than the gods of the Israelites and the Babylonians and the Sumerians and more powerful still, yet somehow bound by strictures outside our comprehension, inscrutable to even his followers, who bow low to the riddles. And blessed be these barriers, as without them, none would need my services, because no one would be around. Marbles.

Years we have battled, as the corpses stacked high. I followed their migration, driving them out of Cathar country, before they turned their sights on London. Old black pudding London, gem of the western world.

In between assignments, I enjoyed my stay in The Square Mile. I took tea and the sights, moving through halls of royalty and libertine gutters. Dipping my toes into the Thames, wondering how many skulls were staring back at me. All the while waiting out the stars. Like both sides had always done. The cosmic chess game played on a terrestrial board. I sniffed the air, avoided the food and sampled the humanity around me, which is a relatively painless process. Relatively. By way of my rather unconventional initiation, I was intimately familiar with the flavor of tainted meat, fouled by whatever their side brought through from far off places and unleashed on our unprepared feedlot.

I had been stationed in London for several uneventful months, when I found the scent, which led me into the East End and the warren of brothels that serviced the bent desires of prim English gentlemen of Queen Victoria's empire. Following instructions taught to them in dreams, the Dark Man's followers utilized discarded street girls to spread their fungal stain into London's population. Death from trash, wrapped in a silken doily, this time using humans as the mules instead of fleas like centuries before. Prostitutes were hired and used, servicing clandestine orgies to keep the master plot hidden. Never one at a time, never kidnapped, as that would draw too much attention amongst the working women, and one can never kill the spread of gossip without sacking a city. They took their hosts from off the streets, and deposited spores into vaginas, mouths, eyes, organs, in a closely scrutinized mating ritual guised as fantasy play. Practicing their miscegenation in plain sight, lit by black candle and smoking brazier. After the wounds were washed and bustles retied and before the drugs wore off, the women were set free to spread what they now carried to the thousands of locals and global travelers that took full advantage of the daylight whore trade of fabled London. Catch and release, to grow the herd.

So I cut those mules apart, finding the bad bits and disposing of the disease as only my people know how. Spores were not just left in the womb, but could be anywhere, depending on the vagaries of the copulation, and the physical capabilities of the sire. Behind the cheekbone, spinning in the intestines, buried in the heart. The hosts didn't need to be quality, just female, and alive long enough for the spores to mature into polyps, and then into something more. Those unfortunate Brick Lane dollymops were just incubators, spider sacks to be sucked dry by the grand scheme of tiny parasites who dreamed of rising tall like their fathers. Prodigies from beyond the stars. That just wouldn't do, so I sniffed them out, tracked them down, and did my business before disappearing into the fog.

Upon seeing my handiwork, draped proud and messy, the local authorities assumed rape, as they always do, but those poor drabs had been raped a thousand times before I ever found them. I was sending a message. To Them. Fucking cunts. This wasn't about murder, this wasn't about a scandalizing of the local whores. That was just collateral damage. My work was about protection, the careful removal of the next generation of those things that lived in the hills and other forgotten spots now shunned by humanity. The intelligent bacteria from far off Yuggoth, that did terrible and unpredictable things when acquainted with human ingredients.

My conspicuous message did the trick, and the fellowship of the Dark Man uprooted again in the middle of the night, booking passage to Chicago by way of Arkham, with private train portage to the heart of America. They thought that I was unaware of their plans, and especially their end destination, but just as they have tentacles, I have tendrils, and the concentrated wealth of the very few and very old can buy a mountain of classified information. Money can substitute for numbers on many occasions. Not on the field of battle, per se, but in the close quarters of global commerce, which is all that the world cares about these days anyway. That and their lust for murder, just so long as it will shuffle out the door in time for brandy and cigars. These church pew sadists probably didn't deserve my work, but orders are orders, and our papers say keep them safe while giving them a circus. The clowns always draw the eye away from the cracking whips and creaking chains behind the tent flap.

And I give them their circus, because it suits my needs and thwarts those of the Dark Man. It did the trick in London, and has moved the game west, across the frozen sea, following the path taken by so many English three hundred years before. Of course, the circumstances seemed different then, but the root cause is not dissimilar. The exodus of the faithful.

A shout goes out, startling me, which is an unfamiliar sensation. I am on edge, and try to blame my seasick stomach. Yet I know something isn't right about the speed of their departure from London, but my pride hides the truth. A force bigger than my art and my kind is at work. I will tell myself that it was what I did on those East End streets that tore them from the city, but I know that I am wrong. Gods help me if I'm startled again. Gods help all of us.

Land is sighted and a crowd moves to the rail. New England off the starboard bow. The ship creaks southward past the lightless blot that makes up queer Innsmouth, bearing west again into the harbor, flanked by Kingsport and Martin's Beach to each side. We head up the sluggish Miskatonic to Arkham, where a waiting train will take them to the middle of the country and the expo that will bring in a million pilgrims a few years from now. What the docks did for London, this World's Fair will do for Chicago. Attracting flies of every species from every country on the planet. I will follow my six measured steps behind, and they will not know I am there, until they set up shop again, and I am *everywhere*.

Snow begins to fall, slicking the deck. It's Christmas time in the dying weeks of '88, but no one seems to remember. No carolers stroll the streets of Arkham. No bells ring in the church houses. This isn't that kind of city, which is why they are passing through here.

The ship docks, and I disembark down the gangplank, slipping with my seventh step. A sailor catches me by the arm. "Watch yourself, miss," he says with a grin, revealing a sporting history in several missing teeth. "Don't want to drown yourself a foot from shore."

I nod, feigning a coquettish blush that hides the burn of anger at my unsteady stride. For stumbling, even slightly, while the black seawater waits and watches below me.

"You arrived from London, then?" the sailor asks while escorting me to the pier, stepping lightly on the plank to not disturb my balance.

"Yes." I scan the wharf.

"Terrible business happening there, with that Jack the Ripper running the streets."

The name brings me back to attention. "Indeed, sir. A woman is lucky to make it out alive."

"Old Bloody Jack wouldn't like your type, I don't reckon."

I arch an eyebrow to the high heavens.

"Begging your pardon, ma'am," he sputters. "Just meanin' that you bein' such a fine lady and all, not like those brothel slags who got carved up proper."

I say nothing, as there is nothing to say.

"A bird's gotta keep her eyes open back home. Never know if Jack's headin' your way."

I can't help myself. "What if he's headed *your* way?"

The sailor is about to respond, but swallows his words. He tips his cap and hurries back to his ship. The fear has spread, as the game continues.

I called myself Jack in Londontown, but that's not who I am. That was just the latest mask, the newest nickname, and just as insipid as the others. And there will be others.

My name is The Truffle Pig, hard trained to root out the fungus. I am your protector, the 42nd of my kind. I was yours truly, and I will be again soon.

So next, Chicago.

BEER & WORMS

Russ placed a six-pack of Storz tall boys, a box of hooks, and a sealed filet knife on the counter and waited patiently. It felt good to just stand there and do nothing. He'd left his watch at home, fingers absently touching the pale ring on his wrist where the hair had rubbed smooth.

He gazed around the store, settling his eyes on the faded Chesterfield poster above the register, which showed Ronald Reagan smoking a cigarette. "*The voice of the turtle*," it announced under his name, followed by "ABC." Always Buy Chesterfield. A forgettable country song filtered through a closed door in the back, blending with the bubbling of the minnow tanks and industrial hum of the coolers.

The door opened and a wiry man emerged, carrying a box. "Land sakes! Russ, is that you?" he said, heading toward the counter.

"Mornin', Joe."

"Surprised to see you in here."

"Oh yeah?"

"You know. Bein' September and all."

"The beans'll grow just as well without me for a day."

Joe laughed. "Ya, I 'spose they will. Prices probably won't, though." He rang up the beer, slowly circling and punching the buttons on the register as if he was trying to remember.

Russ nodded to the hooks. "You got anything bigger than a nine aught?

"'Fraid not, Russ," Joe said, sounding more regretful than one would think appropriate for the situation. "Don't have much call for anything bigger 'round here. Maybe out by McConaughy, where they got them six foot muskies. Take your arm off with one chomp." Joe finished ringing up the items. "No 'crawlers, huh?"

"Not today. Mixed up a batch of stinkbait."

Joe nodded. "Yeah, too hot for bass, I 'spose."

"Too hot for everything but cats."

"Suckers and bullhead. Gar, maybe. Course, the sunnies are always bitin'." Joe thought about this, crossing one of his eyes with concentration, then brightened back to attention. "You headin' down to the Platte?"

"Nah. Goin' after that big sumbuck on the Jansen's back forty."

"Whoo-boy! Ol' Dale says it's gettin' big enough to eat a calf."

"Just as long as he's big enough to swallow a nine aught."

"Got some liver that'll work wonders."

"I'll go with the stinkbait today. New recipe, and all. Wanna try it out."

"You know best," Joe said, carefully putting each item into a separate paper bag. "When I was a kid, we used salmon eggs to catch trout."

"Not much trout 'round here."

"True enough… That was back east. Aunt's place in Delaware."

Both men stood in silence for a few moments.

"That'll be $4.25," Joe said.

Russ counted out a few bills, then dug into his pocket for change. "Throw in some of that deer jerky, will ya Joe?"

"It's coulee. All that's left from last year."

"That's fine. It's not for me anyway."

The whitewall tires spun quiet down the last few feet of asphalt before Dutch Hall Road gave way to gravel, marking the county line. Farm ponds dotted the wilder areas between 80-acre plots of corn and soybeans, collecting the spill-off below terraced hillsides. Most of the farmers didn't fish their ponds much anymore, and they'd be doggoned if they'd let any city folk traipse around their land in fancy hip waders from Cabela's. That meant Russ had the pick of the litter as far as fishing holes, and today he picked Dale Jansen's place.

Tiny rocks pinged off the undercarriage as a thick cone of gray dust billowed up behind the truck bed, where a Fenwick rod rested against a white plastic paint bucket and red metal tackle box. A pheasant rooster strutted across the road atop the next rise and disappeared into the plum thicket choking the ditch. Russ made note of the location, as no matter what this humidity told him, October would be here before you knew it.

Russ turned off Dutch Hall and headed down County Road 23, easing past the slumping houses, rusted trailers, and mud yards of the Kennard outskirts, back out onto the arrow straight line of gravel, until the stand of trees surrounding the Jansen farm came into view.

He passed the dirt driveway, slowed at the cattle grate separating two squared ends of barbed wire, and turned onto the grassy tractor path between the yellowing corn and the scanty shelter belt of piss elm and cottonwood.

The truck bumped along the rutted slope, the tall fescue muffling the sound of the engine as it slithered underneath. He crested the hill and descended the other side, to a low area in the land where four fence corners from four farms converged. The pond that had formed was mostly on Jansen land, but a bit of it bled over onto the other plots, allowing them access. Even so, no one fished back there except Dale, as everyone else that had claim was too old, too concerned about what they would pull out of that pond after years of fertilizer runoff, or dead.

Russ parked a good distance away from the water. He got out of his pickup, the various paper bags in his hand, and hauled the white bucket from the back, grunting under its weight. He chuckled to himself as he picked up his rod and tackle box with two spare fingers, and swished his boots through the brome toward the pond.

Dale sat in a frayed lawn chair just a few feet from the muddy shore, hunched over his line as he threaded an egg sinker just above the swivel.

"You're puttin' all the fish to sleep."

"Well, look at this," Dale said, spinning in his chair but not getting to his feet. Russ walked up and set the bucket next to Dale, who grinned at him from under the brim of his green Cargill hat, squinting through the sun. "Didn't expect to see you out here 'til after next plantin'."

"Brought you somethin'," Russ said, handing him a paper bag.

Dale took it and peered inside, pulling out a hunk of dry, blackened meat. "Okay!" He sniffed the jerky. "This ain't muley, is it?"

"Shoot. What you got there is corn fed Papio whitetail."

"Velvet of the plains," Dale said with a smile and took a bite. He fought a frown. "A little gamey for whitetail."

"You take what you can get in September. Beer?"

"Much obliged." Dale cracked open his tall boy and took a long drink. He burped and set about baiting his line, hooking a greasy shad to each prong. Russ hadn't yet touched his gear, nor opened the beer in his hand.

"Hotter than the dickens out here," Dale said.

"Boy, you said it." Russ stared out at the unbroken surface of the water. The dead branches of a hackberry tree reached into the cloudless sky on the far shore. "Too hot for bass."

"Too hot for everything. Doubt even the bullheads will be bitin' much."

"Bullhead'll bite in a tornado."

"Ya, I 'spose so."

"I ain't goin' for bullhead today."

Dale looked up at Russ, whose shadow loomed over him. "The big cat?"

Russ grinned slyly. Dale returned to baiting his hook. "Figured it had to be a special occasion."

Russ took a seat on the bucket. "Sure is."

Dale set his rod over his lap and took another swig. "Appreciate the beer."

"Don't mention it."

"You bring the 'crawlers?"

"No sir." Russ slapped the bucket under his legs, which thudded like it was filled with cement. "Brung us some homemade stink bait."

Dale whistled low. "Hate to think you went to all that trouble. Fish haven't been bitin' for squat."

"Wasn't no trouble at all. I've been meanin' to try out this recipe for a while. Comin' down here and goin' for the biggun just gave me an excuse."

"Ready to get after it, huh?"

"Figured I would. Got the freezer space."

"Bring the camera?"

"Back in the truck."

"Man's gotta have a goal."

"Nothin' wrong with that."

"Boy, you said it." Dale opened another beer and lit up a Winston while Russ packed his lower lip with Skoal. He rubbed a little on his upper lip, under his nose, stood, and peeled off the lid of the plastic paint bucket. He reached in and pulled out a handful of bait that looked like dark brown cookie dough, peppered with flecks of red and white. Dale wrinkled his nose. "That's ripe."

"Not quite primed, but it'll get there." Russ handed the glob to Dale, who looked up at him. "Give 'er a shot."

Dale shrugged, ripped the three small fish from the tines, and formed the stink bait into a ball around the hook. He grimaced at the odor. "How's Nancy?"

Russ spat. "Well, you know." He grabbed his own wad of bait, pressed the lid back on the bucket, and sat down on it again.

Dale shot a glance at Russ before casting deep, pulling the line up short so the bait fell with a mushy plop a few feet in front of the stand of drowned trees. "Surprised she let you come out, with the season and all." Dale reeled in his line a crank or two, then let it sink to the bottom, anchoring the handle into the sandy mud and resting the reel seat lightly in his palm. "That's some heavy bait."

Russ chuckled. "Used the good stuff."

"Gonna have to give me that recipe," Dale said. "If it works."

"That's a deal," Russ said, throwing his own line into the pond, close to Dale's, but still far enough away to avoid a tangle.

Dale exhaled a hiss of smoke. "The kids?"

"Chris left for Lincoln last week. Won't see him 'til Thanksgiving, most likely. Connie hasn't called for a while. Still got a girlfriend, I hear."

They sat as the sounds of the late summer insects danced in the grass around them one last time.

"You hear 'bout ol' Denny Goetsch?" Dale stubbed out his cigarette in the wet soil.

"A shame what happened to him."

"Hogs took him down to nothin'. Only left the skull and his right foot 'cause it wouldn't come out of the boot."

"Hammer toe came in handy at the end."

"I 'spose. Them ol' boars could eat a tractor tire if you left it in the pen."

"Gotta watch 'em close."

"Shoot 'em if they get too big."

"Shoot 'em all if you've got a bad heart."

"And a hammer toe."

They both laughed.

"A shame what happened to him, though," Russ said.

"Sure is. Wife and kids left without a man."

"Crops still in the field, and he just paid off his combine. Who's going to move them hogs to market?"

"Won't get my auger back now. Denny had it two years. Never brought it up."

"Probably get it back at the auction."

"Yea, I 'spose."

Something large and dark broke the surface of the pond, rolled, and shimmied back to the bottom.

"There's your hoss," Dale said. He put another cigarette between his lips. "He don't seem to like the bait." Dale glanced sidelong at the bucket, then up at Russ.

Russ reeled in slowly. "You got somethin' on your mind?"

Dale took off his hat and wiped his brow. He was sweating more than the heat demanded. "Well, I gotta tell ya," he said, winding up. "I'm just real surprised to see you out here, is all. With the way Nancy got after ya last time you came out fishin' while the crops were still in the field, I—"

"You what?"

"Well, I got a whole lot of respect for you. Doin' what you wanted to do, pissin' on the consequences. Lord knows Nancy can get difficult."

Russ spit, removed the chew from his lip and flicked it to the ground. "I killed her, Dale."

Dale blinked at the distorted reflection of the sun glinting off the pond. "How's that?"

"I killed her."

"You killed who?"

"Nancy."

Dale swallowed hard, smoke sputtering out of his nose. "Good Christ, Russ. What'd you go and do that for? She runnin' around on ya?"

"Nancy? Shoot." Russ snorted. "A guy can get pretty desperate, but I don't know a man alive within a thousand miles that would want to lay down with a cripple."

"Slippin' on her chores, then? She don't move as well as she used to, I 'spose."

"No, that wasn't it, either. She was doin' enough. Doin' what was expected of her, I guess."

Dale clamped his teeth together. "So then what?"

Russ' eyes followed a flock of starlings that were swarming around a lone cottonwood the next field over, fighting for a limb. "Last week, I was sittin' there in the kitchen, stirrin' my coffee, thinkin' 'bout how nice it would be to stop by Joe's, pick up some beer and some worms, and head out here to go after the big one. Then I thought about havin' to ask permission. Havin' to ask permission from a *woman*. What's the world come to?"

Dale shrugged his shoulders a few times, as if trying to loosen something inside of him. Russ reeled in his bait and looked at the ball on the end of the hook. Not even a nibble taken out of it.

"If a man can't fish when he wants, he ain't no man at all."

Dale popped open another beer. Loose Winstons fell to the mud from a shaking soft pack and sucked up the pond water.

"So anyway, I walked up to Nancy while she's fryin' up some eggs, thinkin' 'bout how I was gonna ask her 'bout me goin' fishin', when I should have been tellin' her, and then it dawned on me." Russ opened a beer and set it down without taking a drink.

"What did?" Dale's voice was hushed and failing, as if he started talking at the very end of a breath.

"I'd rather kill her."

"You'd—"

"I'd rather kill her than ask her."

Dale worked his tongue, searching for moisture. The surface of the pond broke with the gulp of a giant mouth swallowing a feather it mistook for something else.

"So she's lying there—outside, you know, because I didn't want her to bleed out all over the kitchen floor. Head wounds spurt like somethin' else, with the arteries and all... and I figure what I done could kill two birds with one stone."

"Russ, I—"

"I need to get rid of the mess, and now that I have all this free time to fish, I'll need money for bait. Tackle I got. That don't wear out. But bait, well, that's another matter. That's out of pocket. Joe don't run tabs these days, and I got that old cob grinder my daddy left me. A few spare buckets left from paintin' the barn..."

Dale's long ash hung from his cigarette like a bent, shriveled finger.

"With the weather bein' so muggy, I figured she'd cure up right in a few days, and make some darned good stink. That was last Thursday."

Dale smelled his fingers, then leaned over and retched, the chair breaking apart, sending him to the mud.

"It's the funniest thing," Russ said. "Human beins' fall just like hogs when you hit 'em square between the eyes. I wonder if ol' Denny Goetsch knew that." Russ reeled his line from the water and dangled the dripping stink bait in front of his eyes like a swinging medallion. "I had to tap Nancy on the shoulder to make sure she turned around first. Then—" Russ snapped his fingers, causing Dale to jump. He clambered backwards toward the grass, in the direction of the truck.

Russ walked after him, guiding the stink bait through the air, twirling it in circles. "Now, the only question is, Dale ol' boy... We gonna keep fishin', or are we gonna do somethin' else?"

Dale wiped the puke from his chin, sat up, and took a deep breath.

"Let's fish."

WHITE FEATHER

T he glass of cider arrived without ceremony, set several feet from the tall figure standing at the counter. The barkeep crossed his arms and waited. The man reached over and picked up his drink, placing a coin in the center of the circle of liquid left on the oaken tavern top. The barkeep made no move to retrieve it.

Chilton held the glass to his nose, working through the alcohol and molasses down to the subtle perfume of Newtown Pippins before they were picked, smashed, and ordered to rot. Back when they first emerged as springtime buds from a lifeless branch, so full of promise. This was the aroma of his home, of a particular wind and soil that knew him from birth and yet held no judgment. He wished he were a boy again, before his father lost his leg and his mother her will, before the responsibilities of adult life solidified a legacy that was as permanent as history written by the bloody victorious. Before his last raid on Nova Scotia.

Chilton wasn't a drinking man, but he wanted very much to taste this cider today. A warm bloom of past life while all in the present was cold and dark and mutely watching instead of groping for his neck.

"Finish that and be on your way."

Chilton opened his eyes with the slow realization that they were closed. The barkeep glared at him, eying the Indian war club at Chilton's waist. Gad Richardson was his name. Little Gaddy, all grown up and bulging his success over imported purple trousers, filling up a bit larger every day inside the walls of the

Broken Pony. The walls Chilton had helped him build. They'd known each other since they were lads, running the untamed forests and creek beds around New London, looking for arrowheads and fighting imaginary skirmishes against the savages. They always played the British then, swaddling themselves in red fabric and brandishing muskets of birch. Today, and ever after, they were strangers. Battle makes heroes, and it makes goats. It all depends on who survives.

"I'll be moving on presently," Chilton said, gazing into the golden fluid, drawn to the dance of sediments arranging themselves in curious patterns at the bottom of the glass.

Richardson wiped down the bar, moving past Chilton. "A good Christian never turns away a thirsty man," he said quietly. "But I don't think all my customers are so charitable in their adherence to Holy Scripture."

Chilton followed the jut of his chin to the patrons clustered in small groups and huddled over their mugs at tables throughout the room. No one spoke, and every eye watched him with varying levels of hatred and disgust. He nodded, finished his applejack in one pained gulp, and headed for the door, shouldering his pack and donning his black felt hat as he exhaled fire, blinking his eyes quickly to reorient the room. Gad spiked his cider with grain alcohol, which kept his tables full and the neighborhood pillory well populated.

"Ger damn 'em bloodybacks what left ye alive."

He recognized that voice, but couldn't find the face in his mind. Everyone was the mob now, every word the jeering Chorus. Chilton's hand pawed at the door latch. It clicked and gave but the hinges stuck tight, frozen over from the icy brine outside, forcing him to put his shoulder into the wood. He banged a few times before the door creaked open, framing a very ungraceful exit for the famed New England Privateer Captain Mark James Chilton.

Chilton stepped outside and clenched every muscle in his body, as much against the bracing cold as the bullet he assumed would pierce him like sackcloth through the back - a leaden spine probe to make sure he still had one. Chilton was curious himself, and almost hoped for the hot stab of whistling death to put his suspicions to rest.

Regardless, his nerves were shot, and his gait unsteady. It was difficult for him to remember the days just before the incident, although they were only a few months prior. The midnight missions up the coast, the sinking of the British frigate after a vicious battle that cost him most of his men and a good portion of his foremast. The Caesar's welcome the survivors received upon limping back to dock, battered but triumphant. Captain Chilton, slayer of the Tories, subject of song and pamphlet churned out to raise morale amongst the rebels, which it did. They now felt like adventure stories written about someone else, read in his mother's voice when only just a sprat, and therefore fuzzy around the edges. But the looks inside the Broken Pony assured him that they were just as real as his last raid on that uncharted Nova Scotian cove. The legacy of the past made the present fall from grace all the more jarring, and the once proud locals all the more vicious. When times are bad and sustenance dwindling, the starving eat their heroes first.

Chilton never wanted any of it, but providence finds those it needs, regardless of cost. Indeed, Mark James, eldest child of native son Elias Chilton and exiled Ulster aristocrat Miss Charlotte Flannery Fitzpatrick, was hailed as the bravest boy ever sired in New London, who grew into the bravest man to ever join the Connecticut militia. On a dare, or even without one, he'd climb the tallest tree to fetch a swarming honeypot, take on a rogue bear with nothing but a patch knife, or drop his shirt and prizefight for a half plug of tobacco. He wasn't much of a shot with a musket, but loved a tussle more than anyone around. A natural born pugilist with a chin made of granite. Old timers would sit back and shake their head with a smile, wondering if he was dropped on his noggin when he was born, or just too naturally muddleheaded to consider consequences. Or too Irish. But Chilton was that sneaky kind of smart that made him a good soldier, and an even better ally, and your worst enemy if you crossed him, which fewer and fewer people did as he added years and the city dug deeper into the forest.

His father Elias was once a gentlemanly farmer of rye, potatoes, and apples, proudly tilling his uneven plot situated as far outside of New London as the counsel would allow. He wanted the challenge of taming the land, and providing room for what he hoped would be a large family. But it turned out that he was too far from town, as a raiding party of Mohegans caught him while cutting trees on the backside of his expanding property, taking off his leg with the same pit saw that felled the acres of maple and birch. The Indians left him to die, or warn the rest of us off the land, or both. Elias did neither. He cauterized his wound in the glowing ashes of a stump fire, dragged himself back to the family home, locked himself in his room with a dusty case of whiskey, and emerged two weeks later a different man. Freed from his cage of empty bottles, smears of dried blood, and piles of human filth, he fashioned a crude wooden leg from the last red maple tree he cut, and went right on farming without another word about the incident, or any word for his family in general. That next harvest, he sold what he needed to rear his family and dumped what was left into the smoking brass still set up in the barn after slaughtering all the livestock and leaving their corpses to rot in the yard, dooming the family for fresh meat. He said the sound of animals bothered him, so he brained each in turn with a bush hammer. Every day after that he'd spend the sunshine hours trudging across the fallow fields, combing the forest for Indians, avoiding human contact, and making rare few trips into town. At night, he'd take turns on his wife and his two children, depending on the moon and the quality of the spirits bubbling into maturity out in the darkness, telling them that it was his divine right as *pater familias* to sleep where he saw fit.

Charlotte took exception to this, and was beaten with a length of firewood until she could no longer speak, or do much of anything aside from drool, her eyes now crossways and the light inside her gone. But she still had enough wherewithal to drown her only daughter in the horse trough, lest Elias get to her one more time. After making a dinner of stewed hare and turnips—her husband's favorite meal—she hung herself from the support beam over the kitchen table that night, discovered by Mark James upon returning from town after selling off the family heirlooms for salt and flour. After taking in the scene, the son stirred the pot over the fire, sending the aroma of bubbling meat up the chimney, sat at the table, and waited.

Mark James, who soon became just Chilton in the absence of Elias amongst the general populace, killed his father slowly and carefully with the same piece of firewood that stole the life of his mother, and eventually his sister, and loaded his battered remains into the still in the barn. He spiced the batch with a pot of stew and added wood to the fire. He took the wooden peg back into the house and carved it down into an Iroquois war club. That morning at dawn, he put torch to the house, mounted the family horse, and galloped into town. He left his father's whiskey fermenting in the barn for the creatures of the forest, both human and not. Everything gets thirsty, especially those that call the wilderness home.

New London gossip whispered about the occurrence at the Chilton farm, but no official inquiry followed. The British Magistrate was unconcerned with the disappearance of rurals, and the underground local leadership committee was uniformly sympathetic to the younger Chilton to a man, while always scornful of Chilton the Elder. An outbreak of yellow fever was eventually blamed in the official account, and the property shunned.

Interest in this local mystery was soon eclipsed by the rumblings of war, as revolution was taking hold amongst the colonies. Forces were agitating in Boston, and more Red Coats were sent in from across the ocean, together with new laws to strangle the unruly subjects back into servitude. Although Chilton cared little about the discovery of those things that took place on the final night at his childhood home, or the capital repercussions, the timing of these major events moved minds away from such domestic matters. Nothing erases memories faster than war, as those within surely band together against those without. That both of these groups were mixed together up and down the colonies just made the growing situation all the more explosive.

Port activity increased during this time of tension, and without family or property, Chilton quickly found a new home on the New London docks. He'd hop any ship that was leaving harbor, often taking lower wages and sleeping on deck amid the elements, just to get away from the sweaty grip of the land behind him and learn his new life as a swab. The salted air was cleansing, at least on the outside, adding color to his cheeks and a sharpness to his round, Black Irish eyes. Standing on the prow in the early morning hours while the rest of the crew slept, he sucked in as much brine as he could, hoping it would take care of what was curled up deep inside him.

After only a few months, he was a dyed-in-the-wool wharf rat, whose already sizable reputation for courage and grit grew with each excursion upon the waves. With this new elevation in profile (which seemed to overshadow his status as a landless orphan), Chilton soon netted a wife—a wispy clothier's daughter named Agnes Warren—and set up house on Bank Street. From this close vantage point to the harbor, and due to the increase in late night smuggling runs, Chilton quickly secured ownership of a merchant vessel he rechristened *Sea Hag*, which he embellished in wide, bold black lettering on the stern, making sure everyone on the docks knew her name. A local artisan painted a terrifying visage of an aged crone, horns dripping kelp, mouth running red with blood. Rumors spread that the moniker was inspired by his notoriously frosty mother-in-law Eleanor Warren, who had provided the loan to purchase the ship, most likely to keep Chilton away from her daughter after Agnes' insistence on marrying him. Two years on, with Chilton spending more time at sea than home, and Agnes without child, the investment seemed to have paid off for Eleanor. Either way, both parties seemed happy, or at the very least mollified.

After several profitable seasons of stocking New London with rum, sugar, and what many thought were unseemly spices from the Caribbean and shadowy spots further to the southwest, Chilton found his livelihood threatened as the Intolerable Acts of the British pressed too deeply on the colonists, and a revolution broke out in earnest. This changed everything. Maritime activity turned from mercantile to martial, as all of New England—and New London—rallied to the saber rattle of war against the British crown, at the behest of a steely Virginian named George Washington.

Chilton was drafted into the newly minted American Navy an hour after he declared his soldiering intentions, and was officially bequeathed the rank of Captain by the Second Continental Congress, receiving his first commission to command the *Sea Hag* as a Privateer against the ravaging patrols of the British fleet off the coast of New England.

Living in New London, Chilton was in prime position to raid the southeast Canadian coast and rebuff hostile moves against the heart and soul of the revolution. It was 1776, and a year into the war, American losses were mounting, both on land and at sea, helped in no small measure by the constant flow of reinforcements from England by way of Canada. After a dozen successful incursions that inflicted notable losses on the crown, the Royal Navy pulled back, avoiding the *Sea Hag*'s usual radius. Sensing a change in the tides, and eager to push the battle lines further into enemy territory, Congress issued Captain Chilton an express order to break up the supply routes and staging areas of Nova Scotia. Chilton rounded up his best veteran crewmembers and a gaggle of greenhorns—inspired by promises of honor, spoils, and a heaping portion of righteous violence—refitted his vessel with new canonry fresh from the smithies of Philadelphia, and set off up the coast to a hero's farewell. The last sight Chilton beheld on New London shores was the stooped and shaking figure of Agnes as she wept into her hands while her mother held her hair. It was the first and last time he saw Agnes cry.

Chilton walked down Pequot Avenue, passing School Street and on to Thames Street Portage. The cider in his belly shot fire down his legs and into his feet, melting footprints into the lightly blown snow and leaving a steaming trail behind.

He avoided a look to his right towards Bank Street and the empty shell he once called his home and all of the ghosts moaning in those empty rooms that had never been filled, no matter how many trinkets and furniture he had stuffed inside. Further out of town, the Chilton farm lay still and quiet, unmarked graves hidden in the overgrown potato field returning the abused bodies of mother and daughter back to the earth. He was glad they were spared the details of what had happened to him to at sea, only wishing that his father still remained to witness what was coming. Chilton touched the club at his waist and felt a twinge of unexpected regret. Pa had died too soon, he decided, with too little horror to aid his passing.

Crossing Thames Street brought Green Harbor into view, and the outline of the *Sea Hag*. Chilton watched the gentle sway of his vessel, noting every slope and angle that was etched into his brain like the body of an immodest lover. His ship was the only craft lashed to the bulkhead at Green Harbor. No others wanted to be within 100 feet of her.

He tightened up his kerchief and continued down the street, passing the tiny Mariners' Church that teetered on a rocky outcropping near the graving docks, between the foundry and the fish house. A set of weathered stairs led up to the doorway, which stood wide open. This let in the cold, but also helped keep the congregation awake, while sending the message that God closes the door on no man, no matter the transgression, either at sea or land immediately adjacent. A resonant voice boomed from the occupied darkness inside. Even though he couldn't make out the words, Chilton knew the sermon was coming directly for him.

"Today's message was to focus on the generous spirit of the Christian soul," intoned the barrel-chested Reverend from behind the pulpit fashioned from prow and rigging. "But, recent developments have moved me to speak about courage, and of cowardice." Murmurs rippled through the congregation, who were squeezed into the four rows of narrow pews. "For a *craven* soul stands amongst us now. A shirker, a soft liver holding up a spine made of Goodie Holman's famed sourdough." Mrs. Holman blushed in the front row, waving off a few laughs and playful nudges.

"It is written in Timothy II," the Reverend continued, his face returning to stone, "that God hath not given us the spirit of fear; but of power, and of love, and of a sound mind. We were born into fear upon receiving the knowledge of good and evil, but through God's divine grace, and his protection, we now... fear...*nothing*."

"Nothin' 'cept a coward," someone called out from the back row.

"Indeed, indeed, Goodman Pratt. For Proverbs states that the wicked flee when no man pursueth: but the righteous are bold as a lion."

The congregation rumbled their consent. Heavy boots and a few walking sticks thumped the floor.

"And forget not the writings of Revelations. Chapter 21, Verse 8: 'But the fearful, and unbelieving, and the abominable, and murderers, and whoremongers, and sorcerers, and idolaters, and all liars, shall have their part in the lake which burneth with fire and brimstone: which is the second death.' I say to thee, good people of New London, that Hell awaits the fearful of all things that are not the Lord our God!"

A laugh cut through the shouts of agreement, turning every head in every pew toward the open door at the back of the church, where Chilton stood, holding a small statue of Jesus on the cross.

"Unhand our Christ," the Reverend commanded, the knuckles on his large, scarred hands turning white as they gripped the side of the lectern.

Chilton glanced around the room. "The last church I was in looked nearly identical to this one." He looked down at the occupied crucifix in his hand, absently rubbing the figure's feet with his thumb. "Except for this."

He shrugged and tossed the cross to the floor, where it landed face down. Half of the room shot to their feet, gasps and curses knitting together in a seething ball of fury.

"Blast ye," the Reverend hissed, pointing down from his place on high. "Blast ye and burn ye."

"Piss on yer coward soul, Chilton," snarled Mr. Pratt, rushing toward the lone man in the doorway.

Chilton pulled a flintlock from his breeches and shoved the barrel into the advancing man's mouth, stopping him cold. Chilton rattled the metal around Pratt's teeth, knocking out a rotting molar that dripped to the floor in a bloody strand.

A woman sobbed, gripping her husband tight. "He wouldn't dare kill a man in church!"

"No, I wouldn't kill a man in church," Chilton said, his voice flat. "But I would kill this one right here, right now, because he be no man, and this be no church."

"You blaspheme!" thundered the Reverend, pounding the top of the pulpit.

"Oh, I do more than that," Chilton said. "I speak the truth hidden beneath the blasphemy, because I surely seen it, plain as day and the stars at night. Hell be no fiery place. Hell be dark, and wet, and glitters with white gold."

Enraged men rushed at Chilton, who cocked the hammer on his pistol. Urine ran down Pratt's trouser legs, collecting in a steaming pool under his boots, creeping toward the statue.

"Hold," the Reverend shouted, stalking up the aisle, shoving aside tensed bodies and unsheathed knives. He stood before Chilton, holding out his worn

Bible like a talisman. "Begone, yellow demon. Your reckoning awaits you, outside these doors."

Chilton glanced behind him. "I reckon it does." He tipped his hat and looked down at the floor, flipping over the cross with his boot, facing Jesus to the ceiling. "He won't be coming down to save you." Chilton took in each pale face in the room, engaging every wide or squinted set of eyes. "Because the other ones are coming up for you first."

No one said a word, the silence broken by the thud of a woman who fainted in the back row. Chilton walked out the door, a black silhouette against the blinding daylight.

Outside the church, Chilton descended the steps, pulling the war club from his breeches and twirling it with his free hand. Below him on the street a crowd waited, lead by a core group of hard-bitten men and a few slatternly women who had followed him from the Broken Pony. They were arranged at the bottom of the stairs in a ragtag formation, pipe smoke dancing up into the icy sky. All of them regarded him squarely, ginned-up courage hardening their bloodshot eyes and tightening their grip on musket iron, daring him to raise the pistol. Even outside, over the breeze, he could smell their fear underneath the stink of alcohol and sweat. He knew that smell, and hated it. His senses were heightened after his last night at sea, and what he saw there. A survivor's wisdom, he told himself, never believing it for a second.

Chilton stepped off the stairs and parted the crowd, heading toward the *Sea Hag* that waited for him.

"A pox on ye, Captain *Craven*," came a gravelly female voice from the crowd.

He turned to the woman, aged beyond her grief by strong drink and late nights in various alehouses around town, and no doubt a few swinging hammocks as well. Chilton's eyes narrowed, drawing up the hollows underneath like two tiny curtains. His lips curled sideways. "A pox on all of us, Widow Embree."

Invectives spewed out of the tavern patrons, while more shocked gasps issued from the church doorway that was emptying out the congregation, encircling Chilton on all sides. Hands fluttered hex signs, while men held their women close and covered the eyes of their children. A few of the more modest citizens of New London hurried on their way, sensing trouble. Most stayed, hoping for the same.

"You speak the language of witchcraft," Samuel Ennis said from the crowd, swinging his musket down from his shoulder.

135

"Oh that witches were real, and their sorcery at our disposal." Chilton casually scratched his growing beard. The crowd moved back several steps in each crescent, as if pushed by an invisible hand instead of the outrage of fear. "But alas, we are alone in this universe of monsters."

Mrs. Embree conjured up a ball of phlegm from deep within her wasted being and spat on the ground as she staggered forward, dragging her gnarled left foot behind her. She groped inside her bodice, digging between flattened breasts, and produced a damp white hen feather, holding it out in front of her body as if poisonous. Stopping in front of Chilton, she reached up and buried the pointed calamus into the loosening wool of his topcoat lapel. He looked down at it, the soft tendrils along the shaft dancing by the cold breeze off the ocean.

"Only medal yer'll ever wear."

Chilton nodded, turned on his heel, and left the crowd standing huddled together, the steam of their quick breathing twisting and disappearing into the whistle of the building gale.

It was thus that the citizens of New London sent off Captain Chilton, who boarded the *Sea Hag* alone, cut the mooring ropes short from the cleat, and headed off to sea.

The *Sea Hag* carved the waves with an almost perceptible eagerness as it headed north, just like it had done the last time, when the deck was crowded with singing mariners busying themselves with battle preparations. Today the ship held only one man, which is all it seemed to have room for now.

At the wheel, Chilton listened to the creak of the rigging, the flap of the topsails, trying to find solace in the familiar sounds. He looked up the crows nest, where young Paul Wiggan once held vigil, day or night, only coming down to eat and often taking his meals high above the planks. He wanted to be a captain someday, just like the brave Mark James Chilton, who assured him that without question he'd be Commodore in a free American republic before his twentieth year. All he had to do was keep his eyes sharp and his instincts salty. Wiggan promised that he would, and meant it, yet when the time came, he never saw them come up from the sea, because he wasn't at his post. No one was, and so no one did, as they moved from sea to air without a sound, parting the water as if a silken curtain and climbing up the side of the ship like bloated crickets. But the day before, the lad was in the nest, keeping constant watch for the dread Nova Scotian Colonel Alexander Godfrey, who never materialized on the horizon like Chilton thought he would. He even had the nights watch burn torches, in hopes of drawing out Godfrey from the blackness, but to no avail. The Colonel wasn't in the area, or if he was, he chose not to engage. A disappointing turn of events for the crew, and no less to Chilton, who was itching for a fight, and a chance to hobble the Brits.

With a strong tailwind and favorable current, they made good time. On their port side passed Massachusetts, New Hampshire and Popham Colony country in upper Mass. The whole of the trip north, they encountered no resistance, allowing them unfettered and almost leisurely ravaging of suspect fishing communities once they hit the islands of Nova Scotia, starting with Yarmouth and working their way up the northeastern coastline, jagged with inlets and the jut of peninsulas piled with massive boulders. While unarmed villagers watched helplessly from a distance, Chilton and his men sank suspicious ships at harbor, dumped a portion of the fish haul, and restocked their barely depleted supplies from available larders as they worked their way to Halifax, where they knew a proper battle awaited, possibly with help from additional American Privateers that constantly prowled the nearby waters. The triplet grouping of Halifax, Spryfield, and Burnside were always fattened by their British masters and begging to be plucked. Chilton was only too eager to do the plucking, and had cleared out space in the lower hold of the *Sea Hag* for pillaged goods. He felt like a proper pirate, a regular John Halsey on a divine mission, and wished there was a little more bend and heft to the saber at his side.

On the morning of the day they were to reach Halifax, Wiggan spied the thin, delicate steeple of a church peeking over the rise of a high cliff face walling off a hidden cove. As sure as an arrow stuck in the ground, the spire gave away the location of the beating heart of a community tucked away from the sea that wasn't logged on any of their charts. This was indeed queer, as they were using smuggled British maps certified by the King's royal cartographer. Chilton immediately took it for a secret British military base, hastily built with the appearance of a bucolic fishing and herding community.

Chilton's heart soared as he instructed his men to arm heavily, loading up extra powder and ball, as what they were about to find on shore would dwarf any domestic goods they burned in Halifax, and they wouldn't give up willingly after going to all this trouble to hide their activities. "We found a nest of vipers, lads," Chilton said with a laugh. "So bring your biggest sticks."

The raiding party arrived on shore in the late afternoon, just hours before sundown. After encountering some difficulty scaling the cliffs that led from the rocky beach, they moved quickly over the dunes of scrub grass into the rundown village. The streets were empty, the houses timeworn and ramshackle, looking barely livable. Everything smelled heavily of rotted fish, although no catch lined the empty stalls in the cramped market square. As they crept from building to building, they found not a living soul, discovering instead several large smelters installed in various innocuous-looking warehouses. The town seemed deserted, although recent habitation was evident amongst the filthy conditions. All was quiet as a tomb. No birds sang from the eaves, no dogs barked behind fences or sniffed the gutters. The trees had been cleared from every rutted sidewalk. Yards were tamped down mud. It was a depressing place, lorded over by the high steeple of the church that sat on the hill just above town, a small belfry window giving a clear view of the sea. The citizens must have seen the approach of the *Sea Hag* and had fled.

The small scouting teams returned to the square and gave their reports, regrouping around their Captain.

"There's nothing here, sir," said Lt. Jeffrey Scott, Chilton's first mate, who was the last to return. "No weapons, no supplies, no—"

"—No people." Chilton's gaze rested on the church. He walked toward it, climbing the smoothed dirt pathway that lead to the plateau above town. Scott nodded and followed, checking the breech on his Brown Bess and affixing his bayonet. The men did the same, pulling ramrods and falling in line behind the man in front of him.

The church was infinitely older than the rest of the town, and seemed to be built right into the granite – or out of it – with the wooden frame and shingles acting as more of a masking agent than necessary architecture. No windows lined the walls, giving the impression of a strong box instead of a house of worship. The twin front doors were shut and no sound came from inside, but the structure had a weight to it, a teeming heaviness that seemed to hum.

"There ain't no cross up there," Wiggan said, squinting at the shape topping the steeple point. "It's a star."

"Byzantines," spat an old wiry sea dog named Squire Boone. "In league with the Tommies."

A slight tapping came from behind the doors. Muzzles rose. Boone moved to the door, and Chilton nodded. Boone turned the iron latch and pulled back the two slabs of heavy wood.

A cold stink issued from the church like a slow shove, squeezing groans from the sailors. Chilton pulled his kerchief up over his nose and entered, waiting for his eyes to adjust to the near absence of light inside. As vision slowly returned, he found what must have been the entire village – close to a hundred people – peering back at him from the dark. Men wore hats low over their faces, women were veiled like brides, their features hidden under gray and green lace, but hinting at large, strangely colored eyes and wide lips. A man removed his hat and smoothed back wispy black hair over the smooth skin of his unnaturally streamlined head. A peculiar smile played on his toadish lips, but it might have been the curvature of the mouth high up the cheek. His hazel pupils were flecked with gold and appeared to push out from his skull with each quick, labored breath he took.

Chilton took a step back, shocked at the unnatural appearance of the faces, the waxen expressions, that stared back at them.

"What's wrong with these people?" whispered Scott.

"Inborns," someone said.

"Celestials," Boone said.

"Innsmouth folk," said a sailor named Rickert, who grew up in the woods north of Boston. His face was pale and his trigger hand shaking.

Chilton had heard of the secretive village of Innsmouth tucked away in a narrow fold of the Massachusetts coast, although he and everyone he knew – save maybe Rickert, by all accounts – had never been there. It was a closed community of religious and cultural abnormalities, founded long before the rest of the colony. The crew must have stumbled upon another outpost of the Innsmouth clan, or perhaps the other way around. Either way, Chilton thought, there certainly weren't any British sympathizers here.

"Look at the ceiling," Wiggan said, his high voice far too loud.

Above them, the vaulted ceiling was covered in images and pictograms set amid a heavenly scene of what first appeared to be aquatic life playing amongst stars and fanciful planets unlike anything Chilton had seen in the schoolhouse astronomy texts. The entire rendering glistened, made entirely of pale gold, studded with gemstones the size of a man's fist.

"We's rich!" Boone shouted. A few of the men cheered.

"Return to ship," Chilton said, cutting through the excitement, trying to keep the creep of fear out of his voice. He had never been afraid before, but the gnawing chill in the pit of his stomach surely must be it. It felt as if the ceiling were watching them. "We have no business here."

"But Cap—" Boone started.

"Return to the goddamn ship," Chilton ordered.

The men hesitantly turned to the door, one taking old Boone by the arm, but the door was no longer behind them. Several of them turned back around, and discovered the way out was now across the room. The congregation just stood and silently watched.

"What is this?" Chilton whispered, his voice rising in pitch.

No one in the room uttered a word. His men began to rile, and Chilton felt as if he had to say something, and was about to blurt either a salutation or an order to fire – he didn't know which – when a small robed figure emerged from the collection of villagers and shuffled toward the sailors. He or she was no larger than a child, but moved with the pained effort of extreme old age. When it reached the men, a hand emerged from the folds of heavy fabric and stretched out to the club at Chilton's waist, revealing a spindly arm covered in flaky, desiccated skin.

"Leper!" Boone said.

Chilton knocked the hand away with the butt of his musket.

The congregation came alive with a sudden eruption of barks and croaks, surging forward like a swarm of gibbering locusts. A boom echoed off the high rafters, and then another, and a dozen more. Smoke choked the air and bodies slammed to the floor.

"Back to the ship," Chilton shouted into the haze, burnt saltpeter stinging his nose. He charged through the confused mass of leaping and fallen bodies toward the last location of the double doors. Something snatched the musket from his hands while the man at his side was yanked to the ground. Chilton pulled his pistol and fired at the moaning figures that shambled out of the smoke, swinging his club at anything that didn't fall.

He reached the doors and kicked them open from the middle, pulling out each of his battling men to the last, before slamming the doors shut and leaning into them with his full weight, soon joined by several of the larger crewmembers.

Hands slapped at the doors from inside, which quickly became heavy lunges. The wood bowed and the thick rusted hinges popped, but the jambs held. Scott and three other men pushed a corroded buckboard in front of the entrance, and the men stood back, breathing heavily while reloading their muskets.

Wiggan's face was pale. "What do we do, Captain?"

Chilton listened to the inhuman sounds coming from inside the church, terror shriveling his insides, stealing his voice, melting the iron that had held up his bones his entire life and draining it out his feet. For the first time in his life, after everything he had done and had been done to him, Chilton was scared, and that feeling horrified him, far more than the inhuman monstrosities that threw themselves against the double doors.

"Captain?" Scott said.

"Burn it," Chilton finally managed. "Burn it all."

The *Sea Hag* raised anchor and crept back out to sea. Chilton stood on the quarterdeck and watched the last rays of daylight frame a dozen funnels of black smoke that joined together into a growing cloud above the burning town. He didn't move until the sun was gone, and the sea and the sky became one.

The crew was silent on the voyage home. No hoots and hollers and drunken brags about feats of barter and sexual conquest once they reached New London. Even Boone stopped talking about the pool of melted gold collecting in the burning ruins behind them, never mentioning a return plan to collect it. The ship was full of plunder, but this was forgotten. The mugs hung empty and the grog stayed in the barrel. Everyone to a man seemed drawn inside themselves, contemplating what they had just seen. Hands made the sign of the cross, or clenched together in rusty prayer. Even after all duties were complete, no one slept. Wiggan didn't climb the crow's nest that night, huddling instead down in the hold. He didn't want to see anymore. Chilton walked the deck, trying to conjure up the right words to share with his men, to reassure them, but he had nothing to say. Instead, he retreated to his cabin while Scott took the wheel.

It was hours into the silent journey home, and just before dawn, when the *Sea Hag* abruptly stopped in the water, pitching man and cargo headlong across the ship.

Ships on open sea, miles from shore and nowhere near pack ice or hidden sandbar, never just stop, but the *Sea Hag* did, freezing on the main as if grabbed by a giant hand below the waves. Sails billowed and the masts groaned angrily, but the craft held fast while everything simply *ceased*. No waves lashed at the waterline. Scott regained his feet, ran to the railing and looked down, finding the sea smooth as glass, like a frog pond. The texture of the water mesmerized him. He could see down deep into the ocean, spying a light that filtered up from the murky depths. A pale silvery glimmer of something deep, and quite vast.

Chilton had been thrown into his dressing closet, and was frantically fighting through the maps that covered him when he heard the first shout. By the time he reached the door to his quarters, the shouts turned to screams.

He dashed out onto deck just as the ship was overrun. Shadows leaping out of shadows, hopping and scuttling, extinguishing torches that reflected off bulging white eyes, slick mottled skin. Musket fire flashed in the darkness, etching scenes of slaughter in stark relief. Lt. Scott was ripped in two, each side of him hoisted over a shoulder like a butchered calf and spirited back to the water. Squire Boone staggered the length of the deck, tripping over his own entrails that slowly unraveled from the inside of his ripped waistcoat. He slipped on the blood that now painted the boards, landing with a plop on his own insides that smeared to jelly underneath him. A second later and his head was missing, yanked from his shoulders by a scaly claw like a child plucking a morel cap from the stem.

This was something that should not be, death like this, from things like this. An impossible sight, ripped from fever dreams buried deep within the brain and deeper in the human race. Dark truths that retreated from superstition outside the caves, waiting and watching for those who remembered the Elder Knowledge.

Chilton shuddered from the inside out, feeling his grip on sanity loosening by the moment, helped in large measure by the fact that the things grabbing Chilton's men and pulling them into the water made no sound at all. They massacred in silence and with a cruel efficiency. All he could hear was the one-sided screams of horror ripped from the throats of his crew, and the splash as they hit the water, carried down by the things boiled up from the deep. Young Wiggan called out to him for help from somewhere in the darkness, his high voice pleading, but Chilton stood frozen in place, his courage rendered down to glue that fastened his boots to the deck timber. He just stood and watched as the ship was cleared, one shrieking man at a time, until all were gone.

After several moments of terrible silence, a lone creature leapt down from the yardarm, landing heavily. It rose partially erect and looked in Chilton's direction, then brought itself to its full height, thin muscles rippling strangely under its glistening skin. As if showing the man it could do it. It could stand like him, taller than him. It could beat him, and did. The face born at the bottom of the sea seemed vaguely human, in some respect. More than the faces of the other ones that had taken his men. Walking in an unnatural, loping manner, it approached Chilton, carrying something small and glittery in its webbed hand. It set it down in front of the captain, turned, and leapt over the rails, disappearing under the water without so much as a splash.

Chilton gazed down at the object resting at his feet.

The *Sea Hag* was empty. All that remained was the Captain, who stood on deck, waiting to go down with a ship that remained afloat.

To live is sometimes to die, to leave behind the world you once knew and to journey, transformed, into the Hell of displacement, separated from everything you knew and loved. This was the hero's true journey, and the course on which Chilton was unknowingly traveling, as the *Sea Hag* sliced through the ocean waves toward that locus of nightmares.

Even before his equipment confirmed it, Chilton knew that he had arrived again at his destination, as his blood seemed to thicken in his veins and the sails suddenly hung limp. He was there, floating above the nest like a fly listing on the surface of a trout stream. This time, the ship lay empty at the start of his journey rather than at the end. This time, he was ready. He didn't drop anchor, as he knew it would never find the bottom. Besides, the ship had stopped on its own.

Chilton went to the railing and discarded his pistol in the water, then the ocean chart he didn't need, his sextant and compass, and finally his club, gripping one last time the piece of wood that had once been attached to his father's body, before casting it into the sea. Everything from the land came from the sea, and everything from the land will return to the sea again. It was just a matter of when.

Chilton busied himself on deck, taking out various objects from his pack. Once prepped, he unmoored a cannon and dragged it to the center of the upper deck. He sponged out the bore and dried it with great care, then packed the chamber with an extra portion of black powder and wadding, before loading the heaviest ball on ship. He cut the wick of the slow match short and wound the strands tight.

Leaning against the cold iron of the neck, Chilton reached into his pack, pulling out a small metallic crown. By its size, it could have been a tin children's toy, or the priceless diadem of a boy king, made of intricately intersecting threads of pure white gold. He removed the white feather from his lapel and stuck it into the top of the crown, before placing it on his head. Then he slowly disrobed, piling his unwashed clothing into a heap that he sprinkled with gunpowder and set ablaze from the lantern he had placed nearby. The oily wool fibers went up like tinder, billowing black smoke up into the dead sails.

His offerings made to the sea, and the signal fire set, Chilton waited.

It didn't take long.

Just enough time for the sun to set over the land behind him, washing the thin clouds in pink and yellow, and once again merging sea and sky.

Then they were there, emerging from every concealed spot on the ship and standing in a loose formation. Like a military raiding party, dripping salt water onto the deserted deck.

Chilton got to his feet, his naked flesh shivering in the biting cold, and looked over the group of creatures. How pale and hairy he seemed in comparison to their colorful, smooth skin, flared with pops of red and stripes of yellow. Natural war paint, just like the natives. When he spotted the one that had given him his crown, he nodded. The creature didn't nod back.

In a blur of activity, he snatched up the lantern and hopped atop the cannon, straddled the lip and forcing down the muzzle under the weight of his body. A monster iron phallus pointed down at the deck from between his legs.

Chilton shot a look at the tall creature. "The land will always rise."

With a triumphant cackle, he smashed the lantern over the wick, and seconds later the cannon fired, sending its charge down deep into the guts of the *Sea Hag* that were packed with a Privateer's fortune of gun powder.

The ship exploded like the floating bomb it had become.

A shower of wreckage descended through the dark water, drifting gently toward the waiting hive a mile wide and built of pearly gold, which was already marshalling for war. The land dwellers would not be prepared. They never were. This would be a revolution of a different kind.

Amid the debris, the small crown tumbled down, the white feather gone.

TRANSMISSION

E ven this far out, away from the light and the bilge and the droning nouveau bullshit lounge music rasping from a purposely old LP, things were
still sort of a blur.

The same blurry party with the same blurry people with annoying hipster
headgear and piercings and tattoos and post-ironic t-shirts and uniformly blurry
beards. The off-brand bottle of blurry liquor in his hand. The blurry, slurry skank
that he had seen before but never recognized, pressing in too close, breathing all
of his air.

The shouting. The broken furniture. The fight. The blood. The weaksauce
ghetto insults hurled from a safe distance as he ran out of the blurry room in the
blurry house on a blurry street in a forgotten Midwestern city that blurred brown
and green but mostly brown under a thousand jumbo jets every single day.

A blur. All of it. And none of it worth a single fuck.

Max scratched at the crusted gash on the side of his face and concentrated
on the tunnel of pavement opening foot by foot ahead of him, trying to clear the
blur from his mind as he drove west, ever west, in a last ditch effort to outrace
the smudge of his past. This was it, he felt. A wagon train of one, fueled by a last
hope for blessed clarity waiting amongst the swaying palms of the Pacific coast.
Failing that, he'd drive off the end of the goddamn continent and drown in the
murk of the darkened deep.

Max blinked his eyes and lit up a cigarette, checking the cheap plastic compass he picked up at a truck stop in Grand Island, Nebraska, stuck lopsided to the dash of his shitty late model Dodge. West, the bobbing arrow assured him. West. He was still heading in the right direction. At last that much was certain.

Max knew he stayed too long at his last stop. He had gotten lazy, and worse than that he had gotten hopeful, figuring roots would sprout from the bottoms of his shoes if he just loitered in the same place long enough. Anchoring him to a piece of ground at last. But the roots never came. Only rot. And that's when he knew he had to get out. That night. That second. By whatever means necessary no matter what collection of beards and bows were in his way.

And so he did.

It made no difference that he had a belly full of poison and eighty-seven dollars to his name. He just knew it was time. And so it was.

And so he went.

Max would keep moving this time, for as far as his shitty late model Dodge would take him. He was pretty sure he had hurt some people pretty badly, maybe even fatally, during his abrupt exit from the blur two nights ago, so going backwards wasn't an option at this point. He just had to keep his head down and keep grinding that wheel, fueled by the last hope of finding his destiny out yonder under western skies, as so many eastern souls had done before him. Get his hands on a bit of true clarity in the fairytale hills. He'd change his name, maybe grow his hair into Viking braids and take up surfing. But most importantly, he lose himself in the crowded anonymity of the city of nearsighted angels, where everyone is too busy squinting into the mirror to spot the disheveled fugitive sitting across the bar.

It wasn't his fault, this wanderlust. It was congenital, ancestral, born out of a thirsty Caucasian soul and dissatisfaction with nearly everything around him, combined with the certainty that new lands conquered would quell all inadequacies and establish contrived dominance in one fell swoop. So Max became a human tumbleweed from the first time he learned how to thumb a ride, spinning from city to hamlet to dusty campsite, in search of something bigger than himself to tie him down and make him *want* to stay, to become part of something outside of himself. Some people looked for God. Some quested for love. Max just searched for meaning, starting with the self and working outward from there if he had time. All of everything that was and would someday be. There had to be a point—a greater purpose—to the entirety of this terribly self-important but most likely utterly meaningless nonsense, and the answer had to be out there somewhere, around the next bend, over the next rise in the road.

But he never found it. Not yet. In all those miles and all those late hours, he'd just found more of the same. He just found more blur.

So here he was, knifing down Highway 50 west of McGill, Nevada, as the last two days and nights—hell, the last thirty-two years—melted into just another portion of an unbroken line of bleary days and blurry nights spent doing nothing with a thousand nameless nobodies, all bored to panicked tears hidden behind masks of sardonic bullshit. Somehow, without knowing exactly where or exactly why, Max had drifted off of I-80, that great tentacle of government-issue cement that stretched the length of this vast, savage land. But it didn't matter. His cheap plastic compass assured him that he was heading west, and that was good enough for Max. That certainty was enough for now. Small victories in the war against the unknown.

Exhaling a small nimbus cloud of smoke into the windshield, Max sat back, and for the first time in what felt like forever, he relaxed and opened the window, allowing the cool dry air to clean out the car. The blur had begun to recede, which allowed him a smile. He was moving again, had been for two sunrises, and the road behind him was growing longer. He was carving a proud wound into the hide of the central Nevada desert, and no one could force him to do otherwise. Max had regained his footing about the time he hit the Rockies, and with the great peaks of the continental divide doing just that between where he currently was and what he had left behind, he found himself feeling the music again, the rhythm of pavement as the highway danced for him beneath the floorboards.

Max turned on the radio, switching immediately from the dead FM presets of his last layover to the strange anonymity of AM. A veteran of the road, Max loved to scan the monophonic dial when moving through the most remote areas of the country. Amplitude modulation radio in major cities was the cozy bed of blustery right wing shitsuckers, sports broadcasting, and Madison Avenue country pop. But out in the forgotten hinterlands, especially in the desert southwest, the bedfellows become more strange, inhabited by a disparate mix of yammering Spanish, mournful cowboy crooning, random snatches of Chinese, thunderous Evangelical sermons, and UFO whistleblowers who always seemed to concentrate in the dried out, forgotten places, using the AM airwaves to vent their spleen and warn the ignorant masses about the alien entities already moving amongst us. The desert seemed ideally suited to a curious collection of castoffs, eccentrics, weirdos, and sociopaths naturally drawn to the dusty fringes. Meth cooks, anti-government militias, New Agey art nuts, murder cultists. All headed to the sandy heat like Jesus himself, looking to face down their demons, or possibly create them, away from the prying eyes of the better irrigated. Owing to the circumstances surrounding his exit from his last stopover, perhaps Max should join this sun-blasted freak show, he thought. Get lost amongst the lost. But he knew something else was out there for him, waiting far beyond the arid wasteland, where the mountains and trees sprang up again along the ocean cliffs, trying to slow the momentum of western trajectory before all frustrated life again ended up in the sea.

Max pressed "scan" and skimmed over an offering of MexiCali accordion music and a low rent advert for industrial shedding, arriving at what he loved the most—the Born Againer martyrdom rant against the encroaching forces of the Antichrist, who was always some eastern hemisphere powerbroker carefully selected and re-christened by each new generation, and then watched like a chicken coop eyes a hawk—albeit a hawk two thousand miles away. No matter what latitude or longitude traveled, Max could find cold comfort in the certainty of religious zealotry flooding AM airwaves in the forgotten places of North America, stoked by paranoia, bigotry, xenophobia and a sort of gleeful fatalism that would have chilled Nietzsche to his knickers. Land of the free. Home of the brave.

"And so the days of the tribulation are nigh, my brothers and sisters," roared the firebrand, buzzing Max's tiny speakers. "And ye shall hear of wars and rumors of wars. See that ye be not troubled, for all these things must come to pass, but the end is not yet here. For nation shall rise against nation, and kingdom against kingdom, and there shall be famines, and pestilences, and earthquakes, in diverse places. All these are the beginning of sorrows!"

The signal faded a bit, but came back strong a few seconds later, allowing Max to continue his front row seat to the theatre of holy fear. "The signs are everywhere, if one knows how to look with the eyes of Jesus and the mind of God! The return of the Chosen Ones to their ancient land, the gathering of crows, the massing of armies…" Hoots and hollers from the unseen audience gave credibility to these ravings that would be deemed insanity in the western world if spewed under a different banner, or no banner at all. "It's all in the Word, and the Word shall come to pass!"

The Word. Max chuckled and lit up another cigarette, shaking his head at the dead-ass certainty of the Evangelical blowhard. How can one be so assured of *anything*? Faith aside, if this were a country settled by Bronze Age Norsemen and founded on the teachings of Odin and his hammer-wielding sprat, Americans would have a totally different outlook on the afterlife, and pine for bloody laurels while ascending to the Halls of Valhalla after being split in two on the field of battle. But this wasn't that country. Thanks to Rome, then Columbus and Cabot and Cortez, pious Americans from every bloodline under the mongrel sun got the longhaired peacenik from Galilee as their redeemer, who Max surmised was more dope smoking flower child than gun wielding capitalist. Luck of the historical draw, as all the books that mattered to posterity were written by the victors. How many times had Max roared some version of this half-baked pundit screed into various living rooms and barroom bathrooms the past ten years like a C-list Beatnik? How many times had no one given a solitary fuck what he was saying? Gospels aside, the Son of Man probably experienced the very same thing, albeit to a better tanned crowd.

Max pushed himself back from his annoying existential meander just in time for the signal fade from the Bible thump. He sighed and pressed scan again, starting the lottery anew.

Outside his bug-painted windshield, the sign for "Fallon, NV – 30 Miles" whizzed past. Max barely glanced, concerned only with how far he was from the Pacific, where his future would be made or broken on the chewed coastline of California. The place of childhood soft drink commercials and 80s beach comedies. Paradise under an eternal sun that didn't burn or wither but lit everyone to camera-ready perfection. He just needed to get through the desert, and he'd be fine. The answers would be waiting for him at the water's edge. They had to be. What was the meaning of life for a flyover boy? California, your honor.

As the radio scan continued to cycle through dead air, Max looked out into the night around him. The range of his headlights hinted at an endless stretch of dried-out nothingness, colonized by scrub grass, creosote bush, cacti, and probably a fair share of bleached bones of varying size and species. Forty days and forty nights in all direction. This wasn't land that had recently gone dry. It looked like it was *born* dry, shot malformed from the ocean to land under a misanthropic sky that refused to grant it any relief, any taste of that wet place where it was formed.

This backcountry was broken by the occasional squatty house, built low and set far back from the highway, as if the structure itself was trying to run from civilization and—reaching the end of its tether—collapsed glumly onto the dusty ground in defeat. Max could never figure out why anyone or anything with any sort of viable option would choose to live in such a God forsaken environment. No appreciable water, daytime heat that could kill a man, and a bloodthirsty landscape populated entirely by flora and fauna that was either poisonous or covered in deleterious thorns, or both; a brutal ecosystem crafted with an eye on repelling or murdering any non-native species that was stupid enough to wander into the neighborhood. And yet, softheads came out in droves to parched places such as this to restart their ridiculous lives, pumped in borrowed water, set up artificial air conditioning, and hunkered down inside their suburban pillboxes, waiting out each day as if they lost a bet.

The radio found a tether and stopped on a fuzzy station espousing the tourist attractions of the area. "—orthern Nevada, some of the most accessible examples of these mysterious petroglyphs can be found at Grimes Point, about twelve miles east of Fallon on Highway—" And just like that, the signal was gone again. Scan...

Max was pondering the important issue of how petrogylphs differed from hieroglyphs when the radio halted its roll at the very far end of the electronic dial. After a brief silence, the weak signal transmitted indistinct sounds, like whispers, intermingled with an odd chanting that faded in and out like a spectral dirge. Intrigued by this strange combination, and hoping for a broadcast of a lonely Indian powwow, Max turned up the volume, but the higher it went, the softer the voice and chant became, going silent. There was no apparent signal, but the radio scan was still stopped, locked in on something.

Perplexed, Max noticed that the compass on his dash began to shimmy in its housing, spinning this way and that, even though the road ahead was straight as an arrow.

The silence was shot through by a booming intonation that blasted from the speakers, startling Max, who grasped at the volume button, barely noticing the brownish, misshapen hulk that lurched onto the highway ahead at the far edge of his headlights, gripping something large in its massive paws. Max mashed the brakes while cranking the wheel away from the creature, which dragged a half-eaten carcass of a deer—or was it a dog? —up the rocky embankment, as the Dodge swerved by, skidding onto the shoulder and burying the front grill into the opposite hillside as the radio went silent again.

The car engine gurgled and pitched under the slightly crumpled hood, then jerked to a stop with a wheeze. Breathing hard, Max fixed his eyes on the compass. It was spinning like a top inside the plastic housing. Was this from the crash? But the car wasn't moving, and probably wouldn't be anytime soon. The radio was again cycling through dead air. And what was that huge fucking thing that ran across the road? Pebbles rolled down the hillside and onto the car like a hundred tapping fingers.

Max sat frozen, blinking his eyes that were obviously playing tricks on him after too many hours on the road. That thing... Was it a desert inbred? Some sort of mutated bear that wandered too close to a nuclear test site? This *was* Nevada, after all, the bullpen of the atom bomb. Max was unnerved, more by what he did know of what he saw than what he didn't. Or maybe it was what he heard. They both happened so fast, so close together. He was sweating, and felt as if the car was closing around him like a tin can prison. He locked the doors, not sure if what was out there was worse than what he heard inside, as he quickly realized what most terrified him was that the radio would again find that baritone chanting that seemed to echo from somewhere impossible deep. He reached out hesitantly to push the off button, when the scan again stopped on the far end of the dial, but this time, he heard...*weeping.* The strange, uncomfortable sound of a man crying, as if profoundly grieved by the tragically occurred or the unfortunately inevitable. This stayed Max's hand, before the sobbing splintered into sudden, spastic laughter. What was this nonsense? What sort of psychotic local pirate station owner or ham radio operator was pranking over the air, scaring the shit out of those who scanned the far end of the dial? This fucker owed Max a new, shitty, late model Dodge. Or at least a ride to the coast.

The laughter then stopped, and in the silence, the mic picked up sounds of papers being shuffled, tapes stacked methodically. Then, a flat voice that sounded distant in tone and emotion began. "You can hear everything in the desert." The voice wavered, as if the speaker needed to stop, to breathe, to collect himself. "The buzzing of insects, the hooting of owls, the mad yap of the coyotes..."

"You got that right," Max chimed in with irritation to no one but the unhearing voice at the other end of the radio transmission, which came to life again:

"Sometimes those sounds fall away by some unspoken agreement, and in that profound silence, the right type of ears can hear, can *sense*, the softer, more terrible noises that lurk underneath the normal nighttime din..." Another pause, another intake of breath. "The desert whispers to me, telling me things I never knew existed, never dared dream, giving up secrets older than the primordial soup... I record these secrets, as I have been tasked, and broadcast them when I can. But the recording is the key, and I have been diligent, as were those who came before me."

Outside the car, dry lightning carved the sky, highlighting clouds that looked like seething shapes forming on the horizon. "If you could rewrite the Bible, the Nag Hammadi, the Tablets of Thoth, directly from the source, would you sacrifice your life to do it?"

Another religious loony tune—this one with a shiny heretical paint job, Max thought, trying to chuckle in spite of a gnawing fear that was coiling in his stomach. He quickly turned the key and tried to give life to a halting ignition while avoiding glancing out into the darkness. He was still shaken by the crash, and nervous that he might be stranded out on this forgotten ribbon of highway with this obviously insane misanthrope and whatever loped up into the hills.

After much protesting and cajoling from Max, the battered engine sputtered to life. He revved out the kinks, then backed out from the embankment and out onto the highway, jammed the car into drive, and drove wobbly on in the same direction he was going, the voice continuing its diatribe, with Max trying not to listen. The compass still spun like a mindless dervish, so it was no good to him. But Max knew where he was going. West. Ever west and as west as he could. He had to leave this weird fucking place behind.

As he built up speed, the radio signal got stronger, and Max found himself listening more intently in spite of himself, finding courage in motion, and increasingly fascinated by this obviously deranged individual who somehow attained access to the radio airwaves. It was like an auditory train wreck, the ultimate metaphysical reality show, and Max couldn't turn his ears away, or move himself to turn off the radio.

"It's late in my mission," the voice said, "and nearly time for me to move on. I'm waiting for my replacement so the work and the message can continue. They tell me that the time of the awakening is at hand, and as such, the preparations have become more urgent than ever before."

The signal started to fade, and so Max slowed. He was now fully engrossed in this mournful monologue, and felt somehow compelled to keep listening, as if guided by a gentle outside force. Nearly losing the signal all together, Max stopped the car in the middle of the empty highway, dropped into reverse, and trundled backwards in the darkness cut open by his white reverse lamps, until the signal increased in strength again. He stopped and idled, leaning forward, as if to better connect with this lone speaker in the darkness.

"The desert tells me to do this, and I do as I'm told, because you never, ever argue with the desert." The voice giggled again, this time with more mirth, but it ended with a terrified edge, as before. "So, now I whisper to you, speaking for the desert, speaking for those behind the desert, and speaking for myself, as my time here has lately become short."

The car engine shuddered, seized, and expired. Max didn't notice.

"There is beauty and horror here, wisdom and madness, and I have drunk deeply of it all. Will you do the same?" The man went silent. Lightning licked the sky. Max, again feeling the car close in around him, began to wonder if this was merely a one-way conversation.

"Will you?" the voice asked again.

"Me?" Max answered.

"You," the voice continued, as if in confirmation. "Will you do the same?" The signal wavered and buzzed, then faded into fuzz again.

Max flung open his door and tumbled out of the car. Rushing to the smashed hood, he pushed against the cracked grill with all of his might, and moved the Dodge backward, gaining momentum as he labored. As it picked up speed, Max ran to the open car door and jumped inside, breathing hard as he turned up the volume. The signal came back in, and Max quickly veered the car off the road onto the graveled shoulder, settled in behind the wheel and listened.

"—slicing open the forbidden fruit forever, peeling back the skin to reveal that essential pulp, as knowledge is not evil, it is the natural progression of humanity, and a realization of what we were placed here to do by the creators. I and others in the service of the truth are just signposts, simple steps forward in the awakened dream. The *work* is the most important thing that humanity is undertaking right now on this planet, battling the old war against those who call madness all things they dare not understand..."

The radio strength dipped, and Max was about to hop out and reposition his car yet again, when it resumed.

"My time with the work is almost complete, as my vessel has been filled to the cracking point... I now wait for another...One who has been promised, who will come to pick up the transcription while I move on..." More fuzzy static. "The work isn't about good or evil, as good and evil do not exist. Those are arbitrary judgment calls, muddied by rationalizations. Only order and chaos are real. Only light and dark. Only knowledge and ignorance. Out of these primal forces spring everything we know. And I now know *just a mere fraction* of what is out there, and sometimes wish I didn't, as in its transcendent power, it has ended me for this sphere... My brain has heard too many whispers, dreamed too many times beyond the First Gate, has seen too much revealed... and now aches for an eternal rest, to exhale after a decade long upload. I seek the silence of the teeming abyss—to rest, and to dream, as has been promised. The veil has been lifted and the bliss of ignorance has been shattered forever, and so now I sit in a state of unsettled wisdom, blinking my watery eyes as if I have looked too long at the sun…the unimagined beauty…the indescribable horror…the unimagined beauty of the indescribable horror…" The voice trailed off in rasping awe, then the man took a deep, shaky breath. "Who out there will take my place? Who dares peek behind the veil, to see the truth in all its many splendors and impossibly endless vistas? Who will listen to the whispers after I am gone?"

Max sat in his car, mesmerized by this voice, hanging on every quaver and sigh. This man was obviously bat shit crazy, but in his insanity, there was a powerful certainty about knowledge and realities that Max could scarcely imagine.

"The work *must* go on, as the truth *must* be told." The voice found strength once more. "We weren't created to live as ignorant insects our entire existence, puttering around our self-made terrarium with our heads dragging blindly in the dust. The lost knowledge handed down from beyond must be brought back, made whole, and again disseminated across our land, if we are ever to rise to the dancing dimensional heights we once knew as a young Arcadian civilization, flush with the magic of sacred geometry and outer technology. These sciences made us gods in flesh. As above, so below. No difference aside from degrees… But the weakness, the jealousies, the things they did not foresee… Our godhood was torn from us, ripped from walls and hidden in the mud not by natural disaster, but by rank superstition of the stolen elect, beholden only to the bureaucratic fear of an enlightened human race and the freedom of that learning. Pearls before swine, kings to beggars… Echoes, echoes, and remnants remain, twisted into cautionary tales uttered by perverts, telling us now to fear the very same fruit that first gave us life, that is the only food we are meant to eat. These echoes remain, and in the hearing, we are lesser for it…"

The voice trailed off with a zigzagging reverberation, as if impacted by an outside interference, before returning again. "For I speak of gods and monsters, creation and eternal life and the destruction of both, the birth of stars and those things living inside them… I speak of the Truth of Truths, of the way and wherefores of all realities discovered by those cosmic entities that whisper secrets to those who refuse to live their lives deaf, dumb, and blind as worms. I speak of transcendence, liberation, and terrible paradise… And now, I await my replacement so the work and the message can continue. The book was stolen from us, the knowledge ripped from our minds, so it is up to us to rebuild the book, and relearn the knowledge… They tell me that the time of the awakening is at hand, and as such, the preparations have become more urgent than ever before—"

—Fssssshpop! And with that, the battery, the last life force of Max's shitty late model Dodge, blinked and died.

Max sat behind the wheel in total and utter silence, scarcely able to breathe, scarcely able to believe what he had just heard as his eyes rimmed with tears. It was as if a water balloon popped inside his brain, drenching his insides and leaving behind nothing but a newly scrubbed view of his destiny. His meaning. He felt reborn, dancing atop a hunger he never knew existed. No longer was he worried about reaching the coast. All he knew now was that he *had* to keep listening to this transmission, at whatever cost.

The increased strength of the signal just before the death of his ride meant that the tower—and most likely the source of the voice—was near. Max scrambled out of his car, intent on finding this strange person and learning more. This broken, impossibly enlightened man knew something, *believed* in something with every fiber of his tortured being, and Max had to figure out why.

Max was out of the car and running up the center of the highway, and soon discovered a weed-choked access road that led off from the main drag and up into the noxious wilds of the Nevada desert. Max's gaze followed what he surmised was the direction of the path up into the hill country, where he noticed a small red light floating in the higher elevations, like a disembodied eye keeping watch over the dead sand below.

Max looked back at his car, threw his keys into the darkness, and set out for the guiding red light that lurked somewhere out there, waiting for him.

Bony fingers of lightning crackled above, strobe-lighting the ominously shaped clouds. Max walked quickly, his path between lightning flashes barely illuminated by a waxing moon, hanging low and sallow over the ring of mountains gnawing the sky like the craggy molars of a monstrous exposed jawbone. His shoes crunched over shattered plates of volcanic stone, pushing out the noises of the desert that the quivering, hollow voice described. The hovering red light was getting closer, and so Max moved onward, continuing his tumbleweed journey by rootless foot. Once again, he found courage in forward motion, scant as it was. The meaning, the meaning…

After nearly an hour, Max spied a stand of stunted trees that seemed to coalesce out of the darkness on a ridge slightly above. As he neared, he could just make out a dilapidated shack squatting amid the gnarled timber, blasted ghostly white by decades, maybe centuries, of enduring the spite of the brutal Nevada sun, which seemed extra angry with this part of the world as if by result of an old and festering grudge. Every hundred yards or so, a rough hewn stone monolith of greenish gray stone—which didn't seem to originate from the surrounding hills, or anywhere on the continent, really—stood sentry, forming a wide, easy-to-miss circle around the circumference of the ridge.

Passing through the loose knit ring of stone, Max quickened his pace and approached the old shanty, which was built up atop an ancient foundation of crumbling adobe, like those found in the ruins of the cliff-face domiciles constructed by the mysteriously vanished Anasazi that Max had explored several years back while tumbling through New Mexico. Anchored by the clay foundation, random building materials were haphazardly pasted and lashed, to keep out the wind and sun and sporadic bouts of furious downpours that sought to wash away those godless things that made their home in the desert.

Max walked to the front door, leaned in close and listened. The faint, hollow voice that was now so familiar could be heard inside. Emboldened, Max tried the door, and found it unlocked. He opened it and pushed inward. The door creaked on protesting hinges and sat open, yellowish light spilling out into the night, momentarily blinding Max. The voice was louder. Nothing moved inside. Steeling his resolve, Max entered.

The small outer room was lit by several naked light bulbs that hung from the ceiling, buzzing with flies and beetles. The raw light cast harsh shadows on stacks of moldering newsprint, boxes of moth-eaten clothes, and various detritus that one would normally associate with a bunker existence. Canned food. Jugs of yellow liquid. A gas mask hanging from the barrel of a large bore sniping rifle. The voice was coming from a back room, sectioned off by a ratty curtain. Max walked through the maze of refuse and pushed back the drape, terrified and thrilled in equal measure to meet the intermediary of this message that had brought him from the known road into the weird wilderness.

Max found no one waiting beyond the curtain. Instead, he discovered a cramped yet deserted room hemmed in by high racks of notebooks and journals, facing a corner heaped with a precariously arranged amalgam of new and incredibly old radio equipment surrounding a makeshift broadcast booth. Analog modulators, reel-to-reel players, a turntable, magnetic cassette docks, CD ports, and a laptop, all wired together in the same haphazard fashion as the shack itself. A DIY broadcast station carved out of overstuffed shelving and countless stacks of yellowing paper.

The old iron office chair behind the microphone was empty. A digital recording was playing, continuing a pre-taped monologue transmitted out into the desert night, into Max's car, into countless other cars, and homes, and minds.

"And so," the recorded voice continued. "The work must go on, even here, at this broadcast station at Grimes Point, built here because here has always been, and shall ever remain, a doorway to what the Early Ones called Star Nation before moving on, what we call The Outer Places, and the Realm of the Elders, where all is nothing and nothing is all in this dance of divine illusion..."

As the voice continued, Max explored the room, picking through the reams of notebooks and folders, blowing off thick red dust that had settled everywhere, and reading a few lines of wildly advanced and esoteric learning—mind-bending formulae, non-Euclidean calculus, quantum physics, interlaced with blurbs of history and a shocking understanding of the universe and inter-dimensional travel. Max moved to the broadcast table where lay an open journal. Paging through it, he discovered bizarrely grouped information assembled into monologues, written out in a sort of movie script format, similar to the ones heard on the radio, similar to the one the voice was relaying at that very moment, which Max followed along with his finger:

"Upon receiving my assignment and arriving here, I spent some time alone among the rocks, discovering the promised doorway that I shall soon revisit for the final time..."

Max rifled through the notebooks and tapes around him, noticing dates that went back several hundred years. This was not just a broadcast booth, Max realized, but a library, a repository of arcane and antiquated knowledge off the scale of human imagination.

Stunned by the implications of what loomed around him, Max then noticed a line of several dozen framed photographs on the wall, of different people manning the microphone, sitting in that heavy chair, moving back through the ages, from color pictures to black and white to muddy sepia tone. Two dozen men and women of varying ages, races, and obvious social standing, all sitting in the same pose in front of the same microphone with the same grim expression and slightly unbalanced gleam in their eyes.

The most recent speaker continued his taped oration, as Max moved in closer and squinted at the last photo to the right, which showed a man not much older than him, staring haughtily into the camera of an unknown photographer, the instruments of transmission glowing behind him. "I felt as though I had passed into a pinhole poked through realty, taking me outside linear time and into the seething void... Grimes Point is a wrinkle in the fabric of this brittle plane, a carefully plotted and placed dimensional distortion allowing access to and from the Place of the Beginning, and the measureless vistas of the Continuing Chaos—a place forgotten or shunned throughout the course of human history. But a place that was also sought out, by those brave seekers who heeded not the fear... This is just one outpost, numbered six, and is one of many, where others like me continue the work to rebuild that which was stolen from us, a primal birthright ripped from our molecular memory. They took from us our knowledge, our book, but we will rebuild it, and again teach the truth through the written word, through the electronic ether, through the television and the radio waves... We seek to swing the wrong back to the right, through darkness and light, and ready the awaiting flock..."

The fly-spattered light bulbs flickered, and Max looked up, noticing perplexing lines and curves etched into the ceiling, surrounding what appeared to be several intricate, overlapping star maps. But, the maps didn't feature any of the known constellations, or none with which Max was familiar.

"I speak of what was whispered to me, through the sounds of the desert, of elder mathematics—the language of all creation, the root and the key of what we know as eldritch magic. That which sank R'lyeh, raised Atlantis, and built the sacred pyramids and other abandoned monuments to the Outer Gods across our crowded sphere..."

Max sank slowly into the stout broadcast chair and gazed wide eyed around the room, as if a sudden realization clicked in his head, giving confirmation to something he had always surmised but didn't dare believe, and rarely ventured to dream. West, ever west... Out into the Pacific... Fate or drown. Fate or drown...

Max's eyes bulged as he listened with every atom of his being, taking in the words as the voice went on to tell of the Outer Gods, who will come and take away those who know how to ask. About how he and others throughout history and prehistory and the dawn of sentient life were mere chroniclers of these impossibly old entities and their epic machinations, from drawings in the primordial clay, to paintings in caves, to those driven mad compiling the Dread Book, to now—transmitting the stories and knowledge into the atmosphere, then out past the charged particles of our finite space. All the same. All working in the same service. Those who chronicle and spread these revealed truths are members of the enlightened few, and are assured a place of exaltation beyond the stars, spared the coming reclamation of this tiny blue rock by the errant overseers who have seeded all of the living worlds in the dimensions of their influence.

The workers at Outpost Six at Grimes Point are the newest members of these few, collecting information imparted in purposely small, disassociated segments to keep the recorder sane for as long as humanly possible. These are the further writers of the Book of Knowledge, continuing the work of Alhazred, von Junzt, The Scribe of Eibon... Mason, Curwen, Carter, and Ward...these are the chroniclers of the Higher Wisdoms to prepare the Earth for the promised coming and the transformation, when the Old Masters return home to check on their children, their forgotten Petri dish prepped and left in a far flung corner of nowhere...

"This is what the desert told me," the voice continued, "and what I and others have recorded for decades, centuries, eons before our poorly-made vessels became too full and started to crack..."

Sitting in the chair with his eyes staring straight ahead while his mind began to venture several dimensions away, Max didn't see the bathroom just off the broadcast room, where a bloody razor and clumps of hastily shaved body hair clogged the sink. Max didn't see the trail of blood that led out the smashed back door, over the dusty yard, past the unnatural mounds and monoliths surrounding the property, and into the sand of the endless desert. Max didn't see the speaker of the voice, just hours before he arrived, standing on the brink of Grimes Point, and flinging himself down onto the curiously arranged rocks below. Max also didn't see the body of the man disappear into the void before it hit the craggy bottom, warping away to a swirling, unnamable infinitum of places unknowable, where he would join the roiling mass of omnipotent chaos that probed for a way back into our tiny plane of existence, settling in the meantime for psychic missives sent from the Beyond. Measured portions of the ultimate truth transmitted to our time, place, and space in hopes of teaching one of us the correct formula to open up the dimensional gaps dotting our universe just wide enough for something substantial to come through, to return to a place unvisited in a billion years, but never, ever forgotten.

Max didn't see these things, because he was sitting at the microphone—his new post at Outpost Six—taking in The Words in preparation for continuing The Work. The voice in the darkness had sliced open the forbidden fruit and offered a taste to Max. He took a reluctant bite, and was now changed forever—a doomed man enslaved by this terrible growing wisdom, joining all those curious souls who had been drawn to this place before him.

"So," the speaker in the picture, the speaker who dove into Grimes Point and into the boundless, structured abyss just hours earlier, concluded in his strange, hollow voice. "I leave this sacred burden to you who have found your way to this humble temple of the Outer Gods, the true rulers of this universe and many others, who have revealed themselves to those who were forced to forget... They are there, and They are waiting, watching, and whispering... Tend to your task with seriousness, and be mindful in your work, for the destruction and rebirth of all we know demands rigorous attention and strict vigilance…" The speaker's voice began to give, but he mustered enough strength to continue, if only to breathlessly croak: "Fare thee well… and worry not… for understanding beyond measure is nigh! A replacement draws forth, even now! Signing off…and bid this forgotten place goodbye…knowing that you are already on the doorstep…and the cycle…continues…"

The voice gave out and the transmission ended.

In the dead silence of the tiny shack, the noises of the desert began to creep in, as well as those softer, more terrible sounds that lurk underneath the normal nighttime din.

Max was listening.

MR. LUPUS

A straight razor scraped across soapy flesh, taking with it stubborn gray whiskers and leaving behind a slug trail of scarlet. Blood shot to the surface and dotted the patch of new skin. It was thin and bright. Certain fluids quickened while the rest of the machine slowed.

"Blast," the old man muttered, rinsing the blade under the faucet and holding a towel to his cheek. He fussed over the metal with his fingers, wiping off the blood and making sure it was sucked down the rusted drain in a spiral of water, taking it to God knows where, but hopefully far down river.

He blinked into the mirror as he worked, noticing the sag of his eyes that were once a dark, commanding brown but were now gauzy hazel, tinted with the jaundice of misspent age. His hair was wild, shooting sidewise in wisps of silvery white. A bird cackled strangely from the landing outside the bathroom window, and his mind drifted to thoughts of blood oranges and tropical flowers. The playful laughter of his wife as she reclined naked on a white chair set incongruously in the middle of a primal Malaysian jungle, unsullied by cartographers and the grim industrialists pulling their strings. How pale she looked amid all that exotic darkness, how like an untamed thing born out of the dripping milk of the moon. She was never like that, but here she was. Like that. And so was he. Naked. Savage. Adam and Eve, prancing through a hidden shard of unwritten Eden. They were to live forever there, together, before he lost her to the woods.

The man returned the cutting edge to his face and paused. He gazed at the entirety of his face, features he hadn't recognized for decades, and then moved the blade to his neck, lining it up with dozens of light scars running across his throat. He paused there for what felt like a second lifetime.

He set down the razor on the sink top and the old man shuffled into the hall, twisting off the electric light as he left. Fluttering wings beat against the bathroom window.

In a stuffy bedroom that smelled just as it looked, he sat heavily on the bed indented on only one side of the mattress and pulled up bright green stockings over sagging calves. He felt ridiculous, as he always did this time of year. A clown hawking treasures to monsters. Pearls before little pink piglets. The man slipped into stiff spat boots, purchased new for the season, buttoned them up tight, and rose to his feet. He stretched out his arms inside the garish peddler's frock and etched on a toothy smile. "Ta-da!"

Heavy heels clomped down the staircase, slowing as they made their way to the bottom. Casting aside a velvet drape, the old man emerged into a show room packed from floor to high ceiling with toys and novelties of every stripe, size, and level of handicraft. He moved through the store on the groove worn into the old floorboards, passing by hundreds of frozen eyes. Beautifully grotesque marionettes from the Carpathians and wind up monkeys from Siam held sentinel over animal skin drums from the Congo, music boxes from London, muslin dollies from Appalachia, popguns from Texas... He'd been all over the world finding his premium toys, and never came back empty handed, even when he brought back nothing to sell. He was a collector of souvenirs, after all.

The old man walked to the draped front window display arranged like a diorama of a centuries-old town populated by carolers, holiday revelers, and jumping dogs frozen in mid leap. A train track snaked through colonial homes with cramped windows and peaked gambrel roofs. The entire scene was dusted with artificial snow that appeared so realistic one often wondered if pools of water collected on the floor underneath. He flipped a toggle switch and the scene came alive. Singers swayed, dogs leapt, and a festive locomotive piloted by a rotund, waving, red-clad figure chugged around the town, emitting tiny puffs of ultra fine powder that served as smoke.

The man checked his pocket watch, took a deep breath, and pulled back the heavy blue curtains cloaking the display from the outside world. As suspected, he was greeted by two dozen fat little faces bunched together like eggs in a carton pressed against the glass. The fog of their hot, quick breath froze in pale circles.

He could hear the *oohs* and excited squeals from inside, and his blood jumped just a little. He hated children, yet loved them all the same. Especially the ones with negligent parents, and there were so many these days. The unbathed ones with uncombed hair and hidden bruises, who appreciated the attention afforded them during a private tour of the stock room because daddy died in the Moncrief mines or just ran off into the night in search of different flesh, leaving mommy with only the cup to keep her company. Male or female, fair or homely, complicit or "difficult"—it didn't matter. They all kept him fed, as every child ended up in his toy store eventually. It was the only one in town.

The man moved to an easel next to the window and flipped a placard from 5 to *4 Days 'Til Christmas.*" High-pitched cheers erupted from outside. He gritted his teeth and worked through the half dozen locks securing the front entrance. The massive oak door swung inward and he stepped grandly into the threshold, hands on hips, frigid morning air rushing past his viridian leggings to rob the coal in the basement. Above him hung a large wooden sign proclaiming *Leopold's Curios & Novelties* in proper Prussian lettering painted a bright, cheery yellow. Plumage.

"Good morning, Mr. Leopold," said a rosy cheeked woman holding her child by the collar of his jacket. His feet clattered for a propelling grip on the icy sidewalk. Mr. Leopold uttered a few convivial words while looking past her, to the dingy faced child standing all alone, playing hooky from school with thoughts of spending the day inside the warmth of Leopold's Curios & Novelties. The old man smiled his first genuine smile of the day.

Up and down the street, a chorus of bells arose from all corners of the mercantile district, buoying the rim of the rising sun as it attempted to push back the unnatural darkness billowing from a thousand smokestacks that had held sway over the sky for as far back as anyone could remember. These weren't the heavy peals of a pendulous clapper banging against a thousand pounds of grim, church sanctioned copper. This was the light ting of brass bells brought to life by the wave of a hand—the unmistakable sound of Christmas on the street.

Men in crisp red jackets with white piping appeared at every other street corner, smiling under their military style hats, ringing their bells and nodding politely to passersby. The metallic jangle rose, sank and overlapped, sometimes finding a rhythm inside each other, creating the impression of a tinkling chorus, a movement in the barren yet beautiful symphony written for the sprawling city that so very much needed it, as all cities do, no matter feast or famine.

This was a time of famine.

But Christmas knows no want, especially here under the watchful eye of the Moncriefs, and so lush holiday decorations hung from every street post, power line and storefront, framing the morning thoroughfares already packed with dead-eyed commuters and hopeful shoppers. Most were heading to unremarkable jobs in one of the endless industrialized office complexes standing sentry over the river's edge downtown. But some were clutching shopping bags and tiny mittened hands.

Lording over it all were three tall buildings, blocking the eastern view of the Fenris Mountains beyond the bend in the sluggish runnel. The center structure rose just above the other two, as if standing on its toes. These were the Moncrief Towers, which gave life and death to everything crawling down below.

The bells continued to chime, and the ants continued their march.

In the skylight suite of the middle tower, just below the layer of smog gifted to the city by his family, James Moncrief looked out the tinted glass window at the urban sprawl below, holding an unlit cigar in his left hand. His large blue eyes swam atop dark circles that perpetually seemed on the edge of tears. He heard no bells up this high, only expensive silence. On the walls around him hung the mounted heads of two-dozen wild and monstrous animals from various remote outposts of untamed wilderness. Elephant and rhino and a long necked giraffe that stretched up to the mosaic of constellations on the ceiling. A stuffed polar bear stood guard in one corner. A massive red wolf, captured mid lunge just before total extinction, bared its teeth in a murderous snarl next to carved double doors.

Behind him, a marginally pretty but utterly forgettable woman pulled up her stockings and hid the rips under her cheap, tight fitting dress, absently arranging her hair like a chastised little girl. The pale skin of her face was flushed, more so out of the slow creep of modesty than amorous exertion. It hadn't lasted long enough for that.

"Button me up, yeah?" she asked, her accent giving away a waft of the docks.

James said nothing. He could sense the bad fabric covering something cheaper within. He was disgusted for her, and doubly for himself and his venal weakness that continually brought him to such gutter depths this high up. The woman was about to say something when he spoke. He didn't want to hear her voice again.

"Ms. Talmidge will see to you."

As if on cue, the double doors opened, and a no-nonsense woman who seemed to live her life under a tight bun and neutral colors strode inside. Ms. Talmidge beckoned to the young woman with the harried manner of a school marm attending to a student and smoothed out the wrinkles on her jacket, licking her finger to dab at an opaque stain.

The woman smiled shyly at Ms. Talmidge, then addressed James without looking at him. "Give me a lift home?"

He hadn't moved from the window. "Mr. Barrows will take you where you need to go."

Ms. Talmidge shot a raised eyebrow at James' back. If he felt it, which he always did, he showed no sign.

"Come on, dearie. We'll take you out the back."

"The back," the girl murmured, pulling her collar tighter around the red finger marks on her neck. "Like a delivery of bread."

"Or discarded seafood," James said, putting the dead cigar into his mouth.

Ms. Talmidge handed the young woman her hat that was two seasons behind trend, fluffing up the goose feathers painted to look like ostrich. "How about we put on a smile, then?"

The woman took the hat and forced a sad grin, turning to the shadow in the window. "Goodbye, Mr. Moncrief," she mumbled, searching for something else to say. "Thank you."

James turned to her, leveling a cold stare. "Don't mention it."

The young woman did an awkward curtsy. Ms. Talmidge ushered her out into the hallway and to a waiting attendant, then returned to the room, closing the doors behind her. James was at his desk, poring over a stack of paperwork as if he had been deep in the books all morning. That famed Moncrief compartmentalization. She walked over and took the cigar from his hand and tossed it into the base of a nearby artificial banana tree. "You're not going to find what you're looking for by stealing the virtue of strangers."

"She wasn't strange to me," he said, not looking up. "I know her uncle, Mr. Briggs. Runs a textile concern over on Water Street."

"Her last name is Brixton," she said flatly.

"At least it started with a 'B'."

Ms. Talmidge sighed and crossed her arms. "Are you ready?"

"For what, exactly?"

"It's December 21st." No reaction from James. Her eyelids fluttered with irritation. "The fourth day before Christmas."

James' face soured as a realization struck him. He deflated in his high back chair that always made him look like a child. Behind him, a huge, Renaissance style portrait of a portly aristocrat smoking a cigar at the same desk overlooked the room. The man looked like James, only doubled in stature. "Is it that time again?"

"It is."

He tossed papers across his desk, scattering them like toys, although each cramped page held the fate of families, companies, Third World nations. "Such a ridiculous, antiquated notion, this Christmas."

"How rude of it to come around every year just to annoy you."

"One would think an evolved society would have grown out of it by now."

"People never grow out of Christmas."

"I did."

"Yes, well... You grew out of a lot of things." He looked at her evenly. She returned his gaze. "We go through this every year. Don't spoil the season for the rest of us, especially the children. It's a magical time, and people need it now more than ever."

He laughed. "I don't believe in magic."

"You don't believe in anything."

"I believe you're trying to get under my skin."

"I would if I thought there was anything underneath." Ms. Talmidge held out his bowler, her lips stretched into an impish grin. "I'd burrow deep, do a little redecorating."

James got to his feet and took his hat. "You specialize in handing hats to those on the way out."

"We all have our duties," she said, waiting in that insufferably patient way that always infuriated and comforted James in equal measure. "And our crosses to bear." Exhaling grandly, he threw open the doors and disappeared into the hall. She closed the doors behind them, a satisfied look on her face.

The tank-like Packard limousine barreled through the narrow streets powered by a dozen oversize pistons specially built to move 4,000 pounds at high speed with little regard for braking. High-walled melanoid tires ate up the cobblestone. Traffic and pedestrians gave way in deference or just fear of the Moncrief family crest on the move. Several bawdy women waved to the car, blowing out crude promises underneath the steam of their breath, either to garner attention or perhaps jog a memory of a brief tryst at the top of Towers. Everyone wanted a piece of James, the last remaining heir to the billionaire Moncriefs, but he gave them nothing, even as the machinery of his family gave them everything.

The limousine lurched to a violent stop in front of the Orpheus Theatre, and the waiting press corps dropped cigarettes and closed in like a cloaked swarm of hungry locusts. This was front-page meat for every paper up and down the river, pushing last night's knicker shot of the local tin heiress from the headlines. Camera flashes popped and crackled as James exited the back of the car. He blinked and waved, peeling back a megawatt smile to rival the exploding bulbs that always bothered his eyes. Reporters called out unintelligible questions as James nodded and focused on his grin, the steps in front of him leading up to the entrance to the Gothic structure. Hideous stone gargoyles leered past sword wielding angels to watch the scion of the Moncrief line trudge up the wide stone stairs. "Santa Moncrief!" a reporter bellowed from the depths of his jowls. Avuncular laughter erupted.

A child hopped up and down, pulling on his mother's cloak. "Is that Santa?" he asked with confused wonder.

"No lad," she said, her face drawn. "No it isn't." The little boy frowned.

Press and populace crammed quickly inside the auditorium, jostling for seats. Two sketch artists expertly captured the foundations of the scene in quick slashes of charcoal. Atop the stage hung a banner that read *The Moncrief Family's 73rd Annual Santa's Little Helper*. Below it was a single steel podium bristling with a dozen microphones, wires leading off the stage and into the darkness like wiry tentacles. The twin griffins of the Moncrief family crest stamped the front of the lectern.

James strode out from side stage shadows and mounted the dais, regarding the crowd with practiced ease. He cleared his throat and spoke in a voice denoting rote memorization more than actual conviction. "As is the Moncrief family tradition, every year in the week before Christmas, we select one letter written to Santa Claus and answer the wish contained inside. Santa might be great at his job, but the jolly old fellow needs a little helping hand every now and then, don't you think?" The crowd laughed as they always did at this part, a little too loudly, as everyone in attendance hoped to catch the eye of the man on stage and use any familiarity for future gain.

James held up a single letter. The eyes of the children in the front widened in unison, like tiny opening shades. "Just arrived from the North Pole," he said, blowing fake snow off of the envelope decorated with a blue fish scale pattern. "And the lucky letter writer this year is..." James squinted at the ornate calligraphy. "*Calliope*," he said at last, then smirked at the crowd, who laughed reactively. "Looks like we have a bit of a fancy lass." James chuckled to himself and slid a serrated silver letter opener across the seal, breaking through the red wax stamping. He removed the folded piece of delicate paper and glanced over it, noting the carefully painted artwork of fairies and butterflies dancing around Santa seated on a golden Egyptian throne. Jesus and the Hindu deity Shiva stood on either side of the jovial old man, a hand resting on each shoulder. "Ms. Calliope would like..." James read on, his brow furrowing. "She would like the end of sadness, and the return of snow... If that isn't possible this year, then she would like a pink unicorn."

The cavernous room went silent. James looked at Ms. Talmidge, who just shrugged. The quiet was eventually broken by a guffaw, which spread like a wave, undercut by the buzz of future headlines taking shape. James held up his hand and the assembly hushed. "Well, I uh..." James was at a loss. "Since we can't stop sadness, nor control the weather, we'll just have to get Ms. Calliope a unicorn."

Audience members looked at each other. Ms. Talmidge began to clap, and the gesture was quickly taken up and broadened into a roar of applause by the congregation.

The Packard crossed the Dismal River and roared east out of the city with a full police escort, followed by a Moncrief Stables horse trailer housing an albino Shetland pony procured from the city petting zoo, hastily painted a pale fuchsia, nearly matching its queer eyes. A portion of carefully fluted wooden lathe was affixed to its head with an industrial epoxy that would no doubt eat into the brain of the poor beast and kill it just after Christmas, well after the migration of the press corps, and, naturally, of Santa Moncrief. Two stable hands were seriously injured in the transformation, and thus paid handsomely to recuperate in silence at home, away from nosey cameras. Behind the trailer wound a caravan of media sedans. Bets were already being laid about how this would go down. The calamity crew had the odds. Either way, it was a header piece, and pocket flasks tipped in anticipation of top fold bylines.

Alone in the rear hold of the car, James looked sightlessly out the window as the suburban neighborhoods ringing the city like needy children abruptly gave way to the rowed nothingness of stubbly fields lying fallow for the winter. Miles clicked by as the Fenris Range grew in the distance. Wherever Calliope's family lived, it certainly wasn't municipal. Post offices outside the tax radius weren't dying fast enough, apparently.

They passed through the insular agricultural towns of Nithsdale and Lower Weed, where the rugged citizenry bound themselves in fashions of previous decades, and the cramped, low-slung buildings reflected a time much older than that. The industrial march of the Moncrief brand had yet to make it out this far into the rural areas, even though it had name recognition. James took mental note of this, plotting a new advertising campaign appealing to the rustics. He'd spin chaff into gold and build another tower.

A flock of chattering corvids passed over the sun, casting the route in shadow.

The road became rough as it rose into the sparsely populated hill country festooned with stands of aspen that looked like bleached bones buried into the ground, in the lea of the occulted mountains that hadn't seen snow since the Moncrief stacks began blowing progress into the stratosphere. James' mother came from this area, and once she was plucked from the brambles by Augustus Moncrief after a moderately successful boar hunt in the lowland forests ringing her village, she dusted off the hayseeds and never looked back, citing vague references to Sodom and Gomorrah and the wife of Lot. Odette Moncrief, nee Mabus, was a singularity amongst her rough rural tribe, with skin the consistency of cream and strikingly black eyes, framed by a cascade of auburn hair. She stood out from the ruddy skinned, light-eyed chattel of her kinfolk like a burning torch in a snowdrift, and was therefore accused of all manner of nefarious dealings after sunset. Jealously does twist the mind into surprising shapes. After more than a decade of private scrutiny and public shunning, Odette couldn't wait to flee to the city. James was certain she planned the seduction of his father well in advance – years, maybe – if only to escape for one night into the folds of velvet Society. Then again, intimately familiar with his mother's preternatural confidence and fabled sensuality, she must have known that her escape would be permanent after that initial night of lost honor. A small sacrifice to seize the iron crown. The dowdy Moncrief hens were brutal in their gossipy pecking. Odette absorbed the beaks and arrows, and then proceeded to bend them all in half, one by one. Country girl made Villain Queen, arched eyebrow and all. This was the stuff of fairy tales, if such childishness was true. She didn't even need to change the monogram on her dowry chest. O.M. Augustus was amused and allowed latitude, until he lost interest and moved on to new distractions, just before his mother did the same. Distraction coursed strongly in the Moncrief blood. James knew this only too well.

His parents had been gone three years now, moldering side by side in a marble mausoleum the size of an aircraft hanger; and while he didn't miss them, as the familial fire had gone cold years before, he often wondered about them as one would ponder dead icons. The ultra-famous he learned about from press releases and scandal sheets. Mostly, he wondered what his mother thought when she looked up into those mountains that she often warned him about after she dipped too deeply into the brandy. The truth always came out when she got into her cups… Strange fires burning on the high peaks every equinox. Black masses. Wolves that decimated traveler campsites. This was haunted country, and now James was heading right into the mouth of the nighted and strange. Down his mother's throat.

The car was abruptly enclosed in darkness as a high country coniferous forest converged around them, swallowing the trail of motorized drones. James wasn't superstitious, but shivered anyway. The wilderness was a lordless brute, and his inheritance held no sway this far out from the city.

After several more miles of piercing deeper into the eternity of trees, guided only by the increasingly narrowing road that disintegrated into a muddy logging trail, the Packard slowed to a crawl. The window separating the cab from the back dropped and Ms. Talmidge's austere face filled the void. "We're here," she said, holding up a yellowed map that looked like a museum prop.

James glanced out the windows, and saw two intersecting road signs, battered with age and the elements. The wooden slat on top read *County Route 7* in official albeit dated lettering. The directional below it was hand painted. *Mermaid Lane.* Erected along the road was a vine covered postbox, carved from wood in the shape of a buxom, topless woman with the tail of a fish, the mail slot a vertical cleft set just below her bellybutton.

"Bohemians," James sneered. "I guess that explains the envelope." The partition window rolled up with a hum of front seat disdain.

The car paused, contemplating the turn, then banked onto a long driveway marked by knee high brown grass only slightly lower than that carpeting the tunnel through the trees along the crude path. The caravan followed hesitantly, several of the smaller sedans swallowed under by the uncut brome. Cigarettes glowed from inside rolled up windows. The liquor had run dry, and the barracuda were getting restless inside their aquariums.

The trees thinned out and transformed the further they traveled up the track, allowing in the sun to dapple tiny spotlights on the approaching visitors.

Pines gave way to stout oaks and maples, and then an assortment of species not normally found in the area. Banyan and cypress tree commingled in spots, dropping venous roots into the unusually black soil. Every ten yards or so the path was guarded by a teapot baobab, looking like hulking brown casks with mad wires sprouting from their tops. Further back from the driveway, arranged like living sculptures, were pliant sycamores shaped as saplings into baskets and double helixes. Ladders leading up into nothingness. Dancing scarecrows. It was a surreal sight, this collection of growing oddities. A circus sideshow of exotic timber hidden away from its audience.

James almost didn't notice the clearing up ahead until the limo slowed to a stop, and the engine died. From the front he heard Ms. Talmidge gasp, and followed her gaze to the opening in the strangely arrayed forest, where loomed a most curious structure.

He exited the car and looked up in genuine wonder at what appeared to be a giant size replica of a gingerbread house rising three stories from the close-cropped grass, still green even in the dead of winter. Adornments painted to look like gumdrops and licorice decorated every joint and edge, while gable boards hung heavy with carvings of twirling bears and frolicking fairies. A series of clerestory windows grinned down at them from the jetty. Delicate baroque carvings rose above oxeye windows along the dormer, giving the impression of drooping, decadent eyelids. Natural salts leached from the stout foundation stones and chimney brick, crystallizing with a powdery efflorescence that looked like a coating of snow.

James moved forward, compelled, and found the grass spongy. He bent to touch the turf and discovered a thick thatch of moss covering the entirety of the clearing. Nothing was frozen here except for time and a decayed sense of storybook whimsy.

As the mutter and winding cameras of the disembarking press corps brought him back to the matter at hand, James realized that he had been holding his breath, and he inhaled deeply. The coarse pungence of the air was startling, tearing a hole in his cocoon of urban ennui with hints of an eternal spring. He could smell the earth, and the secrets that were buried there. He suddenly didn't care what sort of child awaited him, or if the tiny nag stood up as a unicorn. He was just glad to be here, and to know that such a place as this existed.

"Looks just like where I grew up," Ms. Talmidge said at his side with a smirk.

James seemed genuinely confused. "What do we do?"

"Well, unless you want to drop down the chimney like a proper Santa," she said, nodding toward the tufts of lazy white smoke escaping the chimney, "I'd say you knock on the door."

James mounted the granite porch slab and faced a stout oaken door fastened by ornate, paumelle hinges forged in brass. On either side, bubbled panes of stained glass swam with images of the smiling sun and frowning moon and other swirling planets and heavenly bodies that weren't familiar to him. A large onyx bird claw gripping a crystal orb served as the knocker. James lifted it and rapped twice. There was no answer. No sound of movement within. He looked at Ms. Talmidge, who just shrugged. He knocked again. Nothing. He tried the doorknob that was the cast iron head of a smiling pig. The door clicked and opened, swinging inward without a squeak.

The colored light entering the house under the high arched ceilings gave the impression of entering a church, as dust played in the red and yellow sunbeams. The sumptuous furnishings were overstuffed, embroidered in garish colors and stitched with strange glyphs. Two red stockings hung from the stout beam mantel of the great fireplace, which was flanked by a cozy, pillow-strewn inglenook looking out into the backyard, a kite winder staircase leading to the upper floors. A large, long dead Christmas tree decorated with the disparate trappings of every conceivable holiday loomed under the stairs. Multicolor glass bulbs mingled with antique wooden Easter bunnies, painted hearts, jack-o-lanterns, and four leaf clovers. More surprising still were the bookcases that covered every visible wall in the house, lined with thousands of well worn, ancient leather tomes stretching from floor to ceiling.

"Hello?" James's voice thudded off the comfortably stuffed acoustics. "I'm... here to see Calliope." He held up the letter, as if it would call forth his intended. Nothing stirred. The reporters peering inside from the front door had never been so quiet in the history of the medium.

A sound came from a back compartment. James strode through the arched entry and looked around the vast room, finding hundreds of homemade dollies arranged in various states of play and domestic chore around a canopy bed draped in pink silks and artificial vines in a recessed corner. But what gave James pause was the large silver cage that hung from a vaulted ceiling joist in the center of the room, equidistant from each wall. Roughly ten feet square, it contained a neatly bound bedroll topped by a circle of rope, a breadbox, and a tea set arranged on a tiny table. Freshly cut purple flowers wreathed the top. A little girl's playland inside a sparkling prison six feet off the ground.

Ms. Talmidge stood in the doorway, cocking an eye at the suspended cage. "What do you suppose *that's* for?" James wondered aloud.

"Sometimes it's better not to ask."

James emerged from the house and faced the reporters who were scattered about the property, as if forgetting the occasion. Some of them clowned around like school kids. The stable hand held onto the bridle connected to the sad-eyed pony, looking pathetic as the paint began to fade on its fur, streaking the pink with muddy brown.

"I guess nobody's home," James announced to the group.

"Are you a stranger?"

James jumped slightly, and looked up in the direction of the voice. In a mammoth cypress tree to the left of the house crouched a girl, perched on a branch like an owl, watching the confused collection below with large, curious eyes. She wore only a diaphanous white dressing gown, covered to the narrow waist by long tresses of raven hair descending with serpentine symmetry, occasionally braided with the same purple flowers that decorated the cage inside. Around her neck hung a simple brass key on a chain. She hopped to the central trunk, where just below her bare feet bulged an enormous knot resembling a trapped head, the branches serving as a horned diadem. Yellow eyes were painted on raised lumps, swirled with turquoise irises, protruding over an upturned crescent ridge colored bright red. It was a ghastly image. The girl and the face in the tree stared down at James, fixing two sets of large, unblinking eyes on the perplexed man.

"I, uh..." James fumbled.

The girl scuttled down the tree like a lizard, alighting on a lower bough, but still remaining at a cautious distance. "Grandmother says never talk to strangers." She looked at the group of men closing around her. "And so many," she said with quiet trepidation.

"No, I'm not a stranger. I'm... I was sent here to give you something."

"Really?" She hopped closer on her perch.

"Do you live here?" James cringed at the stupid question.

She laughed, a pure, musical sound. "Not here, silly goose." She swung from the branch, landing on the soft ground and stood in front of him. Closer up, she wasn't a girl, but a young woman, although her age was difficult to discern. Her skin was so pale it was almost translucent, making her large brown eyes all the darker. "I live in *there*." She pointed to the house. Before James could stumble out a reply, her gaze caught the tiny horse grazing by the jumble of parked cars. "*No*," she moaned, grabbing James by the arm. "Could it *be*?" She ran to the Shetland,

and reached out to touch it, but pulled back, afraid to break the spell. The press scrambled, grabbing cameras and pulling pencils from behind ears as they gathered around the scene they all skipped happy hour to cover.

The young woman closed her eyes and shook her head, loose ringlets undulating like a coil of beautiful serpents. "It can't... It just *can't*..." She popped open an eye. "Can it be?" She opened both eyes very wide. "A unicorn!" She jumped up and down and clapped as a triangulation of flash bulbs strobed her every movement, chopping it into slow motion fragments of unbridled joy. The flashes terrified her, and she yelped and ran behind a tree.

"What's wrong?" James asked, moving toward her.

"Why do they shoot lightning?" James turned around, confused. "Are they wizards? Agents of Zeus?"

James paused, thinking that she was jesting, but then laughed as he concluded that she wasn't. "It's okay. Just flash bulbs. For photography."

She poked her head out from behind the trunk. "Pho-*tos*? I've heard of this magic..."

James was befuddled. "Magic?"

She crept from the tree, gazing at the pony with disbelieving awe. "How did you know what I asked for?" A realization stole over her and froze her limbs. She turned to James. "Who are you?"

"I was going to ask you the same thing."

She held out her hand. "I'm Calliope."

James took hers in his. "*You're* Calliope, the little—the girl who wrote this letter?" He held up the envelope.

Calliope curtsied. "At your service, my liege. Was my penmanship acceptable? Our quills have grown frightfully dull, and pencils just wouldn't do."

James began to see the scene for what it was, and why this strange girl was just that. "No, it was... It was perfect."

"And you are?"

He fumbled a bit, as he couldn't remember the last time he was forced to introduce himself. "I'm James Moncrief... Santa's Little Helper."

She took a few steps backwards, awed by the proclamation. "You work for Lord Cringle..." She paused, raised her chin and screamed into the sky. "I knew it I knew it I knew it!" Ms. Talmidge stood next to James, bemused. "I *knew* I had been a good girl," Calliope continued, "and Santa would bring me exactly what I wanted!" Just then, she became still as sadness crept across her face. She looked up at the overcast sky again.

James bent to her. "What is it?"

"This means that my other wishes didn't come true."

James thought for a second, remembering the letter, then smiled. "We'll work on those for next year."

"The snow and everything?"

He nodded. "Absolutely."

"On your oath?" she asked, holding out her tiny fifth finger.

James took her delicate digit in his own pinkie, intertwining with hers.

"Say it," she entreated. "It won't come true if you don't."

"On my oath," James repeated with a conviction that surprised even him. Ms. Talmidge looked on in wonder—not at this strange, childlike girl, but the effect she was having on James, who seemed to soften around the edges, his shoulders melting away from around his neck, a new sort of smile dancing around his mouth.

She nodded. "I believe you," she whispered, so only he could hear. She turned to the group, her face brightening. "You all must come in. We haven't had visitors in such a spell. Our tea party will be the subject of song!"

The entire room was packed with bodies, sweating in the cramped space that swirled with exotically spiced incense smoke wafting from cast iron braziers hanging in the corners.

James and Ms. Talmidge sat across from Calliope. The press corps, to a man, awkwardly held dainty teacups, glancing at each other in disbelief. Several hid laughter behind their lapels. Some looked positively uneasy. The Shetland was tethered just outside an open window. It banged the clumsy horn against the wooden frame. Calliope giggled and swooned. "I just can't *believe* my present! Moons and stars! What a Yuletide this is going to be!"

"How old are you?" James asked. Ms. Talmidge shot him a look, which he ignored.

"Older than the tadpoles. Younger than the trees." She began to hum a curious, vaguely familiar tune.

James gauged her age at around twenty, although she could pass for far younger, depending on her expression, which were animated and mercurial. She was lean, almost wiry, but possessed of a softness in the curves of her tiny frame.

"Where are your parents?" inquired Ms. Talmidge.

Calliope shrugged. "Holding council with Buddha and Jesus and the Great Old Ones. Grandmother tended to me since I was a seedling."

"Is she here?"

"She disappeared two moons back. I do miss her so. Perhaps she's gathering herbs and mushrooms and got lost. Or checking on the Three Little Pigs. She forgets her way, sometimes." A dark cloud passed over her face, then she brightened. "But I'm a patient girl. She'll be along shortly."

"So you're all alone out here."

"Oh, I'm never alone, Mr. Moncrief. I have so many friends that look in on me from time to time."

James didn't like the sound of this, although he had no idea why.

A reporter leaned into the next room. "What's with the cage?"

Calliope's face became serious. "It's my safety place." The journalist shrugged and dumped a flask into his teacup.

"Safety from what?" James asked.

"From Mr. Lupus," she said, sipping her tea with a now slightly shaky hand.

James looked at Ms. Talmidge, who shrugged. Pencils danced over notepads. "Who's Mr. Lupus?" James said.

Calliope went pale, which seemed impossible with her coloring but happened all the same. She looked both ways, leaned forward and whispered. "He's the big, bad wolf."

A snort and several drunken giggles came from the back of the room.

Ms. Talmidge spoke up. "Did your grandmother know about this Mr. Lupus?"

"She most certainly did, Ms...."

"Talmidge."

"She most certainly did, Ms. Talmidge. She had the cage built when I was a wee one, after the night I got lost in the woods, hiring the kindly silversmiths who live beyond the mountain. When Mr. Lupus comes calling once a month, I'm to get inside the cage for a night and two days. He won't bother me any if I'm inside. It might seem dreary, but what a time I have in there," she said cheerily.

James just watched her as she delicately cut through a stack of crepe paper with tiny, rough-hewn shears, the tune she hummed escaping through partially opened lips. He was enchanted. She let out a little squeal and opened up the paper. A garland of connected elves holding hands, with two large figures on each end. "This one is you," she said, pointing to the front silhouette. "Leading the merry band." She smiled at James, who had never seen such an expression of untainted joy. It was beautiful, and difficult to endure. He looked down at his watch and stood.

Outside, Calliope walked the group to their car, hugging each member of the press before moving onto the next. Grizzled old men and young go-getters all stood silent and watched her go, exchanging glances of bewilderment and wonder, a sweeping singularity amid this hard-bitten crew. Hats were pushed up and heads shook. No one even lit up a smoke, preferring to wait until they had cleared this hidden pocket of unsullied mountain paradise.

Calliope made her way over to James and Ms. Talmidge, and hugged the older woman tightly. "Give your children my best," she whispered into her ear. Ms. Talmidge seemed momentarily shaken, something James had never seen before. She quickly got into the car, her face flushed. Calliope stood in front of James and took a deep, contented breath. "Mr. Moncrief... Please convey my deepest gratitude to your employer, and give him this for me." She handed him a note sealed with a wax stamp. She hugged James, and his eyes closed involuntarily. Her hair smelled like the first blush of spring, tinged with honeysuckle and the vitality of newly awakened life. James' head swam in a new sea he never knew existed. He wanted to drown.

"Farewell, Mr. Moncrief."

When James opened his eyes, she was almost back to the house. He had to steady himself against the car. Glancing down, a strange image from the tree line reflected in the window. He turned and saw three squatty, pink creatures standing at the rim of the clearing, mostly concealed by a tangle of underbrush. They had piggish faces and long snouts, and seemed to be staring at just him with their yellow, oddly human eyes. A shout caught in his throat as James looked for Calliope, who was tending to her "unicorn" by the house. She held up her hand, which was covered in pink paint. She looked back at James, who quickly got inside his car, glancing at the tree line as he did. It was empty.

The ride back to the city seemed to take longer, or shorter. James couldn't tell. All he knew was the last look Calliope gave him was that of a swatted puppy.

He broke the seal on the note and read the carefully painted wording in the dying sunlight that plummeted behind the mountain peaks:

"Reverend Claus, your dignitary is a truly fine gentleman. Please consider giving him a raise in wages. Warmly Yours, Calliope."

James put the paper to his nose, catching the vaguest hint of incense, and carefully refolded the note. He didn't see the face of Ms. Talmidge in the partition window the entire way home.

◎

After making a fruitless attempt at work, and dithering through a dozen social engagements, James broke by the dawn of the third day.

Less than an hour later, the Packard was retracing the route up through the hinterland hill country and into the mountains crawling with unnamable things that birthed old wives' tales and frightening urban legends like fraternal twins. Maybe those old wives didn't want their husbands to know about creatures such as Calliope.

The Shetland was washed of its pink paint and grazed free on the dense moss that made up the yard.

James bounded up the step and rapped on the door. There was no answer. He tried several times, and was about to find some other way of entry when he stopped. Calliope regarded him from a partially opened window to his right. Her face was unreadable, although the slight elevation of her dainty nose gave him a clue as to her present disposition.

"Calliope, I—"

"—You shirked."

"Pardon?"

"You shirked your duties, sir."

"I'm afraid I…"

She disappeared from the window. A moment later, the door flew open and Calliope marched outside, backing up James as she strode forward, her tiny hands clenched into fists.

"You are blessed with one of the most important jobs on this earth, and you absolutely *disregarded* your calling, putting in the bare minimum and trying to fool the children who look to Santa to make their dreams come true? Foul! Foul! You are a *foul* man, Mr. Moncrief!"

Scrambling backwards in the face of this wee ball of fury, James stumbled and fell to the ground. Calliope was advancing so determinedly, her momentum took over and she fell on top of him. Her angry face was inches from his. "You hurt my feelings."

"I-I'm sorry."

Calliope searched his eyes, probing deep inside. An electrified current snaked through him, finding the core, agitating the marrow of his bones. She was so light on top of him, although the various curves and soft spots particular to women did register as they made contact. It felt as if her eyes extracted from inside James, and she blinked. He exhaled.

"I do believe that you are."

She rose to her feet and held out a hand. He took it and she helped with up with surprising ballast for someone so small. "I can't imagine that Santa knows about this."

James found his opening. Being raised in a pool of gladhanding sharks grows one a certain instinct.

"He doesn't, as a matter of fact. Which is why I'm here. I need you..." he trailed off, unable to go on. Expectant suspicion creased her immaculate brow, as she waited for him to continue. "I need you to help me find the unicorn."

Her expression darkened.

"The real one."

Excitement smoothed her expression, and her dark eyes once again danced to life. "A quest?"

"A quest, indeed." James felt like he was dictating a fairy tale in which he was a character. He warmed to it. His nannies read him the same books that lined Calliope's shelves.

"Like *A Thousand and One Nights*! *The Odyssey*!"

"It's nearly Christmas, and I can't leave my task unfinished. I failed in my search, so I cheated, and for that I deeply apologize. Now I need your help. I'll lose my job if you don't."

Calliope turned and stared off into the forest at the spot where James thought he saw those three horrid swine squatting in the underbrush. "I need to wait for Grandmother."

"We'll just be away for a day. Maybe two."

Calliope fidgeted, pulling at her sleeves.

James walked to her and took her by the hands. They were moist, warm. "We'll have you back very soon."

"In two shakes of a lamb's tail?"

"Maybe in one." He smiled.

She forced a small grin and ran into the house.

James caught up to Calliope as she padded into the back room, past the shadow of the hanging cage, and drew back a sash. A blackboard was sunk into the wall, on which a moon was drawn in chalk, allowing for waxing and waning to be filled in manually to chart the progression of the night. The white ecliptic was nearly complete, with three empty thin striations cutting the remainder of the circumference.

"I must be back home in two days."

"You will be."

"I have to be inside the safe place before the full moon."

"And so you shall." She looked at him. "I promise," James said.

Her face fell. "Just like the unicorn."

"This is different. This is your life. This has nothing to do with my job. And our quest."

She smiled. "I'm sorry for what I said before. You're not a foul man, Mr. Moncrief. I can see that now."

"Then you'll come back with me?"

"Yes, I do believe that I will."

James clapped his hands in jubilation. Calliope joined him.

Calliope exited the house, wrapped in a brilliant white fur draped to her ankles, brushing against her bare feet. James followed, hoisting a timeworn steamer trunk over his back. As a Moncrief, he wasn't accustomed to stooping his shoulder under such a task, but considering the circumstance, he took to it with zeal, following the petite green footprints left in the frost covering the mossy ground. A quest...

Calliope arrived at the waiting limousine and the waiting Mr. Barrows, a giant of a man who buried his expression inside a thick moustache, heavy brow, and deep-set eyes. Calliope looked up at Mr. Barrows, then to the black car coated in a fine layer of reddish dust.

"And you are, sir?"

"This is Mr. Barrows," James said. "He's my driver."

"A noble profession, goodman Barrows. Every prince and princess needs a carriage driver. I do hope that you have one someday, and your little princes and princesses as well."

Mr. Barrows opened the door for Calliope, who curtsied and peered in at the dark cavernous back compartment. "Where are we going?" she said, almost as an afterthought as James huffed to the car, setting down the trunk with a thud.

"To the city."

Calliope's face froze as she turned to James. "The *city*?! I cannot go to the city, Mr. Moncrief! I absolutely *cannot*!"

"What? I don't—"

She spun around, eyes filled with terror, her voice dropping to a choked whisper. "Mr. Lupus lives there." James crossed his arms, pondering this. "Grandmother said I was to never, *ever* go to the city, as that is where Mr. Lupus makes his home."

"You needn't be worried," James said. "We have Mr. Barrows." She was confused. "I fear Mr. Lupus as well, you see," he confided.

"You do?"

"Of course. Everyone does. Which is why I hired Mr. Barrows. He's undergone certain… *arcane* training to guard against such creatures." James glanced at his driver, whose expression didn't budge.

She looked again at the giant man, his massive shoulders and tree trunk arms bulging beneath his fine suit. "He'll protect me?"

James stood next to his man and crossed his arms. A cub leaning against a boar grizzly. "We both will. And besides, I live in a cage of my own."

"Is that so?"

James nodded and smiled. "Stretches all the way to the clouds. You'll see. It's quite stout, and provides plenty of room for tea parties."

Calliope worked through all of this in her head, her face a swirl of emotion. "Santa does provide strange accommodations for his workers," she said to herself.

Before she could take the next mental step, James nodded at Mr. Barrows, who opened the door. James held out his hand to the girl. "Shall we?"

Calliope looked from Mr. Barrows, to James, to the house, and back to the car. She nodded ever so slightly. "To the quest."

And with that, she took James by the hand, and he helped her into the car. She sat stiffly on the seat as James sat next to her. "This contraption is safe?"

"One hundred percent bullet proof."

Calliope didn't understand. James laughed as Mr. Barrows closed the door. "To the towers, Mr. Barrows."

The entire way back to the city, Calliope sat next to the door, often putting her head out the window like a jubilant puppy, taking in the sights and scents of a land that slowly evolved from its natural state to that reshaped by industrialized man. Passing tractors terrified her, tilled fields filled her with curiosity. She marveled at the villages and bridges, wondering aloud about hiding trolls, and was audibly confounded by the preponderance of so many people as they moved into the suburbs. During it all, she kept up a constant chatter, as her every excited thought leaked out of her mouth.

James sat back in astonishment, quickly learning that her entire worldview came exclusively from the pages of archaic children's books, spoken fables, nursery rhymes, and religious books, both orthodox and occult. It was extraordinary. He was bearing witness to an unsullied brain newly born into a spent, cynical civilization. Sitting with her in the back of a two-ton horseless carriage, James was allowed, for the first time in his life, to see the world through unjaded eyes, and the effect was intoxicating.

Before he knew it, they were pulling up to Moncrief Towers. Calliope hid on the floor, refusing to look up at the skyscrapers. James laughed while quietly cursing the end of the ride, knowing that he would now have to share this rare find with the machine that was waiting for them.

The first cog stood in front of the entrance in the form of Ms. Talmidge, tapping her foot on the pavement as a way to vent the aggravation that came as close to rage as she'd allow. James had gone missing that morning, and was hard to track down the two days prior, ghosting through his schedule and disappearing for hours on end. Ms. Talmidge has been tasked with keeping James on the path set a dozen generations prior. Erratic behavior from a Moncrief never turned out well, and often led to disastrous consequences. James was being impossibly erratic, and she feared it would only spiral as he hopped from the back of the Packard, leading by the hand that peculiar girl they found in the wilderness.

"I'm taking the rest of the week off," James said. "And you are, too."

"You don't take days off," Ms. Talmidge countered, looking Calliope up and down.

"I do now."

Ms. Talmidge was at a loss for words, which startled her.

"Where's your Christmas spirit?" James winked. She sputtered. "Ms. Talmidge..." James put his hand on her shoulder. "Bonnie..." He had never uttered her first name. No one did. Not even she, in her most private of thoughts. "I won't be needing you for a while." He kissed her on the cheek. "Merry Christmas."

James held out his hand to Calliope, who smiled sweetly at her. "Merry Christmas, madame governess."

Left alone on the sidewalk, the madame governess stood for a long while. The limousine was gone, replaced by the ringing of bells. Then Ms. Talmidge began to walk. She wasn't sure if it was the right way home. She couldn't remember anymore.

At the far end of the lobby, James stood inside the elevator car next to the boyish attendant, who held open the doors, trying to look inconspicuous but clearly fascinated with the situation. James was trying to coax Calliope, who stood just outside, anxiously twisting her hair. "It's a levitating box," he said. "It floats to the top."

"Magic?"

"With a mechanized edge. My grandfather helped invent this thing. Made a fortune. Made a lot of elevators, too."

"Will you ask him if it's safe?"

James looked to the ceiling, mumbled, and smiled. "He promises."

Calliope nodded, took a deep breath, and stepped into the elevator. The attendant allowed the doors to close. James handed him a key, which unlocked a metal latch revealing a blank ivory button. The attendant pressed it and the trio began to swiftly climb.

The elevator doors opened at the top floor penthouse. Calliope was crouched down, holding onto James' leg. He pressed a fold of cash into the young man's hand. "The savvy forget." The attendant nodded, mouthing the phrase he had heard so many times before. The doors met, and they were alone.

The elevator shaft served as the center point of the huge, domed loft that was James' living quarters. It was lightly but expensively furnished, owned mostly by vaulted space lined with iron rib supports, but the appointments that did exist were conspicuous and comfortable. No art decorated the dark walls, which pushed all eyes to the far end of the room made entirely of glass. The Moncriefs, young and old and long since decayed, couldn't hide their hereditary obsession with looking down from their gray towers, as a reminder of where they began, and where they now stood.

Calliope crept hesitantly toward the arched windows like a seeker approaching the edge of the abyss. The layer of smog blanketing the city looked ghostly and beautiful just under the burgeoning moon.

"We're walking among the clouds..." She whispered, testing the textured rug with her dainty toes, then turned to James. "You live on Olympus."

James laughed and poured himself a drink from a crystal decanter at the free standing bar. "Nothing quite so divine. Care for a drink?"

"Milk, please."

James paused, scratching at his jaw. "I'll have to order up."

Calliope removed her fur wrap and arranged it into a little nest on the enormous antique chesterfield anchoring the sitting area. She curled up cross-legged and gazed around her, soaking up all the newness with her fathomless eyes. James sat opposite in a wing back chair and just watched. After several minutes, she began to speak, asking an endless string of questions that James was only too eager to answer. He felt like an ambassador, or a well-traveled uncle, or something far different. He wasn't sure. Calliope disjointed him, fracturing something deep inside that he knew would never heal nor allow him to return to the blasé status quo. He wasn't accustomed to being uncertain; but with her, he questioned everything about himself, and by increments the reality around him.

And so they spent the entire night this way, until the sun crept over the mountains of her discovery, where she was hidden away for years amid the irregular trees that weren't supposed to grow there.

After many hours, she put her hands to her head, complaining that it was too full. James poured her another warm milk and another brandy for himself. Calliope sat quietly then, pondering so many new mysteries, until sleep seized her like a spell. Bidding him a good night, she curled up into a ball like a pale fawn, looking one last time out the wall of glass that caught the top edge of the rising ball of cosmic fire. "It can't be so bad... We both have the same sun," she murmured, before drifting off to sleep.

James drained his glass and tried to remember his meeting schedule for tomorrow, but coldn't. A slow weariness crept over him, but he didn't want to close his eyes, fearing that this was all a waking reverie, and she would evaporate into the nothingness like a beautiful specter of a forgotten dream. Her breathing became even, and he could smell her stirring bouquet from across the room. It was the fragrance of honeysuckle.

The next morning, Ms. Talmidge found James' office empty, and the door to his penthouse locked. Neither of these things had ever happened in the past. She paced the floor for what seemed like several hours, every so often stealing a glance at the two robin's egg blue teacups spider webbed with gold resting on the otherwise empty desk.

She stopped and looked at herself in the indistinct reflection in the tinted windows, unconsciously bringing her hand to the bun in her hair streaked with poorly concealed gray. She didn't recognize this lusterless person she saw, this aging woman of unerring practicality. Turning on her now conspicuously sensible heels, Ms. Talmidge decided to go home for the holidays, and possibly longer. Not to her deserted apartment a few blocks down, secured two decades ago to provide quick access to the job that was to become her life and surrogate pedigree, but to her parents' cramped cottage on the outskirts of the rundown western suburbs. She had grown weary of cold, echoing spaces, and felt a keen craving for confinement. She thought about her nieces and nephews, and the viability of her forgotten womb. The Moncrief seal that covered too much of her insides and the stiff world around her would have to be removed by the marvels of modern medicine. She had wanted to be a doctor once.

Ms. Talmidge left the office, avoiding the searing gaze of Augustus high above. She left the double doors open and disappeared into the hall, wondering if she'd ever return to close them. By the time she reached the elevator, she knew the answer.

James and Calliope walked down the sidewalk in the city center, the pedestrian herd parting like winter wheat as recognition spread up and down the block. Parallel to them in the street, Mr. Barrows kept pace in the Packard, an imposing arm hanging out the window.

Calliope cautiously ate an ice cream, nearly squealing with every lick. As she passed each street corner, she would drop coins and bills into the tin buckets held by the bell ringing Samaritans clad in their pressed red uniforms.

James strode just behind her, allowing a view of her mesmerizing movements and reactions to this crowded new world.

She stopped, lowering her eyes, allowing the white liquid to streak down her tiny hand.

"What is it?" James asked.

"Everyone is staring."

"The city does love a new showpiece."

"The city disquiets me, and I keep wondering…" She trailed off, peering down alleys, as if expecting something to be waiting there.

"We'll have you home soon, my dear."

"'*My dear*'…" She blushed, looking down at her bare feet peeking out of her newly purchased and specially tailored cocktail gown. "You overstep your position, Mr. Moncrief."

James paused just slightly, coughing. "I never was possessed of much dexterity."

Calliope smiled coyly. "Yet you are artful all the same."

James was about to reply with a hastily cobbled together witticism, when her cone splattered on the cobblestones. She brought her sticky had to her mouth and gasped as James followed her line of sight to the shop window. In it stood a plush stuffed unicorn. Calliope crept towards the window, as if not wanting to spook the mythical animal.

"Is this a deception, like before?"

"It doesn't appear to be."

She moved even closer, increasingly aware that she wouldn't scare it away. Her voice dropped to a whisper. "Is it dead?"

"It never lived. It's a toy, Calliope."

She moved her hand toward the window. "Can I touch it?"

"You can do more than that." James opened the door to *Leopold's Curios & Novelties*. "Shall we?"

She narrowed her almond eyes. "Did you arrange this?"

"I wish I could take credit, but alas..."

Inside the shop, James took the unicorn from the display and set it down in front of Calliope, who touched the toy's nose and began cooing to it in a strange language he couldn't understand.

"I'll fetch the shopkeeper," James said, heading deeper into the store, when her voice stopped him.

"Mr. Moncrief." James turned back to Calliope, who smiled. "Thank you for answering my letter. Your employer will be most pleased... as am I."

James returned her smile. "Thank you for being patient."

Calliope turned back to her unicorn, speaking to it like a child does to her dolly when playing the game of mother and baby.

James moved around groups of children and their mothers, trying to look inconspicuous but attracting whispers and points as he passed. The array of odd toys lining the shelves seemed more ghoulish than playful the further he walked. After reaching several dead ends, he retraced his steps and returned to the front of the store, but Calliope was nowhere to be found. Panic quickened his blood. He rushed through several aisles, finding her, standing prone against a line of wide-eyed hula dolls. An old man was squatted in front of her, pressing the stuffed unicorn into her midsection, the horn angling down between her legs.

"Calliope, come to me."

She turned and walked quickly into James' arms, putting her mouth to his ear. "I know this man... I've smelled him before." Her eyes communicated a name to his brain that her mouth needn't utter.

"Mr...." James began, turning to the shopkeeper.

"Leopold," the old man announced, holding out a hand. James noticed that his nails were long and yellowed. A sallow band of gold choked his ring finger on his left hand. Mr. Leopold looked at Calliope, his nostrils flaring, as if unconsciously taking in scent. "Your daughter is a very curious girl."

"She's not my daughter."

"Oh?" Mr. Leopold's interested tone hung in the air. He smirked, oily lips pulled tight over graying gums. "So young…"

James bristled, then fell back on furious pride. "Do you know who I am, old man?"

Mr. Leopold squinted, cleaned his glasses, squinted again. He went pale. "Mr. Moncrief, I-I'm so very dreadfully sorry."

"I want to leave," Calliope said quietly.

"Not until we get the unicorn."

Calliope ran from James' side and out the front door. James snatched the stuffed animal from Mr. Leopold's hands and leaned into his face. "Bill me."

James burst from the store and looked both ways. Down the street to his left, several people stood and pointed behind them with worry. He ran in that direction, calling out her name.

After bumping through the crowd and knocking over an elderly man who cursed him as he hit the street, James spied Calliope, and caught up to her moments later, grabbing her by the shoulders and spinning her around. "Why are you running? What's wrong?"

"I want to go home! I want to go home!" she cried, pulling away from him.

"I don't—"

"—I told you I've smelled him before. Every month. That smell. He's Mr. Lupus. You took me right to him."

"But how? You said Mr. Lupus was a wolf."

"Don't you know? The wolves wear the skins of humans to hide, until the full moon compels them to strip down and hunt! He said that he knew me, that he knew everything about me and would teach me…" She shuddered and wrapped her arms around herself. "We must flee this place and never come back."

James' mind raced. "Okay, we have another day. We'll leave first thing tomorrow morning. I'll go with you. I'll *stay* with you, until your grandmother returns. We can shut down operations for the holidays."

"No, it must be tonight!"

"I can't leave tonight. I have something I must attend to, arrangements to be made. Tomorrow. We'll take you home tomorrow. On my oath."

Calliope was about to say something, as was James, but both fell silent. When Calliope spoke, her voice had been stolen of its music. "Very well. Tomorrow it will be."

◎

Back at the loft, Calliope was curled up inside her fur on the floor, facing away from the view, as she had seen enough of this new world from the top of Olympus. No amount of persuasion would get her to rest on the couch, or his bed across the room. The windows were black, and no moon cut through the thick clouds, billowing in extra measure to feed the demands of the season. A sprinkling of white ash from the chugging potash factory upriver dusted the glass, carried down to the city by a cold northern wind.

"Look," James said. "It's snowing." He pressed his fingers against the window, as if he could touch it. He dipped his lie in white, hoping to make her happy. "That's two from your list. Now, if we could just work on…"

He turned to look at Calliope, but she was already asleep. He placed a glass of warmed milk next to her, and covered up her bare, ivory shoulder with the fur. He leaned down to kiss her on the head, but stopped and straightened.

Minutes later, dressed in a simple merchant's cap and plain woolen jacket, he picked up a leather bag, the contents of which clanged slightly as he hoisted it over his shoulder, and quietly left the loft.

James exited the towers out the back entrance like so many shameful secrets before and moved up the wide alley filled with refuse and the skittering of rats. Emerging on the main street several blocks down, he looked back at the main entrance, where the Packard was parked, waiting for orders. James imagined Mr. Barrows sitting inside as he always was, and wondered when the man slept, and with whom. As with Ms. Talmidge, whom he had avoided all day, he couldn't remember a time when he didn't know Mr. Barrows, yet at the same time knew absolutely nothing about him. James wouldn't need a ride tonight.

He lifted the wide collar on his jacket tight to his face and headed off into the darkness on foot, the limousine growing smaller and formless behind him. The bells in the street were silent.

◎

Just before dawn, James stealthily re-entered the loft. He was without his hat and jacket, and the bag hung heavier in his hand. His eyes were bloodshot and wider than normal, casting suspiciously around the room. He moved gingerly to the living area, making sure that Calliope was still sleeping on the floor. He saw her small shape wrapped underneath the fur, and breathed a shaky sigh of relief.

He placed the bag just outside the partitioned washroom, and drew himself a bath, cranking the hot water that steamed out of the faucet. James disrobed slowly, as if in pain. His forearms were scratched, and the blue smudge of a new bruise crept along his back. He lowered himself into the scalding water and bit his lip to keep from screaming.

James emerged from the bathroom as the sky lightened outside the windows, wearing a white robe. He was coiffed and scrubbed, but the new look that fired his eyes remained undiminished.

He went to Calliope and stood over the lump under the fur, noticing that it wasn't rising and falling with the gentle breath of slumber. Worried, he quickly unwrapped the fur and found the stuffed unicorn staring up at him with lifeless eyes above a blank smile.

Hastily dressed and untucked, James ran from the front entrance of the towers, holding the bag while still sliding on his shoes. The sidewalks were empty, as were the streets. The limousine, and Mr. Barrows, were gone. James shook with frustration, anxiety, pacing back and forth in short bursts. Just then, a lone jalopy, back seat stacked with newly printed newspapers, turned the corner and creaked toward him. James darted out into the street and stood in front of the car, which ground to a prolonged, raspy stop on weathered brakes. He rushed to the driver's side window and grabbed at the man behind the wheel.

"I need your car."

"So do I." The man spat chewing tobacco out the window, his gaunt face showing more curiosity than fear

"How much do you want for it?"

"How much you got?"

James fished into his pockets. "Do you know who I am?"

"I certainly do," the man said with the cock of an eyebrow as unfolded bills began to collect in James' hand.

The car chugged off up the street as fast as its tired engine would take it, leaving the man standing tall on the curb. He tossed back a fine Moncrief scarf, waving a hand decorated at the wrist with the finest timepiece in the city. "Merry Christmas!"

With the city hunched under its permanent cloud cover far behind, the old rattletrap wheezed up the climbing country roads into the hill country. What

took them a few hours just days before was now taking him most of the day. He felt like he was crawling across the dirt on the back of a beetle. Seeking to lighten the load, James tossed newspapers out the window with his free hand, leaving a trail of fluttering pages dancing in the morning breeze like a loose flock of clumsy birds. He didn't seem to gain any speed at all.

James gritted his teeth as he ground the clutch, trying to squeeze every last bit of power out of the overheated engine that outlived its generation. Smoke began to waft from under the dented hood, but he didn't ease up. He'd ride this nag dead to the ground.

A few miles out from the long, overgrown driveway he yearned to reach, the car seized and died. James slammed the door so hard it broke free from its frame. He buttoned up his jacket, picked up the bag he brought from this loft, and ran up the narrow track as the car sparked into slow flames behind him. Burning oil and consumed metal shot pitch into the graying sky. The day was dying, giving way to the time of the moon. Everywhere the Moncriefs went, they brought smoke and fire and annihilation with them. James was no exception.

He ran for what seemed like days. Unaccustomed to such physical exertion, he heaved and stumbled in his slick bottomed shoes, concentrating on keeping his legs churning, moving forward, moving upward. Explosions of white shot across James' eyes, only angering him further, feeding the inferno that sustained him. Smoke and fire. The quest…

Rounding a bend that somehow looked familiar, James noticed a collection of crows and buzzards squawking in the trees above a small glade just off the road. Dozens more were fussing over a large shape propped up against a massive uprooted tree, partially burned in the fallen leaves and pine needles. The blood froze in James' veins. Calliope…Mr. Barrows…

James dashed off the road and clambered over fallen logs, trying to push the image of a gargantuan hand closing around a wan, fragile neck. He dove through brambles and battled back the huge black birds that cawed and shrieked at the wild-eyed intruder. James bent to the corpse, and let out a shout of relief when he discovered that it was someone who had obviously been dead for a few weeks. Maybe a month. The meat of the face was chewed off and the eyes long since plucked. Stringy strands of long white hair were left untouched, like a stylized wig adorning a partially skinned skeleton dressed mockingly in an old fashioned black dress, as if a prop for All Hallow's Eve. It was the body of a woman, but an elderly one, and only half, as the lower portion of the corpse under the ribs had been completely removed. The right hand was devoured to the wrist, the left was shriveled into a claw. Dangling from one of the remaining fingers was a ring stamped with the image of a mermaid.

James, in his exhausted delirium, rose mutely to his feet, grabbed the bag, and returned to the trail. His mind pulsed as quickly as his heart. The sun was nearly down.

An hour later, James had to nearly crawl up the driveway, tamped down by the recent creep of wide, luxury tires. His body was giving out on him, but what lived below it wouldn't allow him to stop. He saw Augustus scowling down at him and dipped into another hidden reserve. Almost there...

He broke into the clearing, and found the Packard parked on the edge of the mossy yard. Mr. Barrows stood with his back to him, facing the house. A faint and flickering light filled the windows. The bizarre trees around the property seemed closer somehow, leaning in and holding their breath amid the deathly quiet. The yellow staring eyes from the knotted trunk burned through the dusk to watch this stumbling new arrival.

James staggered his way to Mr. Barrows, heaving and gulping for breath. He grabbed the larger man by the shoulder and tried to turn him. He was un-successful, so he angled in front of him, finding it difficult to look imposing on legs turned to jelly.

"Why...did you...bring her back here?" James gasped.

"Why did you take her from here?" Mr. Barrows's voice was a rumbling baritone. James took a step back. "She doesn't belong with us." Mr. Barrows leaned forward and allowed James a look into his usually hidden, deep-set black eyes that glared at him balefully. "She doesn't belong with *you*."

James fell back toward the house, searching through the branches for the moon. Mr. Barrows crossed his arms but didn't pursue. James spun and entered the front door, closing and locking it behind him.

The entire dwelling was lit with black guttering candles that he hadn't noticed before, casting everything in leaping, threatening shadows. As James walked to the back room, a rhythmic sound from outside stopped him. For a mo-ment, he only heard the pounding of his own heart in his ears, made louder inside this thickly silent place. Then nothing. The creak of a metal chain deeper in the structure brought him back to action, and he ran to the back room, where he dis-covered Calliope crouched inside the suspended cage, arranging her belongings with rote efficiency, mumbling to herself in that strange, inscrutable language.

"Calliope!"

Shaken from her trance, she spun toward him like a frightened animal, not recognizing him at first. She whimpered and backed up into the corner, cowering at the sterling bars.

"Calliope, it's me. Mr.— It's James."

"James?" Neither the name nor the face seemed to penetrate her fog of fear.

"Let me in. I have something to tell you."

She struggled to remember. "I know you…"

"Yes, you do. I'm Mr. Moncrief, from Olympus. Remember?"

"Yes, Mr. Moncrief… Walking in the sky."

He stood below the cage. "Please allow me inside. I have such news for you."

Calliope peered down at him for several moments, as the mist drained from her eyes. She smiled shyly, stood, and walked to the cage door. Taking the key from under her blouse, she leaned in close and unlocked it. "Hurry," she warned, fastening the rope from her bedroll to a clip on the doorframe and lowering it to the floor.

James slung the bag over his shoulder, gripped the rope and climbed up with difficulty, the squared enclosure swaying under his weight and struggle, iron chain links protesting above. He pulled himself into the cage. Calliope retrieved the rope, shut the door and locked it, concealing the dangling key under her top.

James sat back, resting his legs for the first time in hours. "I need to tell you something. Two things, actually. One bad, and one very, very good."

Calliope was still suspicious, and narrowed her eyes. "Bad first."

James took a deep breath and nodded, deciding how to continue. "I found your grandmother."

She gasped and put her hands to her mouth. "I don't believe you."

James set the mermaid ring on the table. Calliope took one look at it and screamed with delight. "You *did* find her! How can that possibly be *bad*? What did she say? Where has she been?"

"I discovered her in the woods."

"How wonderful! Is she okay? Did she ask about me?"

"No, I'm afraid she didn't."

Calliope looked around frantically. "Where is she? *Grandmother!*" she called out to the gloom. "Grandmother, I'm in the Safety Place, like I'm supposed to! Where are you?" Hearing nothing and becoming confused, Calliope looked at James. "Where is she?"

"She's…" He squeezed her hand. "She met with Mr. Lupus." James' grimace brought Calliope to her knees with a tortured sob.

"No. No!" She wailed through her tears. "Gods *damn* the beast! Gods damn the beast to the Outer Gates!"

"But I met with him, too."

She turned to him, eyes red and tears streaking her face. "You...what?"

"I killed Mr. Lupus." He unzipped the bag and pulled out the matted, blood smeared head of Mr. Leopold and placed it on the dainty tea table. Deflated eyes leaked from their sockets, a fattened tongue pressed between missing teeth. James placed the serrated letter opener that once opened her letter next to the head and sat back. "I stole his life with silver."

She stammered, forcing the words through her mouth. "Y-Y-You... W-When?"

"Last night. While you slept."

Calliope couldn't form another word, and just sat on her knees, staring at the head that leaned on a bloated jowl fringed with roughly torn shreds of skin and tendon.

"I took him down into his basement," James said in a hollow voice. "Where he had stacks of children's clothing, pictures on the walls. So many pictures, from so many places..." James shuddered and wiped his eyes, fighting laughter as he tried to stay mentally balanced while facing the full brunt of memory. "He begged for his life, the coward... He lied. He told me his wife was bitten on a trip to Asia. He said she was pregnant, and ran off into the woods. He said he was innocent... Looking around at his cellar, and what was collected there... Looking into his eyes, I knew he wasn't." James turned to the head. "So I killed him... I killed him for you."

Calliope approached the severed head and sniffed. Her eyes grew. "It *is* him..."

"Now you're free."

Calliope flew into James' arms. "I am?"

"You're free to do whatever you want. Live wherever you want. *Be* with whomever you want."

She pulled back and looked closely at James, holding on to his lapels like the little girl everyone took her for and forced her to be, instead of the grown woman that she was. He brushed the hair back away from her face, gently removing tiny strands that stuck to the tears dampening her cheeks. He touched her full, quivering lips. He leaned in, closing his eyes, while hers stayed open.

"Shhh," she whispered. "Do you hear that?" She disengaged from him and stood, looking toward the darkened window.

Now James heard it. The beating of drums. The syncopation was wild, primal, yet somehow not totally unfamiliar. It was the rhythmic anticipation that fueled a Witch's Sabbat, serial psychopaths, and eaters of the dead as they descended 66 stone steps into the waiting charnel house. It unnerved him. It excited him, speaking to certain antediluvian rites abandoned by modern man that still dusted his most basic genetic makeup.

"The death of the sun, and the rise of the moon," Calliope said as she stood, positioned herself in the middle of the cage and began to remove her clothing. "We have to take off our clothes, and sit perfectly still inside this circle." On the floor of the cage was painted a pentacle, surrounded by a circle. An 'X' was painted in the exact center of the design, placing it perfectly equidistant from the bars on every side. "You must sit in the medial of the ring, as his arms are long, and have great reach, all the better to rend you with."

"Calliope…"

She tore off a piece of cloth from her silken slip and stuffed it into her ears. "You must plug your ears and close your eyes, so you neither hear nor see the things he does to trick you."

"Calliope, he's dead!"

She stopped, casting her gaze on the decomposing head on the table. The realization sank in, and she leaned into his chest, closing her eyes, almost talking to herself in quiet relief. "The drums tricked me last moon, calling me out into the mountains. I never made it into my cage."

James closed his eyes, imagining her walking amid a dewy forest meadow, her hair animated by a gentle wind. She was his Fairy Queen.

"Grandmother found me and hid me away from him in the forest near the Forbidden Trail. The next morning, when I awoke, I was back here, and she was gone. He must have taken her instead of me… Poor Grandmother…" She wept softly.

James opened his eyes, processing her words. He lifted her away from him as the hair stood up on the back of his neck. She looked at him through heavy, wet lids, falling into a daze. Behind them, outside the window, the clouds parted and the light of a full moon streamed into the house, lighting up both of them in a ghostly sheen that sucked out all the color and replaced it with a lifeless pallor. Her skin became porcelain. Her eyes went hammerhead black in the colorless beam. "I'm all alone now," she said, her voice growing husky, edged with an impish snarl. "Will you stay with me forever?"

James released her and backed up. Calliope's face was backlit and shadowed, framed by that swirl of serpentine curls that now writhed over a featureless void.

"What is it, my dear?" she growled. "You are my *dear*, aren't you?" She seemed to enlarge, or perhaps James was shrinking, trading places with her, becoming the frightened child. It was difficult to tell, as the beating drums churned his stomach. "For I am yours, and you are mine. *'Ring around the rosy'*..."

James was suddenly gripped with the urge to escape, and crawled to the cage door. It was locked. The bronze key flashed mockingly in the moonlight, just below Calliope's rapidly widening mouth that emerged on either side of her face. "Looking for this?" she growled, ripping the chain from around her neck, opening her mouth too wide and tossing it down her throat. Her tongue licked her stretched, splitting lips, eyes flashing yellow. The cream of her skin was sucked up by an emerging cloak of fur.

"You did it..." James gasped. "You killed your grandmother."

"Spout ye not these lies." Calliope barked with a grotesque articulation that echoed and rasped as if trailing away into a hellish abyss. She moved toward him slowly, hunting by inches, bursting through her underclothes as she expanded in a jerking, bone cracking hunch. The cage swayed on the creaking chain, and the severed head rolled next to James.

"And I killed your father."

A hyena's cackle rippled from her broadening, furry chest as she moved closer to him, savoring the moment. Her—*Its* spine popped, lurching it forward onto its hands that crunched into club-like paws. The creature's nose and jaw, dripping bloody mucous, stretched outward with a rending sound, forming into a canine snout that stopped inches from his quivering face. James, suffocating on his own constricting madness, fought through the grip of paralyzing terror to express the one thought that scattered his brain like a bullet.

"Y-You're Mr. Lu—"

The monster roared and lunged, and James screamed, just before the upper half of his body disappeared into gaping jaws.

Outside, Mr. Barrows stood motionless as a shriek of absolute horror escaped the fairy tale house. The last, muffled scream was cut short, followed by a profound silence. The drumming had stopped. A primal howl filled the air.

At the edge of the forest, the three squatty swine creatures stood and watched, motionless.

After a moment, Mr. Barrows nodded his head, grunted, and got into the car, its suspension groaning under his great bulk. He fired up the engine, dropped it into gear, and drove slowly back up the driveway without turning on the headlamps. The moon lit the way.

FREE FIREWORKS

J acob let loose of his father's hand and took off across the cobblestones of Independence Square, slaloming through the statuary as he headed for the brightly colored booth advertising *Free Fireworks!* William smiled, readjusting his grip on the bouquet of red, white, and blue carnations. Jacob acted just as surprised and excited as he did last year, as he did every year. Children never tire of the familiar.

In Old City, fireworks were distributed free of charge by the federal government, which knew all too well that those who became accustomed to the explosion of gunpowder made for better soldiers. And in this city, as it was in all the free cities that were left, everyone was a soldier.

It was thirty minutes until the parade, and two hours before sundown, but already the crowded streets were alive with pops, flashes, and booms from 60 tons of liberated Mexican fireworks, doled out one bag at a time. Excited hands couldn't wait to bring spark to gunpowder and ring in the holiday with roaring concussion. M-80s and bottle rockets, Black Cats and spinners. Smoke bombs, snakes, and sparklers for the girls. There was a certain power to the dangerous alchemy. War games, played by children, watched by adults.

Across the top of the Square, below the breeze line, tendrils of smoke hung like lazy apparitions in the sticky July air. Jubilant groups of people gathered on stoops and balconies veined with ivy, drinking, grilling, and laughing under strung lines of tiny liberty bells. Revelers spilled out of apartment building doorways and onto the narrow sidewalks, taking the party into the street. Security was high and conspicuous, but citizens were allowed free reign today, and knew it.

This was Independence Day, the most important holiday of the year. The day to howl freedom in an explosive symphony of a million tiny bombs. All other holidays were shadows now, their backstories muddied by generations of tears and rivers of blood.

Jacob clomped back over to William in oversize steel toes, eyes as big as saucers. "Look what I got, daddy!" he said breathlessly, opening his bag. The fireworks were a bit sparse this year. Budget cuts. The war had been dragging on too long. Insurgencies were like that. Ones fueled by religious fanaticism were even worse. Without hope for treaty or surrender, they could suck a country dry while every last zealot with a death wish was pried from a hole and liquidated. Pricey stuff, this business of hunting and killing.

"Let's show mommy!" Jacob said, taking his father's hand. William's wife Abigail was back in their apartment, listening to jazz with the windows closed, a bottle open and curtains drawn. She hated the 4th. Hated the fireworks, and what they meant. Hated that her husband might someday join the parade that started in twenty-five minutes. So she hid her patriotism made poor behind four walls and a ceiling, waiting out the day, especially the night, peering into a glass and drinking what came out. Abigail missed the old days, when the 4th of July was about picnics and skinny-dipping and explosions that would never reach you. William missed the old days too, but knew that looking over your shoulder at the golden glow behind wouldn't change the unlit road ahead when you turned back around.

"Don't you want to watch the parade?" William asked his son, not ready to go back home yet. Jazz always confused him. Made him edgy. Especially that bebop shit. What ever happened to Lionel Belasco? Abigail never could hold her liquor.

A firecracker went off nearby. William jumped and reached for something at his belt that wasn't there. "Can we light these on the roof, daddy?" Jacob asked, holding up a handful of roman candles. "I want to send them into outer space!"

William chuckled, tousling his son's hair. "Let's go lay the flowers first," he said, peering over a sea of heads crowding around a tall bronze statue.

"Okay, dad," Jacob said absently, squinting at the labels of his fireworks, trying to work through the inscrutable Spanish to get at the secrets. "But can we hurry? The parade's going to start any minute!"

William glanced toward the east end of the Square that opened up into the city proper, where a group of disabled veterans and the local battalion marching band were gathering in the shadow of a converted church. A hobbling man, his face pinched and whorled by shrapnel scars, jerked his body in that direction, still trying to come to terms with the rubber and titanium that now served as his left leg. Jacob jumped in front of him, pointing finger pistols at the teetering man. "Pow! Pow!" The old vet staggered dramatically, feigning a mortal wound, then smiled and winked before continuing on.

Jacob held on tight to his father's thick, military-issue belt as they wound through the jostling crowd, arriving at the center of the Square. William laid his flowers near the base of the statue, adding the bouquet to the thousands already stacked wide around the monument. This one was built higher and grander than the other eleven statues arranged in a half moon on each flank. William stood back, taking a moment, before bending to his son and recounting the story he told him every year. Jacob smiled. The magic of the familiar...

This was the statue of Sheik Nazir, the first member of Group of Twelve, a handful of popular, firebrand religious leaders, politicians, and mullahs who turned their back on extremism and joined the side of law and order. This shocking movement flipped the field in the Time of Terror that erupted after the dawn of the New Enlightenment over a decade ago. It was then that the New League of Nations bonded under one banner of unmitigated truth, fighting back against those who shut their eyes and held close to lies taught by the generations that came before. Those who didn't know any better.

A giddy squeal came from nearby, interrupting William's story. Jacob looked over to a group of kids who had somehow hollowed out a pocket of space in the rowdy crowd. They were setting up a line of beer bottles, anchored by pouring in grit through clenched fist dug from a purloined sandbag. Jacob's face brightened. "Bottle rockets... Sweet." He looked up at his dad, who nodded. Jacob ran over and joined in, speaking in the fast, clipped language of little boys.

William looked past the children at the arching line of mismatched statues. These were the Twelve Infidels. A dozen to turn the tide. Their bold organization in a time of chaos helped prop up the flailing collective of hastily treated governments as wave after wave of catastrophic suicide attacks on all free countries nearly brought civilization to its dusty knees. Loaded oil tankers were turned into half million ton napalm bombs. Passenger trains filled with ammonium nitrate burrowed deep into city centers, leveling financial districts. Dirty bombs depopulated seventeen major metropolitan areas, while a massive fleet of truck bombs took out governmental installations in forty-two others. In the outlying areas, groups of heavily armed men burst into shopping malls, movie theatres, and grade schools, mowing down everything with a pulse. Sleeper cells in military platoons fragged fellow soldiers and blew themselves up, taking as much of the brass with them as they could carry. Brother killed sister, only to be killed by father. Ordered society broke down, melted away, congealing in a pool of splattered organs and chips of bone imbedded into bedroom walls. Ultra religious savagery reared the many heads of the hydra, as holy warriors wrapped in death cult dogma sought to plunge the globe back into a new Dark Age.

They came so dangerously close. Two million died that First Day: July 4th, eleven years ago today.

But the infidels fought back on the 5th, spreading hope like a spider web creeping up from the underground to cover the globe. And so the war began in earnest. The new War of Independence. The last Great War, everyone said. Everyone was probably right.

William's modest Midwestern city stumbled to the brink of extinction after the First Day, as the kill ratio was so astronomically high. But the frontier was built on DIY, and the old mettle bubbled up. Soon, a small but determined group of police, ex-military, and even the local football team picked up hunting rifles and used their innate knowledge of deer trails and secret ravines to track down the remnants of the murderous cell that just days before killed thousands of locals. The remaining city leaders decided to pull back into Old City, walling off the blood soaked suburbs of what became known as New City, and hunkered down. That's what people did on the Plains. They hunkered down when the world turned foul, as it often did out here.

That was seven years ago. Pitched battles were fought in the meantime. Bombs of various sizes went off almost weekly. Always testing... Spies were sent, and spies were captured. The stench of waiting death hung over everything, as the souls of the free citizens calloused under the weight of daily, lingering fear. Some trained. Others drank and listened to jazz. A few split themselves open on the cobblestones. Everyone prayed and watched the skies.

But Old City was still free, and today was a celebration of that improbable fact, wrapped inside the stars and blood red stripes of a nation that was now just another wounded part of the wider world. Wave the flag, crack a year old beer, and toast to the Fates. Death came not on this day.

Fight like they do. Die like we do.

And they did, and so did we.

Four bottle rockets fizzed up from the group of children in near syncopation, whistling past the bronze image of proud Nazir, who looked out with fierce eyes under raised, haughty brows to the city skyline, toward the bombed skyscrapers and scooped out remains of New City just visible over the thirty foot concrete security wall. A wickedly curved scimitar was housed safely in its scabbard at his waist, but a knotted hand was on the hilt, always at the ready to take down insurgent filth of any stripe, any tribe. Even his own.

We were all infidels in the image of Sheik Nazir and The Group of Twelve, and we of the free lands wore the title as both a blood oath and badge of honor.

William walked over to Jacob, who was staring at a tiny rocket still resting inside its bottle. "Mine was a dud." Jacob held a smoking punk like it was a stick of incense.

William lifted his son into his arms with a grunt, reminded that the day was fast approaching when he wouldn't be able to lift him up anymore. He pushed back a bit of Jacob's unruly black hair. Hair like his mother's. "I promise that'll be the last dud of the night." Jacob smiled and hugged his father, wrapping his legs around him like he did when he was a baby. With his boy in his arms and the entire city holding them close, William walked back into the crowd, melting into the swirl of citizens, celebrating like it was their last night on earth.

The sun was setting, and the cicadas took up their song. The daylight hours of July 4th seem to last an eternity, adding anticipation to that moment when the night sky first goes from dead to alive, thrilling and frightening in equal measure.

From the rooftop of their apartment building, William took a deep breath, and caught a waft of countryside air, blowing in from the west, pushed on by the sunset. For a brief moment, he could smell the honeysuckle, flavored with fresh tilled loam of the farm where he grew up, where he used to run through the wooded creek beds and crawl through culverts, playing war. It was mid summer now, and the crops would have been growing so quickly you could hear the corn stalks creaking and popping in the fields as they thickened and reached up toward the hazy sun. The beans needed to be walked, and the hogs were fattening in the mud, looking for a low spot in the fence. The bailers would be out, scooping up the first cutting of fragrant alfalfa drying in the fields, exposing a hidden civilization of earwigs and clicking beetles that gathered under the hot wetness beneath. William closed his eyes and took another breath, hoping to uncover more memories, but this time only smelled smoke. A neighbor had just lit up one of those ridiculous cone fountains on the far side of the roof. Children danced around the guttering sparks like wild Indians; like the heathens we all once were. Jacob got up from his contemplation of a late-lingering June bug and joined in.

William frowned. He had grown to hate the smell of smoke, of burning things, which now filled him with horror when it was such a pleasant experience in his youth. He hated that he was an expert in smoke, noticing the nuanced differences of chemicals and wood, rubber and flesh. He hated the things he had done while other things burned. He missed the smell of burning trash on the farm, when the sharp stench of combusting plastic was just a Kool Whip container dripping into the coals, when the odor of burning hair and muscle was just the calcine remains of a bird shot squirrel.

Down below, a muffled hush swept the Square, nudging William from his reverie, as the mournful strains of "Taps" began. This was the lament of the widows and the heartbroken left behind. William looked back at the door leading to the roof. He fetched Jacob and brought him close, listening to the song begat during the Civil War – the first Civil War – but made so common the last few years that it became an Independence Day hymn. It was written by a youth from the North, who ran away from his family to attend music school in the South. There, he wrote a simple, mournful tune. That young man died on the field of battle, fighting for the Confederacy, and the song was discovered in the pocket of the bloodied corpse by his shocked father, who was an officer in the Union Army. The officer asked his superiors if the Union band could play it for his dead son. They refused his request, as they'd be damned if their band would play a tribute to the enemy. He pleaded, and was finally offered a single bugle. The grieving father gave the song to the bugler, who played the funeral dirge to the lone body who had written it. Taps.

William looked down at Jacob, who was watching the veterans' parade with right hand raised to brow in a stiff salute practiced for so many hours in front of the mirror. His grandfather, who fought, killed, and died a little in the haunted jungles of Vietnam, would have been proud. William smiled sadly, wishing that Jacob would run away to music school, to leave this city and this war and this grim and uncertain future behind, but Jacob would have nowhere to run. Music schools were the stuff of fairy tales these days. Music was the drum beat of battle and schools were now campuses of war.

The battalion band took over, playing John Phillips Sousa as the parade proceeded through the Square. A shout went up, and grew. Men saluted. Women threw flowers and blew kisses. Children watched with wide eyes. It was a celebration of those who survived and sacrificed so much to keep this country free.

As the sun dipped below the horizon, bathing the world in that sweet hue of magic hour blue, the first volley of organized fireworks launched into the air, exploding in bellowing showers of multicolored sparks taking on fantastical shapes... Flowers, sunbursts, fiery spirals like the flash of galaxies. Jacob jumped up and down, clapping his hands and trying to whistle through his fingers like his father taught him. Somewhere in their apartment, William could almost hear the dissonant sax music rising in volume. Abigail needed to be up here, but she just couldn't. William understood that, as best he could.

The fireworks continued, unleashing burning glory in the sky. Brief, fiery sketches thrilled the crowd. The Square cheered each glimmering salvo. Bellowed like Vikings. People were drunk now, forgetting their fear in the haze of liquid hope. William watched the burning patterns branding the darkness reflected in Jacob's eyes. He picked up his son, so he could get a better look.

William heard a sound behind him, and turned. Abigail stood in the roof access doorway, holding a lit sparkler in her hand, a tired, bleary smile on her face. He set Jacob down and went to her; took her pale face in his hands and kissed her deeply, like they used to kiss when every second mattered before the porch light came on. He looked into her bloodshot eyes, and pressed his forehead against hers. "Thank you," he said. Her soft hand against his face told him everything he needed to know. She held up the sparkler as it fizzled to a red, glowing stick, then frowned, pouting like a little girl. William laughed and kissed her again, sometimes feeling as much her father as her husband. He took her by the hand and walked her to the edge of the building to their son. Jacob's eyes lit up, but he said nothing as he hugged her tight around the waist. William put an arm around his wife, and brought his son in close between them. For the first time in a long time, it all felt right. The way it was supposed to be. The way it once was. The All-American family, enjoying the 4th of July under a dying sunset, with fire in the sky and without a thought for tomorrow.

Just then, a boom much lower and louder than the others shook the cobblestones. The parade stopped abruptly, the band's trumpeter trailing off like a deflating balloon. Fireworks continued to fly, as the fuses were already lit, but no one was watching anymore. Murmuring silence choked the Square. Abigail looked at William, whose face told her everything *she* needed to know. Another muffled blast sounded, and another. Triangulation. The citywide PA system croaked to life. Orders chattered into the night. Sirens wailed. Abigail fell to her knees and wept. William looked down at her, as if it was happening in slow motion.

A plume of black smoke billowed up from the Old City marketplace, four blocks over from the Square. The throaty belch of a heavy machine gun fire chewed through the din. Screams littered the Square, as the crowd scattered, grouped, rallied.

God damn them. On our holiday. Just like last time.

Jacob looked down for Abigail, but she was gone. His stomach turned. He didn't want to gear up and head out like this. William took a deep breath and turned to the roof door. A hand stopped him. It was Abigail, holding Jacob in front of her. She blinked away tears and smiled, laughing in spite of herself. He walked to her and she kissed him, whispering into his ear. William smiled, gripping the small of her back, re-etching the familiar curve into his memory. He then hugged Jacob and looked into his son's eyes. William wanted to say that he loved him, but he did it so rarely, that he was worried that the boy would take it as a final goodbye. So he just nodded. Jacob nodded back.

Then, only two stood on the rooftop, and William was gone. White smoke drifted over the Square. Black smoke rose beyond. Abigail closed her eyes.

Wearing starchy fatigues, a modified M-240 in his hand and a heavy pack slung over his shoulder, William strode onto the street. He blinked a few times, trying to orient himself to the frantic commotion of the Square after dressing in the silent apartment. All around him, fellow soldiers, male and female, young and old, kissed their loved ones goodbye, while others emerged grim faced from apartment blocks still littered with bottles and trappings of the party that hid them from the outside world just hours before. A banner of red, white and blue dangled limply from the awning of a shuttered storefront. Under it, an old man leaned on a cane and looked up for the stars of his youth. He didn't move, only stared. William looked up at the roof, where he knew Abigail and Jacob were watching, and waved.

Another explosion two neighborhoods over shook the ground and shot red-gutted smoke into the sky. Infiltrators. Spies gone active. Peace had made security soft. Made all of them soft, William thought, adjusting the tight Kevlar vest under his jacket that had fit him so loosely before. He was adding inches, while the city was giving them away. Give them an inch, they'll blow up a mile. Gunfire ripped into the night, sending everyone but the soldiers scurrying for doorways. The man under the striped banner was gone.

William jammed a receiver into his ear and a walkie talkie to his mouth, as he jogged toward the outer wall ringing Old City, receiving intel and barking orders. He had to man his post.

The walkway cresting the wall was crowded with crouching troopers, weapons bristling outward like deadly whiskers, just like the days of castles and keeps that thrilled William's childhood. A teenage private, still a bit woozy after fear burned off most of his drunk, lit up a cigarette. William shot a glare in his direction. The kid blanched and quickly stamped out the smoke under heavy boot tread. William shook his head. A glowing cherry earned you a sniper's bullet exiting the back of your mouth. Some of these guys need more training, more time. There was never enough time anymore.

William returned his gaze down his scope, scanning the frustrating darkness below. He knew they were out there. Knew they were watching, praying to the empty sky. He could smell them. Smell their smoke. Exhaust, campfires, dank Turkish cigarettes... What were they waiting for?

It had been hours since the last of the suicide attacks rattled the city and dawn was on the creep. Insurgent recon was lacking, as they leveled a recently emptied ammo dump and part of the Old City prison, freeing two spies awaiting trial just long enough for proper justice to be rendered with the gavel fall of hollow points. Their slapdash Trojan horse failed to open up the enemy from the inside. Terrorists didn't win many battles. They just wore you down until you gave up and lowered your head. But tonight, there would be no "wearing down." This would be to the death, and whatever waited beyond.

William's earpiece crackled to life. Air support was on its way, but they were coming in from the nearest base in the Rockies, a good thousand miles away. William tested the breeze, hoping to find a westerly tailwind. Nothing. Everything was still. Quiet, within and without. The holiday was over. The air force would be late.

He looked up to the queer stars arranged in new constellations that knew not nor cared not what was happening below. He didn't think he'd ever get used to them, even after all he'd seen. A shooting star carved through a patch of grayish black with a dim trail of stratospheric sparks. Free fireworks.

A commotion went up from the troops manning the west section of the wall. Dots of light appeared on the hilltop about a mile outside Old City, on the grounds of what used to be a high school. William looked through his scope as the sun groaned through the pre-dawn, dimly lightening the sky and giving the first glimpse of what was waiting in the dark.

Flags decorated their front lines. Flags with symbols of religious zealotry and indiscriminate terror. The Crescent moon. The star of David. The Cross. The insurgents—from Pakistan, Korea, Italy, Ethiopia, Iran, England, Indonesia, India, and the barely united States—raised their collection of mismatched firearms and took aim at the city wall ahead. They had a half squadron of banged up tanks. Aging howitzer barrels bristled behind them. A battery of Russian-made rockets flanked each side. Ragtag military equipment patched together with a soldering iron and chewing gum. By the collection of this hard won gear, this looked to be a last stand. We'd send them to paradise, good and proper.

Fight like they do, die like we do.

William sneered and shook his head, as all around him the flags and battalion banners of Old City were raised, catching the growing breeze. These were the flags of organized statehood against those of anarchy. These were the flags of the Twelve Infidels. Those of fang, of eye, of tentacle. That of the Elder Sign, which tied them all together under the primordial bond of The One Faith. These were the believers in the Blind Chaos swirling at the center of Time, as revealed to the bug-eyed world through The Great Priest, who cracked the foundation of the earth and rose from the sea to reclaim his earthly province. To wipe away with an atmosphere splitting roar all the lies that filled the vacuum in Its absence. It came back to remind us all of how it all began, and how it would never end. After bursting from the South Pacific, the Old One straddled the earth for The Three Days, crushing mountains and displacing seas. Destroying certain myths and validating others. One hundred million died in the unnatural calamity, a fitting sacrifice for our forgetfulness, for our arrogant creation of our own gods and fathers, in the absence of alien reality. Then, without a glance at the fleas weeping in the circus below, It leapt into the sky and disappeared into the ether, leaving behind a New Order of Things, staying just long enough to give us a glimpse of stark, mad reality, tended by those Things that awoke with it, crawling from the earth and screaming down from forgotten mountains where they had waited for a billion years to reclaim Eden.

Many did not believe—*refused* to believe—branding the Old One and the Elder Things spawns of the devil, even though the accused progeny were incalculable eons older than their supposed father. These religious extremists clung to their upstart monolithic god and his handful of dirt scratching prophets with violent resolve, spurning an older pantheon, just as they did with the Pagans, the

Babylonians, the Egyptians, the Hindu, the Greeks, the Native Americans.... Where was their god now? Was it cowering in the corner of eternity, or fled altogether? Did it ever exist in the first place? No one knew. There was no proof. There was only the faith of a bawling child, waiting on an errant father who promised to come back and take them to paradise. The paradise was lost before it could ever be found. But still they believed. They needed to believe, because to not would mean they were wrong. That they knew nothing. That they were nothing but a handful of chemicals given mass and the electric spark of life. They wanted back the magic of the familiar.

William's grim musings were interrupted by the deep, humming peal of the curiously shaped bell that one night just appeared in their abandoned church four years ago. He turned back as the Nameless Acolyte of Old City emerged from the cathedral, now a Temple to the Starry Wisdom. He wore a cowled robe of yellow, stitched with intricate patterns that dazzled the eye, even from this distance. No one had ever seen the Acolyte's face, and none wanted to. Old City was devoted to the New Enlightenment adopted by the American federal government and so many others, at the behest of the Twelve Infidels. But that didn't change the fear that twisted the hearts of humanity still coming to grips with this new religion birthed amongst dead stars in a reality not compatible with our own.

The Acolyte raised his wrapped hand, and made several quick, arcing movements, as if carving the air with tortured geometry. These gestures were now familiar but no less unsettling to William, who pulled on his helmet that had the appearance of a cuttlefish, and checked his chamber. His fellow soldiers did the same, as the clarion call of horn and dissonant flutes split the early morning quiet. The Army of Justice and Truth—the Army of the United States of America—took their positions on the wall, taking aim at those far out and below.

William set up at the head of his platoon, and from around his neck took out a figurine carved from a greenish gray stone. He brought the tiny toad-like shape to his lips and kissed it. "Elder Gods protect us on this day from the non-believers," William said, looking up into the dark sky. "May the infidel triumph over the lies of the usurper."

A shout came from further down the line, as three trucks without headlights sped toward the wall, bucking and pitching over the cratered ground. Suicide attack. Grinding trident. The men on the wall of Old City opened up with .50 caliber fire, thudding the turf with heated lead. Several Katyusha rockets whooshed from the ground behind to cover the desperate attack, and slammed into the base of the wall, rocking the graves of smashed strip malls.

One of the trucks spun out and flipped. The other burst into flames. The last truck, chugging lower to the ground under the weight of three inch thick armor plating, withstood the barrage and was still coming. The decoys were dead, but the stuffed duck still remained, moving to within a hundred yards of the wall. Just then, from behind the Old City lines, a boy no more than twelve—just a few years older than Jacob—jogged forward, a LAW rocket launcher bouncing casually on his shoulder. All the men and women parted, allowing the boy to reach the edge of the wall. He hoped up on a box set down for him, took aim just ahead of the truck and squeezed, sending a whistling anti-tank round arcing downward. The truck stayed on course and met up with it sixty yards out, unleashing a mini mushroom cloud fueled by five hundred pounds of C-4. The terrible boom blew back the fighters on both sides. A mobile bomb that would have torn a 30-foot wide hole in the wall. A Hail Mary in every ironic sense.

As everyone picked themselves up, the cottony silence after a huge explosion was filled by a clicking and chattering coming from the sky, peppered by piercing shrieks. Many on the wall smiled. Many more shook off a shiver. The terrorists sometimes had choppers, even an occasional jet, but the free nations also had things that flew. The air force had arrived.

William looked up into the sky, where winged, insect-like creatures—inkblots against the bluish smudge of the Milky Way—moved in bizarre but graceful formation, sizing up those on the ground below.

Small arms fire rang out from the enemy position, before the anti-aircraft guns mounted on the back of pickups roared to life, pouring death into the heavens. Phosphorous tipped tracer rounds stuttered across the sky, trying to bring down those Things that flew above. Some took bullets and crumpled, falling with unnatural speed to dent the earth with a monstrous impact. But others found their targets, swooping low to rend metal and flesh, scattering survivors and sanity as they swooped back up into the unquiet sky.

William crouched low and took aim, squeezing off rounds into moving figures that could be friends and neighbors, but who had all become The Enemy. Fuck 'em. The worms would eat them all just the same.

Bullets rattled the wall, as defenders dove for cover. William reloaded and reengaged, when an RPG exploded to his left, blowing him onto his side. His ears rang, his eyes bled, but he could still see flashes of fire, the rockets red glare, the bombs bursting in air, that were lighting up the sky above the city, carving rivulets of light over the towering bronze effigy of Sheik Nazir and as his eleven fellow infidels. A Baptist missionary. A venerated Vatican Cardinal. A

Micronesian king. A Muslim scholar. Three Presidents, two rabbis, a swami and a Mormon leader. All those who lost their faith in the lies of the One God, and embraced the horrific but undeniable proof of the Many Gods.

The fighting increased, as both sides vented their righteous hate through sizzling metal. William got to his feet, clutching the figurine around his neck. All he could smell was smoke. July 5th: the day the Twelve fought back.

William looked up, unbowing his head. Tracers and explosions ripped across his view into the universe that was closing its eyes, turning away. Showers of sparks from exploding shells took on beautiful, terrifying shapes, creating a new show, an encore of brutalism and death that danced atop the sky, below the mute stars that saw nothing.

Free fireworks.

LOVE SONGS FROM THE
HYDROGEN JUKEBOX

D oyle had only been back on the Hill for two days when he already
planned his next escape.

He disappeared three weeks ago from a reading at City Lights, hitch-
ing to SFO and flying twenty-three hours to scratch an itch in some Indonesian
shithole. Screaming through the jungle, devouring the local medicine, taking
full advantage of lax prohibitions on deviant behavior. He always went alone,
and came back looking like he had grown an inch, with a couple of new scars, a
bag full of bizarre trinkets, and enough stories to tide us all over until his next
disappearance. I didn't blame him for skating, at least not that night. The poet
was garbage, mixing tenses and mushing up metaphors without knowing exactly why. Must have sucked down his scoop of melted Ferlinghetti back in Boise
through a game of telephone. The girls thought he was sharp, but I suspect only
because he looked like Tab Hunter. He could have looked like Borgnine and
the birds still would have been chirping, just because he was standing a few feet
above the rest of us, shadowed on the illuminated roof. Everyone's supposed to be
beautiful when heated by the spotlight. I thought he belonged further down the
coast, where blond hair and a football chin earned you a paycheck and the pros
write all the lines for you. Still, he scored pretty sweet that night, saving his best
verse for after the show.

In Doyle's absence, North Beach seemed to hold its breath, more out of anticipation of his return than the government spooks who were poking around the filthy dives and unheated squats that cloistered together on Telegraph Hill, hoping the rest of the tourist world would pass on by and head to the Golden Gate. The feds made their best attempt to blend in, wearing Hawaiian button ups and dungarees, trying to score a lid or making conversation with the street corner glamour boys, rummies, and shirtless Negro kids who cross-stitched the streets on their modified Schwinns. But we knew what these deadbeats were up to, combing the area for reds or fags, or the nightmare scenario for every Betty Crocker American—the homosexual communist. We could spot the stiffs as soon as they arrived, even before the whoops from the street told us there were fleas on the dog. Because no matter how deep their cover, how much research they did on the Vagabond Tribe, those Washington Joes couldn't help tucking in their costume shirts, and their footwear was always showroom clean. A square can't fake an octagon no matter how many angles they play. Not enough degrees.

We told Doyle about the Hoovers when he got back, but he brushed it off as he launched into a mad tale of getting bent on shots of deep bush nutmeg stirred into Coca Cola while a Sumatran mountain witch unfolded from a steamer trunk and pulled seven rusty nails out of the spine of some crippled child. It was wild, like all of Doyle's stories, and no one knew where the facts ended and the ball of yarn began. No one cared, either. He was our Shaman, even to those who didn't know what that title meant. He cured us with his words, wiping away the disease of home and the poison of memory. We were all going to make a new go of it on Telegraph Hill, so we naturally needed a gathering point. That point was Doyle, who seemed to be here before any of the rest of us arrived.

As he told the story of the mountain witch, Doyle passed around one of the spikes to the group gathered in front of him like a prayer circle, settling in between the roaches that disbanded their three-week circus and skittered back into the walls. This was holy time, and no one—not Jack or Allen or any street corner messiah—could touch him as he spun his silk into day-glo tapestry, hovering a full six inches off the floor. Still, earlier in the day, I saw something in his eyes when the agents were mentioned. A flash of rage that cut rare in his wide, placid face that always danced on the verge of a private wink. He knew things that we didn't, even about ourselves, and that seemed to include why the government was sniffing around the Hill. But after that day, it was never mentioned again.

His homecoming shindig was a real blowout. Everyone in North Beach knew Doyle, and held him up as their golden calf, molded in the desert under the gaze of a fickle God to give them something tangible to trust. No one knew exactly where he came from, but he had an air of Back East breeding, tempered with something carved raw boned in the wilderness. The symmetrical features, the aristocratic nose. Hair that woke up better than your entire newly pressed outfit. He obviously had money, as his frequent jags to Peru and Afghanistan and a hundred other obscure destinations showed, but he lived like a pauper, dressing in worn-out trousers and a navy t-shirt. And he never wore shoes. "I like to feel the earth moving beneath me," he explained to me the day after I first arrived while we blew through some choice Hawaiian Tai stick. He was a strange cat, Doyle, but that was why we all loved him. "Hero of the outcasts," a junkhead we all called Raggedy Man croaked one night before vomiting into a bucket on the porch. The beat-down tramp, who lost his real name in a bloody cow pasture in eastern France twelve years back, just wiped his mouth, smiled, and nodded out, knowing no one would hassle him until he ventured back into the streets. We were the Outcasts, every dancing one of us, and we were all under Doyle's protection from whatever wars haunted the outside world. Just as long as you were within his circle, and so many of us were. We'd fight to stay within the insulating glow that leaked out from behind his eyes, and probably do other things, too. Everyone needs a family, and we were all Doyle's.

At the party, the girls whipped up some mean sandwiches with fresh sourdough and end cuts of Italian dry from Molinari's, while the fellas mixed a batch of jungle juice in a bathtub half buried in the back yard. Doyle owned the house, a sweet three-story Queen Anne Victorian just off Columbus Ave, but not a car. Said he didn't like to squirm through life inside a greasy fish tin. The sidewalks told the best stories anyway, and the love songs playing from the cracks held the sweetest harmonies. Six inches off the ground, no matter where he went.

"*Nellll*-son," Doyle called out in a singsong voice. I turned and found him reclining on the cinder block retaining wall next to the alley, staring up into the murky night sky. The bricks must have only been a foot wide, but he made them seem like a king-size mattress. "Nelson Barnacles," he mused, as if tasting the words. My last name was Barnes, but I was thrilled that Doyle gave me something new. Something that came from him. He gave lots of people nicknames, and now that included me. The glow around me suddenly grew brighter. I felt protected in a way Raggedy Man never could, especially because Raggedy Man ended up with his head caved in and missing both eyes and his left arm when he was fished up from under the wharf last week. Dumb bastard ventured too far out of the radius and ended up behind enemy lines. Just like in that cow pasture in eastern France. "Come check this out, Barnacles."

I downed my glass and walked over to Doyle, drying my hands on my pants like a school kid called to the front of the class to receive a ribbon. I always hoped that Doyle liked me because I was interesting or special in some way, but deep down I knew it was most likely because I slept in my '48 Buick Roadmaster, which was the last working ride on the block. Never mind that it was the only home I had on earth. I probably could have crashed at Doyle's pad, but I didn't want to intrude. Anyway, I had wheels, which meant Doyle did too.

He gestured to the sky. I looked up, and couldn't see anything through the incoming fog that reflected the light from the city back down upon itself like a golden canopy. "You see what I see?" Doyle asked, more to himself.

"Yeah... Yeah, I think I do." I saw nothing, but it was very important for Doyle to think I was on his level at all times, even though I couldn't find his floor if you built me a golden elevator.

Doyle exhaled a perfectly shaped nimbus cloud of spicy smoke that he was holding in the entire time. It didn't smell like grass. It didn't smell like anything I'd ever come across. His voice dropped an octave. "Nelson, we need to find the hydrogen jukebox." He turned his electric blue eyes on me. "We need a cleansing."

I paused, then nodded. "We sure do."

He stubbed out the narrow joint on his tongue and swallowed the roach. "Fire up the sled and let's burn."

I waited, expecting him to continue, but Doyle just stared at me, looking stone-cold sober, like a professor waiting for an answer. "N-now?"

"If not now, then when?"

I thought for a minute, climbing through the gauze that spread from my stomach until I discovered that his question was rhetorical.

Doyle waited for me to say what I was supposed to say, what anyone would say, but I didn't, so he smiled and hopped down off the ledge, landing lightly on his bare feet. "Meet me out front in thirty," he said as he disappeared, taking the light with him.

I stood in the dark for several seconds. "Where're you going?"

"Provisions!"

◎

Thirty-two minutes later, we were rumbling down the Hill like a dull spear thrust into the slow rising sun, just as the city was shaking off the regret of the night before.

Sugarboy rode shotgun, rolling an Atomic Fireball across his stunted teeth and awkwardly jerking his head to the Kay Starr song on the radio, a gut full of bennies beating a hole in his heart. Doyle was in back, sitting between Cincinnati and some cat I'd never seen before. He called himself Escofet, which could have been a first or last name. Didn't matter, really. Just another punter riding the carousel. I took him for a queer, with his sweat-stained silk shirt open to the waist and long lashes that fluttered over black eyes that looked perpetually on the verge of tears, and presently seemed to be locked into watching me in the rearview mirror. A lurid tattoo of something ripe and naked peeked out from behind the row of pearl buttons. Doyle brought new faces and names in and out of the group almost daily, and it never mattered the color or persuasion. He had an interest in all of it, and tried every inch of it on for size.

In between sips of Old Fitzgerald and necking pretty heavy with Cincinnati, Doyle called out directions just as each turn was almost behind us. I yanked and careened, lurching the Buick through three lanes of traffic and a hailstorm of curses, catching the I-80 out of the city. My dad would have had a heart attack with the way I was beating this car. Doyle howled above each tire squeal, instructing every disgruntled commuter in turn to sodomize various family members in a variety of creative ways. Cincinnati giggled like she was seven instead of twenty-four and nowhere and drunk, while Escofet kept watching me in the mirror. Sugarboy popped another handful and lit up a joint, lost in the world just outside his window as he ground his nubs further into his gums.

We crossed the Red Bridge and invaded darktown Oakland like roaring barbarians, waving to the mothers heading to the salon and nodding to the hard-eyed neighborhood toughs manning their posts under the eaves of shadowed stoops. By this time, I was dipping into the road whiskey, and after a few slugs stopped wondering where we were going and focused on how capital it was that we were getting there. "Tapping in and letting go," as Doyle so often called it. Tapping into the lizard brain to learn the secrets of the reptiles, and letting go of the ego of the sapien. It wasn't easy for a boy raised between hay bails.

The row houses ceded ground to rugged hill and Spanish fir, and we soon made our way onto the 24, passing Emeryville and Upper Rockridge as time seemed to speed up while the fish cans around us slowed like unwound toys.

◎

The highway thinned out, the energy in the car plateaued, and an unspoken silence crouched just below the radio backbeat and the roar of the pavement. I watched the painted signs pass above us, looking for clues. No one said a word for a long time, going through what they were going through. Escofet's eyes made the minutes into hours.

"Where're we headed, anyway?" Sugarboy asked as he turned to the back seat, his bloodshot pinpoints darting from Escofet to the creep of Cincinnati's dirndl skirt that showed just a hint of rounded cotton. He had pulled himself back together long enough to ask the question I had been meaning to bring up back on the Hill, but didn't have the guts. I wanted to seem the bold adventurer, tearing off in the pre-dawn slate without a destination in mind or a care in my soul. I wanted to be Dean Moriarty. But I was just Nelson Barnes, all smooth hull without texture, and what I was most concerned about was the five-body wear on my wheezing shocks.

Doyle took another belt from the bottle and grinned, squirting a rivulet of warm liquid between his teeth onto the back of my neck like a spitting cobra.

"Up into the rim. Forehead of the Western world. We gotta get a better view of things, you know?"

I had no idea what he was talking about, and neither did Sugarboy. The back seat, on the other hand, seemed drenched in understanding. The unifying power of liquor and forgotten modesty. I tried to join in with a chuckle. "We going mountain climbing? I didn't bring my boots."

Doyle started humming, or gurgling, deep in his throat. It was a terrible sound. "*The songbiiiird waits, at'er top o' Deeeevil's Moun-tain, openin' them brown arms wiiide,*" he sang in an off-kilter voice, then hit the bottle again.

Sugarboy knitted his brow and cut his eyes to me. I just shrugged. We didn't know each other well, as he ran with the Night to Day crew in the house while my hours were more in line with a college professor. But on this trip, it seemed like the dividing line between camps was separated by pale blue vinyl seats. Escofet and Cincinnati just grinned knowingly. "We are about to be enlightened," Doyle pronounced before throwing on some grandma shades and leaning back in his seat.

My copilot twitched a few times, casting lassos through his orbiting brain, then turned back around and popped a Tootsie Roll into his mouth.

I swallowed a few times. The whiskey was wearing off and left something hungry and hollow in its place. "But what does that mean?"

There were a few moments of silence. I couldn't see Doyle's eyes behind his dark lenses, but I could feel Escofet's latching onto mine, as if he was watching for the man next to him. "How's that, Barnacles?"

I cleared my throat, wishing the bottle would make its way back up front, but Escofet was holding it with two hands, blowing into it like a jug player. Licking the opening. "Enlightenment, I mean. What are you getting at?"

Doyle lowered his sunglasses and looked at me with an expression I'd never seen before. Finally, he broke into a smile, then a laugh. His backseat chorus joined in, cackling like they were watching Jack Benny.

"Do I need to break it down for you? Our brothers are dying in the streets, bodies chewed raw from the filth of Korean rice paddies. Our sisters are locked in cages by husbands turned bosses… *slavers*, while the rest of us stare at our glowing squares, worshipping Cronkite and Lucy. Laughing inside the flames." Doyle grabbed the back of my seat, wrenching it back toward him, his eyes flaring. He was strong. "What we think we know is *bullshit*, and what we don't know is our salvation. The West ain't the best. The West is a gerbil wheel. Knowledge from the older places is what we need right now. I'll be good goddamned if we scorch ourselves off this marble and leave only a black smudge with nothing underneath. I want to go deeper, find out how to rise above."

"Right on, big daddy!" Cincinnati hooted and lit up a cigarette, pushing her limp blonde hair behind her ears. She was such a brown noser, made worse when her underwear was warm.

"We're going to see the man with the plan." Before I could ask, Doyle sat back in his seat, as if exhausted. "Take the first exit."

I drove for five more miles, and was about to turn around, when I saw the small green sign on the side of the highway. Mount Diablo State Park.

The Buick veered onto the 680 South. That was the path to Devil's Mountain, where an angel awaited.

After sliding through the foothills, we began to carve up the mountain on a fib of a road that degenerated into the truth of a barely paved switchback. I had to sit up straight and man the wheel like a Clipper captain amid a furious gale, lest we split open on the rocks below that waited at the bottom of a thousand-foot gorge, grasping at the tires just inches from the edge of the spotty asphalt marking the trail like flattened, black popcorn balls.

Within minutes, we were totally disconnected from civilization, as the sequoias closed in like colossal spires around us, eating the sun with arms a thousand feet high. The radio had faded to static, and Doyle started to hum again. That hideous, tuneless sound, as if intentionally missing notes. I wondered if we'd ever be able to turn around and head back down. Forward or die.

The road straightened and leveled off, ruts smoothed by wear and some level of primitive upkeep. I rolled down the window, and in between gusts of Cincinnati's cigarettes, I could smell a dedicated wall of pine and ancient soil, worn down from the mountains to birth a million wooden titans. This was a different sort of smell than Nebraska loam, which had a damp odor of retreated ice, shallow streams, and clumsy agriculture. Up here lay the bite of primal dust, clinging to the backs of slumbering giants, full of wisdom born way down deep.

I looked into the rearview, hoping to catch Doyle's gaze but expecting to find another's, but I saw nothing. I pivoted in my seat, and found Doyle whispering into Escofet's ear. He was leaning into the side of the car, eyes closed. Cincinnati pouted and picked at her nails, flushed ears poking through straw.

"Watch the road, man!" Sugarboy screamed, grabbing the wheel and wrenched it to the left as the right tire nearly slipped off the edge of the trail. The car found the road again. "You almost *killed* us!"

My face drained and my ears pounded. I was terrified of heights, and here I was, piloting a crew of hopped-up ragtags to the rim of the world on a broken spider web. Doyle just laughed behind me.

Further up the mountain, the asphalt degenerated to a dirt path. A pair of figures stood on the edge of the tree line, holding hands. It would have been hard to tell if they were male or female, as they wore matching plastic Wanda the Witch masks. But they were both naked, both male, and totally erect. Their heads turned as we passed, hollowed out eyeholes pouring darkness into the car.

Sugarboy jammed his hands to the side of his head, wagged his fingers and made a face at them through the window. They slowly imitated his hand movements in unison.

I looked at Doyle, who frowned at the naked pair like a disapproving parent. I had never taken him for a prude. Maybe he objected to their cheap costuming. "Is this some sort of orgy?" I asked, hiding my discomfort with a lame attempt at humor.

Doyle shrugged. "It'll be what you want it to be. But it'll be something, that's for sure."

"I'm ready for anything!" Cincinnati squealed, hugging Doyle, who had craned his neck to watch the two men run back into the forest as if being chased.

Mismatched automobiles and campers were parked on either side of the road, stretching as far as the eye could see into the shadowed depths of the forest ahead of us.

"Pull in behind the last car," Doyle said.

"So many people," Sugarboy muttered through clenched teeth, scratching his neck raw as the car squeaked to a halt.

"Grab the tent," Doyle said to Sugarboy, who was about to protest when Doyle tossed him a baggie full of pills. His mouth cracked into a jack-o'-lantern grin, and he threw open the door and hustled to the back of the car.

The rest of us piled out into the unnatural dusk, accept for Escofet, who was sleeping in the back seat. "What about him?" I asked, half hoping he had over-dosed on a noxious stowaway Doyle secreted back from the jungle.

"Leave him. He'll catch up later."

"What's he on?"

"I don't know, but I wish I had some." Doyle put his ropey arm around my neck and grinned, projecting that glow out of his mouth and eyes like a blanket. "We'll have to ask him later."

We walked nearly a mile on a gentle upward incline, joining a procession of travelers from all stations of life and what looked like a hundred countries across the globe. Many of them spotted Doyle and offered greetings of various sorts. He responded in turn, like some sort of pilgrimage ambassador. This was Doyle's Christmas card list come to life and congregating on one California mountain. An advert for international brotherhood right out of central casting. His mystery deepened, if that was possible. Between multilingual salutations, we all trudged toward the locus of light dead ahead that would lead us out of the forest and back into the sun.

We breached the womb of trees and emerged into a vast clearing, and I could have sworn we stepped into a medieval carnival. Thousands of people clad in outlandish garb or some far-flung native dress danced, spun, and congregated in tight groups on the tamped-down grass. A tent city was set up at the far end of the glade, while gaily festooned vendor booths fronted the trees to the right. Lording over it all was a massive central structure built out of a mountain cliff that rose up into the clouds. It was a hundred feet high and a football field wide, erected from mortared stone and thick wooden planks, topped with an onion dome that could have been ripped from eldest Siam or reddest Moscow. Narrow windows dotted the sides, giving the impression of a church, or perhaps a fort.

By the weathering and veins of creepers crawling up the sides, whatever this place was, it must have been here for a while.

"Crazy, man…" I breathed, soon realizing that Doyle was waiting for my reaction. "What is this place?"

"This is the Listening Place," Doyle said, taking all of it in with the appraising eye of a construction foreman. He glanced at me and winked. "One of them, anyway."

A smiling woman with striking yellow eyes and skin tanned from a faraway sun skipped over and hugged Doyle before handing Cincinnati a flower. It looked lush and tropical, shining as if made of wax. Just like the woman who gave it. "Power to the children," she said in a dreamy voice.

Cincinnati brought the flower to her nose and gasped. "Wow, it smells like… like… my grandmother's farm." She giggled and cooed, and I saw a glimpse of the little freckle-faced girl from Ohio, before she traded everything certain and safe for a chance to chase kicks and wild boys in the weird hothouse of San Francisco.

Sugarboy was eying vendors' row, which was insulated by a coterie of patiently waiting customers. "Y'all sell candy around here?" he asked the woman without facing her. She handed him an identical flower before padding away, liming the magic hour sky with the serpentine curls of her black hair. Sugarboy glanced around sheepishly, then inhaled the glistening petals. A wince escaped his lips and he staggered. Swallowing a wave of emotion, he threw the flower to the ground and stomped it flat, before skulking away with that hitched, agitated gate of his.

"What did it smell like?" Cincinnati called after him.

"Aftershave," Sugarboy murmured, as his mind tumbled backwards to those places he had tried to leave buried in the west Texas sand of east Lubbock. *My stepfather's aftershave*, he thought, hoping his mouth didn't move as he worked the words across his swollen tongue.

I watched Sugarboy melt into the crowd. "We're gonna lose him."

"Probably," Doyle said. "He'll get what he needs here, or he'll go home."

I stood back and marveled at the scene, again noting the smiles and bows shot Doyle's way. This wasn't like Telegraph Hill. This was an international procession of young and old. Mostly old. Yet all of them respectful, and often near reverent. "Why does it seem like everyone knows you up here?"

"Not everyone," Doyle replied cagily, eying a pretty girl with red hair twirling like a Dervish on an open patch of ground nearby, her bare feet tamping down a perfect circle in the grass and her beatific face aimed up at the sky.

"How'd you find this place? It doesn't seem real. It's like… like a play, or something."

Doyle took me by the arm and we walked like country gentlemen, Cincinnati falling in behind us, still holding the flower to her nose, grazing her thin lips as she inhaled deeply, eyes lidded heavy. A little girl again, almost beautiful. Almost.

"Have you ever traveled, Barnacles?"

"Me? Yeah, of course. I ended up out here, didn't I? I mean, in the city."

"I don't mean *moving*, I'm talking about *traveling*. From this plane, to the next, and the next, and to the billion billion beyond."

I felt silly, small-minded, as I often did around Doyle. Like a child trying to hang out with the older, cool kid. "No, I guess I haven't."

"You should give it a shot sometime. You'll be surprised by what you find."

"But what is this place?"

"It's… *here*. It's now. But it isn't, you know?"

My silence told him that I didn't.

Doyle took in the scene, eyes coming to rest on the mountaintops capped with snow. "The Indian tribes shunned this place like the plague. Called it The Place of Too Many Secrets. The Armenians who arrived here after the genocide named it *Hetch Hetchi*. Nothing of Nothing. The white-bread mapmakers, hearing a few of the watered down legends, labeled it Devil's Mountain, which is a fucking joke on so many levels. But I guess they didn't know how else to describe what goes on up here, and other places like this."

"What goes on?" I asked with a bit of trepidation, remembering the two naked men standing in the forest. Masked and pale.

Doyle gestured with his chin to a bearded man wearing only a loincloth, blowing soap bubbles at a group of children who jumped and laughed, snatching the bubbles from the sky. Catching rounded rainbows. "You see that guy? That's Randy, an ex-Marine from your government's army. He killed three men and two women outside Pusan, then raped the ten-year-old daughter of the mother he brained with the butt of his rifle two minutes before."

I reacted with horror, feeling my stomach tighten with nausea. "What a monster."

"Yes, he was. A monster not born, but made by the territorial army of the United States of America. Transformed from lamb to lion in the space of one tour."

"What the fuck is he doing up here?" I said, my voice rising. "Around all this? Around *them*?" I pointed at the children.

"He's transforming back," Doyle said. "On that day in Korea, in that burning slaughterhouse, he stared into the void, and found himself alone. He didn't see what was really there, waiting for him, watching him, encouraging him. Randy was blinded by programming, which only exists to take away the true eye, and make us blind to the Father." I never took Doyle for a religious man, but what he was laying down sounded like the Sunday sermons I'd heard as a kid. "He came up here, traveled counterclockwise down the spiral of what we call the mind and what hides there underneath, and found what he was looking for. His eyes were opened to the truth, within and without. He's become a child again."

Once again, I didn't understand what Doyle was talking about, and this time, I didn't try to hide it. Instead, I shook my head and collapsed onto the grass, burying my head in my hands. "I don't know what's going on," I said, embarrassed, figuring that this was the end. Maybe it was that weird stuff Doyle smoked, giving me a contact high that I couldn't shake. Whatever it was, I knew I didn't have the ingredients to stand with Doyle, so I figured I'd end the charade on my ass.

He sat down across from me, crossing his legs and sticking a blade of grass into his mouth. After almost a minute of him not saying anything, I looked up, and found him gazing up at the huge structure across the meadow, that grew out of the mountain like a distended belly. "When I was rolling through the Hindu Kush, looking for prospects," Doyle began, taking on a practiced tone, as if he had told this story before, although I'd never heard it. "I caught whispers from the local Sufis of this bizarre medicine man who sat on the summit of the highest mountain in Kashmir, in search of this empty state of mind called 'nirvana' that waited for us all behind the illusion of this meat suit we call The Self. Didn't eat for thirty years. Thirty fucking years, can you believe that, Barnacles?"

"No," I said.

Doyle's grin dropped. "Well, it's the fucking truth. The body can be told lots of crazy things if the mind knows how to say it."

"Yeah, I get that."

Doyle looked closely at me, probing behind my eyes, waiting for a spark of something akin to understanding. Finally, he went on. "So anyway, while this cat was up there, communing and listening and not eating or thinking about anything other than what could lay beyond the roof of the world, a strand of Knowledge happened across the mountaintop, pouring into him like a lightning bolt finding a key on the kite. Flesh made antennae. ZIIIPPP!" Doyle snapped his fingers and laughed, but there was no music it in. "Old man didn't find nirvana, he found something DIFFERENT. Something older than Allah or Shiva or Yahweh or any of those bullshit cartoons. Waiting out there in the dark, with so many secrets to share. And shared they were… Now, our Punjabi friend is passing on what he learned, one person at a time. He's a cosmic guru, this one. Fully legit, and I've checked out a few. He's got the sight."

"Guru?"

"Holy man. Shaman. Professor of the Divine. Whatever you want to call it, it's the goddamn same. Always *has* been. We just put new labels on it that we recognize, like a can of fucking soup. Same soup, same can. Different packaging. So we eat it like good hungry Christians, you dig?" Doyle lit up one of those strange cigarettes of his. "This guru – The Nightjar, they call him, after some Indian bird that nests on the ground but flies in the air – climbed down from his high-altitude perch like Jesus fucking Christ himself who spent time in India, by the way. The perverts in power won't tell you that, Barnacles. No fucking way. Too *Eeeastern*… " He drew out the last word in the flat accent of a disgusted Middle American, took another drag and exhaled, the smoke twisting into ghostly seraphim around us. "So anyway, cat starts to wander, talking about the REAL deal. News spreads across the north, and in a matter of weeks he's tearing the country sideways, pissing on religious hierarchy and giving the finger to madrassas and false holy places, gathering his followers around new ones, carving away at the status quo from the inside, like a life-giving cancer. The Hindus hated him, and the peacenik Buddhists weren't much kinder. The police in Uttar Pradesh put a bounty on his head. But the villagers *dug* him, all the way through Nepal and into China. They remembered the stories of the elders, the ones told around cave fires after the dinosaurs died. This guy was telling them again. Everything old is new again…"

Doyle handed me the smoke, but I waved him off. He took another drag and went on: "The heat got so bad, with the police roundups at gatherings and death threats, his disciples had to sneak him into Pakistan, wrapped him in a shroud and hid him among the Muslims, hoping to get him to the sea at the port of Karachi. Instead, he disappeared and visited eight villages in four nights. Local Imams burned down each one after he left, once they heard what had happened." Doyle's eyes burned, and not with that normal protective glow. This was something more intense, much more private. "When the Nightjar opens his mouth, opens his *arms*, what flows out of him is righteousness from the way, *way* back. This is wisdom from the Beyond, the House of the Old Father, and what he's teaching is cutting the nuts from everyone who bleeds humanity dry with threats of eternal damnation in fairytale land. He's read the poetry of the universe, listened to the music of dead stars, and took in everything that was out there waiting, his body serving as a vessel. Writing a song. A love song from dear old dad. Once he came down from the mountain, hollowed out and filled up again, he gifted us all by sharing this solitary thing with everyone he met."

"What's that?" I realized I hadn't swallowed since he began his story. Maybe I believed more than my mind would allow.

His dilated pupils danced above his white, perfectly straight teeth like two black dimes ringed in blue. "The embrace."

"I don't get it."

"Don't you ever get tired of saying that?"

"Yes," I said, and meant it.

"Then stick around, and you won't ever say that again."

The low register peel of a great bell rang through the valley, issuing from somewhere deep inside the onion dome. It repeated, shaking through me like the vibration of a bass string as big around as my arm.

Doyle sat up straight and cocked an ear to the repeating sound, seeming to find new things in each chime. He grinned over at me. "Time for the service."

Thousands of people stood patiently in a queue that spiraled around the structure, looking inside the doorway, hoping to get a glimpse of what lay beyond. As they waited to reach the door, men and women, nearly indistinguishable from each other due to the lack of facial and cranial hair, walked up and down the line holding bins labeled *Donations to the Father* in pink, bouncy letters. As each pilgrim walked past, they dropped in wallets, watches, jewelry. Some even tossed in their clothes, returning to the line in various stages of undress as the shadows of trees and peaks cut slowly across the clearing.

I walked past the line with Doyle, heading toward the entrance. Just like with every joint on the Hill, Doyle never stood in line. VIP all the way, regardless of the geography. "Why are they doing that?" I asked, motioning to the rapidly filling bins, trying to avoid the sporadic nakedness, as my blush would surely out me as a prude.

"You can't enter the temple burdened by the outside world," Doyle said. "Cuts down on the transmission, like lead between an X-ray. But aside from all that," he added, shooting me a mischievous grin, "everything's better when you're naked."

I looked around at the variety of mostly unclothed flesh, noting the variety in shape and size and skin tone and hair density. "I don't know about that."

Doyle laughed and threw his arm around my shoulders, kissing me on the side of the head. "You're a real peach, you know that, Barnacles? If I didn't like pussy so much I'd marry you tomorrow."

We walked to the front of the line and passed through the wide doorway. The side of my head where Doyle's lips touched it throbbed with a liquid warmth. Neither of us had removed any clothing, but I felt more naked than I'd ever felt in my life.

Inside, people were seated on a dirt floor in evenly spaced lines, just inches apart from each other, like a mosaic of humanity. The air was heavy with burning incense that billowed from giant copper braziers hanging from thick chains bolted to the vaulted ceiling of the dome, that wasn't as naturally sloping as one would expect from the outside, but possessed a hyperboloid geometry that made me dizzy. Or maybe it was the smoke, which smelled just like Doyle's strange little cigarettes.

The hushed congregation was facing a low stage built at the front of the cavernous space, backed by heavy curtains of a thick and lustrous fabric. Doyle led me to the far end of the room, just in front of the rise, and squeezed my shoulder. "Wait here," he said into my ear, "and don't get on stage, no matter what I say."

The bell chimed again, startling me, mostly because it seemed to be coming from directly underneath the room, somewhere deep under the mountain, and not from a hidden steeple. *This is the church, this is the steeple, open the door, and see all the people...* I realized after a few fuzzy moments that I was staring down at my waggling, intertwined fingers. Perhaps I was becoming a child again, as well. I looked up to show Doyle, but he was gone. The recessed lights hidden in a gutter circling the high walls dimmed at that moment, and the tolling of the bell abruptly stopped. I could hear the beating of my heart in my ears. It was a slow, syrupy rhythm. The sound of an organ in mid-dream.

In the heavy silence emerged the creak of rusted wheels. All heads turned in unison to the right, as another of the hairless men pulled a rope attached to a rough wooden cart, atop which was seated a small, gnarled figure dressed in thick, simple robes the color of clotted cream, a hood covering its head. That cart was led in a narrowing spiral around the stage, then brought to a rest in the center, facing the crowd. The hairless man walked to the backing curtain and pulled it aside, revealing Doyle, now changed into a ceremonial robe of rich burgundy brocade. The crowd moaned softly, a thousand strong mouthing the sound "*oooooo*" which grew in subdued strength, compressed volume amplified by the identical pitch of so many vibrating throats.

Doyle strode forward, raising his arms, as he did just before story time on Telegraph Hill, but this time without a Mason jar of Jungle Juice in his hand. A circle stitched in shiny black silk adorned his chest. No, not a complete circle. It was broken, lacking a finishing piece on one rounded side. The corrupted symmetry somehow unnerved me, and I suddenly grew nostalgic for the small crescent of Regular Family that gathered around in a complete circle on the dirty cement of the old Victorian. That seemed like a simpler, quainter time of a long gone nostalgic past, even though it only happened twenty-four hours prior.

The crowd gathered here gave off a different vibe than the one living on the Hill. This group, although similar on the outside, was infused with a frantic yearning buried shallow, just under their whimpers and supplications. Doyle strode to the cart and unceremoniously pulled back the cowl covering the crouching figure's head, revealing folds of leathery bronze skin heaped over the skull and face of a tiny man. He resembled a rotten potato, or a deflated balloon wrapped over a doll.

The man raised his chin from his chest and regarded the crowd through eyes pressed shut by deep wrinkles. One of his sockets pulsated, then opened like sliced flesh, as a sticky orb the size and consistency of a martini onion bulged from his face. Hazy, pus yellow and grown over with cataracts, it seemed totally sightless, but it moved across the crowd hungrily, his wasted body turning with great effort.

Doyle placed a microphone stand in front of the seated man and turned it on hot. Feedback squealed through the room, fading to a low drone.

The shriveled man began to hum along with it. The audience took up the vibration, and the whole vaulted structure filled up as the strength of the thrumming increased in texture, creating an invisible mass in the air that pressed against everyone. The acoustics of the building were perfect, absorbing the sound and amplifying it back without echo. The ground beneath my feet felt as if it was coming unmoored from the foundation and rising from the hardened skin of the mountain. And still the braziers smoked…

The sound of tablas began in some hidden place, pounding sharp and fast, interspersed with a metallic keening. The shrill piping of disjointed flutes joined the backbeat, bringing a frantic, zigzagging melody to the rhythm. A song was building, coalescing into something tangible, but no less chaotic, hitting the inner ear at an odd angle, unbalancing the brain. All that remained were the lyrics.

"Who among you will sing?" the shriveled man rasped into the microphone, his lips barely moving. The voice sounded like the shifting of sand, the scrape of great boulders. The accent was strange, undercut with a clipped hesitancy. Not exactly central Asian. Not exactly from anywhere.

"*I will,*" a voice shouted from the crowd.

"Your Father loves you," the man said. No speakers were present on the stage or dangling from the arched ceiling, but his words boomed out into the room.

"*And we love Our Father,*" the congregation replied as one.

"Your father waits for you."

"*And we wait for Our Father!*"

"The Father is a Child to his Father, and to his Father before him. We are all the Children."

"*We are all the Children!*"

"Who will enter the holiest of holies?" the man barked through rubbery lips. Doyle was nowhere to be seen. "Who will be baptized and born new, ready the truth of paradise?"

The crowd rose to their feet, reaching their hands to the stage. "*We will! We will!*"

"Who will feel the embrace, the hug of the servant?"

"*We will! We will!*"

"Who will be first? Who will be first to be last?"

The drumming and the piping and the ping of metal stopped. I felt a hand on my shoulder. I turned, expecting to find Doyle, but it was the shaved man from the stage.

Doyle's voice, cut through the sudden stillness of the room. "My brothers will!" He stood now on the ground with the rest of us in front of the stage. Escofet and Sugarboy were at his side, both stripped naked, both standing stiffly at attention. The acne on Sugarboy's back seemed to wink like tiny, diseased eyes in the weird light of the room.

"They've come to learn the song," Doyle said, gripping them tightly by the shoulder with each hand. "They've come to feel the embrace. They are the children waiting for their father's arms."

"Approach," the man croaked, his one open eye fixed greedily on the two men.

Doyle led both to the stage and climbed the low stairs, walking them to the seated man, who slowly raised his arms, holding them out wide. "The father seeks to provide the attention and care we all should have received as children," the old man said. "The father seeks to right the wrongs. Restore the balance."

The crowd moaned again, a sound of longing, expectation. Sugarboy and Escofet got to their knees and nuzzled in close to the man's torso, clinging to him like two kittens pawing at the teats of their mother's belly. Sugarboy shook, sobs wracking his body, undulating under his jutting ribcage. Escofet just smiled, like he was home. The wrinkled man's arms emerged from their cloaking and wrapped around both, enveloping them in his embrace. His wingspan seemed too wide for someone of his stature, his fingers too long and knuckled in too many places. He hugged Sugarboy and Escofet firmly, drawing them into the parted section of his garment, into the wrinkled skin of his chest and stomach.

His grip tightened, the sinews of his distended arms bulging taut, and the men slowly disappeared inside the man's robes without a sound. First the faces and heads, then torsos, hips, and two sets of bare feet were drawn inside the seated man like pouring melted butter through a sieve.

The hidden bell tolled. The crowd gasped, clutched at each other.

"The children have gone home," the tiny man said. His eye closed, and his head lowered once again to his chest.

Doyle walked to the front of the stage and bent to the microphone, his eyes shining like sparking embers. "Thus concludes tonight's service."

The crowd began chattering at once, breaking the silence with an explosion of confused noise and animating a thousand formerly sleeping corpses. Many of them rocked back and forth. Several more shot to their feet and thrashed in some violent dance, before falling to the ground, speaking in gibberish like an old revival tent meeting. Some joined the dance, others heading quickly for the doors, expressions ranging from dreamy wonder to masks of horror. Many of them cried and held each other. I wasn't sure if this was out of disappointment or trauma. Possibly both.

I couldn't wrap my mind around what had just happened, if I was just witness to a magician's trick or something much deeper. My brain felt funny. I had a difficult time remembering yesterday, how we had arrived at this place. I just remembered locomotion, travel. A gray jumble of freeway concrete that led to this place high above the regular world. There seemed to be no going back, because forward was the only thing that made sense, and wasn't shrouded in an anxious mystery.

Nelson.

Somehow I heard Doyle's voice above the din, the slap of bodies and weird chanting. Doyle was standing on the stage, the microphone gone. *Nelson*, he said again, his lips not moving over a curious grin that lit up his face. Did I imagine it? He held out his hand. The full force of that glow enveloped me, and instead of heading toward the door, I walked towards him, the crowd parting in front of me. Pleading, envious faces looked up at me, and I couldn't help but feel special. Blessed. He had called me by my first name. Not my name from the Hill, but my real name. He knew me.

That name climbed inside of me, just as we climbed the stairs to the stage, hand in hand, and followed the man on the cart through the opening in the curtain. I didn't care what anyone else in the room believed. Doyle was my guru, and I'd follow him to the ends of the earth, and probably beyond.

The light slowly faded with the sound of the crowd behind us until we were in total darkness. All I could hear was the squeak of the cart wheels, and the pounding of my own heart. I couldn't feel Doyle's hand in mine anymore. I couldn't feel my feet touching the spongy ground, and yet I had the sensation of moving downward in a tight corkscrew, although I never brushed up against a wall or ceiling. I was adrift inside the throat of some great beast perched on the lip of the outer void, moving toward the culmination of all of my wandering. I was about to travel.

The sound of the wheels ceased and I felt the air change, growing more damp and cold and constricting, pressing in on me as would the steam in an over-heated room. There was a sensation of the material world reconstituting around me, and then I felt the ground under my shoes. It was uneven, ridged, and I had to readjust my weight to stay on my feet as my brain seemed to find my body underneath it again.

"Bring us some light," I heard Doyle say. I couldn't tell where he was. His voice sounded clear, but muffled, as if he spoke directly into acoustic tile.

"As you wish, Mr. Wolverton," someone said.

Torches flared to life one by one and started to move, as more of the shaved men emerged from alcoves in what the flickering firelight in their hands showed to be an enormous cavern with craggy walls, twice the size of the room we had just left, roughly hollowed out by tectonic shifts or some other blind elemental force that found rock to be nothing but deluded clay.

As the torches grew in number and the light brighter, I realized that the walls weren't jagged cave rock, but a tapestry of bones. Millions and millions of bones, in various shapes and sizes and species, from a dozen eras of planetary history, fused together from floor to ceiling with the mortar of time and glacial ooze of living rock. And although the bones were scattered and the body structures vague, it was clear that whatever living things they had once been, they were all individually facing—*paying eternal homage to*—one singular object: a wide sheet of raised, jet-black stone in the center of the cavern, which jutted at a 45 degree angle from the cave floor, like an insect display, and held in stasis a half-exposed fossilized spine of what looked to be a giant snake, but topped with a massive skull that more closely resembled a Tyrannosaur. Or a dragon. It had died in a loose, nearly perfect circle, open mouth and teeth facing its tail, but not quite reaching it... The broken circle pattern on Doyle's robe, here calcified and memorialized by an innumerable pattern of dead pilgrims... Ouroboros before it could complete its mad autosarcophagy... Failure of the Eternal Return, frozen for all eternity in a half layer of volcanic rock that must have been a billion years old. This was the elephant graveyard for every vertebrate creature that slithered, walked, swam, and flew across this planet since the cooling of the primordial soup.

I stood, mouth agape and mind spiraling, still somehow rooted to the bones under my feet, while the shaved men busied themselves around me, paying me no mind as they sorted through the donation bins, grouping, counting and labeling each item down to the last sock and faded penny. Others packed up documents and took down draperies that had formed impromptu tents within this hollow in the earth—basically moving house, if one's house was a traveling circus of the damned.

"I'm sure you have a few questions," Doyle said, suddenly at my side. He shook out a stiff, leathery suit as one does after pulling a wet blanket from the wash. He began to fold it carefully, trying to smooth out what wrinkles he could in more of a nervous habit than anything actually effective. It then dawned on me what it was in his hands, but I couldn't bring myself to believe it. But, just moments later, I was taking it for granted and speaking around it, as if it could have happened, and *does* happen. A man holding the flesh suit of another man, in a cave made of bones. The surreal had become reality. Nightmares more tangible than the outside world, which seemed so far distant from where I was standing at that moment.

"What happened to him? The Nightjar," I said, my voice feeling as if it came from someone else and I was listening to it as one would a stranger. I gestured to the suit as Doyle fussed with a zipper, digging skin out of the teeth so it would glide properly and find purchase.

He glanced up at the ceiling, which was pocked with openings that could easily accommodate a person. Or something the size of a person. "Oh, he's around here somewhere."

"What *is* he?" The stranger with my voice spoke again.

"A servant. Just like me. And just like—" A tittering hiss filtered down from the warren of holes in the ceiling of the cavern, and Doyle just grinned, laying the haphazardly folded skin suit to the side, which was solemnly picked up by one of the hairless men and ferreted away to one of the quickly filling wooden storage boxes. "Well, okay, he's a *lot* different than any of us, but let's just say he plays for the same team."

My jaw worked without sound. I needed water. I needed to drink every gallon of goddamn Lake Ogallala, where my family went camping every July 4th. The fireworks looked so beautiful reflected in the lake. Like cosmic spiders, revealing themselves in an explosion of terrifying light and sound for only a few seconds, before burrowing back into the dark. Nebraska was so far away now. Everything was. "What happened to Sugarboy and... that other guy?" I said, feeling my voice return to my throat. "Your friend."

"Now *that* I can't tell you. I mean, I would tell you if I knew, you dig? But I don't, so I can't."

The inclusion of the *"you dig"*—something the old Doyle would have said, the Doyle who wasn't some pseudo religious leader—set my already chattering teeth on edge, and seemed to focus me, ripping me away from the saw-blade edge of awe and possibly insanity at the existence of such a place, of such things, and dropping me closer to a more rational state of mind tethered to reality by the familiar nudge of irritation. It was blasphemous, the new mouth saying these old words. More so than anything that was said out on that stage, than what was buried here under this mountain.

"Why did you bring me up here?"

"I wanted you to see," Doyle said, reclining against the hipbone of some great forgotten beast. "And then I wanted you to decide."

"See what? A buried museum? Some space-case, bourgeois religion? A cheap magic trick?" Even though I said the words, I didn't believe them, not in the dismissive way they came out. I was embroiled in something huge, and way beyond my comprehension. But I wanted to insult him for lying to me, thinking me a dupe. I probably wouldn't make it out of this cave, but I wouldn't go out like a chump.

Doyle couldn't believe my words either, judging by the expression on his face. "Magic trick? *Magic* trick?" he snarled, air expelling from his lungs in shock. "Do you think what you saw up there was a fucking parlor game?"

"I don't know." I crouched down, trying to get small. "I don't know what I saw. I don't know what any of this is."

His face became deathly calm. "Let me clarify it for you."

Doyle nodded his head, and one of the shaved men walked forward and stopped, still as stone. Doyle snapped his fingers, and something large landed with a heavy thud behind the man. There was a ripping sound, followed by a gentle lapping. The man's face held its concentrated expression as sweat beaded his forehead, then poured down his face. His body shook, then started to writhe, as his skin expanded outwards like a stretched, veined sausage, facial features and muscles popping, before every inch of him burst, showering a twenty-foot radius with a spray of blood and meat. What bone and chunks remained were choked down in segmented jerks by a massive, squirming worm the general shape and color of a garden grub but the size of a jersey heifer, cross-mated with a jungle variety centipede.

"The fuck!" I screamed, wiping gore from my eyes and scrambling up the wall as far as my worthless feet would take me, which wasn't very far.

Once it finished eating, the slug emitted a shrill scream like the folding of metal and slithered its way back up the wall to escape the light in a hitched, coiling motion, evidencing a total disconnect with movement on land, or possibly three dimensions.

"What *is* that?" I ducked down and shielded my head as the worm disappeared back into one of the holes in the ceiling, yowling in a rising, halting pitch that sounded like madhouse laughter as it buried itself deeper into the primeval granite behind the skeletal arabesque.

My mind swam, the pattern of bones all around me twisting and diving in a stuttering pattern that made me nauseous. I dropped to my knees and vomited. I wanted to expel everything I had seen and now knew. I was sure this was all the result of something Doyle had given me. This was all a hallucinatory dream.

It *had* to be. Oh fucking yes, I needed this to be true, or else I'd bash my fucking brains out with a rock. With a dragon bone. "What is that thing?" I asked, playing the role in my waking dream, this inverse déjà vu, bile dripping from my quivering lips.

"A Servitor," Doyle said, gazing up with a smile of pride at the now populated tunnel in the ribcage of the world. "A Pure One sent here as a missionary to spread the ballad of Old Leech." I stared up at Doyle, not understanding. "You know, the song that gave us speech, taught us math, physics, how to split the atom."

"I don't— This doesn't…"

"Okay, call him the choir. Or maybe the A&R rep. Our tiny Punjabi friend here, or…" Doyle looked around, not finding the skin suit. He shrugged. "Wherever he is, climbed the antennae of our planet looking to hear something, *anything*, reaching **WAY OUT** from his mortal shell to hear the truth amid the dead silence of the universe, and OL found his frequency." Doyle looked at the circular arrangement on the black stone slab and smiled. "He called, dialing the right number, and someone answered. The rest is history, or soon will be. He's just one of many."

"Then what are you?"

Doyle cocked his head to the side, as if he had never considered this question before. "A fundraiser, I guess. Bandleader, maybe." He laughed. "With pedigree, of course."

"I've never heard of this… leech. Is he your god?"

"No and yes. If he is a god, he's yours, too. You just don't know it yet. Not knowing the truth won't stop it from existing, or doing what the truth does."

"Which is?"

"Finding its way to the light. In this case, Old Leech isn't too keen on all that illumination, so it's going to do a little major redecorating around this corner of the multiverse, make it a little more cozy for when he stops by for a visit."

I looked around the room with eyes opened just a little bit wider, taking in the gravity of the eons of animal and human bones stacked on top of each other, showing a devotion stretching back so far my brain couldn't comprehend it all. The hidden god of the mountains, worshipped in secret under the mountain. Humanity didn't know a goddamn thing, maybe didn't want to. Ignorance is bliss, bliss in ignorance, my crown for just one more second of ignorance. "Your god is coming?… Here?"

"Oh yes," Doyle said, his eyes gleaming in the dusky torchlight. "That's always been the plan. My family, and a few others, have made it a point to roll out the red carpet when he arrives."

I curled up into a ball, dislodging a femur of some early hominid in my hand and bringing it close to my chest like a little girl's dolly. Fetal position, longing for the womb. Lord, birth me again, far away from here. Or shoot me out stillborn, slimy and blue. Anything but this.

"I want to die," I moaned, fighting back another wave of nausea.

Doyle walked over and crouched down in front of my face. "Like hell you do," he said, breathing into the side of my head. "We're just getting to the good part." He stood up suddenly. "The time of the Arrival is upon us, and you could help lead the charge, my brother! We need good people, good men." Doyle fixed his gaze on the circular skeleton across the cavern. "Old Leech is patient, but he's also an impulsive motherfucker."

"I don't underst—"

He dropped to his knees again and took my by the shoulders. "Of course you don't, you fucking barnacle!" Doyle's face looked feverish, sweating madness. "I don't either, really. This is a birthright, and who can gauge the history of a family that stretches back to the time of the mastodon? The first tribe? Back when the play of the universe and the earth were more closely connected? Back when the Dark walked, or slithered, on our planet each and every night? What I *do* know is that a brigade is being put together. The foot soldiers are cozied up in the barracks all around..." Doyle swept his hands to the tunnels dotting the ceiling. "And in a dozen other outposts scattered across the planet. I've dropped in on them all, and everyone – everything – is ready and waiting. Now we need the generals." Doyle took my face in his hands, tossing that lasso again. This time, the rope was on fire. "I know that you know that I know what creeps deep inside of you. That thirst for *experience*, the taste of the edge. For the command of things that have no name. You and I are the same, Barnacles. We want to exterminate the status quo, and kick the doors in on a new era of enlightenment that will move our species from the apes we are to the earthly gods we are destined to become!"

He was squeezing my face now, and I ripped my head away from his grip, bringing fingers to my bruised cheek. "You've lost your shit."

"Have I?" His face fell, eyes becoming cold as a reptile as he stood up. Even their shape seemed to change. "Sink or swim. Song or meat. It's your choice." He held out his hand. I just looked at it. "It's going to be everyone's choice soon, so consider yourself getting in on the ground floor."

After several moments, I sat up, looked him in the eye, grinned ruefully, and took Doyle's hand. He gripped it and brought me to my feet, pulling me in for an embrace. I leaned in close to his ear, smelling that clean sweat of his and strange incense clinging to the nape of his neck. That intoxicating aroma of my former guru... In my mind, I saw myself running through the woods. I was followed, above and below, but I didn't turn around, because I knew if I did I'd want them to catch me. To kill me, because what was following me was worse than what I had seen inside the mountain. There were worse monsters still that hadn't yet been revealed, and I wanted to live in ignorance or die from the knowledge. The drums. The flutes. The song. In my mind, I ran...

"Meat," I whispered into Doyle's ear, before burying the bone into his neck like a dagger, driving it so hard it poked out the other side with a crimson blurt. He jerked away from me, pawing at the bone lodged just under his jaw, stumbled backwards and fell on his ass, blood spurting out from between his fingers, his teeth.

"You did it, Barnacles," he gurgled as he fixed a horrible smile outlined with dark red. "You... really did it..."

I staggered backward, horrified and proud of my action in equal measure, completely unaware of where my motivation to murder my friend, my teacher, my everything, had come from.

As Doyle fell to the floor, his life draining out of his grinning mouth, the black stone slab rippled like ink, or maybe flesh, and a sound – a voice – arose from inside all that endless black. It was quiet at first, vague, but built quickly to a terrifying volume. It howled, it roared, it yammered in a language I couldn't possibly understand that nearly split my eardrums and fried my brain like an egg.

And then it sang, and I stood there, listening. Song or meat. Both Doyle and I had our role now, and I dragged his body toward the pulsating slab of rippling black that lapped up and over the bones. Shrill barks and clicks came from the holes in the mountain. Things emerged from the openings, and watched the procession on the ossuary floor below. The song from the black slab grew louder, and I started to hum, as it started to make sense. Vibrations became words, stitched together into stanzas. New real estate in my brain began to map itself out. New synaptic connections were made. New notes discovered in a sonar range I never knew existed.

The first verse in this psalm I already knew. It was born inside me, in my lizard DNA, and I just needed to be swallowed and reborn to remember:

For one to transcend, one must kill their heroes. This is the way of Old Leech.

Thus concludes tonight's service.

TWINKLE, TWINKLE

Emily carefully re-positioned the Celestron 1400 HD telescope, a gift from her father for her recent eighth birthday. It was far too expensive, and she begged him off for as long as she could. But he was insistent, and she thankful, especially considering why he bought it.

She scrolled to the left, in the direction of her mother's writing hand, moving to a deeper, blacker section of the glittering cosmos while humming the tune to "Twinkle, Twinkle Little Star," as she always did every night while setting up. Her father had advised her to check the darkest areas—the "cold spots"—because that was where the new stars popped up. These empty voids would be the best places to find her mother, who died three weeks and four days ago tonight.

"Find her yet?"

Phillip stood in the doorway to the rooftop balcony, clutching a full glass of wine that never seemed to leave his hand these days. Emily smiled sadly at him. "Not yet, but I will," she said. "She's got to be out there somewhere by now, right?"

"Yeah, I would think so," Phillip said, taking a healthy pull from his glass. "But sometimes the journey takes a little longer for some."

Emily thought about this, then brightened with an idea. "Maybe the angels are holding onto her, and won't let her go."

Phillip nodded, scratching his three week and four day old beard. "Yeah, maybe.... Wouldn't you?"

"Yeah, I would for *sure*," Emily said, returning her eye to the telescope, gripping the pencil in her right hand. "I'd squeeze her so tight she'd never get away."

Phillip found himself nodding as he stared off into the empty gloom, blind to the stars, before turning back to the open balcony door, not sure where he was going, or what he was going to do once inside. "Don't stay up too late, monkey," he said. "You've got school tomorrow."

"I won't," Emily said, as she continued scanning and humming, finally quietly breaking into song:

> *Twinkle, twinkle, little star,*
> *How I wonder what you are.*

Emily adjusted the refractive lens to probe deeper into the cold spot, marking down her position with each recalibration.

> *Up above the world so high,*
> *Like a diamond in the sky…*
> *Twinkle, twinkle, little star,*
> *How I wonder what you are…*

A bright smudge centered in her finderscope. Emily sucked in a breath, her eye widening past the black rubber hood. "Daddy," she cried. "*Daddy!*"

After a few moments, Phillip ran out onto the balcony. "What is it?" he asked, slightly winded.

"I found her." Emily said in an awed whisper, a joyous smile spreading across her tiny, perfectly symmetrical face, nearly dividing it in two. "I found mommy."

His brow knitted above a dubious frown.

"I *found* her. Come look!"

Phillip stepped unsteadily to the telescope, as Emily bounced around him. "Look," she said, guiding him to the eyepiece. "That part of space is always dark. *Always* dark. See?" Emily grabbed a sheath of vectored paper and showed Phillip the intricate star maps she had been compiling since her birthday two weeks prior. She moved her finger past meticulously charted and labeled celestial bodies and pointed to a vacant part of the lower right of the page, somewhere between Eridanus and a stellar grouping called Fornax. He'd never noticed these particular constellations in the weekly horoscope section of the Sunday paper. "Eridanus! The Supervoid of Eridanus, Dad! That's where we're looking, where the CMB couldn't find anything, and now mommy's there."

"The...CMB?"

"The cosmic microwave background map," she said with that tone of exasperation particular to little girls of a certain age.

Phillip's blank expression caused her to shake her hands in frustration. "Never mind. It's supposed to be dead space, a billion light years across. That's where they made room for all the new souls, and now mommy's there! She's *there*, Dad! Can you believe it?"

He couldn't, and wished that he could, even for one second, ashamed at his envy of her blissful ignorance. Her faith.

Heaven's suburbs, Phillip thought. He was incredulous, of course, which was a gentler offshoot of a deeply held cynicism only made worse the last few weeks. But then again, this was Emily. He knew better than to doubt anything she did, even if it was impossible that she had located her mother's detached soul in the deepest reaches of deserted space.

"Are you sure?" he said, vocalizing a different question than how it came out.

"I'm *positive*—it's Mommy. It's Mommy *for sure!*" Emily raised her arms above her head and did several graceful pirouettes while Phillip double-checked the map, then looked through the scope. He didn't really know what he was looking at on the page, but sure enough, a fuzzy, grayish shape hovered in the midst of nothing but black far up above.

"And that wasn't there before? In that particular area?"

"No. That's what I'm trying to tell you, Dad."

Phillip straightened, eyebrows raised. "Well..." She waited for him to continue, faced animated with expectation. "This is amazing, Emmy."

She beamed, for the first time in what seemed like forever. "It really is!" Emily exclaimed and hugged her dad, who was thinking more about what could possibly be his daughter's first legitimate astronomical discovery, at the wizened age of eight years and two weeks. She thought she had found things before—unnamed comets, rogue asteroids, alien spacecraft—but this somehow felt different. He'd check into it, of course. He'd been doing it for years, from the time of Emily's first StarNav at the ripe age of three. She always seemed to find something meaningful up amongst the stars, regardless of the equipment at hand.

Emily ran back to the telescope, and looked up into the heavens again. "You were right, Daddy. You said she'd come, and she *did*. She did!"

Phillip sat back in his chair, no longer worried about what this could mean for Emily's future at JPL, instead filled with satisfaction that he had somehow made his daughter happy. A fanciful set-up created in vain desperation was somehow paying off. He allowed himself to smile, as the occasion seemed to call for it.

"I have to mark down this reading, so we can never lose her again." Emily picked up the map and plotted out the cosmic position of her heavenly mother. "I *knew* it would be somewhere around Alpha Eridani, because that's the place where the double stars died and all the ghosts live in the Supervoid." She jotted down the coordinates on the graph paper, chattering to herself in a sweet, high-pitched voice.

Phillip wasn't really listening as he watched her with that rare sort of amazement that never seemed to abate. Like a clear dawn that forever kept its magic to the caveman who feared the death of the sun each night. This little creature, spreading her music and flame, lighting up a dark world. He had felt that way about Emily's mother, who taught him against all odds that love was shockingly and unquestionably real, and also the source of the greatest pain ever felt inside the fragile shell of the human body. Phillip's daughter had what her mother had, a fascinating differentness that changed the air in any room, no matter how stuffy. This unique ability, of course, also set her apart from the other children, who contented themselves with Barbis and garish cartoons while Emily was watching documentaries on William Herschel. She was always alone amongst her classmates, and now even more so. The singular always remain single, or at least singled out. It must be so hard for Emily, Phillip thought. He lost his wife, the only woman who laid bare his soul and made a wooden puppet into a real boy, but this little girl lost the only mother she'd ever know. She was half orphaned, and the sadness of that somehow helped distract Phillip from the searing knife slowly sawing through his guts, screaming for a bullet but settling for wine.

"Done!" Emily announced proudly, before looking up into the sky, trying to spot the new star with her naked eye while measuring with an antique sextant her mother had picked up for her at their favorite antique shop in Vermont. They had a cabin there once. Before the sickness. Now it rotted away with the damp leaves in the woods. "She's too far away," Emily said, disappointed.

"That's what telescopes are for," Phillip said, gathering Emily close to him and inhaling deeply the scent from the side of her head that only smelled like she did. "To watch our mommies."

Emily liked this. "Can we watch her again tomorrow night, Dad?" she asked with a hopeful smile, leaning her head back on his chest and looking up.

"Of course we can, Emmie. Every night from now on."

She hugged him close and went back to the telescope, gazing into the infinite reaches of space for what seemed like hours, as Phillip dozed off in his chair, praying for dreams.

The next day, as he had done several times in the past, Phillip took Emily's position reading to his old college buddy who now worked in the astronomy department at Cal Tech, hoping that Emily could have possibly discovered a new star, a spinning chunk of ice, or even far flung planet, and that she could name it like she did all of her stuffed animals. Each one was named after the moons of Uranus, her favorite planet, partly because of its interesting physical makeup, but mostly because it was tragically underappreciated by astrophysicists in general. She thought about things like that. She thought about so many things a girl her age shouldn't, or shouldn't have to. But she did, and by her logic, why would someone have a doll named Sally when she could have an Umbriel, Miranda, or Titania?

Across town, Emily tried to sit through school the best she could, watching the sun trundle like a lazy snail across the sky, silently cheering its slow creep from horizon to horizon.

When the final bell rang, she raced out of the building to the curb, where Phillip was waiting to pick her up in his faded beige Subaru.

Emily opened the door. "Four hours and thirty-seven minutes to sundown."

Phillip grinned while putting the car into drive. "I'm not even going to imagine how you know that."

Emily looked out the window and up into the sky, cleverly stained blue to hide the real world beyond. She imagined her mother sleeping the day away behind this silken veil, stretching her long, pale limbs at the first blush of twilight, and emerging, hand in hand with the darkness, to look down at her daughter and husband who missed her so incredibly much. Emily turned to her father to tell him her theory, but found him blinking back tears. She wasn't sure if they were the happy or sad kind, and didn't want to ask. He wasn't used to crying, but was getting better at it.

Emily ate her dinner next to the kitchen window, keeping one eye on the sky, and another on the clock above the microwave. "T-minus fourteen minutes," Emily said, just as she had sixty seconds prior, and each of the last seven minutes before that. Phillip chuckled tiredly and poured himself another glass of caber-net, his uneaten food sitting cold in front of him. He liked his wine bone dry these days. And cheaper. The labels all looked the same now.

The sun slipped down behind the neighborhood's western tree line at Lake Avenue and headed toward the ocean, washing the valley in that distinctive Pasa-dena azure that kept cinematographers tinkering late into the night. Phillip liked this time of day best, when he and his wife would sit on the deck, hatching schemes and making outlandish travel plans that seems totally plausible during the hopeful haze of magic hour. Emily raced from room to room inside the house while Phillip stood on the deck, sinking into his slippers, feeling more alone than he ever had in his forty-two years. She seemed to be taking all of this better than he was. Amazing what faith can do. Even faith in fairy tales and the gentle lies that keep them afloat.

At last, the dwindling daylight gave way to darkness, heralded by a "*Yaa-hoo*!!" from the doorway as Emily clattered outside, wearing her mother's favorite Louboutin heels, Bebe sash, and Tiffany hoop earrings. Gifts from Phillip, as his wife never asked for anything, so Phillip naturally wanted to give her everything. All the way to the end. He would now do the same for his daughter, protecting her from pain and tears and death, battling the inexorable with every fiber of his being, every tool at his command. The world would close in soon enough and spoil the dance, but all the while Phillip would push back with the force of Atlas unburdened

"It's time," Emily said. "It's time to see Mommy again."

Phillip eased back into his chair with his wine, absently tapping the silver band on his left ring finger on the side of the glass. Emily buzzed around the patio, skipping the warm-up humming tonight and launching straight into the second verse of her song as she carefully arranged her map and made a few last minute adjustments to the telescope.

When the blazing sun is gone,
When there's nothing he shines upon,
Then you show your little light,
Twinkle, twinkle, through the night.
Twinkle, twinkle, little star,
How I wonder what you are!

"You're my mom!" Emily laughed, answering the lyrics, then looked into the eyepiece.

In the dark blue sky so deep
Through my curtains often peep
For you never close your eyes
Til the morning sun does rise
Twinkle, twinkle, little star
How I wonder what you are.

Phillip took a long drink and listened to his daughter sing, realizing for the first time how profound, and slightly unsettling, the lyrics were.

"Mommy isn't alone."

Emily didn't continue, and his finger stopped tapping. The extended silence shook Phillip from his thoughts, and he looked at his daughter. "What do you mean?"

"She has friends now," Emily said, her eye glued to the finderscope.

Frowning, Phillip got up from his chair. Emily stood aside while he squatted on creaking knees to have a look for himself.

"See?" Emily said. "*Lots* of them."

Phillip squinted into the eyepiece, and noticed that the fuzzy, gray shape from the night before was a little brighter, a little bigger, and now surrounded by several other formless shapes equally gray and fuzzy.

"Mommy's got friends," Emily said. "Lots and lots of friends. Isn't that wonderful?"

Phillip pulled back, wondering how a formerly vacant block of space could now be populated by a number of new, obviously enormous objects. "Did you adjust the lens to look further out?"

"Of course not. I didn't want to lose Mommy. It's in the exact same position as last night."

As Phillip pondered this, and Emily set about naming all of her mother's new companions, his cell phone rang. Phillip fished it out of his pocket and noted the number of his friend at Cal Tech. He answered. "So, is she gonna be famous or what?"

A loud, terrified voice crackled through the phone, babbling quickly, punctuated by shouts. Hasty explanations. Phillip's face went pale and he slumped back into the chair. His brain tumbled over what he was hearing.

After less than a minute, ending with pleaded commands, the dead phone fell from his hand and Phillip looked at Emily, who was talking in hushed tones to herself. The city had gone quiet, but he dared not look up. He pressed a quivering fist into his lips, digging into his teeth, looking for pain, slowly swallowing the words that his brain was struggling to understand. He could hear himself say it, and then fought to bring the words back inside. But he hadn't said anything, hadn't moved. Hadn't done a thing when everything around the balcony seemed to drain of color and form, leaving these simple wooden planks fully realized amidst a hostile smear of gray dotted with pin pricks of light. But they weren't just light. The light was just a reflection of what they really were.

And yet Emily kept smiling and naming her mother's new friends, which kept Phillip moored to the chair, to this reality. *Demeter, Hestia, Hypnos, Thanatos.* Did she know what she was saying? How many were up there? How many were coming? He downed his wine in one gulp, hoping that he would gag, but knowing that he wouldn't. She rattled off several more names, jumping to new pantheons, her voice becoming muddy in his ears. The music was all wrong. Sweat broke out on his brow, and it felt like blood pooling into his eyebrows.

"Is everything okay?" Emily stared at him with concern.

Phillip looked at her and worked his jaw, but nothing came out of his mouth. He could never hide anything from her. She was too smart. Way too smart for her age. What could he say? He knew that anything that slithered from the hole in his face would choke him and he'd die. And she'd be alone. For this last little while, at least. He'd let her down, just like he did her mother. In the end, he wouldn't be able to do a goddamn thing.

A tiny, moist hand rested on his arm. "Daddy?" Emily's eyes brought him back to here, to her, and he somehow forced a smile, feeling as if his neck would snap and send his skull bouncing to the cedar deck.

"Go look at Mommy," Phillip said, wiping his eyes. "And all her friends."

She returned his smile, and hummed, warming to the last verse.

Phillip fought back his voice, the insanity roiling in his stomach and the cackled scream on his lips that curdled the wine twisting in his guts. He would say nothing, granting her a least one more night of innocence. Gifting her, like with the telescope. Goddamn that thing, and what it saw. But then again, what did it really see? It found Emily's mother, allowing a child a tiny bit of satisfaction that closure brings the grieving. Another gift, however brief, before reality would shatter everything forever. Emily's future life flashed through Phillip's mind, making him dizzy, wrenching shut his eyes. Must not look up. His skin crawled.

His brain grew fingers, picking through what he was told. So this was what it was like to go insane.

As tears began to course down his cheeks, Phillip leaned back his neck that popped with each angle, and opened his eyes to the sky.

Emily, her left eye pressed to the scope, cast her happy gaze high up into space, finishing out her fairy tale mantra in complete and utter joy. That of an innocent calf, just outside the slaughterhouse.

In the dark blue sky so deep
Through my curtains often peep
For you never close your eyes
Til the morning sun does rise...

From the end of the telescope, where Emily's blinking eye peered out into the darkness, the angle and destination of her magnified vision shot up into the stratosphere, out into the solar system, zipping past the gas giants, past the twin ice giants, through the Kuiper Belt and out into the far flung, scattered reaches of unnamed space, where the once tiny smudges refracting off the tiny mirrors in Emily's Celestron 1400 loomed and grew as they neared.

At first, it looked like a cosmic cloud, or even a small swirling galaxy moving at a speed that that appeared glacial at a glance, until the size of the object was fully realized.

Twinkle, twinkle, little star...

The cloud moved closer, determined, and details materialized... Grasping tentacles... Swirling gaps that could only be mouths, capable of swallowing stars, lined with grinding teeth the size of moons... Slowing blinking eyes as large as Jupiter, glaring out into an unprepared and barely remembered dimension.

And this was just the first, as behind it an armada of similar creatures of immeasurable vastness followed its slug trail of wrecked planets and digested suns. This impossible swarm had awoken from a billion-year slumber at the center of infinity, and were now moving through our corner of spatial plane, devouring entire constellations, consuming the very fabric of our universe, leaving a nothingness of collapsing space in their wake.

How I wonder what you are.

Somewhere far, far away, a little girl too old for her skin laughed and spoke her mother's name, while a father sat silent for as long as he could.

THE MISSION

I knew by the sound of the scream that Biggs was gonna kill the Indian.
It was well past dawn, and I overslept again, on account of my recent bout of
nightmares that afforded me no rest, neither waking nor in slumber. Yanked
back into the morning air by that unholy holler, I jumped from my bedroll and
reached for my smokers. They weren't in my holster. They were in Biggs' hand.
Both of 'em. Goddamn a thief that shakes your hand first.

The rest of the party was already on their feet and taken sides, leaving me
out of it, as they knew I wouldn't, or more rightly couldn't. Biggs had Ebke and
Whittle. The Indian, called Sam by us palefaces and Laughing Fox by his Lakota
kinfolk, had the big Negro Jefferson standing behind him. Larsen, the Danish
farm kid who spoke less English than Sam, stood back from the group, gripping
his Springfield like a rudder, trying to figure out what the hell was going on.

Neither group was properly armed, as each man's Spencer was ringing the
old cottonwood shading the camp, just where I ordered them left the night before. Jefferson had a knotty tree branch resting over his shoulder, waiting to sam-
ple some white intellect. Sam, stripped to the waist, certainly had a blade or two
hidden in his britches. Still, no match for the two oiled-up Colts waving at Sam's
vitals - peacemakers given to me in a time of war by my uncle back In Omaha an
hour before hopping the wagon bound for the western wilds of our brand new
state of Nebraska.

Biggs screamed again, spitting on the ground under my irons, shaking so hard that he'd probably lose another tooth from that gangrenous mouth of his. He was a filthy man, inside and out, perfect for this sort of work in which we were now engaged. Men without honor or proper hygiene were ideally suited for this business of hunting and killing out on the Plains. Biggs always screamed when agitated, which was so regular you could set your timepiece by it. Regardless of regularity, it unnerved the hell out of me every single time.

"The fuck is all this?" I asked, startling Biggs.

"The red bastard tried to softpaw my tallywhacker!"

Both sides flexed at the accusation. I just rubbed my head, trying to wipe away the dead shell of unresolved sleep. I couldn't get any rest out here.

"That just don't make any sense," I said.

"It's true, Captain," Whittle cawed in that high pitched voice, licking his thin lips as much out of excitement at the thought of killing an Indian as the fear of doing just that. "I seen it. That Injun tried ta' jerk off Biggs."

"Pig try piss my face when I sleep," Sam said, flipping a razor-edged palm knife into view between his fingers, just like I knew he would. Sam wouldn't call Biggs anything other than Pig. "I miss."

"Fuck this prairie coon, Cap," Biggs said. "Let me do 'im here, and we can get on with our bidness. I reckon he be sendin' smoke signals to his brethren whiles we all sleepin'."

"Stand down, private," I said.

Ebke snorted. He had no dog in this fight. Didn't care for a damn thing in the whole wide world, including his own hide. The kind of man who was just born hollow, who just went where he was supposed to. Didn't matter, though. When the chips were down and the dander up, it's always light versus dark. To hell with this New World.

"But Cap—"

"I said stand down, private!" I snatched my pistols from Biggs, who didn't release them without a stubborn tug, like a child letting go of a toy that didn't belong to him. I checked the chambers. Both hot. "Biggs, how'd you get my sidearms?"

"I was jus' lookin' at 'em is all. Whiles you was sleepin'. Then this red fucker and his sideboot came at me, grabbin' where they shouldn't'a."

"Jefferson?"

"I was asleep. I woke up and found what you did." Jefferson said no more. He didn't expect anyone to believe him anyway. His whole life after '65 was borrowed time.

"Bluegums don't tell the truth nohow, Cap. Ain't in the slave nature."

The veins in Jefferson's neck bulged as he bellied another helping of unrequited murder, just like he'd been doing his entire life. Someday, he'd throw it all up, and bodies would be stacked high as a haystack in tribute. "War's over, Annie Reb," Jefferson growled.

"War'll never be over." Biggs spat on the ground. I checked for rotted ivory. "Not til all ya's get back under the whip."

Jefferson shoved Biggs so hard his legs came up over his head before falling like a scarecrow onto the tamped grass. In a blink he was on his feet and running for the cottonwood, but Larsen got there first, aiming a cocked and ready .50 caliber round into his face. A squeeze of the trigger would take his greasy head off at the shoulders. And it wouldn't be clean. I'd seen it happen at Gettysburg, which ended any hope I'd had to grow old without knowing that the body keeps moving for a spell even when the brain's gone. No chance of that after Gettysburg.

"*Fuck!*" Biggs shrieked, looking about for something to bash into Jefferson. I was mighty glad I took back my pistols, and that Larsen was quicker than he looked, being all thighs and thick wrists. Whittle bobbed up and down, nearly foaming at the mouth. Ebke jerked his eyes back and forth, laying wagers with himself.

In this uneasy moment, when all the insects hiding in the sod held their legs close, Sam stole my attention. He was squinting up the ridgeline that rose above the camp with an expression that I had learned to trust after serving with him for the last six months. Just as I was about to say something, a series of low whistles bled down the ravine and stopped everyone in their tracks.

"Well I'll be damned," I said, cutting the silence. The rabbits were waiting for us over the hillside, waiting for the wolves to catch up. Or maybe it was the other way around. This was like no game I'd ever encountered, and I'd hunted my fair share. They always ran scared. Every warm blooded critter on God's green, two legs or four. These were different, though. They didn't seem scared at all. They seemed amused.

"Tha's them!" Biggs scrambled for his gear, the tussle forgotten as the outside world and what waited there poured back in. There wasn't much glory in killing a fellow soldier. Just court marshal and a rope. Not that Missouri border trash like Biggs thought that far ahead. But any soft skull knew that dragging back two escaped Indians, dead or alive, from the land of their ancestors was a feather in the cap. Big chief eagle feathers. Especially since one of them was a major deal medicine man. Cheers and extra whiskey. Maybe a promotion. Maybe a few tanned ears to send home to pa, packed in salt to keep away the maggots.

I walked over to Sam, who hadn't taken his eyes off of the ridge of box buttes that rose to the east about a quarter mile out, topping the scrub brush like a row of busted teeth chewing up from the prairie. This was uneven country, shot through with hidden gorges and sudden peaks. It was nothing like the butter fields back home. "They up there?" I asked.

Sam shook his head. "Not there." Sam pointed behind us, away from where the whistles came. "There."

"I don't get it," I said. Sam shrugged and went to pack his bedding. Larsen readied the horses while Biggs checked and rechecked his Spencer. Ebke pulled out his pecker and took a piss on the fire, giggling the whole time. Weird fucker.

"Which way, sir?" Jefferson asked. I looked back at Sam, whose face was blank as slate, and nodded my head in the direction of the whistles.

"That way."

As we pushed our horses east, I glanced back at Sam, who was turned in the other direction. Goddamn that Biggs for putting thoughts into my head.

We spied a trail about a mile over the hill. Larsen found it, which just didn't sit right. Too easy. Farm boys ain't exactly expert trackers. Good to have at your side in a saloon dust up, as those coffee can fists always found purchase, but rosy-cheeked plowboys weren't born bloodhounds like those with a more suspicious nature. Sam hadn't said anything since we broke camp, which wasn't peculiar for him. But it was the way he wasn't saying anything that got to be worrisome. He knew something. I just needed to figure out what that was.

A few hours later, the trail went cold, but we kept riding anyway. Didn't have a choice. Just when I thought we should double back and recalibrate, Ebke shouted out and pointed. On top of a bluff, two figures on horseback stood facing forward, looking like a pair of black lizard eyes cut sharp against the pale blue of that infinite sky. It was so far away that the riders had no solid posture, but I knew that set of eyes was looking right at us. Probably right through us. Indians just have that way about them.

"I'll be damned if they ain't toying with us," I muttered.

Sam nodded. "If my people no want be found, they no be found." He spat on the ground, one of several bad habits he picked up in the Army. "They want be found."

"It's a trap, sure as rain," Ebke said nervously. He said everything nervously, but the added threat of kill or capture, from either side, had made him nearly spastic.

"Bet breed here's in on it," Biggs sneered.

"Unless ol' Sam can communicate with someone's mind, you're talking nonsense," I said, not totally sure that they couldn't.

"What we gon' do, sir?" Ebke inquired, more curious about my decision than the outcome. And the way he called me 'sir' always felt like an insult, because it was.

I took a mouthful of deer jerky. It tasted like funeral parlor sawdust. Musky and not properly cured. Muleys never were good eating. Goddamn Sandhills and all their unfit creatures. I missed the Papio Creek whitetails, getting stout and creamy off old man Neumeyer's corn.

"We follow 'em." I tried to swallow, but I couldn't, so I just kept chewing, fixing my eyes on Sam, who was getting harder to see by the hour.

It was late afternoon when we saw the creek. It seemed like a mirage at first, as it lay open and glistening on top of the rolling prairie like a fat, newly born serpent winding and sparkling in the hammered out sunshine.

I gotta admit that we were mighty glad to come upon it, as our horses were lathered something fierce, foamed over and gasping for water. Our canteens were sucking the ass end too, so a ragged cheer rose from our rode-hard band. But as the jubilation wore off, a peculiar feeling set in. No trees lined the banks, no algae collected in the side pools. It just wound wild, a quicksilver tentacle that didn't feel the need to carve its way down into the sandy soil like any other proper creek. Gratitude overcame our unease, as could water our horses and maybe wash off some dust before we kept on. The Indians were just a few hours ahead, and we were gaining on them, so a quick respite was sure as hell in order.

We guided our mounts to the water's edge, which was crusted over with a glaze of something white and brittle. The horses nuzzled the brook and then reared back, grousing and stamping the mud.

Biggs dunked his head in the stream and jumped back, choking out a mouthful of foam. "Fucking— s-salty!" Spittle dangled from his chin.

I bent down, cupped some water, and brought it to my mouth. Sure as shit, it was salt water, and colder than I thought possible. I turned to Sam, who was nodding slowly to himself.

Jefferson tasted it and hacked. "How we get salt water way out here? Ain't no ocean for…"

"Thousands of miles," Ebke finished for him, backing up from the stream. Larsen squatted by the water's edge and just stared. The water was deeper than it appeared, like a controlled canal that was set up to not eat away at the land. As if it was waiting to spread out over the Sandhills and drown the world if given the word.

"Sam?" I said. I didn't know what else to say.

The Indian mumbled something. Everyone waited for him to repeat it, even Biggs. Sam struggled to find the words in English. "Salt… Creek."

"Where does it come from?"

"Big water. Old water. Down." Sam pointed to the ground and walked away. "No good here. Bad things in old water."

"What we gon' drink, Cap?" Biggs shouted, kicking at the salt crystals that had formed curious patterns in the low grass. "Even the water out here's poison!"

I ignored Biggs' bellyaching and sent Jefferson and Larsen to scout from the nearest hilltop.

"This place ain't right, sir," Ebke said, blinking quickly. "I'm tellin' ya… I lived in Nebraska Territory all my life, and I don't recognize this place no more. Darkies 'n reds suppin' next to God fearin' white folk. Salt water coming out of the ground like we on a boat with a hole in the bottom… Shit ain't right, sir."

"We're a state now, and this is how states act when they're united."

"I ain't united with shit," Biggs said, letting the last of his canteen drip into his greedy yap.

"That's treason, private," I said.

"That's the truth, Cap."

I was about to kick Biggs square in the ass when a shout came from the hillside. I turned just as Jefferson barreled down the incline to the creek. "You see 'em?" I asked.

"I ain't seen our ghosts, but I—," Jefferson was breathing hard, but that was only half out of exertion. "You gotsta' come see."

We all stood on the crest of the hill and looked down at a substantial row of buildings hugging close to narrow streets in the flatland below. It was surprising to see a settlement like this so far away from the railroad. So far away from anything, as there wasn't a river or advantageous trail within a hundred miles, not counting that strange creek. But there stood a boondock with all the sturdy trappings of a proper town.

"What is this place?" I asked, mostly to myself.

"Dunno," Ebke said, poring over a worn railroad map of the area, scratching his jaw. He wasn't worth a lick in battle, but that skittish fucker knew maps better than the best Union Pacific survey team. "Ain't even on the map. This place don't exist."

I took out my glass and scanned the layout of the town, noticing that the buildings didn't seem like they belonged out here. They looked old fashioned, *Old World*, like they were scooped up from some forgotten European mountain village and set down in the middle of the Great American Desert. Stranger still, the main thoroughfare was paved.

"What you see, Cap?" Biggs asked.

"I don't know." And I truly didn't. I stowed my glass and got to my feet. "But I reckon we're about to find out."

Our horses clattered on walnut brown cobblestones worn smooth with age or use, or both.

"Where a place like this get stone streets?" Jefferson asked, giving word to what everyone was thinking.

Biggs spat chaw onto the thoroughfare. "Gotta be rich folk 'round here."

"Must have imported 'em," I said. "No stone like that 'round here."

"Yeah, but from where?"

"I don't know, Jefferson," I shot back, irritated. I hated being asked questions when I didn't have the answer. Worse was when any answer I had didn't make any kind of goddamn sense anyway.

We rode through the main promontory, which was deserted and clean as a church floor. The place looked like it had been here for years, although it mustn't have progressed much past its founding. The unmarked houses and buildings flanking each side of main street gave away no purpose or use, like the unfinished sets for a stage play. Structures were gaunt, built up three stories high and seemed to lean inwards over the ground below. Protective-like. Or ready to pounce.

A few men dressed in simple, plain suits appeared in doorways and alleys and just stared. No womenfolk or children were within eyeshot.

253

We stopped off at a trough outside the general store, but stayed mounted while the horses drank. At least I reckoned it for a sundry shop, based on the few meager supplies gathering dust behind the windows.

"What are you doing?"

We all turned to the voice and found a man standing behind us in the middle of the street. He was unusually tall, and wore a pressed black jacket and pants that contrasted against white skin and limp, silvery blonde hair. Small blue eyes looked us over with suspicion, but no fear.

I suspected he was enquiring about something a bit deeper. "We're watering our horses."

"Without asking permission?"

"Water's free, fella," Biggs said, spitting in his general direction.

He fixed Biggs with a penetrating stare as his pupils dilated, blue melting to black. "Nothing is free, stranger."

Biggs pulled his rifle from the saddle holster and slung it across his shoulders. "Ain't very neighborly of ya, citizen. We the *U*-nited States now. Everyone 'sposed to get along."

The man cracked a weird smile. "Is that so?" The small paned windows all around us were now filled with pallid faces.

Biggs grinned, showing his rot to the sun. "Sure as shit *is*, ain't it Cap?"

Pegging me for the leader, the man turned my direction. "What brings you here?"

"To be honest, we're not rightly sure where *here* is. This place ain't on any maps." The man said nothing, so I got to the point. "We're lookin' for two Indians that passed this way. Big ones, would have looked rode hard."

"Have not seen them." The man spoke in a very proper but stilted way, with a tinge of an accent that was hard to place. Like he learned English later in life, knowing all the words, but not how to knit them together properly. Obviously an immigrant, as the prairie was full of them. But living in a town so obviously old...

Larsen said something in Danish. The man shot a look at him and narrowed his eyes. He barked a few words at Larsen before walking away.

"What did he say?" I asked

Larsen shrugged. "German, little bit. Think say...'traitor.'" Larsen shrugged again.

I ambled my horse after the man. "Sir, we're soldiers in the United States Army, on an official—"

The man spun around, his face suddenly animated. "Don't bring your outer wars to this place!" he hissed, walking up to the horse, which whinnied and was about to bolt before I got her under control. The man stood just below me, but seemed to tower face to face. "*You don't belong here.*"

"Do them two Injun we be chasin' belong here?" Jefferson called from behind us.

The man turned to Jefferson, his face reforming into a placid mask. "No, they do not." He folded his mouth into a smile, a horrible expression that looked unnatural over that oblong skull. He raised his long arm and pointed right at Jefferson. "But *you* might."

The man started to laugh, a dry, raspy sound that set my teeth on edge, and did a little jig with his feet. I don't know what Jefferson thought, but he turned his horse and charged as fast as those four legs would take him out of town. The rest of us followed, trailed by the wheezing laughter of the gangly man, dancing on the stones. "*But you might!*" he trilled in a falsetto that echoed off the dead prairie.

We were a mile out of the unnamed town before we caught up to Jefferson, who jumped off his nag mid gallop, tumbled and skidded on the balls of his hands, vomiting into the grass before he came to a stop. We positioned our horses around him, staring down as he heaved everything inside of him into his bleeding, shaking palms. For once, even Biggs had nothing to say, looking as haunted as everyone else in the group.

I dismounted and went to Jefferson. "What's gotten into you?"

"I seen that man before…"

"What, I don't—"

Jefferson jerked his face up at me, lips covered in bile, terror in his bulging eyes that looked big as milk saucers with two black marbles quivering in the middle of each. "I seen him in my *dreams!*"

The sun was starting to set, and I figured we'd ridden enough for the day and everyone was pretty spent from the queer happenings. We made camp on a high ridge plateau, marked by the thick arms of a squatty bur oak, giving us a view of the town. No lights came from the houses or buildings, letting the night swallow up the frontier community as the sun died behind us in the west.

I posted a guard and allowed a fire, as I knew that they knew where we were, so no sense in trying to hide. Problem was, I didn't know who "they" were anymore.

That night, as I prayed for sleep like I always did, I thought I heard bells tinkling over the prairie. Bells that sounded dented and off-key, yet delicate. The insects stopped their droning song, listening as I was, waiting with me. All was still.

I looked out into the dark for what seemed like an age, trying to pry apart the blackness to see what I knew what was out there. Finally, the dance of bells filtered into the camp, louder this time, tying me fast to my bedroll with each discordant note. Unable to move, the ghostly outline of tall, wiry figures topped by antlers stepped lightly just outside the firelight of my waking mind as it reached to tear the veil. The figures carried rough-hewn boards over their shoulders, bells dangling from each end. Others dragged great beasts lashed to stretchers of fresh cut branches. Aquatic creatures, trailing oozing tentacles, slicking the flattened grass with a slimy ink. They were heading to higher ground for a gathering. Prepping for a feast. A mass.

I tried to blink, but my eyes were closed. This was the creep of Flatland Madness. I wished for my wife. I wished for whiskey. I wished for a bullet to my brainpan if it meant rest and an end to the feeling of dread that was pinning me to this cold, hard ground. I didn't want anything to do with the ghosts of the prairie, just like they didn't want anything to do with me. We didn't fit, and this unnatural pairing was ripping me asunder without bothering to make a starting wound. Some earthly places weren't made for living things, at least the way we knew life to be. But man is an arrogant ape, and so here we are, disturbing the Old Ways, while bashing out the brains of every fellow human being that doesn't look exactly like us, or bow to the same flag, sing to the same savior. Ridiculous, arrogant ape, swinging a club like a demigod.

The jangle of bells faded away, and my mind went with it, leaving something hollow behind, which draped itself in black.

In the morning, Ebke was gone, and Jefferson was dead.

I recount these occurrences in this order, because I don't rightly think Ebke was the cause of the latter, but I somehow think he was active in the former, and without much prodding. All of us were spooked. He was the one who deserted.

At least that was what I thought at the time. I feel much differently now, knowing what I know. We all should have left, and headed back to Fort Robison, reporting a failed mission, and getting back to our dreary routine. At least that made sense, as shame was better than what was waiting for us. We all should have left.... The foresight of cowardice, versus the ignorance of courage.

Sam shook me awake, his copper face hard as granite. I wasn't sure that I had even slept, as I remember the sky starting to lighten as I lay frozen, waiting to be dragged off to the top of an ancient bluff, the sound of distant drums joined with the frantic beating of my traitorous heart. I felt like I awakened from a long hibernation that had absolutely zero to do with sleep. Sam's eyes told me nothing. They stopped doing that a few days back.

I walked over to the shade of the stunted oak and stood next to Larsen, who was looking at the pair of purpled, swollen feet swinging gently in the breeze, already drawing flies. Jefferson's boots were gone. He died without them. Whittle sat in the grass nearby, arms wrapped around his knees, rocking forward and back, muttering to himself.

"Holy shitfire! Whittle kilt the nigger!" Biggs sat up in his bedroll, wide yellowed eyes going back and forth from the accused to the side of meat that was Jefferson.

"I ain't killed shit," Whittle mumbled into his sleeves, so quiet that it screamed the truth.

"Ebke," Larsen said. His cheeks were flushed, hands gripping at nothing.

"Ebke couldn't take down that black buck," Biggs said, scrambling to his feet and circling Jefferson's body. "If it weren't Whittle, it were them Injuns. You said it yourself, Cap. They been gamin' us. Prolly waited 'til we bedded down, then snuck in, strung up Jefferson, and took Ebke with 'em for brefess. Prolly got a sign from ol' Sam here." Biggs unsheathed his knife. "Right, Sammy boy? You send up them smoke signals to yer kinfolk last night?"

"It was them townspeople," Whittle said. "They spooked Jefferson somethin' fierce... Set me off my feed a little bit, too."

I remembered Jefferson's terrified face and felt the short hairs on my neck stand on end. "You see anything last night?"

"No," Sam said, his lip quivering, maybe out of grief for Jefferson, but more than likely out of embarrassment that someone snuck into camp and did their business while the proud Lakota brave had his guard down. Sugar and wool were making him soft.

"Ebke had last watch," I said. "Maybe he killed Jefferson then run off."

"No," Sam repeated, then unsheathed his Bowie knife, long as a child's forearm, causing Biggs to stumble backwards. Sam walked up to Jefferson and pointed up to his swollen face, the coffee bean brown of his skin pushed out smooth by the gathered fluid underneath. "No fight."

I examined Jefferson's body, looking at his hands. "Ain't a mark on him."

Sam nodded.

"Close ol' eight ball's eye, could ya?" Biggs said with a grimace, staring at the yellowing sack bulging from Jefferson's face. His other socket was hollow and clotted with blood, awaiting the maggots. "Givin' me the heeby jeebs."

We broke camp and planned on heading back to that queer town, in hopes of contacting Fort Robinson and sending back Jefferson's remains, if they had any sort of freight service. We couldn't stop our mission, not now, and I wasn't going to bury Jefferson out on the prairie, for the coyotes and beetles and whatever killed him in the first place to take him any lower in death than he had been in life. He'd been through enough. His family would get his body, and give him the good Christian burial of a free citizen. It was the least I could do for a good man.

Larsen and I wrapped Jefferson's body in his bedding, and lashed him near the rump of his horse. In this heat, he'd start to turn something fierce in a few days, so I was hoping we could get him couriered back to Robinson while we caught up to these murdering Indians and finished what we started. Something told me that we were nearing the end of the game, and the time was past nigh to start playing for keeps. This chase needed to turn back into a hunt.

We found our trail through the grass that lead us back to the town, but as we followed it, it seemed to just take us in a circle, and we eventually ended up back near our campsite from the night before. The town seemed to have vanished. This didn't make any kind of logical sense, and as Whittle and Biggs started to jaw about all sorts of superstitious nonsense, the circle of turkey vultures that seemed to materialize out of the pale blue to the east drew everyone's eyes to the sky, tracking the lazy twirl of a half dozen shallow V's. I didn't even look at Sam. I knew there wouldn't be a point. He'd changed, as we all had. The prairie had taken something out of us, while putting something between us. Instead of seeking the counsel of my friend, I just took off after Biggs, who had charged ahead toward the locus of the world's loosest, slowest tornado, his unfastened gear scattering behind him.

The vultures brought us to a sticky red trail that just appeared out of nowhere, as if it touched down from the clouds. We followed the trace and found parts of Ebke, left like breadcrumbs. Chunks of meat here and there, bits of bone, but always staying on that straight red line carved down deep into the buffalo grass.

After dragging our protesting horses a quarter mile, we came across what remained of Ebke hanging from a wooden X made of unfinished planks, buried into a slight depression in the ground near the bottom of a draw, like a shallow basin servicing a drainage groove. A collection bowl. Ebke's privates were modestly covered in a swaddling knitted of his own intestines, which also wrapped the top of his head like a crown. I expected to find bells attached to the wood, but there were none.

Biggs was already there when the rest of the party arrived, sitting on his knees, cursing through the strings of snot swinging down over his chin. "Look at this shit…" Biggs sobbed, pulling at his face while his eyes took in the full view of Ebke's limbless torso, and the parts of him hanging from the planks like gruesome Christmas ornaments. He turned to me. "Look at this shit!"

I dismounted and didn't move any closer. Whittle vomited in the grass, while Larsen wiped away tears. Sam seemed far away, even though he was within arms' reach.

"What're we doin' out here anyway, huh?" Biggs continued, rising to his feet and pacing. "Fuck these Injuns, fuck *all* y'all. Let's get the hell out of here, Cap! Say we couldn't find shit. Reds be like worms, disappearin' inta the ground. They'd believe us. They'd believe you!"

I tore my gaze away from that bloody X and remembered my station, my duty. "We're out here to accomplish our mission," I said, regaining my stomach, trying to sound stern, even as I was starting to doubt the sanity of any hostile action taken in this godless land of nightmares and blood and an endless green that blanketed this land like a death shroud. "We do that, we can go home."

"That stinkin' fort ain't my home." Biggs mounted up. "I ain't endin' up like Ebke. I ain't endin' up like any y'all. I'm hightailin' it to Missourah and gettin' the *fuck* outta Nebraska. My momma warned me…" He cinched up his saddle. "Y'all Yankees can kiss my rebel ass and eat my d—"

The pistols were in my hands before that filthy mouth could finish. Hammers drew back with a double click. "You desert, you die." The horseflies buzzing loudly around the remains of Ebke seemed to undercut my point.

Biggs laughed, his eyes wild. "I stay here, I'm dead anyways!"

"You head out by yourself, you'll die faster. And you'll die alone."

Biggs ran through this scenario so quickly it looked like a vein popped right above his temple, where the mange had shanghaied his hair. "Fuck you!" He turned to Sam. "Fuck you, and *all* yer kind!"

Sam smiled. It was a fearsome sight. "Now think like we do..." Sam grabbed Biggs by the ankle. "...'bout *you*."

Biggs kicked away Sam's hand. "Fucking savages, all ya's." Biggs was ranting, limbs flailing, his horse skittering underneath him as my pistols followed. But he didn't leave. He wasn't gonna call my bluff, because there wasn't a damn bit of bluff in what I had waiting for him inside those two smokers. "How could y'all do somethin' like this?"

"Your people do worse," Sam said, approaching the body.

"Oh yeah? Then why's you with us, huh? Our people is *your* people now, and don't you forget that shit."

Sam examined the state of the dismembered body. "My people no do this."

"Who did it, then? The coyotes? The mother fucking prairie chickens?"

Sam said something in his native language. I looked at him, hoping he'd translate. He didn't, until my glare forced him to bunch up his lips, searching for the right words in English. He got close enough. "Other People."

"Them townspeople."

Sam started to laugh. I looked at him. I'd never seen him laugh, but there he sat, high in his saddle, roaring like a loon.

A humming mass buzzed past my ear, followed by the sound of punctured meat. Larsen wheezed and crumpled as the crack of a rifle shot reached us, echoing off the ridges and up from the brambled draws.

"There they is,!" Biggs screamed. We followed his jabbed finger to the two riders on a bluff a hundred yards to our right. Always above us, always too many steps ahead to count. One of them - the shooter, no doubt - was rearing back on his mount, thunder stick held high, long hair whipping against the horizon, like he was posing for the cover of one of those Frank Starr dime novels. The image was beautiful and terrifying. Majestic. These lands were their lands, and we were just clumsy boars, rooting up holes and laying poison seed all over this prairie that didn't want a thing from us, and would kill us to keep it that way.

Sam took a shot back at them, and they seemed to sidestep the bullet like it was swimming through molasses. Laughter arose from the duo, followed by a string of what could only be counted as Lakota insults, judging by the hardening of Sam's jaw.

"You missed on purpose," Biggs said, taking a hasty plug of his own. He was a lousy shot. A lousier soldier. I wished Jefferson was at my side instead of rotting over the back of a jittery horse. Without him, down Ebke, and Sam burrowed deep into his own reservation... Goddamn.

The two riders dug their heels into ribs and charged down the hill toward us. Whittle tried to load a cartridge, but fumbled and dropped his gun. The butt hit the ground and fired low, blowing a hole into the sod under hoof and throwing him from his horse. He landed in a heap next to Larsen, his face so close that he could hear the last breath the farm boy took as his eyes locked into a surprised expression—a postcard from the Great Beyond. Whittle moaned and crawled to his feet.

The two Indians kept coming, cocking their old Henry rimfires. Heavier guns than ours. More accurate, too, even mid-gallop with a belly full of freedom. Sam threw off his woolen jacket, ripped open his uniform, and unsheathed his knife, going AWOL without taking a step. His papers said U.S. Army, but his heart was branded in a language older than figures scratched on parchment. Primitive as death, in communion with things civilized progress was in a hurry to forget.

I took aim at the lead rider, and prayed to the Christian God that my worried slug found purchase. I measured high, right at those bared teeth, calculating that the drop of the land and the weight of my bullet would take my shot right into that broad, painted chest. Salt water on the grass... Horned figures... Tentacles... The cackle of the gaunt man dancing over the smoothed stones...

I pulled the trigger, when I should have squeezed. The stock dug into my shoulder, filling in the space that nerves left loose, and heat spit back into my face. I rubbed my eyes and saw the riders had separated just before my shot, and were circling back up the hill.

"Let's ride," I hollered, chambering another round. All I could do at this point was give loud, empty orders, because nothing else meant shit anymore.

"What about Larsen?" Biggs asked, sending off another worthless round.

"Leave him! We'll come back." I wanted to believe I meant this, that I truly planned on coming back for the mortal leavings of one of our own, but I knew that this was a lie. Biggs knew it too. His face told me as much.

I dismounted to help Whittle onto his horse, but he wouldn't move. I tried to lift him, but all that fear and surrender inside made him heavy as a boulder. "Let's mount up, solider," I said.

"This don't feel right..." Whittle said, his voice small, far away. "This don't..." Whittle looked up at me, tears streaking the dust on his face, like war paint carved sad. "They's *playin'* us, sir. They's playin' us into a trap."

"Got cunny in yer veins, Chris Whittle," Biggs sneered.

"You scared, too," Whittle said, staring at his shaky hand smeared with Larsen's blood. "You just too scared to say you scared."

"Horseshit. Ya got cunny in your heart, where's I jus' got it all over my mouth." I waited for Ebke to snort, but he didn't. How in the hell could he? His tongue was nailed to a board under the shade of a hundred vultures, his own guts covering his eyes.

"We got our orders," I said.

"Fuck them orders. This don't *feel* right!" Fear was making Ebke repeat himself, as he scratched at the side of his jaw that was starting to open up like a sore.

"What do you expect us to do?" I shouted, the fury of frustration roiling up from my boots. "March back to Robinson with piss down our legs and tell the Lieutenant that we gave up the search because they were too close? Because we were *scared* like schoolgirls?"

"They's gettin' away." Biggs' balls seemed to grow the more desperate this situation got. Bedding down cozy in the chaos and blood.

I offered my hand to Whittle. "Let's finish this."

Whittle blinked, nodded and wiped away the tears, smearing his face. "Yeah," he said simply, forcing the resigned smile of a man standing alone on the gallows.

The tattered remains of my squad followed Sam up the hill, riding as hard as we could allow ourselves. Whittle was right. I was full aware we were being pulled forward instead of pushing by the strength of our own authority, but the chase was coming to a close, and I just wanted to know where it would end. I'd get my answer less than five miles away.

The trail left by the two riders was so obvious no one said a word. We knew we were the mice now, always had been, and that the spring holding back the iron bar was quivering, ready to give.

With my eyes focused on the ground, I nearly ran into the back of Sam's horse and sent us over the edge of the sharp drop. Regaining balance, I looked down into a deep wooded valley below, crowded with trees of a size and shape I'd never seen before in all my years on the plains. Trunks two hundred feet high and what must have been twenty foot across threw up a great canopy covering the land a mile wide with a spilled lake of unnaturally dark green paint. These were trees from another place, another era, just like that town, the accent of that man...

"Like dinosaur times," Biggs said, somehow sounding passably educated, and possibly reading my mind. Anything was possible now. "What you think, Cap?"

"I've never seen the likes," was all I could muster, pushing my cap up over my forehead, overcome by the majesty of this uncommon forest choking off the floor of a valley deeper and more severe than what seemed possible for the Sandhills. Like God himself took a chunk out of the living ground with a desperate hand and tossed it up to the stars as an offering.

"They waitin' fer us down there," Biggs said, filling his lip with chaw. "This is where the game ends. Bet my rations on it."

"Yes," Sam said evenly. "They wait."

"Well, let's not keep 'em in suspense," Whittle said. I looked at him, and he still had that same weird smile. He turned to me, and I wish I never saw what I saw in his eyes. Larsen took him along, wherever he went.

We picked our way down the steep decline and into the sprawling valley, checking our gear and increasing our speed, heading straight for that towering darkness. Before we broke the treeline, I thought about praying, but gave up as soon as the sunlight winked out above. The shade took my words.

There was no sound inside the forest other than what we brought to it. I kept waiting for the boom of a rifle, the whoop of a leaping brave, but I couldn't hear anything but us, and we weren't saying a word. Heartbeats and shallow lungs, squeezed tight to keep small and unseen.

All was dusk under the high canopy that let in just enough light to keep us moving forward. Giant ferns nodded over a thick carpet of rotted leaves, with fungi the size of wagon wheels fanning out from underneath. Strange succulents in a variety of vivid colors scarcely muted by the dark seemed to quiver amid a spider web of bloated creepers. I expected to see giant lizards push up from the earth, but nothing aside from the plants seemed alive here. Nothing with meat. Not even us. We were ghosts. No birdsong filled the air. No insect chirped from hidden places. This timber was the thickly furnished waiting room in an empty funeral home.

After what seemed like hours, but clearly couldn't have been, the trees broke abruptly without thinning, and we stood back under the mad glare of that pregnant setting sun, bearing down on us one last time before it turned its back. We blinked away the glare, finding a vast meadow stretching out before us. Several hundred yards ahead, in what must have been the dead center of the clearing, a structure stuck out queer from the landscape like a knucklebone.

"The fuck is that?" Biggs asked. "A fort?"

"Powerful old, if it is," I said, noting its thick, low construction, the mortar and mud reinforcing stone walls.

"Sure ain't one of ours."

"Sure ain't," Sam said, a tone of unsurprised certainty in his voice.

We approached cautiously, rifles trained at whatever we thought was a hiding place. It was made of large hunks of limestone, clay, and old cracked timber that must have come from the forest behind us, judging by the size of the logs. It had a steeple, but it was topped by an Oriental onion dome decorated by a ring of carved figures, hands joined in dance. Arrow slits were carved vertically into the walls that had turned a greenish color, with a horizontal opening near the top and the bottom. They looked like double black crosses stamped into the ramparts, either right side up or upside down, depending on which vantage point you had.

A large arching portico stood vacant, probably once secured by a gate. Just inside, I could make out the opened door held up by thick hinges. On either side of the door were upturned arms screwed into the thick beams of the frame, cast of iron and bent at the elbow, fingers arranged in curious gestures. The curved lintel over the top of the doorway was adorned in a carved phrase in an old language that I reckoned for Latin. I never paid much attention in Latin class at college, so the words *Imo ad summum terrae* didn't mean a damn thing. Dead languages never interested me much. The living ones were hard enough.

The sound of a soft whinny jerked all of our barrels toward a lone horse that wandered over from the side of the building. It lacked a saddle and was painted with intricate symbols on its pale brown fur. Aquatic symbols, of fish and other inscrutable things. They seemed familiar somehow, bristling the hair on the back of my neck.

"Where's the other one?" Biggs asked, dismounting and using his horse as cover from anyone inside the structure.

"Watchin' us," Whittle said in a flat voice. He was good as gone. I wondered when his body would follow, and who would pull the trigger.

"Everyone get down," Biggs called. "The Injun inside can pick us off like fish in a barrel."

"Either of them can," I said, scanning the wall of strange trees standing sentry around us any direction I looked. The curve of the breakline made me dizzy.

I reached for my nearly empty canteen, more thirsty than I could ever remember being. "But they haven't yet." I didn't feel like taking cover. Didn't feel like doing much of anything other than finishing that canteen, and hoping there was a well on the premises that had something in it other than salt water.

"What're we doin' then, Cap?" Biggs asked.

"We're going inside."

"*Fuuuck* that!" Biggs said, starting in. "You want us to walk into a firin' squad, be my fuckin' guest, but I ain't—"

"—We're going inside, Biggs," is all I said. Biggs was about to continue, then knitted cracked lips over those uneven teeth and nodded. He checked to make sure the chamber was heated, and stood at the ready. He might make a soldier after all.

We all stared at that open door, that black rectangle that seemed to suck in the bleeding sun with an almost audible sound.

"Let's start a fire," Biggs said, the sack between his legs constricting just a bit. Courage sometimes takes a while to set, even when fueled by crazy. "Smoke 'em out, or burn 'em inside. The way they done to us in Mud Springs."

"We ain't burning down a church."

"This ain't no church."

"Sure as shit is," I said, pointing at the inscription carved above the door. "That's Latin, making this here dwelling most likely a Catholic church." I walked up to the front door, inspecting the outside of the structure, noting the roof, and the empty bell tower. I looked for a cross, but only found a spike of rusted iron pointing at the sky.

"Careful, Cap," Biggs warned. "Red probably got a barrel on you right now."

"Then shut your mouth and keep your eyes peeled for a muzzle shot to return fire."

Biggs aimed his rifle at the old church, waiting for it to make a move.

More inscriptions were scrawled along the doorframe, but they were weathered beyond recognition in some places, and swallowed in other places by what seemed to be a thick, chewing moss, or maybe algae. A few words remained uncovered. A realization struck me. "Spanish…" I said to myself, almost forgetting the gravity of this place in the wonder of such an architectural oddity. "This is a Spanish mission."

"*Spanish?* Never heard'a no Spanish 'round here."

"Ya, that's the queer part… Spain ain't never held territory this far north. Farthest they got was Texas, from what I can remember." I touched the raised text along the doorframe, my eyes drawn to the hand gestures bent from iron. I forgot that something was waiting for us inside the open door. Worse, I couldn't wait to get inside and see what it was.

"*Emo ad...sum...*" Biggs squinted at the inscription, slowly approaching the door, rifle trained into the darkness. "Fuckin' ooga booga. You was a school teacher, wasn't you, Cap?"

"For a little while, before the war. Just primary, though."

"What's that say, then?"

I shook away the strange feeling and rubbed the back of my head, hoping to pry something loose as I stumbled over the ancient tongue I never paid much mind to study.

"'Top... of the bottom... of... the earth', or somesuch."

"What you reckon that means?"

"Heaven, I guess."

"Shit, if this's heaven, I'm pissin' in a preacher's eye."

"Green Church," Sam uttered, walking up and unsheathing his knife, waiting to go inside. He looked more resigned to a promised fate than eager to fight.

"You know about this place?" I asked.

Sam grimaced, remembering. "My grandfather say old church... made bad medicine. Big, big bad medicine."

"You people would, godless heathens."

Sam laughed again. It was becoming a bad, unnerving habit. It was clear he didn't care anymore. "Got more gods than you." He turned to Biggs and narrowed his eyes. "Meaner, too."

"Ain't none of them worth a fuck, and all of them sound like good eatin', 'cept maybe the jackal." Sam turned away, waiting. Biggs returned to aiming his rifle at any opening or shaded spot in the structure, hoping for movement. The gun came to rest, aimed at Sam's back, hoping for something else. "Why ain't you afraid of this place like they is?"

"I not... *them* anymore. I nothing."

"Then welcome to hell, fucknut."

Biggs was about to squeeze the trigger, when a shot split the air and a piece of the wall behind my head sizzled and spat. We all turned, and found the two dismounted Indians sprinting towards us, powder smoke trailing behind. The leader cocked and fired again, while his companion dragged a giant cut log with surprising ease.

"Inside!" I yelled.

"But they—" Biggs began, jerking his gun from Sam to the approaching braves.

Twin bullets peppered the wall behind us to reinforce the obvious. "They ain't *in* there, you idiot!"

We scrambled inside the church, Biggs dragging a nearly comatose Whittle, and it took both Sam and I to push shut the massive wooden door. It boomed into place, bent arms now outside, drowning us in darkness. After a moment punctuated by gunshots from outside, we could see well enough courtesy of the narrow openings in the wall, and the circle of stained glass in the ceiling, which warped what little light we had into pulsing beams of red, green, and yellow, broken by the swirls of thick dust kicked up by our shuffling boots.

We took up positions at the arrow slits, which barely afforded room for a barrel, and fired half blind toward the oncoming Indians, who kept charging toward the front door. Bullets thudded into the stout wood, the clay walls, sounding like the deadly output of a dozen weapons instead of just two gunned-up braves. I figured this for a full tribal ambush. We mice were now eating the cheese, fattening for the kill inside a hole in the wall.

Sam narrowed his gaze and took aim, muttering under his breath. He closed his eyes just before he fired, and the armed Indian fell and rolled, bare feet and hair pinwheeling above the grass before disappearing from our limited view. The other one, a stout fucker, lifted the log above his head and grinned, picking up speed.

"Here'e come!" a voice shouted. I couldn't tell who it came from. Whittle? Ebke? Jefferson? Didn't matter. It came from all of us. Ghosts and the living and the living ghosts. The veil between it all was slipping away. *Imo ad summum terrae*… Bells in the darkness… two crossed planks…. My God, was I mad? Would I know it if I was?

"Gon' ram the door!"

I aimed for the man's legs, knowing that a body shot wouldn't slow down this force of monstrous nature, but he was moving too fast, kicking up sod like a charging bull. The log seemed like tinder in his giant hands. He looked like Sam. He looked like every Lakota warrior who had ever laid eyes on me, and hated what he saw.

We all kept firing until he was too close to head. Cursing, I pulled my Spencer from the wall and ran to the door, leveling my weapons just to the left of the inside jamb, which I reckoned would splinter first, exposing this savage demon to a noble death by Army steel. "Get in position," I said, "And rain down hellfire once he comes through!"

Four tarnished steel barrels trained on the door and waited for the crash, the splintering of rotted wood, and the figure which would stand before us, accepting the baptism of lead that we were so willing to bestow on this heathen who was better off dead by our hand than alive on his own accord. This was a Godly house, and we would show him how we dealt with transgression.

But no concussion sounded. Instead, a span of impossible silence, followed by the slow descending scrape of wood against stone, ending with a final click. Such a precise sound caught me off guard, and I looked at Sam, whose eyes bulged. He seemed to be surprised, for the first time in weeks.

This terrified me.

Outside, the Indian ran off, whooping and zigzagging so he wouldn't make an easy target. No one shot at him, as all eyes were on the door, the last sound still echoing in all of our ears.

"The fuck just happened?" Biggs said, giving voice to all of our minds.

I went to the door and pulled on it. Didn't budge. I put some leg into my effort and yanked again. Not even a shimmy. The door was fastened tight, from the *outside*. The log in the Indian's hands was dropped into place in the crook of the upturned arms, barring our exit with three hundred pounds of arcane timber hugged tight to iron. "They locked us in," I said, dropping into a creaking pew and rubbing my hair that hadn't seen soap for weeks. I pulled a worm from behind my ear, held it up and looked at it. It was a maggot. Feaster of the dead. I flicked it to the floor, wondering which one of my soldiers it had consumed, before squashing it with the toe of my boot.

I looked up to the front of the church, hoping to find a statue of the crucified Jesus, his face pointed skyward with a look of peaceful resignation. Anything to give me comfort. Even if it was Catholic. Instead, I found a cross knocked on its side, the two stone slabs now intersecting like an X instead of a T, identical to the one that we found on the prairie. It was stained a dark color that seemed to eat into the pale stone like a sponge. It was empty, but that only seemed temporary.

Biggs checked every corner of the sanctuary for a way out with the panicked gibber of a trapped animal, fighting cobwebs thickened by what was probably centuries of dust. At least I hoped it was that long since this place had been used by a congregation, but something deep in my marrow told me I was wrong. This was a place of recent ceremony, and those rituals didn't need a clean surface.

"Gotta be a way outta here," Biggs whined. "Ain't you fuckers gon' help?"

Sam was sitting across from Whittle, looking at the man who had slumped into one of the pews, chewing on a moldy biscuit, most of which crumbled onto the front of his stained uniform. I just stared at that downed cross. Biggs continued to overturn the room, kicking through wooden screens and bringing down empty cabinets. The air filled with dust, caught and briefly held by the last few rays of tinted sun ebbing through the stained glass above. In the dying light, a ring of Latin phrases embossed in the pinkish yellow of Black Hills gold came to life just below the ceiling, circling the room. *Summa imis...Laquearia tenebrarum... In loco ubi animae sunt a ludibrium...Quaeritur Deum enim mortem, et non veniet.* Somehow, I felt glad that I couldn't puzzle out what any of it said.

"We wait 'til sundown, then we break out of here," I said, negotiating with the stubborn sun to flee from this place, if only so those words on the wall would disappear.

"You got some dynamite stuck up yer ass? Cuz that's the only way we's gettin' out this place." Biggs pushed over a chair and went to piss in the corner. "You say this a church, but I ain't seen Jesus Christ once... Pope-lovin' shitbricks." Pulling down his trousers and relieving himself, he glanced over at what looked like an interlocking chain of carved crosses hanging from the wall like garland. He squinted at them. "These ain't crosses... They's claws." Biggs was startled by the sound a rifle hitting the floor, followed by Whittle sobbing.

I ran over to Whittle, who cowered below one of the openings in the wall. "What is it?" He babbled and snotted. I shook him. "What *is* it?!"

"An Injun...crawled up to the wall, and just kep' staring at me. I was—I was gonna shoot 'im, b-but...the way he stared at me... Stole my iron."

"What'd he do?"

"H-He pointed at me, and..." Whittle looked like he was going to faint. "His face..."

I shook him. "What about his face?"

Whittle's voice solidified, dreamy. "He was smiling, sir. But not happy-like. Smiled like... like he knew we was already dead."

I released Whittle, and he slumped to the floor.

"Cap!"

I heard him, but said nothing, as nothing would come out.

"Goddamnit, Cap!"

"What is it?"

"A trap door!"

269

I joined Biggs' side behind the chapel alter and looked at a staircase leading into a yawning blackness. "Ain't no other way out than down."

On the wall above the opening, a phrase was written in the same pinkish gold. I read it aloud. *"Foramina terrae sunt occultata Veritate."*

Sam laughed again.

◎

We wrapped a pair of broken chair legs in the spidery fabric of a sacrament tablecloth, anchored by strips of my soggy undershirt, coating the torch tops with wax melted from the sconce candles lining the vestibule. Two would bring the light, while the other two would keep rifles at the ready.

Without much formality other than a few grim looks, I lead the foursome down, forced to bring toe firmly to stone, which was worn so smooth I nearly slipped on the first few steps. The stairs twisted like a corkscrew as we descended, hugging tight to a wall that shifted from brick to hard-packed dirt, and got progressively more damp as we went. This was a summer of drought, as all summers in Nebraska seemed to be, but here we found the water under the ground, slicking the rocks and choking the air, keeping selfish any designs on helping mankind.

After declining a few hundred feet, we arrived at a landing. I held my torch high, and the flames danced off a glistening mosaic floor, the light dying out above us in the lee of what must have been a very high ceiling. It was evident where the foundation of the mission was grafted onto a natural cavern hollowed out of the earth probably tens of thousands of years ago, and maybe longer than that. The built-up walls were honeycombed with small arched openings, occupied by moldering remains. This was a mausoleum, a charnel house for fallen church members. The cool air smelled dank, of wet earth and old rot, but also spiced with a fishy brine I hadn't breathed since my trip to Boston as a sprat, which hung especially strong as we passed a run-down fishing village up the coast north of the city. It was the sort of uncanny odor that had a certain mass to it, a meaning. And it was just as repellant now as it had been then, and filled my stomach with knots deeper and more concerning than the usual pangs of hunger.

The texture of the floor under my boots brought me back to the room, and I brought my flame low. The work was a mix of colored tiles and opaque seashells, arranged together into strange symbols that seemed to be a form of exotic writing. Arabic, or something similar. Older. I moved across the floor on my knees, hands slipping on the slimy film that covered everything. Groups of people were depicted—not people, but fish-like figures, going about the business of trade and religious rites, in what seemed to be an underwater world, somehow backdropped against constellations, planets, burning orbs. Funeral ceremonies were depicted. Humans buried with animals. Groups interred together, in embraces. A child entombed inside a giant, spiny clamshell. Carvings of humans copulating with sea creatures, flying things, demons...

I stood up, looked at the arched holes in the walls, and knew who and what was resting there, and felt the grip of fear. Then it all snapped together: the scene splayed out below me, this textbook of stone, was fixed inside a map of the continent, and the center of aquatic activity was set dead center in the middle of the American Plains, with the busiest hub located in Nebraska territory. Right goddamn here.

I took a step back, grit scratching under my boots. Sand. The Sandhills. Sand from the bottom of an inland sea that once covered the breadth of this flat expanse from the Ozarks to the Rockies. We were standing at the bottom of a dead ocean, drained and exposed and waiting for whatever might dig down into the surface to get at the past.

"Cap!" Biggs' urgent voice should have echoed, but was now muffled, like something soft was hovering above us in the dark.

I looked up, and found Sam staring at me, an almost eager look in his normally placid eyes. He was waiting for me to say something, or see something. Expectant.

"Cap, come look at this," Biggs implored.

Sam just nodded. I knew I'd never forget that one simple gesture for as long as I lived, and didn't. After a moment, I walked past the Indian, never taking my eyes off of him, and joined Biggs at the far side of the room.

He and Whittle were standing in front of an opening in the cavern that was more a natural gap in the earthen wall than a proper door. Whittle was now a husk of a man, following along like an unstrung puppet that only found its legs. "This is the way out," Biggs hissed. He was sweating. We all were, even in this damp chill. I pulled out one of my pistols in my spare hand, held the torch out in front of me like a protective shield, and stepped through.

The twin torches lit up the small, conical antechamber, revealing walls covered high in thousands of pairs of elk antlers. Two balls of quartz hung from rusted iron chains from the apex of the sharply pointed ceiling. Lower to the ground, the space was ringed tight with the identical tusks of some great beast, the ancient ivory faded a veined shade of brown. I reached out to touch one.

"Elephants," Biggs breathed with awe.

"Mastodon," I said, looking over to Sam, who was watching me with narrow eyes, waiting for me to put it all together.

Moving my torch deeper into the room, it illuminated a thick pylon of black rock four feet wide and about twelve feet high jutting out of the ground at a slight angle. Glyphs were carved into its surface, worn nearly smooth by the grind of wind, or more rightly water. In front of the megalith was an opening in the ground, its circumference framed by what appeared to be shaped bricks, but on closer examination turned out to be solid rock melted into a plume. Like the top lip of a tiny volcano I'd seen in my science books.

Whittle circled the opening and began to hum. An unnerving melody that didn't seem to hit any recognizable notes, but had a definite and repeated arrangement.

"I found Jesus," Biggs said, inspecting the back of the stone pillar. "Why they hide him way down here?" I joined Biggs and held my torch near a small carving of Christ reclining suggestively on a throne. A tiara rested on his brow, made of silver and that pinkish Black Hills gold. *RESURGAM* was embossed in the crown.

"I shall rise again," I murmured, unaware of how I knew this. Biggs whispered a prayer. Under his crown, the Christ figure's face seemed out of proportion. I leaned in close, and spied a pair of toadish eyes slightly distended from the head. The robes that Jesus wore were a draping of fish scales. His face was clean-shaven and supple, showing no signs of the rigors of crucifixion. He seemed to be grinning in a knowing way. My quavering hand nearly dropped my torch, scattering shaky light around the chamber, setting antlers and tusks dancing.

Sam put his hand on my shoulder. Aside from a handshake, he had never touched me before, and the weigh of his grip was nearly crushing. With his free hand, he pointed higher up into the chamber. I stood back, and the darkness above receded and revealed its shape: a creeping mass of tentacles encircling the room, disappearing behind the horns and arranged ivory. From this vantage point the two quartz globes were positioned perfectly to be the glinting eyes of some gigantic, squid-like beast holding back the earth around us. We were standing right below the maw.

"What is that?" Biggs whispered. "Dinosaur?"

"That ain't no dinosaur," I said.

"There's something down there."

We all turned. Whittle was looking over the edge and down into the well. Sam slammed the stock of his rifle over his knee, snapping it in two. He tossed the ruined gun to the tile and melted back into the darkness. Sam was truly gone.

I reached out to Whittle just as he dropped off the edge and vanished into the nothingness below. I ran to the well and looked down. No sound echoed back up. No scream, no impact. Just a silent consumption, coming from a lightless hole in the earth that seemed so utterly black it was almost a new color.

Biggs ran to my side and shouted Whittle's name down the well. I slumped down to the ground and pressed the heels of my hands into my eyes, hoping they'd pop out so I wouldn't have to see any of this anymore. Grit dug into my skin. Sand.

Biggs paced around the chamber, pulling at his hair, tearing out chunks. Blood was coming from his mouth. "What the fuck is this place?!" Biggs screamed. "**WHAT THE FUCK IS THIS PLACE?!**" He screamed this over and over again, and the words ran together into a wall of manic sound. Biggs always screamed, but this pitch came from someplace newly discovered way down inside of him. He screamed until his voice tore and gave out and he collapsed into a heap next to me. Gurgled, broken sobs twisted out of him, winding down into a shuddering whimper.

We both huddled there, unable to move. I slipped both pistols out of their holsters. I placed one on the floor in front of Biggs. I put the barrel of the other in my mouth. I thought about my wife, and tried to picture her face, but I couldn't. Maybe I didn't want to bring her down here with me, to be a part of this place. I willed her face to form in my mind, but all I could see was Sam nodding. My shoulder burned where his hand had rested. I clicked back the hammer on my Colt. The sound of it brought Biggs' face up from its burial place in his arms. He drew in a ragged breath, and held it. The open barrel grazed the back of my mouth. My eyes began to water, and I wished they were tears.

In the silence of that moment, I heard something come from the well. A soft, hollow voice, pushing up words that pieced themselves together after several repetitions. "... the fuck... this place?" the voice questioned, echoing the last utterances from above. But it didn't sound like Biggs, nor did it sound particularly human. It sounded like those sideshow bellows made to mimic sounds. "What the fuck is this place?" it said again, getting stronger, more defined.

I looked at Biggs, whose eyes were bugging out of his head. I put my guns away, too terrified to pull a trigger, even on myself.

"*What the fuck is this place?*" the voice boomed, shaking the cavern.

I scrambled away from the well, dragging Biggs with me, then pressed against the far wall, the tusks cradling my back like a rocking chair. I pointed both pistols at the opening in the floor. The voice had gone silent, accenting the clatter of my shaking Colts. We waited, Biggs and I, frozen with dread, pressed against each other like bait fish cowering together at the bottom of the pail. After a spell, a queer noise filtered up from below. A squish of water... scratching... a slapping of feet against rock... claws and clammy flesh. Something... many things, climbing *up*...

I ripped myself from the wall, dashed to the well top and chanced a look down into the dark, holding the torch above me like a protective beacon. I saw nothing at first, then... I saw movement. The flop of awkward limbs. Bulging eyes looking back at me.

I burst through the opening the wall and onto the tile, hauling Biggs who flailed to keep his feet. I hit the stairs first and climbed up, taking two and three stairs at a time, misjudging the distance in my panic, nearly falling several times. Biggs was right behind me, pushing forward, keeping me on track when the floor could have taken me, keeping me alive just long enough to witness the horror of what was coming up out of that hole bored into the planet.

We clambered together out of the trapdoor behind the alter in the sanctuary and ran toward the front door, only noticing after we were outside and under the scrutiny of a very low and bone white moon that the door was wide open.

Biggs fell to the grass, clutching at it, kissing the blades, crying and laughing at the same time. He was cracked, from the inside out, but he was free and back out under the sky and the humid August air. It was then that I saw Sam, standing next to the other big Indian, a wound patched with bloody buckskin just below his huge bare chest. Behind them, torches flared to life, and a hundred more figures stood at the edge of the woods. I saw masks, antlers. Exposed genitals. Nakedness. Pale skin standing side by side with brown. All with white eyes staring out from swaths of black paint and the gentle tinkle of bells weaving throughout. One of the gathered was taller than the rest and wiry. I remembered when he danced on stone and killed Jefferson with a laugh.

Sam walked slowly toward us, a rifle in each hand, trailed by his companion, who rested a giant, rusted felling axe over his shoulder. This man wasn't a soldier in my Army. This man, this so-called Sam, wasn't my friend. Never was, even with both of our best efforts. How could he be? We were as different as the sun was to the moon, sharing only a similar shape but next to nothing else. He was from a strain of human so far removed from me that I could have been a garden slug. Sam was connected to this place, these beauties and horrors. It ran through his veins like eye color, and here we were, trying to gloss over this birthright with the whitewash of our flimsy cultural advances, as permanent as a coat of paint. None of that mattered out here, away from the sheen of illusion of towns and buildings and laws and so-called civilization. We'd forgotten, but Sam's people hadn't. They couldn't, any more than I could forget that the sky was blue. These were the facts of existence, and my people didn't do well with those things, so we invented our own, writing a new history right over the carved symbols that were already there. Sometimes, those pages didn't hold up so well, curling and falling to dust, while the words written in clay stayed on, held their meaning, because it was all true, even if we chose to forget. The townspeople had decided to remember, so here they were too, gathered to worship at this church of horrors, hidden away in an impossible forest far out in the Great American Desert. This was the Green Church. This was their Mission, not ours.

Sam came to a stop in front of us. He lowered one of the two rifles at my head. "Do you want to live?" he asked in a clear voice, his English nearly perfect, but somehow off, just like the tall villager who waited somewhere in the darkness behind him, smiling through his greasepaint.

I leaned forward into the barrel, pressing it into my forehead, feeling the coldness of the metal against my skin. I waited for the click, and then whatever came after that. Anything but here.

Sam pointed his other rifle at Biggs, and repeated the question.

Biggs nodded his head slowly, moaning, a bloody tooth stuck to his slimy chin. He grimaced, exposing nothing but gray gums. "Yes," Biggs croaked. "I... wanna live..."

Sam glanced at the waiting Indian, who strode forward, flipping the axe around to the poll side and broke both of Biggs' arms, snapping the bones like kindling.

Biggs collapsed with a tortured snarl, toothless mouth biting at the air, fingers clawing at the roots of the buffalo grass as the Indian broke both his legs at the knee. The cries then seized up in his throat and he didn't make another sound while being dragged by his ankles back to the mission and through the open door.

I looked at the trail of blood in the flattened grass. It was a familiar sight now, marking this land like lines on a map. I turned my face up to the moon. I didn't dare look at Sam. I was afraid he wouldn't be looking back at me.

ABOUT THE AUTHOR

T.E. Grau is an author of dark fiction whose work has been featured in over two dozen anthologies, magazines, literary journals, and audio platforms. His limited edition novellas *The Mission* and *The Lost Aklo Stories* were released in late summer 2014 by Dynatox Ministries/Dunhams Manor Press. T.E. Grau lives in Los Angeles with his wife and daughter, and can be found in the ether at *The Cosmicomicon* (cosmicomicon.blogspot.com). *The Nameless Dark* marks his first collection of short fiction.

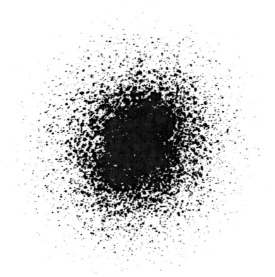

CPSIA information can be obtained at www.ICGtesting.com
Printed in the USA
LVOW11s1404210915

455058LV00002B/306/P